SLICE

SLICE

a novel

ANGIE CAEDIS

For everyone who is chasing their dreams—don't stop.
This one's for you.

THURSDAY

🌴 BEC 🌴

The plane shook a little, jostling the white ceramic mug of jasmine tea she'd barely touched. Bec pressed her fingertips against the tray table and stilled the soft clatter. Usually the slightest bit of turbulence would send her nails digging into the armrest, but today it barely fazed her. Her mind was miles away from the vast ocean below the wings of the plane. She felt like she was still back in the overpriced airport lounge rather than 30,000 feet above the ground, propelling towards her destination at a dangerously fast speed. Her eyes drifted out the window and found the stretch of green that held steady in the distance. They'd be landing soon. Fingers brushed up against her cheek, pulling her attention reluctantly to the seat next to her.

"How are you feeling?"

Bec gave the man next to her a small smile. It was the type of thing you gave to someone as you squeezed your way past them in an aisle. Short. Curt. She quickly picked up the cup of cold tea and took a long sip. At this rate, it was only a matter of time before he realized something was off. And when he did, she wasn't sure if she had it in her to lie anymore.

"Fine," she mumbled into the cup. "I think I heard them say we'd be landing in about twenty minutes."

"Good," he replied as he brushed his thumb against her cheek again. "I can't wait for you to see what I have planned."

Guilt hung heavily in Bec's stomach. But it wasn't anything new—she knew the heft and sway of its weight well by now. It only seemed to grow heavier with every touch and longing look that Tyler offered her. Bec quietly inched her way towards the window and away from him. Any more and the weight of her guilt would drag her through the floor of the plane into a gut-wrenching freefall before her body hit the harsh surface of the ocean and snapped like a twig. Somewhere deep inside she felt like it'd be what she deserved.

"You know, you really didn't have to do any of this," she muttered as she gestured loosely around them. She watched as a flight attendant came down the aisle with a tray of hot towels. "We could have flown coach." Bec ran a hand through her hair, the strands feeling dirty from the past nine hours of travel. "Seriously," she breathed, "—I mean we could have just stayed home for my birthday and gone to dinner or something."

Tyler leaned over to her, his lips gently brushing against her ear. "You deserve something a little different this year," he whispered.

Bec looked at her boyfriend for what felt like the first time all day. She'd done her best to avoid any kind of conversation for the majority of the flight. It had been a miracle she'd managed it. Her inexperience with international travel had been a valid enough excuse. She was tired, she'd told him. Exhausted. And it was true—she was. But waking up at 2 a.m. wasn't the real reason that she'd pretended to sleep the entire flight as they were whisked away to a mysterious, romantic getaway.

"I don't deserve all this."

Tyler looked at her with the same intense, passionate look that had sucked her in the first time they'd met. It was the confidence, the cockiness really, that had made her give him a chance. He wasn't her type. If anything, he was the opposite. But there was something about Tyler that made you want to give him what he wanted. Maybe it was the brightness in his eyes or that coy smirk that was permanently plastered on his face. Or maybe he was just good at convincing you that you wanted the same things he did. She didn't know. But whatever it was, it was the sole reason she was sitting in first class about to touch down in Nicaragua.

"You deserve every minute of this trip," he said, a flicker of satisfaction flashing in his eyes. He leaned into her and kissed the top of her head. "You'll realize that soon enough."

She leaned away from him, pretending to watch their descent through the window as the pit in her stomach grew. This was a mistake. She shouldn't be here. As she fixed her eyes on the city that appeared below in tiny specs, she knew it was too late to back out. Her jaw clenched as she felt the plane descending faster now. She hated this part. She forced a small, silent breath from her lungs. What had she gotten herself into? She had no idea what this trip even entailed. She'd asked Tyler a few times, her questions growing more persistent over the past week. Every time she'd been met with the same answer—it's a surprise. They could be swimming with sharks for all she knew. Or sailing around the coast on a giant yacht. It was all a big question mark.

She didn't even know how it had happened. At first, he'd just teased the idea. She'd tried to casually shut down his suggestion of a once-in-a-lifetime trip for her birthday. But every excuse she'd given him had come up short. When she'd told him she couldn't afford it, he had told her that he'd never allow her to pay a cent. When she'd argued that Stevie, her best friend of over fifteen years, would be pissed if she wasn't included in the big 30th celebration, Tyler had told her Stevie wouldn't care. Oddly enough, when Bec had asked her, Tyler was right. Stevie had told her to go have some big adventure, they'd celebrate when she got home. So without any excuses or the nerve to tell him no, Bec had agreed.

Now, as Nicaragua greeted her from the fingerprint-smudged airplane window, she wondered if she could handle the next week alone with Tyler. A flicker of nausea slithered through her as the landing gear whirled and whined. She wasn't sure. The only thing she did know was that she couldn't stay in LA another second. Her eyes darted down to her phone where it was nestled between her thigh and the plush cushion of the seat. She considered checking the message again—just to be sure. Her fingers brushed the air but she didn't pick up the phone. There wasn't any need for confirmation, not when she'd already read the text a dozen times. She swallowed the heaviness in the back of her throat and withdrew her hand. She couldn't decide if this was all bad timing or some sort of divine intervention. Bec forced another deep breath from her lungs, her stomach heaving in rhythm with the plane's wheels as they bounced harshly off the tarmac. For better or for worse, she had to ignore her latest problem for the next few days. She didn't know what would happen when she got back home or even what would happen here with Tyler. Neither situation felt comforting. But what she did know was that something was coming. That was for damn sure.

"I feel like I'm melting," Bec said as she fanned herself with her hand.

Tyler shot her an amused look. "You said that already."

"Well, it's true," she muttered.

Bec dug around her backpack until she found the water bottle she'd bought before they'd taken the cab here. Correction. Tyler had bought it. Just like back home, he wouldn't let her pay for anything. Not the water. Not the triple espresso she'd gotten when they'd arrived at LAX that morning. And definitely not the trip. But as they both knew, she couldn't have paid for it anyways.

The humidity felt like it was seeping into her bones. It was hot in Los Angeles, but here her body felt heavy with warmth. It seemed to weigh her down into the hot pavement that boiled under her sneakers. She popped the cap off the water bottle and quickly downed half of it. She pulled at her tank top, desperate for the flow of air against her skin. The fabric clung to her stomach with a damp stickiness, growing worse with every minute they continued to stand in the sun.

"Ty, please tell me what we're waiting for," she half-laughed, half-moaned.

He shot her a secretive smirk from where he was leaning against one of the concrete barriers that bordered the road. "You'll see."

"Come on. You know I don't like surprises."

"Then you're really dating the wrong guy." He smiled.

Bec's stomach rolled. She knew he was joking but she still searched his face for a hint of knowing. There was nothing there but amusement and sweat. She offered him a soft smile but it fell flat on her face. She chugged the rest of her water, looking away. It was too hot for the anxiety and shame that was currently eating Bec from the inside out. After touching down in Nicaragua's capital, Managua, they had quickly boarded another plane and taken a flight to the Caribbean side of the country. The plane ride, although only 45 minutes in duration, had proved more bumpy and unsettling than the first. Even Bec's own mind, full of what ifs and dread, hadn't prevented her from clawing at the armrest this time. With a queasy stomach and the stink of plane exhaust clinging to her clothes, a short cab ride had taken them on the next leg of their journey. Bec had expected to be dropped off at a hotel or Airbnb. The thought of an icy cold shower had wormed its way into her mind with sweet longing the minute the humidity had licked at her skin. Even now, as she closed her eyes, she imagined the chill of a hotel room's air conditioning instead of the heat that threatened to bake her in her skin. Or maybe she'd be down at the pool, sipping on the first of many cocktails. But to her dismay, the cab had not dropped them off at their final destination. It had left them thirty minutes ago in the place where she stood now—an empty parking lot in front of an even emptier marina.

Her eyes wandered over the gentle waves that lapped against the hulls of the few fishing boats tied to the dock. What was Tyler waiting for? Bec looked at an expensive-looking boat that bobbed further down. A man rested against the railing, arms folded across his chest. His gaze hovered on Bec and Tyler before wandering out towards the road. He was the captain. Their captain. That, at least, Bec had put together. When they'd first arrived, the man had walked down the dock with a dazzling white smile on his face and a bead of sweat on his forehead. Tyler had spoken with him for a few minutes before the captain had given Bec a cheerful nod and sauntered back towards the boat. She hadn't heard any of their conversation. Of course, she didn't speak Spanish. She blamed her shitty, public school education on that. But from watching the conversation, she hadn't gotten the impression that the captain was behind schedule or unprepared. On the contrary, he seemed ready and eager to go. But for some reason, Tyler had stayed put in the parking lot.

Bec scooted her way next to Tyler and sat on the concrete divider. His tall frame provided a sliver of shade from the sun but the heat radiating off of his body, among other things, kept her from leaning against him. Instead, she rested her elbows against her thighs and dropped her chin into her hands. Fuck, it was hot. Bec's eyes drifted down Tyler's skin, tracing the ornate black lines and shading of his tattoos that glistened in the glare of sun and sweat. She let her eyes unfocus as she stared off into space, her eyelids growing heavy. Her body leaned into Tyler sleepily, or maybe he had leaned into hers. She wasn't sure. It was a subtle intimacy that should have felt normal after dating someone for a year but the very touch of his skin against hers set Bec on edge. Her mind yelled at her to pull away immediately but the heat made her complacent. As much as she wanted to move, her body refused. Maybe this was the cure? Maybe she could slowly find her way back to him in moments like this. Moments where she pushed her instincts aside, where she quieted the shame, and let herself be with him. She closed her eyes as she tried now. Her body fought at first, anxiety fluttering in her chest as her mind screamed and berated her. But after a few minutes, she settled. Her breathing steadied, syncing up with Tyler's. The slight heave of Tyler's body acted as an indicator for Bec's body to do the same. A breeze trickled by, spiked with the salty waft of the ocean. It was almost peaceful. Bec nestled her head against Tyler's arm. Maybe she could do this. Maybe if she pretended everything was normal, sooner or later, it would be.

Tyler's body tensed up, jolting Bec back to consciousness. The slam of car doors and the murmur of excited voices filled the once-quiet marina. As Bec turned to look, the sultry tone of Tyler's voice slipped into the air.

"Surprise."

The screams came next. Bec blinked the haze of her interrupted nap from her eyes, barely registering the figure that came barreling toward her. Before she knew it, her body had teetered backwards before being pulled off the barricade in a tight embrace.

"Happy-fucking-birthday," a familiar voice sang in her ear.

Bec stared ahead blankly for a few moments before she realized what was happening. When she did, she clutched onto her best friend and let loose a wild, gleeful shriek as they both jumped up and down.

"What the fuck?" Bec said as she pulled away and held Stevie at arm's length. "What are you doing here?"

"We're here for you, of course." Stevie smiled devilishly as she gestured behind her.

Bec looked over Stevie's shoulder at the five others on the street, luggage rumbling over the cracked concrete behind them. Her eyes lit up as she looked at them. It was only when she saw the person who brought up the rear of the group that she felt her newfound excitement instantly drain from her body. Her eyes tore back to Stevie, who gave her a knowing look and dropped her voice to a whisper.

"I promise I didn't know he was coming until I came down to the hotel lobby this morning."

Tyler met the group halfway, leaving Bec and Stevie secluded in their conversation.

Bec let her eyes roam over the group one last time before taking a deep breath. "Fuck," she whispered.

"I got your back," Stevie said, draping her arm around Bec's shoulder. "You ready?"

"No." Bec took a deep breath and nodded. "Let's go."

The two walked over to the group, which Tyler had led towards the dock. Every step tightened panic in Bec's chest but she managed to slide a smile on her face as she reached them.

"Well, how do you like your surprise?" Tyler asked with a glimmer in his eyes.

"You flew all of our friends out to Nicaragua just for my birthday?"

"You haven't even heard the best part yet."

"There's more?" Bec flashed a playful look at Tyler but couldn't help the hint of stress that slipped from her lips as she spoke.

"We're spending the week on a private island."

Bec stared at him, a sickening sensation sliding up from her gut as excited yells rippled through the group.

Tyler stepped forward and slid his hand against the small of Bec's back, pulling her closer. "I'm going to make sure this is a birthday you never forget."

Bec stood at the front of the boat, flanked by Stevie and the two other women who'd made the trip. The sea breeze fluttered through her short hair, keeping away the sticky humidity as it tickled her neck.

"Take a picture of me."

The youngest of the group, Eleni, abruptly shoved her phone towards Stevie and took position at the bow of the boat. Before Stevie could even angle the camera lens towards her, she was already posing. Stevie snapped a few shots of Eleni before attempting to hand the phone back to her.

"No, a few more," Eleni insisted, trying a different pose this time.

Stevie tapped the phone screen five more times before casting a look back at Bec. Eleni didn't notice, continuing to toss her hair back and forth and look dramatically off the edge of the boat.

"Oh wait—let me get one like this, too."

Bec stifled a laugh as Stevie's eyes went wide. She silently mouthed the words 'save me' before snapping a few more pictures.

Monique, the only other person aside from Stevie that Bec considered a close friend, watched the impromptu photoshoot that Stevie had gotten suckered into with a tight gaze.

"Okay, Ms. Supermodel," she interrupted, waving a hand dismissively towards Eleni. "I think she got it."

Eleni shot her a sour look before taking the phone back from Stevie. She scoured through the camera roll, her face puckering one second and lighting up with excitement the next.

"Oh-my-God," she swooned as she zoomed in on one of the photos of herself. "I'm posting this as soon as we get there."

"Good luck with that," Monique said before taking a sip of champagne from the short, plastic glass in her hand. "Benny heard from Tyler that this place is totally remote. No service at all."

"Seriously?" Eleni groaned. "What if my agency calls?"

Monique gave her a sideways glare that went unnoticed by Eleni, whose eyes were still buried in her phone screen. The hostility wasn't missed by Bec who shot a curious look at the two of them. In the time since Bec and Tyler had started dating and their mismatched friend group had formed, Bec had found it difficult to bond with Eleni. She knew Stevie also found the self-proclaimed country club brat hard to bear—but Monique? Bec had assumed that Monique got along with Eleni the best out of all of them. The two had worked together on a few photoshoots. As Brand Director for her company, Monique had practically gotten Eleni the modeling gigs. They were friends, right? Now as Bec watched the two shoot silent scowls at each other, she wondered if something had happened. Surely, Monique would have told her if something had? Bec watched carefully but the moment passed by without any more dramatics. She furrowed her brow as her gaze wandered out to the ocean. Maybe she didn't know Monique as well as she thought.

The endless glimmer of the blue water quickly distracted Bec. She found her mind wandering peacefully as the low roar of the boat gliding across the waves drowned out the world. She sipped on what remained of the champagne they'd all cheersed with as they departed the marina. There had been a fleeting moment when they'd drifted out past the other boats and into the open ocean that Bec had wondered if she could escape this. She'd imagined telling the captain to stop, to turn around, and take them back. She'd convince Tyler to change plans to something else—anything else. But as she had turned towards the back of the boat where the captain steered them forward, she had locked eyes with the person she had hoped to escape most of all. It was in that moment she knew there was no stopping this. She'd made her bed—there was no getting untangled from the sheets now.

Stevie leaned into Bec's side and gave her a soft nudge. "Hey," she whispered. "You're not pissed at me are you?"

Bec sighed as she pulled her focus to her best friend. "No, I'm not mad at you, but a heads up would have be fucking appreciated," she said, nudging her back playfully.

Stevie frowned and brushed a piece of fiery orange hair out of her face as the wind blew it every which way. "Shit, I know, I'm sorry," she said as she leaned in closer. "I really wanted to tell you but Tyler made me promise. He said I'd ruin the whole thing if I told you what the plan was."

"And you listened to him?" She laughed but the joy slipped from her face quickly. Bec took a sharp breath and gave her friend her best attempt at a smile. "I'm not mad, Stevs. I promise."

Bec looked over her shoulder towards the back of the boat. The guys were absorbed in their own conversation, laughing with half-smoked cigars hanging out of their mouths. Bec's eyes wandered through the group carefully, looking for him. It didn't take long. He was staring right at her. His gaze seemed to cut the distance between them. His dark eyes bore into her with an intensity that made her cheeks flush. She felt like she might get pulled to him like opposite magnets attracting each other. She looked away quickly.

"This is fucked," Bec whispered, taking a big swig of her champagne.

Stevie looked back to where Bec's focus had been. She let out a deep sigh.

"When was the last time you talked to him?"

Bec let out a breathy laugh, the slightest bit of cynicism seeping from it. "Last week."

"What?" Stevie's voice raised a few octaves above a comfortable whisper.

Both Bec and Stevie looked around. Monique and Eleni had put more distance between themselves. Monique was up ahead, her arms leaned onto the railing as she drank her champagne. Eleni had made her way across the right side of the boat where she was now sitting on the netted floor and taking selfies on her phone. Neither was paying attention, let alone eavesdropping.

"I thought you blocked his number?" Stevie whispered harshly.

Bec hesitated.

"So that's a no?"

"It doesn't matter." Bec let out a deep sigh before chugging the rest of her champagne. "I thought this trip was going to be hard enough to get through with just me and Tyler."

"Fuck," Stevie said.

"Fuck," Bec confirmed.

A silence took up the space between them. They both stared at the ocean for a minute before Stevie looked up at Bec. "What did he say?"

Bec bit her bottom lip absentmindedly before shaking some stray thoughts out of her head. "Nothing important." Stevie didn't need to know how much she'd truly failed at remedying the mess she'd created. Bec gave her a curt smile as she lifted her empty glass. "Do you mind filling me up? I really don't want to go over there right now," she said, nodding her head to the back of the boat.

"Anything for the birthday girl," Stevie replied. After a few seconds, an unusual seriousness drifted its way onto Stevie's face. "You know whatever happens, I'm going to be on your side, right?" She gave Bec a long and hard look as she took the glass. "No matter how badly you think you've fucked up? Or how many times?"

Bec let a small smile flitter across her face. "I know. We're locked in for life, remember? 'Til we die."

Stevie let out a loud laugh as she made her way over to the makeshift bar. "Til we die," she yelled into the ocean air.

Bec heard the guys welcome Stevie over and resisted the urge to look. She knew he was still looking at her, she didn't need the reminder. She just hoped he wasn't deciding if now was the perfect time to confront her. Before that moment could become reality, Bec walked over to the railing and peered over the edge. The water rushed under the boat as they jetted forward. Bec looked back to where they'd come from. The mainland was just a smudge of green in the vast blue behind them. They'd been out here for an hour, maybe close to two already. That was her best guess, at least. She'd stashed her phone in her backpack and ditched it in the galley with the rest of their luggage. There was no use for it. She'd gotten a notification from her carrier the minute they'd touched down. No service available. That's what she got for buying the cheapest phone plan possible. How remote was this island anyway? And why did Tyler insist they celebrate here?

The air around Bec shifted as someone came up behind her. It wasn't Stevie, she couldn't bear to be that silent. The hairs on the back of Bec's neck prickled as a hand slipped around her waist. The touch was both delicate and rough, pulling her close against a firm body.

"Miss me?"

Bec's heart crawled out of her stomach as she recognized Tyler's voice. She told herself that the feeling that heaved in the back of her chest now was surprise, not disappointment. She turned around and offered Tyler a smile, pushing the heavy twinge of shame away as best she could.

"Hi."

She raised up on her tiptoes and planted a quick kiss on his lips. As she pulled away, she felt a quiver of repulsion inside of her. Not for her affection, but for the way she had so easily slipped back into normalcy for a moment.

"Thank you for this," she muttered, waving her hand around the boat. "You really didn't need to do all this."

"It's your 30th birthday," he said matter-of-factly. "A surprise party at your apartment seemed vastly underwhelming."

"For you, maybe," she stressed, her voice soft. "Not all of us grew up with galas and summer trips to the Amalfi Coast."

Tyler pulled her in quickly, hoisting her up onto the railing before she could react. Her fingers dug into his arm instinctively as she teetered on the edge.

"I thought you deserved something a little more... memorable."

The roar of the water below pulled Bec's attention as she balanced on the edge between the boat and the churning deep. For a second, she was mesmerized. One shift of her weight and she would be over the edge, dropped into the depths below. She could swim but she doubted that would do much good. The thought of being sucked under the boat and diced up by the propeller made her mouth go dry. Even her own guilt had limits.

Tyler stepped closer, his body pushing its way in between Bec's legs. His lips breathed hot air into her ear as he spoke.

"I want you to remember one thing."

His hand caressed the back of her neck, ever so slowly leaning her backwards. Bec's hand gripped his shirt. He had total control of her bodyweight, holding it delicately on the outer edge of the railing. She looked into his eyes, their green hues flashing back at her with wicked excitement.

"You deserve this."

Bec felt her body drop backwards. Her stomach heaved, preparing for the fall before Tyler lifted her off the railing and back onto the deck. Her heart thumped in her chest as she grabbed hold of the railing, eager to steady herself.

"Señor," the captain yelled up at Tyler, his voice rising above the whip of the wind.

Tyler and Bec both looked at him before following the direction of his outstretched hand. Ahead of them laid an island, the only dot of life in the endless blue landscape.

"Wow," Bec said under her breath.

The island slowly came into view. A long dock rested on wooden stilts and a sandy path seemed to wind up through the trees. Deeper into the interior, the shape of a roof poked out through the palm fronds that surrounded it.

A wide grin stretched over Tyler's face as he looked ahead. "We're here."

Their footfalls crunched in the sand as a short, middle aged woman guided them up the path. Palm trees and overgrowth crowded the narrow trail, requiring the group to push a stray frond out of the way from time to time as they made their way forward.

"This path from the dock will lead you straight to the house," the woman continued. "There is another that leads from the house to the beach."

Monique yelped and swatted at a dragonfly that buzzed near her head, resulting in a low chuckle from her husband who was close behind.

"There are many paths that lead away from the house..."

The woman's voice drifted away as she rounded a corner, slipping from view. Bec sauntered along with the rest of the group. She let her gaze drift through the jungle around them, taking in the lush vibrancy of it all. Sand turned to pebble as the path turned to something more manmade. As Bec rounded the corner the woman had taken, the vegetation opened up to a large house with a pristinely manicured lawn in front.

"Jesus," Stevie muttered from behind Bec. "This place looks straight out of an HGTV show."

Bec looked back at her with raised eyebrows. "You watch HGTV?"

"Not by choice," Stevie said, trying to defend herself. "But when I was dating—" Her voice tapered off, her words dropping under her breath cautiously. "You know..."

Bec shot a look ahead of them. She had been so wrapped up in her own bullshit she'd forgotten she wasn't the only one stuck on an island with someone she'd rather avoid. She resisted prying into Stevie's thoughts about the whole thing and instead nodded her head towards the house.

"You're right, though. This place is beautiful."

Bec let her eyes take everything in as the group maneuvered up the rest of the path. While Bec had never been forced to watch extravagant home-buying shows by an ex, the sight in front of her did bring back memories. It looked like something out of the travel magazines she'd read at the library as a kid. She'd flipped through so many pages of lavish homes and tropical getaways, she was sure she'd seen something exactly like this. Maybe it had been one of the photos she'd torn from the magazine and shoved in her pocket to later tape to the back of her closet. She'd looked at those many times when the desire to escape her life had grown too strong. She would have filled the entire wall with pictures of places from around the world if her aunt hadn't caught her and threatened to drag her back to the library to fess up. Bec smiled as she stared at the house ahead. If only her 8-year-old self could see this now.

The house's crisp white façade gleamed out from under a red tiled roof. Large windows ran across the front, reflecting the glare of the low sun. Her friends filled passed, no doubt eager to set their bags down and start their vacation after countless hours of travel. Bec, however, seemed to be stuck in place, her feet glued to the path underneath her. Never in her wildest dreams had she ever imagined herself in a place like this.

She caught a glimpse of Tyler, who was enthusiastically chatting with Marta, the woman who had led them to their new home for the weekend. He glanced at Bec absentmindedly as Marta talked. A soft smile worked its way up the corners of his mouth. It was a cocky thing. The type of thing she had seen slide across his face a million times. But something about the way it looked now, mixed with the churning guilt making its way through her insides, made her pause. Tyler was good at surprises, secrets too. He'd kept this whole trip under wraps for who knows how long. Who was to say he wasn't smart enough to see through what was going on now? Who was to say he hadn't figured out her sins before she'd even considered the repercussions?

As Tyler turned back towards Marta, Bec pushed the thought from her mind and closed her eyes. The setting sun hit her skin with a tinge of warmth that competed with the soft chill of the sea breeze tickling her cheek. There was something about the island that made the humidity almost lush now. It was like her skin was soaking up every inch of the moisture and radiating outwards, despite the rot she felt within. She took a deep breath in through her nose and let it out softly. The crunch of pebbles behind her stole the moment from Bec and her eyes snapped open abruptly.

"Hey."

Bec didn't need to turn around to know who it was. She took a step towards the house but her body was tugged backwards as a firm grip wrapped around her wrist. The touch felt like electricity against her skin. It was equal parts danger and bliss.

"Please, we need to talk."

She whipped around to face him. "Are you fucking crazy?" she seethed in a whispered tone as she yanked her wrist away. The loss of his touch hit her like an ache in the chest but she ignored it. Bec's heart raced as she looked over her shoulder. Tyler was facing the house, still discussing things with Marta and a short man who had joined them.

"He's right there." Bec widened her eyes at him harshly, like she was scolding a child and not a grown man.

Her vicious stare only drew a smile from him. It was the kind of thing that had melted her time and time again but now it only drove panic through her.

"He's not even paying attention. Plus, we're all friends here, right? We can talk."

Bec took a sharp inhale, trying to calm down. Was she overreacting? After peering over her shoulder one more time, she took a small step towards him and dropped her voice to no more than a whisper.

"Why are you here, Miles?"

He let out a soft laugh, like the question was unbelievable to even consider. "Because it's your birthday and I wanted to spend time with you." He leaned in closer, his breath hot on her cheek. "And you gave me no other option."

She shook her head. "You shouldn't be—" her voice rose quickly but she stopped herself.

She looked around again. She was paranoid, but for good reason. Everyone was busy checking out the house. Everyone was preoccupied. Everyone except for one person. A tall, burly man stared at her from the patio, his eyes glaring. Bec pulled her gaze away from him quickly. Fuck. She would undoubtedly have to deal with Benny later. The trip was going to be up in flames within the first ten minutes if she wasn't careful—if he wasn't careful. She glared at Miles.

"This isn't the time. We can talk about this when we're back in LA. Just—" She took a deep, ragged breath. "Just enjoy the trip and keep your distance. Okay?"

Before she could lose the sliver of strength she had managed to find, she picked up her bags and walked away. Her fingers gripped the strap of her backpack a little too tightly, her knuckles going white. A flurry of thoughts ricocheted around in her head as she crossed the yard to the house. This was bad—really bad. Part of her wanted to believe that he would keep his distance, but who was she kidding? He couldn't stay away from her any more than she could stay away from him. That's how this mess had started. Bec lugged her bags across the patio and squeezed passed Benny. She refused to look at him but could feel the heat of his stare on the nape of her neck. When she'd put some distance between them, she dropped her bags down inside and took it all in.

The house was impressive, but she wouldn't expect anything less from Tyler. The main room consisted of a fully-equipped kitchen and large living room. To her left was a long hallway, which her friends bobbed through giddily, claiming rooms for themselves and dumping their luggage. Wonder and delight ripped through the air like electricity. But it was all missed on Bec. The uneasiness that had clung to her the moment she'd slinked down the jetway in LAX had only grown more ominous and inescapable throughout the day. Now, as Miles stepped in through the sliding glass door to claim a room for himself, she felt dread's suffocating grip around her throat.

Bec flinched as Tyler's lips found the nook of her neck.

"Pick a room for us yet?"

A sharp breath jumped down into her lungs. "Fuck," she whispered. "You scared me."

He wrapped his arm around her. "Always so jumpy," he teased. "Want me to pick a room and set your bags down?"

She hesitated, her heart still pounding in her chest. "I, um—" She nodded her head and looked down the hallway. "Sure."

He kissed the side of her head before slipping around her and hoisting her bags up from the floor. "Relax—have a drink," he shot back as he disappeared into the room closest to the kitchen. "We're here to celebrate."

Bec watched Eleni and Adrian chat at the end of the hallway. Adrian had picked a room right across from Eleni. Bec could tell by the way his eyes kept slipping down Eleni's body that he was hoping it wouldn't take long for his room to become hers. Bec was rooting for him, too. Adrian was a nice guy, much nicer than Tyler's other business associates. She hadn't necessarily grown close to Adrian in the time she'd dated Tyler, but his presence added a sense of calm to the group. Maybe it was his quiet nature or the fact that he mainly just focused all of his time on trying to gain Eleni's favor. It was nice to have that girl distracted and out of everyone's business. Bec let out a breathy laugh, prying her eyes from Adrian's poor attempt at flirting, as she headed towards the fridge. The weekend might get wilder than expected and for that, Bec needed a drink. A tall man stepped in front of her, casting a harsh glare that made Bec pause.

"Umm, hi. I was just going to get something to drink."

The man looked at her stoically. Bec's eyes flickered across the kitchen.

"Uh, sorry. I'll just—" As she took a step out of the kitchen, the shorter man that Tyler had been talking to earlier appeared at her side.

"Hola. Hello," he declared, a warm smile beaming from his face. "Can I get you something?"

"Um, a beer?"

"Yes, of course," he nodded, quickly sidestepping the other man and dipping into the fridge. Bec's eyes flickered to the taller man while the shorter one popped the cap off her beer. Did the mean-looking guy not speak English or was he just as unfriendly as he looked? The shorter man turned back around, offering her the drink.

"Thank you," she said, taking it from him gingerly. "What's your name?"

"Ramon," he announced, his smile never leaving his face. He pointed back towards the other man with his thumb. "That is Jamari. Anything you need, we are here for you."

Bec offered a soft smile and raised her beer towards them. "Well...thanks."

"Of course," Ramon answered, nodding at her.

He turned to Jamari and muttered something in Spanish before the two men drifted from the kitchen and out onto the patio. Bec watched them curiously as she lifted the beer to her lips.

"Getting started already I see."

The heaviness returned to Bec's stomach as Benny approached her, eyeing her with the same harsh, lingering stare that he'd shot her way earlier. She looked back towards the hallway, praying that Stevie would wander in and save her from the conversation she knew was coming. Benny stepped towards the fridge and helped himself to a beer. He was dressed in a tropical print shirt with all but two of the buttons undone. Underneath the shirt was a wall of muscle and a gold chain. Benny had played two years of professional football before retiring early that year but looking at him, you'd guess he was still hitting the field every Sunday.

"So..." he started. "How does it feel to be joining the 30's club?"

She looked at him carefully. Was he warming her up with pleasantries before he sucker punched her?

"Good. Can't wait to experience the catastrophic hangovers you always bitch about," she replied.

Benny let out a chuckle and leaned back on the counter, downing a good amount of his beer. "Oh, just you wait...I'm sure your next hangover will teach you a lesson."

Her gaze tightened on him as she sipped her own beer. Asshole.

"Speaking of hangovers," Tyler cut in, stepping into the kitchen and wrapping his hands around Bec's waist. "I think it's time we popped open some more champagne and kicked off the weekend properly, don't you?"

"More champagne?" Stevie taunted as she hopped onto one of the barstools at the kitchen island. "Is this a country club fundraiser?"

"I, for one, would love some champagne, Tyler," Eleni cooed as she sat down next to Stevie.

Stevie grimaced at her before slapping her hands down on the counter. "Well, damn, Tyler. You heard Her Majesty. Pop the champagne."

Eleni let out a curt huff before pulling out her phone and pretending to busy herself. As Tyler dug around the fridge for the champagne, Bec found her focus drifting to Marta. She had seemed friendly on the walk up but Bec wondered if there was such a thing as too friendly. Their host hadn't given them a moment to breath since they'd landed on the dock and hiked their way up to the main house. Even now as the group gathered around and began picking at the vast array of fruits and cheeses that had been laid out for them, their host was stationed by the door, her pearly white veneers smiling at them in a Cheshire's grin. Bec gave her a weary smile and forced her gaze away from the woman. She ate a few crackers and flinched at the sudden pop of the champagne cork behind her. Eleni hooted and clapped as Tyler held the bottle up victoriously, foam and bubbles dripping down the neck. Bec's stomach gnawed at her. Now that the stress of traveling was slowly leaving her body, she could feel deep pangs of hunger. She grabbed a handful of grapes, plopping them one by one into her mouth.

"One for you," Tyler announced as he held a glass of champagne out to Bec. She plopped the last grape in her mouth and took the glass from him.

"Thanks."

As he handed out the rest of the glasses, Bec found her eyes wandering back to the door where Marta was still stationed.

"Ty," Bec called out softly.

He handed the last glass to Adrian before heading back over to Bec and wrapping his hands around her. "Yes?" he murmured softly in her ear.

She pulled away from him and rested her hand against his chest. The gesture was the most Bec could manage at the moment without her guilt ripping from her body and spewing out the truth. How could she spend the entire weekend with him when the simplest act of affection set her nerves on edge? Tyler titled his head curiously as Bec's hesitation dragged on. She let out a nervous laugh before shooting a look back towards Marta.

"So is this trip chaperoned, or...?"

Tyler laughed. "No, the staff leaves when I tell them to."

He gave Bec's ass a squeeze before walking across the kitchen towards Marta. As he began talking to her, Benny took a step closer.

"He really cares about you, you know."

"I know." Bec looked at Benny, and his eyes told her that the moment she had been dreading was finally here. "I'm lucky to have him," she added before taking a sip of champagne.

"I'm glad you think that."

Bec could feel his contempt snake its way down into her stomach and take hold.

"He's been my best friend since college and I've never seen him as happy as he is with you."

She should have found his words endearing but they kept Bec's gaze fixed to the tile floor. She knew what was coming, she just didn't know if he had the balls to say it here.

"It's not my business if you don't care about him anymore."

"Benny, I—"

"You might not care about losing him but I do."

Bec swallowed her unease as Benny leaned into close.

"If the truth comes out about that night, we'll both be dead to him. And that doesn't work for me."

Bec's gaze tightened as she looked up at him.

"So don't fuck up." His eyes bore into hers as he gestured his thick fingers between them loosely. "Or we have a problem." He muttered something under his breath before leaving her standing alone in the kitchen.

Goosebumps prickled on Bec's skin despite the hot, humid air filtering in from the open patio door. Her eyes darted to where Benny had joined Monique in the living room and then to Miles, whose eyes hadn't left her since they'd all assembled in the kitchen. He was leaned up against the sliding glass door, half inside and half outside. His eyes seemed to seep under her clothes. A subtle smile danced across his face. He knew what he was doing. Or maybe— maybe he wasn't doing anything at all. Maybe it was Bec's fault that every time she looked at that warm smile of his, she was transported back to the first time she'd met him.

Tyler had hosted a dinner party to introduce her to his friends. It wasn't supposed to change anything but meeting Miles had somehow completely derailed her. A handshake and a smile. His touch had felt like fire against her skin even then. Small talk. Understanding. How could one person feel like home? Lingering stares. A deep need that made her insides crawl. Before she knew it she'd run off the tracks, unconcerned with the damage she'd cause. Now she sucked in a breath as his eyes met her from across the room. With one look, he could see her for all she was. It was like he knew her more than she knew herself—like he'd always known her. The gaze felt too intimate for the space they shared and Bec crossed her arms protectively, looking away.

Crack!

A swift clap shot through the air. Everyone's gaze ripped over to the side of the kitchen as Marta's hands clapped together. As she waited for all eyes to be on her, the wide, contrived smile never left her face.

"Beloved guests," she said in her thick Polish accent. "Before I leave you, I want to inform you more about your stay here with us."

Bec eyed the woman as the words poured out of her like a gravy. Marta wore a stiffly-pressed white blouse and white pants to match. Her feet were slipped into beige sandals that contrasted against the bright red polish on her toes and long fingernails that stayed stiffly intertwined in front of her as she spoke. Her hair was pulled back into a tight bun with a red flower tucked behind her ear.

"...the bugs can be quite a pest at night so I recommend the bug spray and turning off the outside lights when you go to bed..."

Bec's focus drifted to Tyler; he was standing next to Marta, his muscular arms folded across his chest, a pleased look cemented on his face. She couldn't help but think about Benny's comment. At least four people knew what happened that night—and that was assuming Benny hadn't told Monique. Bec chewed on the inside of her cheek as she thought about worst case scenarios. Screaming. Fighting. Silence. It would all make for a very awkward trip. But a part of her wondered if it would be better that way—to clear the air in one fell swoop, like ripping off a Band-Aid.

Her attention jerked back to reality as she noticed eyes burrowing into her. Marta continued talking to the group but her eyes were fixed on Bec. Discomfort grew in Bec's stomach the longer the woman stared. Her attention didn't drift to anyone else for the next minute or so. Bec tried to look away, to shift the woman's gaze somewhere else. But every time Bec's eyes wandered back, Marta's seemed to be waiting for her. Bec took a long gulp of champagne until finally, like a curse being broken, Marta's eyes flickered away. The moment felt so odd that Bec wondered if it had even happened or if she had imagined it. She felt herself let out the breath that she'd been holding as the woman's speech continued.

"...The staff will be here for you until Friday afternoon." Marta took a brief pause to look at Tyler beside her. He gave her a silent nod, prompting her to continue. "After that, you will have the island to yourselves to explore."

Hushed excitement filtered through the group. Stevie said something about an island rager under her breath which caused Monique to shoot an amused look her way.

"Please note," Marta said, extending a finger in the air. "We do have a security guard who stays on the far side of the island." She paused and gave them all a tight-lipped smile. "Felix is mainly there to keep away those who may want to camp or fish on the island."

Marta paused and looked back at Tyler who towered over her. Her gaze was stern. Tyler didn't notice, he was staring at Bec. Excitement dripped from his smug grin.

"It is a few hours' walk to him. He can assist if anything urgent should happen," Marta continued.

Bec's gaze drifted to Stevie whose eyes were glazing over in boredom. As she noticed her friend's attention, Stevie's face lit up before pretending to nod off. Her head bobbed wildly, as if she'd just jolted awake from an involuntary nap. Bec stifled a laugh as she focused back on Marta.

"There is no service or Wi-Fi."

From somewhere in the room, Bec heard a disapproving moan from Eleni.

"There is one boat on and off the island," Marta continued. "The staff will leave with it Friday after lunch service and return Monday before breakfast service. If anyone should need to leave the island, Felix has a satellite phone to use in emergency."

Marta let a silence fill the room as she looked at the group one by one. After an unsettling amount of silence, she nodded.

"Dinner will be served shortly. The staff—" she said, gesturing to Ramon and Jamari who reappeared by the patio door, the waft of smoke and heat floating into the air from the barbeque behind them. "—will retire to the back house after dinner and return for breakfast service." She gave the group one last Cheshire grin while she let the silence drift back over the room. Her voice snapped with a cheerful abruptness. "Please enjoy your stay."

She left without another word. The group looked around at each other with bewilderment plastered on their faces but excitement growing in their eyes.

Stevie's voice broke the silence of the room. "So who's ready for shots?"

Fizzy tartness popped on Bec's tongue as she sunk her teeth into the slice of lime. She gave a shiver, causing Stevie to let out a loud cackle of laughter next to her.

"Ah come on," Stevie sneered. "I taught you better than that."

Bec made a face as she set the emptied shot glass on the counter. "I don't care how expensive Tyler said this tequila is. It still tastes like that cheap shit you give me during your shifts."

"Hey now," Stevie retorted, her eyebrows raising up past the fiery orange bangs that draped onto her forehead. "I give you that cheap shit for free."

"Yes and I love you for that. But can't you..." Bec wavered for a second, her eyes losing focus across the kitchen before quickly returning to Stevie. "Uh, um—can't you sneak me that top shelf stuff from time to time?"

Stevie grabbed Bec's shoulders and gave them a little shake. "You are the only thing standing in the way of all of the free, expensive booze you want."

Bec could feel a 'but' coming.

"You just gotta flirt with my manager. Like I already told you," Stevie stressed with a cheeky grin.

Bec made another face as the thought of cozying up to Stevie's manager snapped through her mind. Although the man was only ten years older than them both, his wandering eyes and scratchy-looking neckbeard were enough to give Bec the creeps whenever she came into the dive bar to visit Stevie.

"No chance," Bec grimaced. "I'd rather drink rot-gut tequila for the rest of my life."

"Speaking of tequila," Monique said as she slid between the two of them. "Who wants to take a shot?"

Stevie's eyes lit up as she smirked at Monique. "Bec does. She was just saying how excited she was to take another."

"Oh, fuck you," Bec laughed as she began arranging three shot glasses in a line.

"Always the instigator," Monique smiled, her eyes lingering on Stevie as she uncorked the tequila bottle.

"Funny how you're the one who suggested taking shots."

"But you agreed, no?"

Stevie let out a breathy laugh before sloshing some

tequila into the three little glasses. "Stubborn as hell. Seems some things never change."

A smile grew on Bec's face as Monique and Stevie continued to hurl snarky, playful comments at each other. She liked seeing them like this. She missed it. They both looked so happy in the moment. It was like nothing had changed, even though everything had. Bec held her gaze steadily on Stevie, trying to read the emotions behind the calculated smirk on her face. Did Stevie miss it too? Movement out of the corner of Bec's eye pulled her focus again. She froze momentarily, catching Miles' gaze as he sipped on his drink from across the kitchen. She had to stop doing this. She couldn't act like a deer caught in headlights every time he looked at her. As she turned to look away, he moved. She widened her eyes at him sternly, as if firing a warning shot across the room. She didn't know where Tyler was. He was probably outside smoking another cigar with Benny. It didn't matter—she shouldn't be anywhere near Miles. But as he stepped closer, she couldn't find the strength to move away.

"Looks like you're having fun."

Bec rolled her eyes at him. "Are you just going to watch me the entire weekend?"

He let out a soft laugh, holding his gaze on her. "I'm trying to do a lot more to you than watch this weekend."

Color flooded Bec's cheeks as he flashed a devilish smile. He took a step closer, brushing his fingers against her thigh. Bec pulled in a sharp breath as his fingers tugged on the belt loop of her denim shorts. Before she knew it, her body had moved closer to his.

"Don't," she whispered.

Monique and Stevie might have been preoccupied now, but Bec knew that wouldn't last forever. She pulled away from Miles' touch slowly, reluctantly. His eyes drifted down her body as she created space between them.

"I miss you." His eyes flickered up to hers. "Do you miss

me?"

Bec's words caught in her throat. Her brow knotted in concern as the question threw itself around her mind. "I—"

Clap!

Bec's heart leapt into her chest as Marta's hands slapped together in harsh unison.

"Guests!" Her voice bellowed over the music that played through Benny's small Bluetooth speaker. "It is time for dinner."

Bec's eyes flickered across the room. Eleni and Adrian were talking on the couch. Monique and Stevie shifted next to her, quickly throwing back their shots before heading to the table. Bec surveyed the room once more, her gut dropping lower every second he was unaccounted for. Finally, Tyler's head popped up behind Marta as he stepped in through the patio door.

"Chow time, everyone," he called. "Come eat."

He caught Bec's eye before he ducked out of the house, flashing her a playful smile. She felt her chest fall in relief as the breath she'd been holding slipped from her lungs.

"Like I told you last week," Miles whispered as he stepped closer to her. "I'm not going to throw this away." He leaned down and reached across her to grab the bottle of tequila off the counter. "You mean too much to me." He was so close that his lips tickled her ear.

Bec stood still as he headed out towards the patio, empty glass and tequila bottle in hand. She closed her eyes and took a deep, shaky breath. *Get it together.* She fought to shake the flurry of emotions in her stomach. It was more than nerves. As she opened her eyes, her gaze fixed on the untouched shot glass resting on the counter. She bared her teeth before picking it up and throwing it to the back of her throat. It seemed to burn up through her nose, sending little signals of pain to her brain. She steadied the gag before heading outside.

Dinner was being served on the lower patio. Although the

patio that rested a few feet from the house was nice enough with its barbeque, wicker chairs, and fire pit, this one held a large dining table. There were small yard lights stuck into the grass surrounding it, giving the space an atmospheric glow. It felt special, private. Bec eyed the table carefully as her foot reached the last of the stone steps. Everyone had already taken their seats. Plates were being set down by the friendly man Bec had met earlier—Ramon. She gave him a small smile as she slid into the open seat next to Tyler. Bec sized up the plate of food in front of her. Seared mahi mahi, grilled vegetables, and rice. Her stomach growled expectantly. Just as she was about to dig into the first real meal she'd had all day, Tyler pushed out his chair. He stood up from the table and raised his glass. As Ramon headed back to the house, Marta hung in the shadows of the palm trees that lined the far end of the patio.

Tyler cleared his throat. "I gotta say, when I first came up with the idea to have this get-together for Bec's birthday…"

Adrian huffed in response. His expression grew dark for an instant before his pleasantries snapped back. He smiled at Tyler. "Man's so rich he rents out an entire island and calls it a get-together."

Tyler stared at Adrian before a small grin flickered across his face. "So rich someone could probably rob me blind and I'd never know."

Adrian dropped his gaze to the plate of food in front of him. His short frame and hesitant demeanor was dwarfed by the 6'5" linebacker sitting next to him.

"Hey man," Benny interjected. "Maybe you can rent out a castle in Ireland for Monique and my one-year anniversary next year."

Benny pointed his fingers in tiny guns at Tyler while his eyes prodded him in jest. His face was flushed from alcohol. Bec hid her irritation as she took a sip of water. Typical Benny. Already seconds away from being blackout drunk.

"Like I was saying," Tyler said with a small chuckle,

ignoring the comment, "when I first came up with the idea, I was skeptical I could actually pull it off." He took a deep breath and shook his head. "I mean, we all have busy lives. We all have a lot going on..." His eyes flickered down to Bec who was sitting on his right. "But we all made time because it wasn't just anyone's birthday."

Bec blushed nervously, her body only relaxing when Stevie, who was sitting next to her, raised her glass and let out a little hoot.

"I'll save the rest for her actual birthday..." Tyler looked around the table at his friends one more time. "...but thank you all for coming. This trip is important and I knew it couldn't be everything I dreamed of without each and every one of you here."

Bec looked around the table. Eleni was sitting on Tyler's left at one head of the table, eyes locked on him. Adrian's gaze was down on the plate in front of him, either hungry or ignoring Tyler's little speech. Benny held her gaze firmly, eyes bloodshot, while Monique gleamed a big smile at her. Bec's gaze stopped at the other end of the table where Miles sat.

"I know we all love Bec..." Tyler continued.

Miles' eyes flashed excitedly before Bec tore her gaze from him.

"...And we all know if she gets any more attention she'll want to die—so I'll end this here. Cheers to Bec and this time we have together." He washed his eyes over the table of friends one more time and smiled widely. "I know it'll be something I'll never forget."

The group raised their glasses and clinked them happily as thank you's and excitement buzzed around the table. Sips were taken and forks clattered on plates as everyone dug into the fresh meal in front of them. As food preoccupied the group, Bec snuck a quick glance towards Miles. He was taking a sip of his drink. It only took a second for his eyes to meet hers. Against her better judgment, she let herself settle into it. One look from him was all it took to ease her most days. Whether she'd had an awful client or a fight with Tyler, she could always count on Miles to be there for her. Even if she didn't want to talk about it, even if she couldn't, he was there. Bec found herself forgetting the world around her. The party. The island. The situation. She was all right. That was, until he shot her a wink. It snapped her back to reality. Bec looked away hastily, the abashed flush of her cheeks contrasting the worry inside of her. It was the dangerous dance between the desire that she had been starving and the panic that ate at her whenever Tyler and Miles shared the same space. Bec's eyes flickered around the table quickly, desperately making sure no one had seen. Only when she was certain the coast was clear did she dare look back. Miles took a bite of food, his eyes still locked on her. Just as she was about to break her gaze away, a hand crept up her thigh. She jumped, startled by the touch. Tyler let out a breathy laugh as he stroked the sliver of bare skin.

"Easy, it's just me."

Bec gave him a flighty smile. "Sorry, you know I get a little jumpy when I drink."

He gave her an obvious look. "Or when you're hiding something."

"Wh—" Bec's throat closed with a dreadful tightness. She fought to catch her breath like she was drowning in a hatch filling with water. "What do you mean?" she choked.

Tyler held her gaze silently, a smile creeping up into the corners of his mouth. The longer the silence grew the more Bec felt a jumble of apologies and testimony climbing up her esophagus with razor-like cruelty.

"You got the gig at Buccellati. Monique told me earlier."

Bec slowly felt herself coming back to equilibrium as the feral panic inside of her subsided. "Yeah," she stammered. "They really liked my portfolio and decided to have me shoot their new campaign."

"That's amazing. I'm proud of you."

The certainty in his gaze made Bec's insides itch. "I just didn't want to jinx it. You know? It's a big job. I mean it's for their entire holiday campaign. Just the stills, of course. Someone else is shooting the commercial..." She felt herself slipping into a ramble as his unrelenting focus gnawed at her guilt. She forced herself to swallow the shakiness in her voice. "I was going to tell you when we got back from the trip." She averted her eyes and chewed at the inside of her cheek.

"Of course, babe." He gave her an amused look before eyeing the plate of untouched food in front of her. "Aren't you hungry? You said you were starving."

"Uh yeah," she stammered, picking up her fork and pushing some mahi mahi around the plate before stabbing a piece. "The jetlag has me a little messed up, that's all."

She gave him a quick smile and turned her attention to the meal. She tried to eat but all she could focus on was how Tyler was still looking at her. Only when she saw him turn away did she allow her shoulders to drop the tension they held. She took a long gulp from her glass, draining the rest of her champagne. Champagne to celebrate. She felt a slap of shame. He had planned this whole trip for her. He had made all the arrangements, convinced their friends to go— no doubt paid for them—and here she was, harboring the nastiest of secrets. She forced a piece of fish down her gullet and into the empty wasteland of her stomach. Like a naive child who'd stolen candy, she thought the guilt would pass. But it had been months and here she was, still swimming in it. Bec kept her eyes fixed in front of her as she ate. She needed to do better. So why was it that she found herself staring at Miles, hoping that he would look her way again?

Marta retreated to the back house with Ramon and Jamari

once dinner had concluded. Bec noticed that the two men seemed to follow her around like guard dogs, waiting for the woman to bark orders in Spanish. The three had left the group with a delicious Tres Leches cake that had been reduced to nothing but crumbs and enough liquor to keep them preoccupied until their return in the morning.

Now that the staff was gone, the air seemed stiller to Bec. For the first time since their arrival, she realized just how far removed from civilization they were. No city lights. No traffic. No planes or helicopters flying above like in LA. The only thing that could be heard was the distant crash of waves on the beach or the soft chitter of animals in the jungle. The group had meandered from the dinner table and now sat in the big wicker chairs on the upper patio. Stevie had constructed a fire in the stone pit in the middle of their circle, making sure to chide the guys about her superior survival skills as she did. The crackle of flames mixed with the champagne's buzz lulled Bec into a content stupor. She looked around, noting that her friends seemed to be equally satisfied.

Monique was chatting happily with Stevie, the slight Nigerian accent she'd inherited from her mother slipping through the more she drank. Bec smiled as she watched the two women throw their heads back in laughter. She wondered what they were talking about. She made a mental note to ask Stevie later. Stevie would try to say it was nothing but Bec would pry—that's what best friends were for. There had been a time when seeing Monique and Stevie sitting together, laughs ripping through their lungs as they joked and teased and pushed each other's buttons, was a normal occurrence. How many times had Bec come home to the apartment to find the two nestled together on the couch? They had probably been watching HGTV all those times. But that was a long time ago. The smile fell from Bec's face. A time before Benny. Back then, Bec had thought what Monique had gotten swept up into with Benny was a rebound relationship. No one expected it to go anywhere. If Monique was being honest, Bec thought she might agree that it wasn't supposed to. But it had. Within a year of meeting, the pair had married. Bec remembered the shock that had ripped through her body when Monique asked her to be a bridesmaid. She had said yes, of course. Monique was her friend. But for the months leading up to the wedding, Bec had dealt with Stevie's turmoil over the whole thing. Stevie had tried to pretend it wasn't because of Monique or the wedding but Bec knew. There had been more drunk nights than Bec wanted to remember. Now, Bec watched as Monique shoved Stevie playfully. She was glad that phase was over but was hesitant what this weekend might mean for her friends.

Benny's voice pierced Bec's thoughts. She turned her head to observe the man whose voice boomed like that of a grown man's but whose mannerism still reminded Bec of the frat guys that always hit on her at bars. He was sitting next to Monique but his chair had been scooted away and pulled closely next to Tyler and Adrian's. The three men seemed to be enthralled in conversation, the pitch in their voices raising and falling as excitement and objection flowed through them. Bec stared into the fire as their talk of investments and stocks dulled her senses. Just before she could fully tune them out and melt into the brainless lull of the fire, her ears pricked up.

"But see, that's what I'm saying," Benny remarked. "It's important to put your money in things that match your values. All these big corporations are too quick to sell away their morals. You need to invest in things that support hard working American people."

Bec's gut rumbled with an uneasiness as she strained to hear more, even though she could already hear the political rant that was coming. Although Tyler and Benny considered themselves Moderates, they always seemed to slip into more conservative tendencies—especially whenever alcohol was involved. Which was often.

Tyler laughed. "Okay, I don't disagree. And what would that be?"

"Local businesses."

"For fuck's sake, Benny," Tyler chided. "Are you really going to give me this pitch again?"

"All I'm asking for is $100,000."

Bec's stomach dropped and she forced herself to keep her eyes on the dancing flames in front of her. She leaned to her left as casually as she could, resting her body against the armrest of the chair in the hopes of getting even an inch closer.

After a few seconds of deafening silence, Tyler spoke.

"Yeah? And what happened to the first $20k I gave you?"

As Bec's brow furrowed, Benny let a puff of air escape from his lips.

"Come on, man. You know that was so I could start working on getting proper training and equipment and shit."

The fire seemed to burn its way into Bec's eyeballs as she kept listening.

"This is to start the business," Benny continued. "I have to rent a space, get something to pimp out the shop, and then do a little marketing. You know, really get it going and get my name out there."

Tyler didn't say anything, just tapped his fingers slowly on his wicker chair.

"You'll get 20% of the company."

Benny let the offer hang in the air for a while but Tyler didn't respond. Bec risked a glance up to the group of men. Benny was staring at Tyler impatiently, his eyes almost pleading. Still, Tyler said nothing. When Benny couldn't take it anymore, he filled the silence.

"Seriously, man. It's not like you need the money." Benny's voice grew more agitated, his words slurring slightly from all the alcohol he'd downed since they arrived. "How much did you spend on this trip?"

The question made Bec's skin crawl. She didn't want to

know the answer; she knew it would be a sickening amount. But still, her curiosity got the best of her and she leaned in a little more.

Tyler let out a breathy laugh. "A trip to celebrate the woman I love with all of our closest friends is a little different than giving you money so you can open up a barber shop."

"Exactly," Benny almost hissed. He sat up in his chair and leaned towards Tyler. "I'm asking you to dip into your trust fund to support your best friend's dream. You'll even make money out of it…"

Tyler smirked, saying nothing as he sipped his drink.

Benny's eyes darted back and forth, drowning in wine, as he waited impatiently. Finally realizing Tyler wasn't going to budge, he huffed before downing the rest of his drink, sloshing a bit in the corner of his mouth.

"We all know I'll be here for you long after she leaves. But fuck me, right?"

Everything stopped—at least for Bec. It was like every nerve in her body turned to stone. All she could do was stay planted in her seat and hope the world didn't come crashing down around her. As for the men, a pause had seemed to wash over them too. Bec didn't dare look up, for fear that one of them would be looking right at her. When she finally heard Tyler's voice, it chilled her.

"You don't think my relationship will last?"

Bec didn't need to see him to know by the tone of his voice that a wicked smile had grown on his face.

"Do you know something I don't, Benny boy?"

Bec's eyes flashed up to Benny. Almost as if he sensed her distress, he met her gaze instantly. Awareness creeped into his eyes as he realized his hushed conversation wasn't as private as he'd hoped. Now it was time for Bec's eyes to be the ones full of pleading. She silently willed Benny to keep her secret, which was as much his as it was hers now. He pulled away from her before anyone else could notice.

"Uh, what? No," Benny said. He shook his head at Tyler

and grabbed his glass before realizing it was empty. He hesitated. "Sorry, I didn't—I didn't mean that." His eyes flickered down into his lap nervously. "Shit. I'm fucking drunk, man. Sorry," he tried to chuckle.

Bec didn't dare turn further in her chair to look at Tyler, but instead kept her gaze locked on Benny. She watched him refill his wine, spilling more than a few drops on the concrete. Fuck—how drunk was he? Nerves fluttered in Bec's chest. He looked guilty as hell. Bec had never thought about how her secret might have affected him. But now she could see that his guilt was as potent as her own. He was going to blow this.

"I'll make you a deal," Tyler started. "You can have the $100k."

The words seemed to shock them all. Bec's jaw fell open. Adrian, who had been quietly listening as he stared into his lap, whipped his head to attention.

"What?" Benny stammered.

"The $100k. It's yours."

Benny's face contorted in drunk confusion as the words were digested.

"But you have to earn it."

Benny fumbled with his words. "Yeah, yeah, man. Whatever you need me to do."

"Prove to me that you deserve it." Tyler gave him a smug grin. "You're right. It's just a tiny drop of money out of my trust fund. If you can show me that you deserve it, you can have it." Tyler emphasized the words, a poisonous tang coming off of his tone. "Besides, I'm sure Adrian will work twice as hard next year to make sure I don't lose any money on my investments. Right?"

Bec stopped listening to their conversation and turned towards the fire. Whatever was going on with Tyler and his friends, she didn't want to know any more. As much as talk of dropping money on trips and giving out $100,000 loans made Bec squirm in her chair, it wasn't any of her business

what Tyler did with his money. In the year that Tyler and
Bec had been dating, it had been clear to her that they saw
money very differently. Where Bec was running up credit
cards and trying to get clients to pay her on time, Tyler was
tossing money at whatever his heart desired. She tried not to
resent him for it, but sometimes it was hard not to. She shot
a look back at Benny, not listening to the words that flowed
from his mouth in a slur of alcohol but rather watched the
lines bend and warp on his face as he talked. Why did Benny
need to borrow that much money to begin with? The last
time she'd talked to Monique, she had mentioned that Benny
was retiring from football to work at a barber shop. Monique
had ensured Bec that everything was fine and that it would
allow Benny to spend more time at home. She had said it
would be easier for both of them. But now? Now Bec wasn't
sure if she was telling the truth.

Monique and Stevie were still deep in conversation and
it seemed wrong to interrupt whatever was going on. Bec
turned her attention to her right. Eleni was facing away
from Bec, her body leaning over the side of her chair as she
chatted excitedly. Bec barely listened.

The topic of conversation was one she had heard many
times before and she wasn't interested in learning anymore
about Eleni's latest photoshoot or how much a brand had
paid her for a social post. Once again, Bec's eyes found
their way to the fire. The orange and yellow hues reflected
against her pupils as she watched them flicker and spit. Bec
wondered why Tyler had even invited Eleni on this trip in
the first place. Bec wasn't close to Eleni, despite her apparent
effort to transplant herself into the friend group. Benny,
Miles, Adrian, and Eleni had all been Tyler's additions to
their joint friend group that had formed after a few months
of dating. The thought of making her friends Tyler's friends
had unsettled Bec. It felt too soon, too permanent. There
was no easy way to back out of a relationship when your
lives were so intertwined. But when Monique and Benny had

quickly become a couple, Bec hadn't seen any way to avoid melding their social circles. While Bec had initially gotten along with Benny and Adrian just fine, Eleni had been a different story. All Bec knew was that Tyler and Eleni were family friends. To her, that said one thing loud and clear. Like Tyler, Eleni was from money. Bec had tried her best to befriend the girl. It had started out fine. They bonded over their overlapping careers—Bec a freelance photographer and Eleni a model. Bec had even run into her on set once. The shoot had been for the launch of a popular brand's 'plus-size' collection. In normal world standards, at a size 12, Eleni wasn't plus size. But in the modeling world, perceptions were distorted. Their interactions during and after that had been fairly pleasant, but little by little, Bec realized that there was something about the girl that just didn't sit right with her. It was like the harder Bec tried to be friendly, the more Eleni looked down her nose at her, which, even at 5'4" Eleni seemed to do.

"What do you mean you're not dating anyone?" Eleni's voice slipped into the air and burrowed into Bec's eardrums.

Bec glanced over and saw Eleni leaning further over the edge of her chair, her cleavage threatening to spill from her tank top. She put her face in her hand and battered her eyelashes at Miles.

"You're way too hot to be single."

Bec felt heat prickle from the depths of her core. She was used to Eleni flirting with Tyler. If anything it was a usual occurrence, despite the fact that Bec and Tyler were together. Bec told herself she didn't care when Eleni flirted with Tyler because she wasn't the jealous type. But if she was honest with herself—which she would rather not be lately—it wasn't that. She wasn't jealous because she'd let Eleni steal Tyler from her. If anything, it'd make Bec's life easier. There wouldn't be a need for secrets and confessions if Tyler left her for someone else. But Miles? Bec listened to the conversation next to her closely, agitation building inside of her with every flourished laugh and compliment that dripped from Eleni's lips. Miles was off limits.

"I can't believe we've never gone out...we'd look good together, don't you think?" Eleni beamed. She didn't wait for his answer, but kept talking. "Are you Greek, too? Or wait," she paused and leaned closer towards him. "Maybe Turkish?"

Miles said nothing as Eleni kept rambling. As she went on, Bec realized that Benny might not be the only one who had imbibed a little too hard on their first night.

"Can you imagine how cute our babies would be? Do you want kids? I would die for like four or five. Like a little Kardashian clan. You know what I mean?"

Miles took a sip of his drink while his eyes danced over Eleni's shoulder. The girl continued to ramble on about how bad the LA dating scene was and how she didn't understand how she wasn't in a relationship already. She was 26, hot, successful, and already owned her own high rise condo downtown. As far as she was concerned, she was a catch. She went on and on but Bec could tell Miles wasn't listening. She could tell because he was watching her instead.

"Take me to dinner when we get back. I'm dying to try this new restaurant in West Hollywood. Apparently, Beyoncé helped create the menu or something. It's amaz—"

"No."

Eleni stopped her endless flow of words. "What?"

Miles brought his eyes back to Eleni. "No," he repeated, finishing his drink.

"What do you mean, no?" Eleni's face contorted into a drunken pout.

"I don't want to date you. Sorry." His apology came across less than sincere, something that brought a vicious flicker of joy to Bec's chest.

"Why?"

Miles ran a hand through his curly hair and took a deep breath. "I just don't want to. Sorry."

The concept didn't seem to sit well with her. "There has to be a reason," she demanded. "No one says no to me. They can't. There has to be a reason. Do you like someone else?"

Bec pretended she wasn't listening, but she was. She gazed into the fire, letting her eyes unfocus as her sense of hearing took center stage. Eleni kept pestering him until finally he answered.

"You're not my type."

"So hot isn't your type?" Eleni scoffed. "So then what is?"

Bec was oblivious to the other conversations that were chattering around her. She raised her eyes away from the fire, looking over Eleni's shoulder. Miles' gaze was already there, waiting for her. The two looked at each other quietly, but while Bec's eyes were full of hesitation, Miles' had a glimmer of mischief. Bec's stomach fluttered in response.

"Sweet. Spontaneous. A great personality. Someone who cares deeply for those around her. Someone who speaks her mind. Hmm let's see…" A smile flickered across his face as his eyes flashed at Bec. "Beautiful. A body that seems like it was molded for mine. Blonde. Maybe like 5'8", hazel eyes—"

Bec stood up abruptly, knocking over the wine bottle that rested on the ground next to her feet. All conversation stopped as everyone's heads turned towards her.

"Fuck, sorry," she muttered quickly, picking up the toppled bottle. Luckily it wasn't broken. The only evidence of her clumsiness was the river of dark red that flowed through the cracks in the patio.

"I'm going to grab a jacket," she stammered. She paused and looked down at the ground. Most of the wine was already staining the concrete with a heavy red splotch, like someone had bled out right there at her feet "…and, uh, some paper towels, I guess."

Bec stepped away from the fire and headed back towards the house before anyone could offer their help. It was a short walk and the crackle of fire and the voices of her friends seemed to follow her through the already-open sliding glass door. The kitchen was full of shadows as she stepped into the house, the only real light emanating from a few lamps in the living room. Already the glow of their bulbs had attracted a few mosquitoes and tiny moths from outside. Bec leaned her body forward onto her hands, planting them firmly on the counter as she took a deep breath. Her mind buzzed with a dizzying mixture of champagne, tequila, and wine and wouldn't still no matter how hard she tried. She closed her eyes and replayed the day in her head. They had only been on the island a few hours but it already felt like days. How long were they even staying here? Bec couldn't remember. Did they fly home on Tuesday? Or was it Wednesday?

Already a dull ache had sprouted in her head. She'd regret taking all those shots. She hoped that would be the only thing she'd regret in the morning. Her mind wandered before she had a chance to stop it. His face, his stupid face with that stupid smile, fixed itself in her head. Miles was going to be a problem. Her problem. A heavy flutter ran through her stomach as she thought of the way his fingers had teased her skin in the kitchen earlier. How he had just described her to Eleni so casually. She swallowed harshly, pushing the thoughts away. No. Stop this. She swore under her breath as she forced her eyes open and shut out the thoughts she desperately wanted to dive into. She needed to forget him. If she didn't, she'd do the one thing Benny specifically told her not to—she'd fuck up.

In an instant, something shot Bec's nerves awake. All was still in the house except for the sound of breathing. As it crept its way into her ears, chills prickled the skin on the back of her neck. A flicker of fear, unknown and instinctual, heaved inside of her. She whipped around quickly. When she did, she was met with nothing and no one. Her brow furrowed as she itched the back of her neck. Without moving, she slowly scanned her eyes across the dim room. Empty bottles, glasses, and red cups littered the kitchen counter along with half eaten snacks. Still, she had an uneasy feeling.

"Hello?" she called out softly.

Her eyes flickered to the left towards the living room and then to the right, towards the hallway that led to the bedrooms. No one called back to her. No movement flickered in the dark. Nothing.

"You're just drunk" she muttered, suddenly feeling foolish about the fear that had buried itself in her chest. She grabbed a glass from one of the cabinets and filled it with water from the sink. After a small swig and a slight puckering of her lips, she thought better of it and opened the fridge in search of one of the water bottles she'd seen earlier. She rested her hand against the door, the bulb from the fridge illuminating the kitchen in a splash of light. Bec twisted off the plastic cap and gulped down the icy cold water with greedy haste. In an instant, a burst of pain snipped through her hand. A soft yelp escaped her throat as she yanked her hand away. The water bottle dropped to the floor with a hollow clatter, echoing through the room. Bec brought her hand closer to inspect it. As the fridge closed, taking the light with it, she caught a glimpse of the mosquito dining on her flesh.

"Fucker," Bec whispered as she slapped the bug.

It was gone in seconds, the only remnants of its life the smudged blood and guts on her skin. She quickly wiped the back of her hand on a kitchen towel before she picked up the empty water bottle. Her head spun a little as she raised herself back up. She closed her eyes briefly as a wave of lightheadedness crept over her again. No more drinking tonight. She dropped the empty bottle on the counter with a rattle before heading for the patio. She hoped everyone was done taking shots for the night. As she moved, a figure emerged next to her from the depths of the hallway. She jumped at the shadow creeping towards her, her heart diving straight into her stomach. An amused look flickered across Miles face as she let out a small gasp.

"What the hell?" Bec rasped. "Were you trying to scare

me?"

He took a step closer to her, his smile growing wider. "No, but I liked that noise you made."

She huffed and continued towards the door. As she did, he stepped in front of her quickly. He stood there smiling, blocking Bec's way as irritation boiled on her face.

"What are you doing?"

"Just trying to steal a second of the birthday girl's time."

"I already told you—" She stopped herself, letting her eyes flicker over Miles' shoulder at the patio. She dropped her voice. "We can't do this here."

"We don't have to talk about that, okay?" Miles' hand snaked its way up to her waist. "Five minutes—that's all I'm asking. Stay here with me and just talk. Talk about anything. The weather. How you've been...I miss the sound of your voice."

"You want to know how I've been?" Bec challenged him.

"Yes. I do."

"I've been shitty, Miles. Is that what you want me to say?"

His brow furrowed. "What? No. I—"

"The funny thing is, I was actually doing okay for a couple weeks there," she continued. "I thought I could move on from this. I thought I could force myself to be a good person for once. But then you had to send me that fucking text." She scoffed, tossing her head back in her frustration. "Why couldn't you just let me be?"

Bec felt the emotions like a boiling vat of acid. She was angry but not just at him. She held his gaze steadily while guilt and frustration wrapped its way around her stomach like a snake with its next meal. He stepped closer and gently weaved his hand into her hair. She stilled, the anger pumping through her slowing down. His fingers drifted down to her face, caressing her cheek softly.

"Hold on," he said. "If you don't want this, by all means, tell me now and it's done."

Her teeth clamped down in her jaw, holding back words

she didn't mean. She could lie about a lot of things, but not that. Bec forced a deep breath from her lungs. Shit. She found herself leaning her face against the caress of his hand before she remembered where they were.

"Goddamnit, Miles," she rasped, pulling herself away from his touch. "He's your friend. Don't you feel guilty?"

"No," he said flatly. "Because you deserve to be happy and he doesn't make you happy. Not like me."

She knew he was right but the realization only made her angrier. "You have no idea how Tyler makes me feel."

"Does he make you feel better than I do?"

Bec glared up at his 6'3" frame as she took a step forward. They both knew the answer but she'd be damned if she gave him the satisfaction. "Yes," she lied through gritted teeth. "Yes, he does."

She wanted him to get angry, upset. She wanted him to feel a drop of the torment she was going through. All he did was smile down at her with that devilish grin of his.

"I know you better than anyone," he laughed, hooking his thumb under her chin. "And you're a horrible liar."

His confidence pissed Bec off but at the same time, it stirred something inside of her. She felt her body yearning to close the distance between them but she forced herself to step away.

"What do you want, Miles?" she spat, the anger she felt for herself spilling out towards him.

He took a step closer. "I want you to stop lying to yourself."

"And what exactly am I lying to myself about? Huh?"

"This. Us."

She didn't say anything for a while. All she could manage to do was look at him and try to bottle her anger. But not all of it was for him. She was the one who had let this go on. She was the one who hadn't blocked his number. She was the one who kept coming back. While she was fuming, Miles was quiet and patient. He seemed so sure. That alone only added to Bec's own confusion and uncertainty. His eyes were alive, filled with excitement and desire. It drew her in, like it had before. She felt her body drifting forward. She knew it wasn't right but it seemed right. He felt right. He was so sure, why couldn't she be too? The soft rumble of laughter from outside snapped Bec back to reality. Her stomach heaved with guilt.

"There is no us," she whispered.

"Wrong," he said. His face grew stern for a minute before a soft smile drifted back into place. "You want this. And the minute you admit it to yourself, you'll save everyone a lot of pain."

Her brow contorted as bewilderment flooded her face. "Jesus." Bec let out a breathy laugh. "You know what, Miles? Fuck you." She tried to step around him but as she did, he laced his hands around her waist and led her back into the kitchen.

"Fuck me?" He leaned in so close his lips almost brushed her own. "I think that's how you got yourself in this mess in the first place."

She let his words sink deep into her bones as his body pressed up against her. This was her fault—her mess. It was wrong, no matter how right it felt. She pushed him away, her body screaming in retaliation.

"So what's your plan here?" Bec hissed. "Annoy the hell out of me the entire week in the hope that I cave? Why not go directly to Tyler? Why not walk out there right now and tell him that you fucked his girlfriend and make the rest of this trip a living hell for everyone?"

"I don't want to hurt you." He lifted his hand up to her face, brushing his fingers against her skin softly. "Things are bound to get messy but I have an easy solution to all of this."

A breathy huff escaped from her lungs. "Yeah, and what's that?"

"We step into my room and I remind you why you've always belonged with me."

Bec's breath caught in her throat. "Yeah, that's not happening," she said, pushing her way past him as she stepped out onto the patio. She couldn't help but play out scenarios in her head as she shut the sliding glass door behind her roughly.

"Shit," she hissed under her breath as she walked across the patio.

The night air greeted her back with a brisk embrace. Bec pulled her arms around her chest to curb the chill. Fuck. Her jacket. The paper towels. She couldn't go back inside now. Miles wouldn't behave, that much was obvious. But she could behave herself, right? The feeling of his hands on her waist had seemed to set her skin on fire. The thought of it now held Bec's breath captive in her chest. She was thoroughly screwed.

Tyler turned around as she slid back into her wicker chair. "All good?" he asked.

"Fine," she replied quickly.

His gaze hovered on her, inciting a quiver of panic through her body. "I had more to drink than I thought so I drank some water and relaxed for a bit." Was she talking too much? Explaining things that didn't need explaining? She offered him a wavering smile before pulling her gaze towards the fire. If she didn't get her panic under control, she'd fuck this up before anyone else even got the chance. She curled her legs up under her, trying to get comfortable despite the sickening feeling that swirled in her gut.

"You see Miles in there?"

Bec froze. She tried to rewind the past five minutes. Or had she been in the house longer than that? The patio wasn't far from the house but surely Tyler couldn't have seen what was happening inside. Could he?

"Umm, no." She gave him an oblivious shrug, her eyes still fixed on the fire. "Maybe he went for a walk or something."

Tyler looked at her curiously before offering a smile.

"Maybe."

Bec stared at the fire until she felt her body settle down, which took longer than she'd have liked. The alcohol swirling her thoughts around didn't help. While the fire had had a tranquil effect on her earlier, now it seemed to taunt her. It popped and sizzled. Rogue flames danced over the stones that contained it. It had a mind of its own. Bec knew if she tried to control it, it'd burn her without hesitation.

A few minutes later, she heard Miles' footfalls reach the patio. Tyler made a joke. Miles responded with some witty remark. Bec didn't hear it. She didn't want to. She was too afraid he might spill their secret. She didn't think he'd do it on purpose but now it only felt like a matter of time before someone said something they shouldn't. For the remainder of the night, Bec refrained from looking at him. She kept her focus on the flames, trying to keep her thoughts from drifting but having no real control over them. The more she thought, the less certain she was of anything. Did she want Miles? Stupid question. But what about Tyler? Did she still want him? The thought made the contents of her stomach sour. Finally, she accepted the fact that she wouldn't come away from this trip unscathed. Whatever happened, whatever she did or didn't do—someone was going to get hurt. Her eyes fluttered sleepily as she curled deeper into the wicker chair. The last thing she thought before the flames lulled her to sleep was that she wished Miles had made the decision for her and carried her off to his bed.

FRIDAY

♨ BEC ♨

Bec was in bed. That was the first thing she realized when she woke up. The second was the cold feeling underneath her. She blinked the sleep from her eyes, trying to pull her awareness back to the living world. An old, brown ceiling fan rotated above her, its worn condition giving it a slight unsteadiness as it turned. Lines etched their way around her eyes as she gazed up at it uncertainly. It looked too familiar.

As she pressed her hand into the bed to push herself upright, she was met with the cold feeling again. Her fingers touched the bedding delicately, realizing it wasn't just cold, it was wet. She looked down to make sense of it. Her eyes grew bug-like as the paralyzing dread of fear pulled at her insides. No. She pulled her hand up slowly, worried that if she moved too fast reality would reach her sooner. No. Her eyes slowly swept to her left, where they found the flesh she knew they would. Stop. Her mind fought against her as she raised her gaze across the body next to her. She had already seen too much. She couldn't force herself to turn away. The blood was just how she'd remembered it. Oozing. Red like cherries. She counted slowly, buying herself time. One. Two. Maybe this wasn't happening. Three. Four. She almost managed a breath of relief before she spotted the fifth stab wound punctured into the torso like it was a slab of turkey. Five.

Bile rose to the back of her throat hotly. She didn't need to look any higher, already knowing what she'd find. But she couldn't seem to stop herself. She had to know, had to be certain. A muffled sob choked from her throat as the sliver of gaping flesh in his neck gleamed back at her. The creak of the floorboard behind her set the hairs on the back of her neck up. His voice seemed to call out to her from the darkness.

"You did this."

Bec bolted upright in bed, gasping for breath. Her fingers clawed against the sheets with a feral desperation as adrenaline ripped through her. The only thing she could hear for the first few seconds was the pounding of her own heart.

Tyler peered out from the bathroom, a toothbrush poking out of his mouth. "You okay?" he mumbled through the foamy paste.

Her eyes flickered around feverishly, trying to understand. It was just a dream. Her heart hammered in her chest and she took slow breaths to try and settle herself. It was just a dream. Bec rubbed her face with her hands.

"Fine," she said breathlessly.

She stared at the wall ahead of her. It was adorned with dried palm fronds and tropical flowers encased in glass picture frames. Her eyes glazed over them as she tried to forget the horrors her own mind had just shown to her—horrors she knew too well. It had been a long time since she'd had that nightmare, but not long enough. After a few minutes, she untangled herself from the sheets and noticed she was wearing her clothes from yesterday.

"You fell asleep on the patio last night," Tyler stated, watching her from the doorway. "So I carried you to bed."

Bec mumbled a 'thank you' as she got out of bed and walked past him. She felt his eyes linger on her longer than she would have liked. The more attention he seemed to give her, the more she could feel her guilt forming into words and sentences. They stuck to the back of her throat like peanut butter.

"Want some coffee?"

She leaned past the shower curtain to turn the water on and cranked the knob toward HOT as far as it would go. "Yes. I would die for some."

Tyler's retreat to the kitchen was barely detectable

over the rush of the water. Bec stripped off her clothes and massaged a kink out of her neck as she waited for the water to warm up. They hadn't even taken the time to freshen up when they arrived yesterday, and she could still smell the stifling musk of travel on her. She darted her hand under the water, eager to strip herself of the grime on her body and the thoughts in her head. The water chilled her skin and she withdrew her hand quickly. The water pattered steadily against the white tile floor of the shower. It seemed to pelt Bec's mind with a rhythmic seduction.

She imagined it cleansing her, past and present. The idea was too appealing. What she would give to forget the past, to wash it away and bury it six feet under. As she stepped into the shower, the beads of water struck her in fiery bursts and she closed her eyes, breathing deeply. The soft burn wouldn't cleanse her of her guilt, but the pain sure seemed to help. Strands of blonde hair fell in front of her eyes in waterlogged clumps. For a moment, nothing existed except her and the hiss of the water pouring from the showerhead.

Bec's mind wandered as she washed her hair, then her body. She thought of her nightmare—of him. Hollowness spread across the back of her throat and she quickly shook the thoughts away. Her mind drifted, like a boat without anchor, to places she knew not to go. She thought of Miles. How stubborn he was. How annoyingly persistent he could be. But as the fiery water numbed Bec's skin, her thoughts shifted. Her anger and frustration with Miles transformed. She pictured him in front of her. How his brown eyes seemed to catch the sunlight like tiny embers, igniting the hazel hues that were dappled into his irises. She thought of how he always seemed to catch her eye in a crowded room. How his presence always grounded her. How he remembered the little things like how she took her coffee and what foods she craved after a night of drinking. How the scruff of his stubble felt against her inner thigh. Bec traced her hand down her body slowly. The water beat against her face as she lifted her head back and let out a soft moan.

"Want some company?"

Bec gasped as her body flinched. She opened her eyes and whipped her head around to look over her shoulder. Tyler was holding the shower curtain open with one hand while the other held her cup of coffee. A cheeky grin grew on his face as his eyes drank up every inch of her skin.

"Want some company?" he repeated.

"What? No, I'm getting out," she said quickly.

"Didn't look like it to me," he said with heavy eyes.

Abruptly she turned off the water and pushed past him. Bec didn't say anything as she grabbed a towel and started drying herself off. As she began wiping the smeared bits of mascara from underneath her eyes, she caught Tyler's gaze in the mirror.

"What were you thinking about?'

"Huh?"

Tyler looked at her steadily. After a while, he snickered softly. "Whatever it was..."

She felt the pressure of his body as he leaned into her.

"...it sounded good."

He kissed the crook of her neck, his eyes fixed intently on her in the mirror as he did. Without another word, he set the coffee cup down on the counter and stepped out of the bathroom.

Once he was gone, Bec stared at herself in the foggy mirror and let her eyes bore into their reflections. Benny's words from the other night flooded her mind. Don't fuck up. She glared at herself for another few seconds before tearing away from the mirror. Four more days on this island. She just had to keep it together for four more days. Something in her gut told her she wouldn't last that long.

When Bec finally made it out of the bedroom, the kitchen was swarming with activity. Ramon and Jamari were busy whipping up breakfast.

Bec saw three pans on the stove. One pan had eggs and plantains frying in oil, creating a delectable sizzle. The other was warming tortillas while the last cooked rice and beans. While Jamari finished the last bit of cooking, Ramon handed out plates loaded with food. Bec gave Jamari a hesitant smile as he looked up from the stove. He met her arrival with cool eyes and a flat expression. Bec took a plate from Ramon, his wide smile harshly contrasting Jamari's lack of one. She was immediately hit with the flavorful aroma wafting from the meal and she breathed in the scent sweetly as the warm steam danced up her nostrils.

"So, what's the plan today, jefe?" Benny asked Tyler in between bites.

Bec grabbed a seat at the far end of the kitchen's island next to Stevie. Tyler said something to Benny about the jungle but Bec wasn't paying attention.

"Good morning," Stevie all but groaned as she sipped a cup of black coffee.

The greeting stirred a chuckle from Bec. "Don't tell me the seasoned bartender is hungover?"

Stevie smiled at the jeer and slammed a bite of plantain into her mouth. She chewed lethargically and swallowed. "Yeah, well...things got a little wild after you passed out."

Bec gave her best friend a hesitant look. "How so?"

"Monique was ready to party. I swear I haven't seen her that determined to slam shots since the wedding."

Food swirled around Bec's plate as she twirled her fork. There was something Stevie wasn't saying. "Okay so what's the big deal?"

After taking a peek around the room, Stevie leaned into Bec. "Benny went in on her."

"What?"

"Yeah," Stevie shook her head and stabbed a bite of egg. "He told her to ease up on the alcohol. Said something about trying for a baby. That's when Monique completely lost it and they started yelling. Benny ended up taking a walk with Tyler."

Stevie chugged the rest of her coffee before dipping a piece of tortilla in the broken egg yolk that oozed all over her plate. "Monique was pissed. And you know, me being a good friend and all, I wanted to be there for her." She let out a sharp laugh and rubbed her forehead. "Which resulted in me and her taking four shots of tequila."

"Good friend, huh?" Bec chided her. "No other reason?"

Stevie didn't look up from her plate as she continued eating. "Nope."

Bec rolled her eyes. "Sure," she said, dragging the word out. She gave her a grin before her eyes darted down the line of plates on the counter until she found Benny and Monique sitting at the far end. They were both eating in silence. She turned back to Stevie and dropped her voice to a low murmur.

"Monique doesn't want a baby yet. She told me a few weeks ago that they're not ready for one."

Stevie's eyes widened. "Exactly. Benny is delusional. Thinks he can just coerce her into having a baby and she'll forget all their problems." She shook her head one more time and finished the last of her plantains. "Like for fuck's sake..." she mumbled.

Bec wondered what problems Stevie could be referring to. Just as she opened her mouth to ask, Stevie cut her off.

"Oh yeah, and one more thing happened."

Bec's stomach knotted. "What?"

"Eleni got drunk and tried to convince everyone to go skinny dipping in the ocean." Stevie barely stifled her laughter.

"Of course she did," Bec muttered before plopping a bit of eggs into her mouth.

"Needless to say the only person who was down was Adrian," Stevie smirked. "And we both know that's the last guy Eleni wants to fuck."

Bec tapped her fork on her plate lightly. "Anything else happen that I should be aware of?"

Stevie stopped chewing and turned to Bec. She swallowed and looked at her firmly. "No. Did something happen that I should be aware of, Rebecca?"

Bec made a face. "You know I hate it when you call me that."

"Well you should have picked a better name," Stevie responded curtly. She waved her fork at Bec, a piece of egg dangling off of it precariously. "But I know you hate it and I also know when you're being shady."

Bec pushed her fork back and forced across her plate as she stalled. "It's nothing."

"Fun fact—I also know when you're full of shit."

Bec took a bite of food and chewed slowly. She looked across the kitchen, avoiding Stevie's impatient glare. Jamari was staring at her as he washed a cast iron pan, hands deep in foamy bubbles. Bec tried to give him a polite smile but his expression was rigid and cold. He kept staring, at her or through her, she couldn't tell.

"Hello?" Stevie quipped irritably, still careful to keep her voice low. "What aren't you telling me?

Bec snapped back to the conversation. "Sorry, um..." She looked behind her, her eyes searching for someone. Miles was sitting on the couch in the living room with his plate balancing on his lap. To his right was Tyler. The sight made Bec's stomach drop. She looked back at Stevie, trying to conceal the worry in her eyes.

"Let's just say someone really wanted to talk to me yesterday..."

Stevie raised her eyebrow. "Bec, please tell me you didn't—"

"No."

The words slipped out quickly.

"But you wanted to."

Bec closed her eyes and took a deep breath. When she opened them and looked at Stevie, there was no judgment in her eyes, only concern. It only made Bec feel worse.

"No. I mean, I don't know." She could taste the denial on her own tongue. "This whole thing is just fucked."

She set her fork down more harshly than she intended and pushed the plate of food a few inches away. Jamari's eyes flickered to the noise. He gave her a hot glare as he reached across the counter and snatched the plate. Bec could still feel Stevie's gaze hot on her neck, so she let her focus wander outside. Adrian and Eleni were out there. It seemed odd to Bec that she only caught the two of them together when it seemed no one else was looking. She couldn't tell what they were doing but Eleni seemed to be ordering Adrian around with wild hand motions. She watched for a minute before Stevie's voice pulled her back.

"What does your gut tell you?" she asked.

Bec sighed. "That I'm a shitty excuse for a girlfriend."

"Because you want to be with Miles."

"Jesus Christ, just tell the whole room won't you?" she said, giving Stevie a wide-eyed look before looking around.

"No one can hear me," Stevie retorted, quieter this time.

Ramon filled her empty cup with coffee, smiling as he did. Stevie gave him a quick 'thank you' before guzzling it down.

"So what are you going to do?" she prodded.

A silence hung in the air briefly. Bec caught herself chewing on the inside of her cheek and stopped. "I don't know," she uttered. "But I think—"

"Oh-my-God!" Eleni sang as she slid open the patio door and burst into the house. "Adrian just took the most amazing photos of me." She tossed her long, dark hair out of her face as she scrolled through her phone's camera roll.

Stevie rolled her eyes and shot Bec a look. Eleni quickly sauntered past the kitchen and into the living room where she shoved her phone in front of Tyler and Miles' faces.

"My followers are going to go crazy for these," she babbled as she swiped through a flurry of photos, making sure to give the two men ample time to view each one before she moved to the next.

"Do you sometimes just want to..." Stevie started.

Bec watched Eleni place a hand on Miles' thigh as she leaned in closer to show him and Tyler the next photo. "Strangle her?" Bec quipped quietly. "Push her down a flight of stairs?"

"Fuck, I was going to say throw her phone in the ocean," Stevie said with a chuckle. "But I guess that works too."

Stevie's eyes followed Bec's gaze until she saw what her best friend was looking at with laser-like focus. "Ah, I get it."

Bec looked away quickly. "What are we doing today, anyway?" she asked.

"I think I heard Tyler say something about exploring?"

Bec shrugged. "That should be fun." She got up and gave her back a quick stretch. She didn't know if it was falling asleep on the patio last night or all of the sitting from traveling yesterday, but her body felt wrecked. "I'll just be glad to get out of this house for a bit."

"We've been here for less than 24 hours," Stevie laughed. "Feeling trapped already?"

Bec looked across the room. Benny and Monique had finished breakfast and quietly headed back to their room. Eleni was on the couch, complaining once again about the lack of Wi-Fi. Adrian was sitting next to her, holding his phone up as if he could magically conjure a signal for her. Tyler and Miles were still on the other couch. She couldn't tell if they were talking to Adrian and Eleni or each other. She wished they would stay on opposite sides of the room.

"Let's just say a surprise party at our apartment would have made me feel less nauseous."

Stevie pulled her into a half hug and shook her shoulder. "Oh come on," she teased. "You're stuck on a private island with your best friend, private chefs, and free booze. That sounds fun as hell."

"Just don't forget the boyfriend and the secret lover."

"Lover, huh?"

Bec tried to give her an annoyed look but Stevie's outrageous grin won her over.

"Fuck, fine," Bec conceded. "Let's go explore the jungle or whatever the hell Tyler has planned for us on this godforsaken trip."

♨ MILES ♨

They were all gathered outside, feet clad in sneakers and water bottles in hand. Miles sat on a rock, perched in the shadows. The shade did little to ease the heat and a trickle of sweat ran down the back of his neck. The temperature had already risen past 80° F. Miles watched Eleni fan herself with her hand while Adrian offered to rub sunscreen on her shoulders. She declined. Miles wished she would throw the poor guy a bone. He looked like an abused, lovesick puppy anytime she was around. A hazy spray of chemicals surrounded Monique as she doused herself in bug repellent.

"I got eaten alive last night and I'm not getting any more bites today," she huffed to herself through the fumes.

"Pass that over here," Benny called to her.

She handed it to him silently before heading over to Stevie and Bec. The corners of Miles' eyes tightened as he watched the interaction. He was surprised how Benny had fought with Monique last night. He couldn't imagine ever speaking to Bec like that, no matter how many times she pushed him past his limits. His eyes washed over Bec she wrapped her arm around Monique's shoulder, comforting her friend. She was good—too good for him. But it only made him want Bec more.

Bec sighed, looking at her friend with those big, brown eyes of hers. "Stevie told me what happened last night. You okay?"

"Oh fine," Monique said. "That man just drives me crazy." She motioned towards Benny with her hand dismissively. "One of these days I might bash him over the head if he doesn't learn."

"They never learn," Stevie chimed in. "That's why I only date women." She beamed at them with a smart-ass look. "No men, no problems."

Miles couldn't help but let out a stifled laugh as he listened in on their conversation. She wasn't wrong.

"No problems?" Bec smirked. "I guess you're not counting the multiple ex-girlfriends who have shown up to the bar to cuss you out?"

"Hey now," Stevie quipped. "All of my exes love me."

Stevie shot Monique a mischievous look which was returned with a breathy laugh and a roll of her eyes. A harsh clap exploded through the air. Miles stopped eavesdropping and turned his gaze to the woman in front of him.

"Guests," Marta began. "We have arranged an adventure through the jungle for you today." She grinned at the group, looking each of them in the eyes, as if taking stock.

"Jamari," Marta said as she pointed to the tall man who stood next to her, "will act as your guide today."

"Is it just me or does he give anyone else the creeps?" Monique whispered.

"We have packed a small lunch for you to eat at a scenic spot along the trail. You all have water already I see..."

Marta's gaze seemed to grow a little brighter as she stared at Miles, finding him on the outskirts of the group. "Do not wander off. It's dangerous to get lost out there."

She clapped her hands one more time, causing Monique to jump.

"We will see you back here in a few hours," Marta concluded. She whispered something to Jamari and motioned for him to begin.

The man stepped forward. Without any greeting he began walking up the sandy path that led into the jungle. "Follow," he said gruffly, not bothering to look at the others behind him.

Tyler slapped Benny on the back. "You heard the man,"

he said. "Let's go."

Miles got up and wove his way into the group. An innocent grin slid onto his face as he passed Bec, locking eyes with her briefly before joining Tyler and Benny at the front. He knew she hated when he was around Tyler. He could see it in the slight panic that flickered through her eyes. But she didn't have to worry, not right now at least. He didn't have any intention of shaking things up for the time being. He knew she'd come to her senses. He'd seen it in her eyes last night. She was slowly starting to realize that there was no avoiding how she felt.

As the group followed in Jamari's footsteps, the jungle quickly enveloped them. Miles looked back and could barely see a sliver of where they had been gathered moments before. Marta's wide grin gleamed back at him briefly until it was swallowed away by the dense greenery. Miles snuck a look at Bec. He hated the distance between them, hated the act he had to put on. He wished the others weren't here. He was tired of pretending. He wanted her to behave like she did when no one else was around—like those late nights when she'd come to him. He missed opening his apartment door to see her standing there, waiting. He missed seeing the hesitation mixed with lust that swarmed into her eyes. Most of all, he missed the way her fingers would twist their way into his hair as she pulled him closer, panting for more. Miles took a steady inhale as he turned away from her and carried on ahead. He'd get her back soon. It was only a matter of time.

The group had split into three. Bec, Stevie, and Monique hung at the back, seeming more interested in the leisurely aspect of the hike. They were about fifteen feet behind everyone else but none of them seemed to notice or care. They were busy snapping pictures with their phones and chatting about the giant leaves and tiny birds they passed by. Miles kept pace with Tyler and Benny who were trying to keep up with Jamari. Miles watched Benny's face grow red and sweaty as they hiked. He had barely been retired six months and already he seemed to be losing the stamina he'd built up for football. Miles glared at the back of Tyler's head as he led them without any noticeable strain or sign of slowing. He couldn't help but resent him. Maybe if the circumstances were different they could have been better friends. Maybe. But Tyler was competition now and Miles had no intention of losing the best thing in his life.

Eleni and Adrian had wound up somewhere in the middle of the two groups. Miles could hear the whine of Eleni's voice behind him. It carried through the jungle with an obnoxious twang and pitch. Fuck, she loved the sound of her own voice. Miles tried to block it out as he walked. Part of him was relieved that Eleni had moved on to flirting with Adrian—he didn't know how much more of her he could take—but another part of him wished she was still trying to fuck him, just so he could see that jealous darkness grow over Bec's face. It was cute—entirely unnecessary considering Miles could barely think of anything other than Bec, let alone anyone. But it was cute nonetheless.

Ahead, Tyler had caught up with Jamari and was trying to engage him in conversation. Tyler had been speaking Spanish to him all morning. Tyler had gotten a few grunts and some one-word answers from Jamari but other than that, the man was a statue. As he led them deeper and deeper into the jungle without a word or a passing glance, Miles wondered if it wasn't the man's understanding but his indifference that kept him silent.

"So, what do you think so far?" Tyler asked Miles and Benny as he fell back into step with them.

Benny blew some air out of his cheeks as he looked around them. "Shit, man," he laughed. "You flew us out to a private island, all expenses paid. I'd say it's pretty great so far." The smile on his face shifted slowly. "I just wish Monique wasn't pissed at me..."

"She'll come around," Tyler assured him.

Ahead of them, Jamari was cutting down the fronds and leaves that obstructed their path with a machete. The whoosh of the blade cut through the air in quick flicks. Miles watched the precision of it. He wondered about the weight of it. How much force did you have to put behind it to slice through the bramble cleanly like that?

"Women are emotional," Tyler continued. "You have to just roll with the punches."

Benny exhaled loudly. "You're right. It's just...she's everything to me, man. I want to make her happy."

They twisted and turned through the jungle. The terrain got steeper and Miles felt the muscles in his legs flex with every step. He savored the strain and pushed onwards.

"When did you know it was the right time?" Tyler asked, his voice mixing in with their heavy breathing.

"Know what?" Benny responded.

"When it was time to propose."

Miles' gaze ripped to the back of Tyler's head. Had he heard him wrong? He must have. His eyes burned into the mass of blonde hair, desperate to hear something else. He kept pace, staying within two feet of Tyler at all times.

Benny was silent for a bit. With a deep breath, he finally responded. "When you know, you know."

Tyler smirked to himself. "I've known for a long time."

"Oh?"

Behind Tyler's back, Benny's eyes flickered to Miles. Miles had never questioned Benny's loyalty. In the few, heated conversations they'd had about Bec, Benny had always made his position clear. He was on Tyler's side in all of this. So now, as they stared each other down, Miles wondered how long Benny would keep lying to save his own skin.

"I love Bec, even though she's...complicated."

"Shit, aren't all women?" Benny laughed.

"Yeah but Bec's different. She's..."

"What?" Benny asked cautiously.

Tyler swatted at a stray cobweb that dangled from a tree

branch. "She's her own worst enemy," he explained. "She self-sabotages."

"Self-sabotages?"

Tyler furrowed his brow as he thought. "Bec does this thing...she feels us moving to the next stage and panics. She gets cold feet all the time. The amount of times we've almost broken up is ridiculous," Tyler muttered. He turned back to look at Miles and Benny, his face seeming more serious now. "It's like she's constantly thinking that things will end badly between us."

Ahead of them, Jamari came to a stop. He finally turned to face the group and motioned for them to stop. "Rest now, then we go," he grumbled.

Miles tilted his head at the sound of the man's clear English. He gave Jamari a long look. So he did understand—interesting.

"You know, I thought Bec cheated on me a while back."

The muscles in Miles' face tensed as he fought every instinct to react.

"What?" Benny croaked.

"Yeah," Tyler replied, running a hand through his hair. "She got really distant a few months back. We had a couple bad fights and she would just shut down every time I tried to make things better."

"And?" Benny whispered quickly as Eleni and Adrian approached. "You confronted her about it or what?"

"No. No. Nothing like that."

"So what?" Benny prodded.

Tyler shrugged. "I learned some stuff about Bec. Some stuff that helped me understand her a little. Gave me some clarity."

Miles narrowed his eyes on him. "What stuff?"

Tyler's face contorted in a slight grimace. "She had a bad breakup a couple years ago and didn't really date anyone until we got together. She said it ended really suddenly. I don't know, just some typical relationship shit I guess."

Miles watched Tyler closely. Bec had confided in Miles a little about her past, small things here and there. For the last year, Miles had worked to carefully crack all of the walls Bec used to guard her heart—all of the walls except those he wanted to break down the most. She never spoke about her past relationships, refused to. How had Tyler done it? Miles' words seemed to jump out of his throat.

"Did she say anything about her other exes?"

"What?" Tyler laughed. "No. It was hard enough getting that much out of her."

"Hmmm." Miles chewed on his thoughts as his eyes buried themselves into the ground.

"Doesn't matter," Tyler continued. "I know what I want. I want Bec." He let out a breathy laugh and smiled at them both. "That's why I'm going to propose to her this weekend."

Benny's eyes widened. "What?"

"On her birthday," Tyler said, grinning.

Benny voiced his support but other than the slight uncertainty in his tone, Miles didn't hear any of it. As the rest of the group caught up, he stared into the green abyss that laid ahead. Everything else around him disappeared. It was like staring into a void, the edges fading into nothingness. Life felt hollow. It was empty. His mind replayed every second of what had just happened but it only made it worse—more real. They couldn't get engaged. That wasn't supposed to happen. His panic smelted down into white hot anger as he stared at Tyler. Tyler wasn't supposed to have her. He was. It was always supposed to be him. If Miles believed in a higher power, he would call what he and Bec had fate. And as fate saw it, this wasn't how things were supposed to go. His jaw flexed as he gritted his teeth together. His focus on Tyler broke as Bec's voice flittered through the air. Miles honed in on her as she joined the group. He watched her, urged her to look his way. When she finally did, the sight of her face anchored him and crushed him at the same time.

♨ BEC ♨

It took the group another hour to reach their destination.

They had taken a few brief rests along the way, each prompted by grunts and mumbled words from Jamari. He would give them just enough time to drink some water and snap some photos before urging them forward. Now, he had stopped once again, and they were gathered in a clearing, awaiting further instruction. His eyes drifted over each of them. Bec couldn't tell if he was doing a headcount or just waiting for them to shut up.

"There is a waterfall up through there," he began, pointing back behind him. "Very beautiful." His enthusiasm was lacking, as if he was reading from a script someone else had written for him. "We stay for an hour, then go back." His gaze cut into Bec. "Don't go too far." His focus shifted to Stevie next. "Meet back here." Without another word he dropped the pack he'd been carrying and situated himself on a rock.

Bec looked at Jamari expectantly, then at Tyler. He looked annoyed, restless even. His eyes were fixed on Jamari. Bec watched the muscles in Tyler's jaw clench as he stared the man down. Jamari wasn't paying attention. He cracked open a pack of nuts, plopping them into his mouth in handfuls. If Tyler expected him to show a little more initiative and take them down to the water, he was clearly mistaken.

"Well, I don't know about you guys," Bec said as she stepped forward, "but I could go for a swim."

"Yes," Stevie agreed, urging Bec towards where Jamari had pointed. "Last one there has to take all of Eleni's Instagram pictures."

Eleni's voice shot out behind them as Bec raced ahead of Stevie. Plants covered every surface, growing up and around each other in chaotic synchronization as she made her way through the overgrown path. The sunlight flickered down through the shaded treetops sporadically. Some places had spotlights of sun beaming through the foliage whereas others seemed to be cloaked in the darkness of the shade. The air smelled different here too. Dense. Alive. Stevie's footfalls crunched behind her.

"How much farther do you thin—"

Stevie bumped into Bec. Bec was fixed to the spot, bewitched. She widened her gaze as she stepped through a tangle of vines and looked at the open jungle in front of them.

"Holy shit."

Bec let Stevie's comment hang in the air as she took another step forward. The air became chilled and a soft spray of mist tickled her skin. She kept walking until she met the water's edge. Licks of water teased the toes of her sneakers as the 80-foot waterfall plummeted down from above, causing the water to ebb against the sandy shore. The dark turquoise water seemed so vast. Bec wondered how deep it was. She strained her eyes to see the bottom but couldn't find one.

"Damn," Adrian muttered as he took a panoramic photo with his phone.

The group filed in closer but Bec's focus stayed on the beauty in front of her. The low roar of the waterfall blended into the chatter of the jungle. Everything seemed alive. Every breath seemed to spark her awake and clear the last of her hangover from her system. Arms wrapped around Bec like snakes, snapping her away from tranquility. She flinched and inhaled sharply as a familiar chuckle rattled in her ear.

"So nervous lately," Tyler teased.

He pulled her in close and kissed the top of her shoulder. She let her body melt back into his, welcoming the affection.

It only took a second for the familiar twang of shame to rear up inside of her. She tried to ignore it. Tried to fight it. She looked out onto the pool which she now realized was a lagoon. Its depth was mirrored by its large expanse which stretched from where they stood to the small cliffs ahead. It was a massive blob that painted a dash of blue among the never-ending green of the jungle. Tyler planted kisses on Bec's neck softly. He held her tightly as their friends stripped to their swimsuits and headed off to explore. Bec received a guarded look from Miles as he brushed past them. Her stomach flipped sickly.

"How's the birthday girl doing?" Tyler cooed.

Bec fought the urge to cradle her head back against his chest. She'd forgotten how good it felt to be held by him. She knew it's what she should be doing. She should be enjoying these moments with Tyler but the flicker of agitation she'd just witnessed in Miles kept her from her peace.

"Great," she said, pulling away from him.

Bec turned back to look at the lagoon, eager to avoid more talking. Her friends were already diving into the tranquil waters and enjoying their little oasis. She took it all in and for the first time since they'd arrived, she actually felt relaxed. It only lasted for a second.

"I wanted to talk to you about something."

Bec's mouth went dry. She turned to face him slowly, dreading whatever was coming.

"Okay."

Bec felt his fingers brush her hot skin softly as he wrapped his hands around her waist. His hand found its place on her lower back, holding her in place. She felt loved—or at least, she should have. But when she looked him in the eyes, all it did was overwhelm her. Something was coming. He almost seemed nervous. Her breath caught in her throat. The heat of the day seemed to stifle her. She felt her heart pound in her chest heavily. She told herself this was the moment. This was the end.

"Remember how you told me you went through a bad breakup with your ex?"

A breakup. Was that how she'd described it? The blood-soaked sheets from her nightmare blared to the front of her mind. She tried to quiet the panic inside of her as she looked up at Tyler but all she could manage to do was nod.

"Well it helped me understand you more. You know," he said, his hands pulling her closer, "helped me understand why you put walls up."

Bec chewed on the inside of her cheek, nodding again.

He smirked, dropping his hands from her waist. "You know, like when you stay silent and stare back at me."

She took a quick inhale before letting it out in what felt like a sad attempt of a laugh. "Sorry," she mumbled. "These kinds of conversations just make me...nervous."

"And I get that," Tyler stressed. "But it would help me if I knew more."

Bec looked back at him strangely for a second. Lines formed between her brows and she tilted her head at him. "More about what?"

"Your ex."

Bec shook her head, little repeated shakes as she looked at the ground and stepped away from him.

"No."

"Bec—"

"No, Tyler."

He caught her arm as she tried to retreat further.

"Come on," he laughed. "Whatever it is, I can handle it."

She closed her eyes, Brennen's blank face flashing through her mind violently. She shook her head again.

"No," she stated. "You just think you can."

She pulled her arm away and tried not to let her mind slip into the dark again. The more she tried not to, the more she felt it creeping in. Dread wrapped around her heart like a damp blanket, weighing her down. It took her into the earth, with the worms and the roots and the dead. Brennen was there in the dark, his big, bulging eyes staring at her, blaming her. She could feel the deadweight of his body next to her on the mattress. She could smell the metallic tang of blood in the air. She could hear the breeze from the open window blowing the curtains against the bed frame. She was trapped there in her mind. It was only when Tyler's hand brushed across her face that she was back.

"Stop," she flinched, her breath jumping from her lungs.

He gave her a concerned look as he withdrew from her.

"Please." Her eyes pleaded with him sternly. "Please don't ask about him."

Stevie hollered down to Bec as she and Adrian climbed up the rock formations that flanked the waterfall. The sight grounded Bec. It felt normal. Safe. Safe for Bec—but maybe not safe for Stevie. She knew Stevie well enough to know she was in search of her daily dose of adrenaline. Bec took a deep breath, feeling Tyler's gaze on the back of her neck as she watched Adrian cautiously follow after Stevie. Bec assumed he was only scaling those jagged rocks to impress Eleni. Bec glanced down at the lagoon. Eleni was bobbing in the water like a buoy. She shielded her eyes from the sun as she watched Adrian climb higher and higher. Bec hoped Eleni was truly interested in Adrian. Adrian seemed like a good guy, she would hate to see Eleni string him along. The twinge of irony danced in her gut but Bec did her best to ignore it. She turned to look at where Monique and Benny were floating nearby. Their expressions were tense as they spoke to one another. Bec furrowed her brow as she realized Miles was missing. Her eyes flickered around the jungle, searching for the familiar head of curly brown hair. When she finally found him, she wished she hadn't.

He was sitting on a large rock at the edge of the lagoon, eyes dark and piercing. He was looking right at her—her and Tyler. Bec swallowed the lump in her throat and turned away. She dug into her bag, looking for her camera, but it was all for show. Something about the way he was looking at her, something about the sheer force of his gaze, made her feel unsteady. It was like every time he looked at her, the impulse to separate herself from Tyler overpowered her. It was the opposite of how things should be. It felt like she was with Miles and every moment with Tyler was the betrayal. Every time, the sensation dug its way into her like a leech until she complied. She knew it was wrong. She was supposed to be fixing things with Tyler—which should have been easy considering Tyler didn't know there was anything to fix. So why was her first instinct to push him away?

She popped the lens caps off her camera and fidgeted with the settings, then lifted the camera's viewfinder to her eye. Miles came into focus through the lens. He was looking up at the cliffs now, no doubt watching Stevie lead Adrian to his glory—or his death. There was a hardness to Miles' face even when he wasn't staring at her. Like time and experience had carved its way into his face and left a tension there. It didn't take away from his attractiveness; if anything, it added to it. She liked the way he saw the world. He'd been through a lot, but so had she. Maybe that's why she felt a peace with him that she'd never found with Tyler. Miles understood her. He knew pain and hardship and loss. He saw her darkness, the amount she allowed him to see, and didn't turn away from it. No, he embraced it. Bec held the camera on him, her finger hovering over the shutter button. Looking at him was like finding something she hadn't known she was missing until that very moment. It consumed her. He sucked her in like a black hole. Bec swiveled the camera towards the water and snapped a photo. She ignored the churning in her lower stomach. She could find him attractive, there was nothing wrong with that. As long as she didn't act on it, it was harmless. She swallowed the lies and lifted the camera up towards the cliffs. She clicked the shutter and captured a photo of Stevie waving down at her. A smile drew across Bec's face before she lowered the camera back down to the water. Maybe she could get a shot of Stevie just before she slid under the surface. As the lens focused on the lagoon, she froze.

"What's that?" she said to Tyler, lowering the camera.

"What's what?" he replied.

Bec watched carefully as the water to the side of the waterfall rippled and fluttered. Her brow furrowed as she tried to make out the shapes. "There's something—"

She pressed the camera back to her eye and zoomed the lens out as far as it would go.

Stevie's voice boomed over the jungle. "Heads up!"

Just as Stevie's foot left the cliff's ledge, Bec saw a sliver of something gliding through the water.

"Wait," she yelled, her eyes tearing from the viewfinder to the air above.

Bec dropped her camera in the sand as Stevie's body slipped through the water's surface like a pin. She rushed into the lagoon with her sneakers on, only stopping when she got shin-deep. As Stevie's head popped to the surface, Bec's voice bellowed to her.

"Stevie, get out!"

Stevie flipped her hair back, sending beads of water flying off the strands. "Five more minutes, Mom," she teased.

"There's something in the water."

"Yeah, fish," Stevie taunted. She began leisurely swimming back to the side of the lagoon, getting ready for another cliff jump.

"I'm fucking serious," Bec pleaded. "Stevie, please get out of the water."

"Shit. Okay, okay, I'm coming."

Bec's heart pounded in her chest with every stroke Stevie pulled through the water. Her mind played out scenes of something exploding from the surface only to snatch her best friend in one shuddering movement. Eleni had scurried from the water once Bec had started yelling. Even Benny and Monique had swum to the side of the lagoon and were now perched on rocks, only their legs dangling into the water.

Everyone watched as Bec urged Stevie forward with urgent eyes. It was only when Bec tugged at Stevie's outstretched hand and pulled them both onto solid ground that she began to feel a little foolish.

Stevie squeezed the water out of her hair and gave her friend a questionable look. "Jesus, Becs," she laughed. "The creature of the black lagoon coming to get me or something?"

Bec took a deep breath and pressed her hand to her forehead. "I—I just saw something in the water. Over there," she said, her breath trembling with adrenaline as she pointed by the waterfall.

Heads turned to look at the spot but the water was still aside from the foamy white that churned beneath the falls. Stevie gave her a comical look, her mouth forming into a smile.

"Okay, well, I'm all good," she said, drying herself off with a towel. "Whatever iguana or man-eating fish you saw, it didn't get me."

Bec took a few deep breaths, the quiver in her hands finally leaving. "Fuck, sorry guys." She sat down and began brushing the sand from her camera. Thankfully she'd brought her old one. "I didn't sleep well and I'm just on edge." She let a small laugh escape her lips as she looked at her soaking wet sneakers. "Fuck, I'm a mess."

Tyler leaned over her, placing his hands on her shoulders. "Maybe take it easy on the alcohol tonight," he laughed. "Yeah?"

"Oh don't be a party pooper," Stevie whined as she sat down next to Bec. "Let the girl have a little fun. She's just watched one too many horror movies is all." She winked at Bec and jabbed her playfully.

As the tension settled, Monique and Benny slipped back into the water. Their voices were hushed but seemed less hostile than before. They treaded water close to each other until Benny pulled Monique into him and sent a happy shriek from her lungs as he swirled them around in the water. Bec smiled at the pair before hearing the scoff that came from next to her.

"Looks like they made up fast," Stevie mumbled.

"Wish that was you, huh?" Bec smirked.

"Shut up," Stevie laughed.

"Hey guys," Adrian shouted from atop the rocks where Stevie had left him. "Can I jump now?"

"Do it!" Eleni cheered from below. She was perched on a rock at the edge of the lagoon, posing like a mermaid.

A smile radiated across Adrian's face as he repositioned his feet on the ledge.

"I'm not watching," Bec laughed nervously. "Next I'll see a Chupacabra on the cliff next to him."

She turned away, meeting Miles' gaze as she did. Stevie hollered at Adrian next to her but Bec didn't hear it. Miles motion towards the jungle behind him with a quick nod. Bec's face contorted. She shook her head subtly, denying his request. He rolled his eyes before getting up off the rock he was leaning on. If he thought she was going to go sneak off into the jungle with him, he was crazy. Even as she sneered at the idea, she couldn't help but consider it. As Miles headed into the jungle, the splash of the water tore Bec's attention back to the lagoon. Adrian came up for air, sputtering wildly. He coughed and hacked as his hands pawed the surface.

"Easy there," Stevie laughed. "What did ya do? Take a breath as you went in?"

As he fought for his composure, Adrian started taking long, slow pulls through the water. "I wasn't expecting it to suck me under," he wheezed, coughing more phlegm from his lungs.

"The fuck you think was going to happen?" Stevie chided him.

"Guys..."

"It's like a 40-foot drop—"

"Guys!" Bec repeated quickly.

"What?" Stevie called out.

"I see it again."

Everyone's eyes flickered to the water, everyone except Adrian. His eyes were fixed straight ahead, unaware.

"Oh shit," Tyler said as he stepped forward to the water's edge.

Both Bec and Stevie got up quickly. Bec felt her heart pounding in her chest as her palms began to sweat.

"Hey, Adrian," Stevie said with a slight quiver in her voice. "I'm going to need you to swim a little faster, okay?"

Monique and Benny had evacuated the lagoon again, but this time, not as much as a toe dangled into the dark blue water.

Adrian gave Stevie an annoyed look, stopping for a second to tread water. "So I can't cliff jump correctly and now I can't swim fast enough?"

Tyler took another step forward, his shoes dipping into the water.

"Adrian, get out of there now."

Adrian's face contorted, recognizing the fear in Tyler's tone. "What the fuck is going on, guys?"

Everyone froze for a second as the water rippled thirty feet to the left of Adrian.

"Fuck, where did it go?" Benny called out.

Adrian's eyes widened as he realized what was going on. "What is it?"

He didn't wait for the answer. The surface came alive as Adrian pinwheeled his arms forward. He took frantic strokes, putting his face in the water and pulling himself towards the shore.

"Where is it? Bec stammered. "Where the hell is it?"

Adrian took a gasping breath as he came up for air. His tired arms moved slower now as he switched to breaststroke. The ripple of scales behind him shot everyone alive once again.

"Swim!" Tyler thundered.

Adrian turned to look back as the crocodile's head

breached the surface fifteen feet behind him. "Oh shit," he choked. His arms thrashed wildly, splashing water into his face.

Everyone watched as Adrian swam for his life. Benny, Monique, and Eleni had all run around to the beach and joined the others. They hollered and begged for Adrian to swim faster as the water behind him swished.

Stroke. Stroke. Ripple. Stroke. Stroke. Stroke. Ripple. Stroke. Ripple.

"You're almost there," Eleni screamed, her voice cracking. "Keep swimming!"

Bec could tell that he was tiring quickly but still, Adrian pounded his arms into the water. The gleam of eyes followed him hungrily. Slowly. Curiously. Adrian was less than ten feet from the shore now. Tyler and Benny stomped into the water, going as deep as their knees and yelling for Adrian to swim as hard as he could. Finally, Adrian's listless hand reached out to Tyler. Monique screamed as the crocodile's mouth reared up out of the water and lunged for Adrian. The water thrashed as Benny now too gripped Adrian's forearm and hurried to yank him out. The three men stumbled backwards onto the sand as the scaly monster stormed up on them. Just as its jaw of long, curved teeth opened up to clamp down onto Adrian's meaty thigh, a flash of silver slammed down against it. Eleni and Monique both screamed as the 18-inch machete pierced the beast's right eye. It writhed in pain and snapped its jaw in rebuttal. Jamari put his boot onto the crocodile's snout and used the leverage to yank his weapon out. The animal snarled and thrashed for a second before quickly retreating back below the surface, leaving a watery trail of blood in its wake.

Jamari cleaned the machete's blade on his shirt with a quick swipe as the group sucked down ragged breaths. Bec stood so still she felt like she had turned to stone. Her heat ripped through her body as her muscles clenched down tensely. A terror she hadn't felt in years pounded through her. Her hands shook as her eyes fixated on the water. It had seemed so peaceful when they had arrived. There were no signs of the crocodile now but a sickly feeling held steadily in her stomach, like the animal would come back at any second to reclaim its stolen meal.

"What the hell just happened?" Adrian yelled amidst the panting breaths around him.

"No more swimming," Jamari remarked, and walked back into the jungle.

☖ ADRIAN ☖

"I said, what the hell—"

"Oh my God," Eleni blurted as her body suctioned itself against Adrian's. "You almost died."

Adrian's rage and fear froze within him as he processed the feeling of Eleni's soft arms around his neck.

"I, uh..." He lost his train of thought as Eleni pulled back to get a good look at him.

"I can't even imagine how traumatized I would have been if I saw someone die."

Tyler scoffed from somewhere behind Adrian. "He didn't die. He's fine."

Adrian couldn't help the flicker of hate that rose up the back of his throat. Of course Tyler didn't care. The man only cared for two things: himself and his possessions. Adrian's eyes washed over the rest of the group. At least they seemed to care. Benny was clutching Monique tightly, panic still streaked through his eyes. Stevie had been stripped of her usual sarcasm and stood quietly. Adrian's eyes locked on Bec. She was pale. Her eyes were wide, glossed with fright. Her hands were shaking softly but she was doing her best to keep anyone from noticing. Bec cared. In some ways, she was more of a friend to him than Tyler ever was. She was always nice to him, kind even. How had Tyler managed to get a girl like Bec?

A sick feeling twisted inside Adrian. Tyler had gotten her because he always got what he wanted. Adrian was sick of it. It wasn't fair. Tyler took and took without concern. But now, it was Adrian's time to take. His jaw clenched as he realized what he was taking from Tyler would never be enough. Tyler would always have more. Adrian titled his head as he watched Bec. How would Tyler react to losing something he truly valued? Something precious? Adrian figured it was about time he found out.

"You're right," Adrian offered. "I didn't die." He walked up to Tyler, his hair and swim trunks still dripping. "But what if someone had? What if it that thing had attacked someone else? What if it had gotten Benny?" Adrian's eyes flashed hotly. "Or Bec?"

In an instant, Tyler's eyes alighted with fury. Checkmate. Adrian savored the way Tyler's face grew red and splotchy. Tyler would never struggle the way Adrian had struggled all his life, but at least Adrian could show him that beyond the power of his money and status, some things were still beyond his control.

"Everyone get your things," Tyler barked. "We're leaving."

♨ MONIQUE ♨

Tyler was up in Jamari's face, words spitting at him with such fury that Monique thought the veins in his neck might burst.

"Why didn't you tell us there were goddamn crocodiles in the water?"

Jamari looked back at him with a slight agitation but went on peeling his mango. "Not usually there," he shrugged.

"Well apparently they fucking are," Tyler spat. "How incompetent are you? What if that thing had bitten off my friend's leg, huh?" Tyler seized up the collar of Jamari's shirt, bunching it into his fist. "What if my girlfriend had been in the fucking water? You would have ruined everything I had—" Tyler stopped himself and forced a deep breath from his lungs.

Jamari's eyes grew darker as a flicker of a smile slid across his face for the first time. "Querías esto, ¿no? ¿Aventura?"

Tyler stared at the man for a second before ripping his grip away from him. He swore under his breath as he stomped over to Bec. He pulled her into a tight embrace.

"Come on," Tyler commanded everyone, including Jamari. "We're heading back."

No one objected, the terror of their encounter still hanging heavy amongst the group. Jamari mumbled something to himself, a flicker of glee lighting up his eyes. It disappeared as soon as Monique caught his gaze. She wished she spoke Spanish. She'd never seen Tyler so pissed off. Jamari walked up to Monique and Benny, pressing little sandwich baggies into their hands before moving on to the others.

"Eat and walk," he demanded.

When he gave the last of the sandwiches to Tyler and Bec, another smile flickered across his face. He pushed past them to take his position at the lead. He was already around the bend before any of them could open their lunches.

Tyler took a deep, aggravated breath and rolled his eyes. "Let's go," he said, rallying his friends.

As Bec took a step forward, Monique heard her foot squelch. Everyone looked down at Bec's sneakers, then to Tyler's. They were completely soaked. Tyler swore under his breath. Suddenly, the thicket of trees and vines rustled wildly. Benny pushed Monique behind him as the snap of twigs grew louder. Monique let out a squeal as a mass emerged from the greenery.

"Where the fuck have you been?" Tyler shouted at Miles.

Miles raised his eyes at Tyler, as if amused by his hostility. "Exploring. Why?"

Tyler ignored the question and turned back to Bec. He caressed the side of her face softly. "If you start feeling a blister, tell me and I'll carry you, okay?"

Bec gave him a hesitant pat on his chest. "I'll be fine."

Monique watched Miles and Bec exchange a quick glance before Bec pulled away from Tyler.

"Come on," Bec uttered. "This place is starting to freak me out."

They walked and ate, quickly scarfing down the steak sandwiches Ramon had prepared for them. Monique noticed the only one who hadn't touched his food was Adrian. He walked quietly, his head down and hands clenched at his sides. She could only imagine he was replaying the image of the croc's mouth opening towards him with every step.

Monique and Benny brought up the rear of the group, walking slowly and silently. During their chat at the lagoon, they had decided one thing: there was no fighting for the rest of the trip. They were here on vacation, celebrating Bec. This wasn't the time or the place for petty comments and arguments. Whatever issues they had, they needed to deal with them when they got back. So now, Monique wasn't quite sure what to say. All she could think of when she looked at him was the fact that he wanted kids and he wanted them now. She hadn't expected that. Even when he'd told her a few months into dating that he wanted a family more than anything, she hadn't taken it too seriously. Of course, she hadn't taken their relationship too seriously either. It had been nothing more than a fling—a way to get her mind off the person who had shattered her heart into a billion pieces. She lifted her eyes from the trail and rested them on the wet strands of hair that dripped down the back of Stevie's shirt. Monique took a deep breath, dropping her gaze back down. She had thought that this trip would be good for her and Benny. She thought it would give them a chance to grow closer, to rebuild some of the damage that had been done over the past six months. But now that she was here, she didn't want to work on her marriage. She wanted to have fun. She wanted to stay up all night with her friends, drinking like she was still twenty-something. She wanted to go snorkeling and read a book on the beach and collect shells to bring back home. But most of all, she wanted to spend time with Stevie. It hurt to admit, but Monique missed her. Monique had spent the better part of the last year avoiding her. She thought if she pretended that her heart hadn't been ripped from her chest that it hadn't really happened.

She'd never told Benny about her and Stevie. As far as he knew, Monique had never dated anyone he knew, never been in love, and never been with a woman. The less he knew, the more she could pretend it wasn't true. It was easier that way—at least that's what she told herself every day. She thought dating Benny would change things. She thought it would change her. To her dismay, it hadn't. Benny pulled Monique towards him and kissed the top of her head.

"I love you," he stated.

She hesitated, watching the fiery hair in front of her sway

with every step. "I love you, too," she responded.

Monique wrapped her arm around Benny's back and gave him a pat. It came across more disingenuous than she meant it and she quickly pulled her arm away and continued walking in silence. Her feet pounded softly against the dirt trail, throwing small puffs of dust into the air. Up ahead, Bec had pulled away from Tyler to walk with Stevie. Monique had noticed it was a thing she tended to do now. There was always a little bit more distance around Bec, like she was keeping the world at an arm's length. But that wasn't what intrigued Monique now. Behind Bec and Stevie was Miles. He was walking briskly, keeping pace with the two women. He whispered something to Bec which caused her to snap her head back at him. Concern riddled her face. She turned to Stevie who then abruptly turned towards Miles. Monique watched Stevie's typically cheerful face grow harsh as she muttered something. Miles immediately slowed his pace, letting distance grow between them.

"What's up with Miles?" Monique asked Benny.

Benny darted his eyes up the trail. "Umm," he mumbled. "What do you mean?"

Monique tilted her head as she watched Miles walk in solitude. "He's been kind of a loner since we got here. Is he normally like that?"

Benny shifted his gaze away from her nervously. "Uhhh, I don't know," Benny rattled. "Maybe he's not feeling well from all the traveling."

She shook her head as she looked back at Miles. "No, that's not it."

Monique watched Bec whisper something to Stevie before marching up the trail. In less than a minute she had hiked up to where Tyler was. He smiled and wrapped his arm around her as Miles caught up to Stevie. They talked in muffled tones. Stevie nodded and gestured her hands wildly in the air. Monique watched Stevie take a deep breath before slapping Miles loosely on the shoulder. She looked back, briefly catching Monique's gaze. Stevie hesitated, stiffening slightly, before turning back and continuing her conversation.

"I think it's got something to do with Bec."

Benny stiffened in response but said nothing.

"Do Miles and her not get along?"

Silence. Monique looked at Benny. He was pursing his lips together, his eyes flighty and uncertain. He gave her a dismissive shrug as he mumbled his words.

"I hadn't noticed."

His eyes met hers before darting away quickly. That's when she knew.

"Benjamin Michael Barbieri," Monique said firmly. She grabbed him by the arm, stopping both of them in their tracks. "You know something."

Benny yanked his bucket hat off his head. His buzzed hair was lightly dewed in sweat. A bead dripped down the side of his face as he looked at her. "Babe, don't worry about it. Okay? It's nothing."

"Don't 'babe' me," she protested. "I'm not going to let you stand there and feed me bullshit. No secrets, remember?"

"Babe, it's—" Benny took a deep breath and wiped the sweat from his brow. "It's not my secret to tell."

"Not your secret to t—" She let out a huffy breath and started walking away from him. "Unbelievable," she muttered.

Benny raced to catch up with her. "Monique—"

She turned back and pushed her hands into his chest. "Tell me." She raised an eyebrow at him, waiting for him to fess up.

He looked towards where the rest of the group was disappearing around the bend and sighed.

"Fine."

♨ BEC ♨

Bec sat on the couch, her wet hair dripping onto her tank top. The first thing she'd done when they'd gotten back to the house was shower. The trek home had left her overheated and her feet wrinkled and numb in her wet socks. She'd shocked her body with icy cold water for a minute before turning the shower fiery hot. The better part of 20 minutes had been spent in there as her body and mind grew deliciously numb. It was only when Eleni had yelled through the house that she was using up all the hot water that Bec had twisted the knob reluctantly and halted the flow. She'd thrown on some clothes and plopped herself down on the couch where she now sat cross legged and dripping.

Bec wanted to go outside and let the sun's warmth dry her hair but Tyler was still out there. He'd gone straight to Marta when they'd returned from the hike, fuming once again while Jamari had slyly crept to the back house. Bec only heard pieces of the conversation but what she'd heard was enough. Tyler was enraged. What wasn't clear to Bec was why. Yes, Adrian had almost been croc bait. A shudder ran through Bec as she remembered the flutter in the water when Stevie had dove in. It could have been Stevie, ripped and shredded by that thing. Bec pushed the thought away and sat up a little taller as she peered out the window. Even so, Tyler couldn't expect them to control the wildlife, it wasn't a zoo. So what had he been arguing with Marta about for thirty minutes?

The woman stood firmly, not at all intimidated by Tyler's six-foot-four figure towering over her. She looked back at him, her face stoic as she spoke. Bec wished she could hear what they were saying. Tyler seemed to have settled down a bit. Bec was happy about that. She'd witnessed his temper a few times, always directed at other people. It wasn't something she wished on anyone. In those brief moments of rage, Tyler wasn't the person she knew. He wasn't the man who'd sent one hundred red roses after their first date or the man who agreed to go to every local art show even though she knew he found it boring. No, in those moments he was the person she'd expected him to be when she'd first laid eyes on him at that bar. Rich. Narcissistic. Cold. In those rare but potent moments, he was the type of man who had no problem reminding people they were beneath him—that his existence meant more. It was the only time her enchantment towards him seemed to dwindle. Well, that and whenever Miles was around. The admission seemed to snap at Bec's side with tiny, razor-like teeth. Maybe that was the solution—get rid of Miles. Never see him again. Problem solved. A nagging feeling in her gut told her it wouldn't be that easy. Tyler finished his conversation and stomped into the house. Bec watched quietly, almost shrinking back into the couch so as to not catch his attention. Only when the bedroom door closed firmly behind Tyler did Bec relax.

She looked back out the window, eager to let the sun hit her face, and her heart leapt into her chest. Marta's stare pierced her through the window pane. For a minute, Bec wondered if the woman even saw her. She just stared ahead, no recognition in her eyes. It was the slow smile that crept onto the woman's face that told Bec that yes—she could see her. A chill from Bec's wet hair rippled across her skin. Or maybe it was something else. Bec tried to smile back but all that came over her was a lopsided line etched into her mouth. Bec looked away. After a few seconds, a feeling pulled at her. She couldn't help herself. She looked back but when she did, Marta was gone. Then a heavy thud bounced the couch, causing Bec to nearly jump out of her skin.

"Shit," Bec breathed as she turned to see Stevie wiggling into the couch cushions next to her.

"Scare ya?" Stevie chuckled.

"Yeah," Bec laughed as Stevie grinned at her wildly. "Today has been…"

"Fucking crazy?" Stevie gave Bec an impish look, extending a hand to her. "Here, this should help."

Bec smiled at her friend as she took the beer. "You are an angel," she said, taking a big gulp. She swallowed hastily and caught her breath. "I was really getting tired of all the fancy stuff." She gestured towards the kitchen. "I mean how many bottles of champagne did Tyler bring along?" She shook her head and took another swig.

"Yeah," Stevie scoffed, leaning back against the couch. "Enough for a whole country club. Next he'll try to get us to bathe in the stuff."

Bec laughed softly into the bottle before tipping it back.

"In all the years we've been friends, I never expected this."

They sat and drank silently for a minute. The rest of the house had grown quiet. Adrian and Eleni were both napping—separately, to what Bec assumed was the disappointment of Adrian. Tyler was in the bedroom. Miles was—she didn't know where he was, but that was probably for the best. Bec had seen Benny and Monique head down to the beach as she'd come out of her room. Monique had given her an awkward smile before shuffling Benny out the door. Something had felt off about the way they hadn't so much as uttered a word to her. Bec had assumed that Benny hadn't told Monique about that night, but maybe Bec was wrong about that.

Bec took another swig of her beer as Stevie's comment nagged at her. "What do you mean?"

"Huh?" Stevie mumbled.

"What do you mean you would have never expected this?"

Stevie sighed and looked at her friend earnestly. "I mean come on, Becs," she laughed. "Look at this?" She waved her hand around the house, beer still in hand. It sloshed around the bottle violently as she did. "Your fancy boyfriend snapped his fingers and got us an island."

Bec gave her a hard look. "And?"

She sighed again. "I just never expected you to end up with a guy like Tyler. That's all."

"I didn't end up with him," Bec snapped. "We're just..." she took a pull from her beer and swallowed harshly. "We're just dating."

"Chill," Stevie laughed, her hands up in mock defense. "I'm not saying you're going to marry the guy. It's just..." she ran a hand through her hair. "Fuck, how do I say this..."

Bec's fingernails ripped at the beer bottle's label as she waited.

"I don't like the guy, okay?" Stevie held her hands up and shrugged. "He's..."

"A lot," Bec breathed into her beer bottle. She tipped her head back and finished the rest of it.

"An asshole," she snickered, grabbing the empty beer bottle from Bec's hand. "Round two?"

Bec nodded firmly. She sat there with a mind full of questions as Stevie grabbed two more beers from the fridge. When she got back, Bec curled her legs underneath her and turned to face Stevie.

"So me and Tyler," she dropped her voice lower, "you don't approve?"

"I have to approve?" She laughed and rolled her eyes at Bec. "What does it matter if I like the guy? I'm not the one dating him."

"It matters to me," Bec insisted. "You're all I've got, Stevs." Bec tapped her beer against Stevie's lightly. The result was a soft clink. "I trust your opinion more than my own most times."

"As you should," she winked. Stevie took a sip of beer.

Her gaze seemed to harden as she thought. "Fuck, you really want to know?"

"Just tell me."

"Here's the deal," Stevie said, scooting closer to Bec. "Tyler is the type of guy you date for the experience. Like that one guy on the lacrosse team I dated in high school before I came to my senses and dove headfirst into—"

"Okay, okay," Bec laughed. "Get to the point."

"He's the guy you date to find out what doesn't work for you. Trial and error, you know?"

"So you're saying I'm better off with someone else?"

"Yes," Stevie laughed as she took a sip of beer. "Literally anyone."

Silence floated in the air between them. Stevie eyed Bec curiously as she fidgeted with the new bottle's label.

"You're taking this well." Her gaze tightened on Bec as a smirk slipped across her face. "It's almost like you've already come to this conclusion yourself."

Bec's eyes stayed fixed in her lap as her fingers worked to peel away the foiled paper around the bottle. She ripped a long piece off like a hangnail.

"I don't know what to think."

"Yes. You do," Stevie prodded. She sighed and leaned back into the couch, her beer resting in between her legs. "The answer is obvious, you just don't want to admit it."

Bec's face contorted into a slight scowl. "If it's so obvious then tell me."

"Miles."

Bec's brow furrowed deeper. "You're serious?"

"Are you?" she laughed in response. "I mean come on, Bec. You two look at each other like you're ready to fuck on the kitchen counter."

Bec downed the rest of her beer and set it on the coffee table with a harsh thud. The giant slab of wood in front of her looked more like a piece of art than a coffee table. It curved and twisted wildly, gleaming back at her with its glossy veneer. It probably cost more than her rent. It was ridiculous—just like this conversation.

"So what? You think Miles is good for me?" Bec challenged her friend.

"I did not say that."

"So what are you saying then?"

Stevie gave her a stern look. "Cut the attitude and I might tell you."

Bec rolled her eyes and waved her hand at Stevie, gesturing for her to continue.

"I don't know if Miles is a good guy. Honestly, it was kind of fucked that he agreed to come on this trip, knowing it would probably cause problems for you."

"Okay, so what's your point then?"

"You want him."

The urge to deny it welled up in Bec's throat. Her skin itched but she forced herself to sit still. It was pointless to try to defend herself because both she and Stevie knew it would be a lie. Bec gave Stevie a careful glare and said nothing.

"You want him but for some fucking reason you just won't let yourself have him. It's mind boggling."

Defensiveness reared up inside of Bec with an ugly fury. "And you?" she quipped at Stevie. "You're just going to keep pretending like you're not in love with someone who's already married?"

"Way to deflect," Stevie muttered into her beer as she took a sip.

"So you're saying it's not true?"

The muscles in Stevie's face tensed as she pulled her gaze from Bec. "It doesn't matter."

"So you're just going to keep pretending everything is fine?"

Bec watched the anger and hurt spread across Stevie's face as she raised her eyebrows and leaned closer to her.

"Yeah, Bec. I am. Monique made her decision."

"And you?"

Stevie swallowed harshly. Bec knew she should stop. Stevie didn't talk about Monique anymore—not like that—and for good reason. They had broken up and Monique had moved on. Cut and dry. End of story. Bec knew Stevie still loved Monique but this wasn't about them. This was about Bec slinking away from her own accountability. It was her best skill. Distract them and run away. She knew it was wrong but she couldn't stop because when she did it would be her turn again.

"I made my decision the day I fucked up and told her she was too much." Stevie's voice grew softer as did the look in her eyes. She nodded at Bec. "And you?" she retorted. "When are you going to stop pretending you don't know exactly what you want? Who you want?"

Tension prickled Bec's forehead as she considered the question. It had been one of the many things she'd been avoiding. But something about hearing it come out from Stevie's mouth seemed to shock her system. She looked out towards the hall, at her and Tyler's closed door. She wondered what he would say when he found out—if he found out. Would he be mad? Or hurt? A deep pit grew in her chest as she imagined the pain in his eyes.

"I'll stop when it's no longer an option," Bec said softly.

Stevie let out a deep breath, the tension falling from her body. "Yeah, me too. Me too," she muttered.

The two stared ahead, letting the silence of their own defeat fill the space between them. Bec snatched the beer from Stevie's hands and took a long sip, draining it. It was probably all backwash, something Bec realized as the last drop slid down her throat. When she was done, she set the bottle back in her friend's hand.

"Fuck," Bec breathed.

"When you're ready to admit that you want to date Miles," Stevie said. "I'll be here to help with a plan to ditch fancy-pants."

Laughed spilled from Bec. She couldn't help it. It was

absurd. The conversation. The tension. Both of their situations. Yet, she felt like something inside of her had awoken. It was like she'd been trapping rogue thoughts in the shadowed basement of her mind for months. All it had taken was Stevie pulling the little cord to turn on the light and show her what was there all along.

"How long have you secretly been calling him fancy-pants?" Bec asked, her brow arching as she stifled another laugh.

"You don't want to know." Stevie smiled.

♨ MILES ♨

He had to do something.

Miles was walking fast, his feet pounding into the trail as he put as much distance between him and the house as possible. He didn't know where he was going, just that he needed to get away. From all of it. From her. He felt like letting loose a guttural yell, slamming his fists against a tree trunk—something. This wasn't how things were supposed to go. When had Tyler decided to propose? When had things gotten that serious? Bec had dragged her feet through their entire relationship. Anyone with eyes could see that. So how could Tyler possibly think she'd say yes? Miles stopped abruptly, his feet skidding against loose rock. She wouldn't say yes, right?

He clenched his jaw as he stared out against the blurring green of the jungle. No, she wouldn't say yes. He'd make sure of it. Miles let a harsh breath slip from his lungs before turning around and heading back to the house. He could tell that Bec was stressed and overwhelmed but it wasn't because she didn't want him. Quite the opposite, he could see her need for him in every tiny reaction of hers. Every passing glance. Every hitched breath. Every prolonged touch. She wanted him just as much as he wanted her. Miles just needed to help her relax—to see things more clearly. He took another deep breath, letting the tension in his shoulder go as he did. As his mind worked at the problem with every step he took, a faint smile drifted across his face. Yes, he had to do something and he knew exactly what to do.

♨ STEVIE ♨

It all seemed too perfect. The soft coastal breeze that wafted across the patio and chilled her freshly-tanned skin. The stark white tablecloth and napkins adorning the table. The steaming hot meal that was placed in front of her. Stevie took it all in, looking for something that might be out of place, because in her mind, something had to be.

The only thing that caught her eye was Marta. She was standing on the edge of the patio, watching Ramon and Jamari with sharp eyes as they set down the rest of the plates. Stevie didn't like her. Maybe it was the way her eyes seemed to sink into you like teeth or the way her smile looked painted on like a doll's. Like everything on the island, her appearance was perfectly curated just for them. But to Stevie, perfect was a lie.

She hadn't always known this. There was a time when she thought her biological father was perfect—a hardworking blue-collar man doing what he could to support his family. He'd slave away during the week, working late into the night, but always showed up when it counted. He was at every gymnastics meet and volleyball game and parent teacher conference. He made every birthday perfect, too, until the one that changed them all.

The illusion was shattered by a shiny silver bracelet with tiny diamonds. He had given it to her on her eighth birthday. It had been perfect. The way it dazzled in the sun. How special it made her feel. She had been so young that she didn't even think about how he could have afforded it. All had been well in little Stevie's world until her mom had come to her tight-lipped and red-eyed. She had to give it back. Stevie was confused, screaming and crying until finally the full truth came out. Daddy hadn't bought it down at the shops like Stevie had imagined. He had taken it from the family whose bathroom he had re-tiled the week before. Perfect had tarnished at the edges then and as Stevie got older, perfect slipped further away. The fighting. The cheating. The divorce. It had all been hidden in plain sight the entire time, she'd just been too distracted by perfect to notice. So no, Stevie didn't like perfect. Didn't trust it at all.

Her eyes flickered across the table to Tyler. To her, he was the ringmaster of all this perfectly orchestrated bullshit. Flying all of them out here, planning this extravagant surprise for Bec—it wasn't genuine. It couldn't be. But then again, Stevie was biased. From the first ten seconds of knowing Tyler, she had known she would never like him. It was the way he'd slid up next to Bec with the drink he'd ordered just for her and that cocky grin on his face. Bec usually hated those types—the ones that assumed some overpriced, fruity drink could win a girl over. But somehow, against all odds, he had charmed her. That was the thing Stevie had come to hate the most about Tyler. He always seemed to get what he wanted. She had tried to be polite, for Bec's sake, but the longer Bec stayed with him the harder it was to put on a good face.

Tonight was different, though. Instead of tucking away her disdain as usual, Stevie smiled at him. But it wasn't with the same fake politeness she reserved for drunk assholes at work. No, it might have been the most genuine smile she'd ever smiled at a man. It was full teeth and scrunched cheeks. It was a happy smile because something had changed. Bec had finally shown Stevie what she had seen coming for a long time. Tyler's grip on Bec wasn't going to last forever—or very long, for that matter. The satisfaction of knowing that made Stevie almost giddy. That rich asshole was done for. Cooked. All that Stevie had to do now was give her friend the support she needed to finally kick him to the curb. The sly smile was still plastered on Stevie's face as she turned her focus back on her plate. Everyone else was already eating what Ramon had explained to them as a Nicaraguan-style tamale. It was some sort of dough stuffed with meat, potatoes, and herbs. Stevie typically tried to avoid eating too much meat but the enticing smell of it and the hunger that resided deep in her stomach drove forkful after forkful.

"You know there's pork in that right?" Bec whispered.

Stevie shrugged happily and stabbed another bite with her fork. "When in Nicaragua," she sang before plopping it in her mouth.

Bec shook her head with a laugh. The scrape of forks and knives clattered across the table. It was just them now; Marta, Ramon, and Jamari had slipped away just as quickly as they always seemed to appear. No one had seemed to notice their absence, everyone too tired from the day and ravenous with hunger. It wasn't until Adrian cleared his throat that everyone's eyes lifted from their plates.

"So, uh—" Adrian started. "Thanks for not letting me get eaten by an alligator today."

"Crocodile."

His brow furrowed as he looked at Tyler.

"It was a crocodile," he said between bites.

"Yeah, well...thanks," Adrian grunted.

"We should be thanking Crocodile Dundee," Benny laughed, gesturing towards the house where Jamari had likely disappeared to.

"He's the reason we were almost croc bait," Tyler objected.

The tension in Tyler's tone seemed to halt everyone's forks in mid-air, pieces of food dangling off them. Monique was the first one to break the silence.

"He couldn't have known it was in there. It was an honest mistake."

Tyler shot her a dirty look. "There should be no mistakes

with how much I'm paying them."

Stevie chewed her food as silently as she could, eager to not miss a second of what was unfolding in front of her. Monique flashed a look at Benny, as if instructing him to put his friend in check. He gave her a shrug before shoveling more food into his mouth. Stevie snickered silently. What a pussy. Stevie would have put Tyler in his place in an instant if Monique had looked at her that way.

"I keep having flashbacks to that moment," Eleni said, inserting herself into the conversation. "It was so close I think I'll have nightmares for a week."

Monique let out a soft jeer, barely keeping it under her breath. "Were you even in the water?"

Eleni held Monique's gaze silently. Stevie almost laughed out loud at the girl's attempt to look intimidating.

"Yes I was," Eleni snapped as she lifted her glass to take a sip of wine.

"The girls are fighting," Bec murmured to Stevie, driving a smile to her face.

Stevie felt energized as she looked across the table. Tonight was going to be a good night—she could feel it. She finished the last bite of her food and washed it down with a swig of beer.

"So Tyler," she started, a sickly smile spilling across her face, "what thrilling adventures do you have planned for us tomorrow?"

He shot her a deadly look from across the table. Stevie knew the animosity she'd always felt for him was mutual. She'd push his buttons from time to time and he'd retaliate by stealing Bec away for a weekend trip or by guilt tripping her into canceling plans. Sometimes Stevie felt like they were in the middle of a custody battle. But with Tyler now on his way out of Bec's life, Stevie wanted to make every last, irritating moment count.

"The staff is cooking us a big brunch before they leave for the mainland," he said flatly before addressing the group with a friendlier display. "After that we can relax on the beach, hike, go snorkeling, anything we want."

"Sounds fun!" Eleni blurted out.

Stevie almost choked on her beer as she watched Eleni blatantly kiss Tyler's ass. She was beaming at him like a schoolgirl with a crush on the playground.

"Do you still know how to snorkel?" Eleni cooed.

"Of course," Tyler said coldly.

It took all of Stevie's restraint not to say something. Instead she bit her tongue and watched the show.

"Remember when our families went to Bora Bora and we got to snorkel with all of those sharks?"

Tyler inhaled deeply. His eyes flashed to Eleni—a silent warning between the two of them that Stevie relished every second of. She didn't really understand Tyler and Eleni's friendship. Tyler seemed to hate her, openly so. There was always a weird power dynamic between the two—but shit, was it entertaining.

"No."

"Oh my God. Yes, you do," Eleni said, her voice dropping into a playful whine. "I was like twelve or something. You kept telling me you were going to feed me to the sharks. God, you were so moody back then," she laughed, her eyelashes practically batting at him.

Wild hysteria splashed across Stevie's face as Eleni kept talking. The girl flashed her flirty eyes across the table as Tyler sat tensely. She quickly moved on from the Bora Bora trip. She began telling everyone how Tyler had left her in a cafe in Paris when they were teenagers, forcing her to take a cab back to the hotel alone. Stevie sat through the whole thing brimming with sadistic glee. How many times did Tyler have to ditch Eleni or threaten to push her into shark-infested waters before she got the hint that Tyler wasn't into her? Stevie tightened her gaze on Tyler as a thought prickled through her mind. Maybe Bec wasn't the only one in her relationship with secrets.

"I didn't know you two knew each other since you were kids."

Tyler looked at Bec quickly. He gave her a soft nod before cutting a piece of tamale with his fork. "Uh, yeah. Our parents have been friends since college."

"We grew up together," Eleni declared. "I probably know Tyler better than anyone here."

Stevie didn't like the way Eleni was grinning at Bec. She doubted Bec liked it either. Just as she was about to make a snide comment to wipe that look off her face, a shadow rolled over Stevie's shoulder. She flinched and swore under her breath as Jamari towered over her. He set down a small dessert plate before swooping away like a bat in the night.

"These are Buñuelos," Marta said, seeming to appear out of nowhere. She accentuated each sound through her thick accent. "Like little fried donut balls." She stood off to the side of the table and looked at them attentively. "Enjoy and good night," she smiled before nodding at Jamari and Ramon to follow her.

Stevie watched the little group walk back into the house to clean up the kitchen. As Marta turned around to slide the patio door shut, she caught Stevie's gaze. She held it there for a moment, pausing with her fingers around the door's handle. A deep smile etched its way onto her face. Stevie yanked her eyes away, a chill sliding down her spine. Thank fuck they were leaving tomorrow. She'd rather eat PB&J's for three meals straight than go through the weekend with Marta's eyes chewing into her skin. A thought pulled at her suddenly. Stevie hesitated, her fingers halfway curled around the fork in preparation to stab one of those little fried donut balls.

"Hey, Tyler."

He looked at her with an irritated quiver of his lip, most likely expecting a joke at his expense. "Yes, Stevie?"

"Why are they leaving tomorrow?"

Her question seemed to catch him off guard. It took him a

second to answer.

"I asked them to."

Most of the table turned to look at Tyler. Only Benny kept on eating the Buñuelos, seemingly uninterested in what Tyler had to say.

"Why?" Monique probed. "You said earlier you paid them a lot of money, why have them leave?"

Tyler chewed and gave her a casual shrug. "Figured we'd prefer some privacy."

Monique didn't seem to be too convinced by that answer, her eyes sliding to Stevie uncertainly.

"I could definitely use some privacy," Tyler hinted, raising his eyebrows at Bec from across the table.

Stevie stifled a groan and finished the last of her beer. As she pulled the bottle from her lips, she noticed Miles shift in his seat. He was sitting next to Tyler but his focus was aimed dead ahead. There was a covertness to the look on his face but Stevie knew the emotion well enough to name it. She saw it every weekend when someone's boyfriend tried to hit on her, oblivious to the fact that she was more interested in the girlfriend standing next to them. The look in those poor girlfriends' eyes was the same look that Miles was barely containing now. It was a vicious jealousy, the type that could eat you alive if you let it fester. Stevie passed a subtle look Bec's way, but her friend hadn't noticed Miles' intent gaze.

Bec was listening to Monique, captivated by the story she was telling about the disastrous sailing expedition Benny had taken her on during their honeymoon. Laughter erupted through everyone at the table, everyone except for Miles and Stevie. The more Stevie watched Miles, the more an uneasiness flickered inside of her. She had seen a glimmer of Miles' exasperation on the hike today. He was tired of Bec's indecision—desperate even. Looking at him now, Stevie wasn't sure how much more he could take. He was at his breaking point, she could see it in the way his jaw muscle tremored whenever Tyler rested his hand against Bec's thigh.

Part of her felt bad for him. She understood. To watch the person you wanted be loved by someone else was a different type of torture. So when she watched the way his eyes burned into Bec now, oblivious to anyone or anything else around him, she didn't judge him. She'd had that look in her eyes when Benny had dipped Monique in that silky wedding dress and planted a wet kiss on her lips. She'd had that look when she'd watched them dance and cut their cake. She'd had it when they'd driven away in that stupid vintage car. So no, Stevie wasn't judging Miles. If anything, she was rooting for him. Because if he was able to steal Bec from Tyler for good, maybe there was hope for Stevie yet.

♨ BEC ♨

Benny threw another piece of driftwood on top of the flames, sending embers cascading into the sand. The fire popped and cracked as it settled around its new sacrifice. The bonfire that had started as a measly pile of twigs placed atop a freshly dug hole was now a hot inferno. Benny stood back and took a good look, pride and inhibition swirling around his face into a grin. Bec could tell by the look on his face that he didn't plan to let whatever happened last night deter him tonight. He would get shitfaced again. Benny sat heavily into the sand and wrapped his arm around his wife. Bec at least hoped that whatever happened, he wouldn't ruin Monique's night again.

"Just call me king of the wilderness," he proclaimed.

"Easy there, city boy," Monique laughed as she patted him on the chest. "You soaked the entire thing in lighter fluid before dropping the match." Her tone felt somewhere between playful and antagonizing. Bec watched her give Benny a sideways glance before Monique's eyes wandered to Stevie.

"Pass me that bottle, will ya?"

Stevie pulled the bottle of wine from where it rested in the sand and passed it to Adrian who passed it to Eleni who passed it to Monique. When she finally got it, she poured a hefty amount into her cup.

"We should play a game," Eleni blurted out.

Bec withheld a groan. She could only imagine what type of game Eleni wanted to play. Spin the bottle? Strip truth or dare? Eleni clearly wanted one thing and one thing only on this trip—attention. Bec dipped her toes into last night's memories, the thought of Miles turning Eleni down bringing a shiver of satisfaction to her stomach. Bec glanced across the fire at him, expecting to find his gaze already on her. The excitement swirling in her gut fizzled out when she found his eyes elsewhere. She waited a few seconds but he kept his gaze focused on the fire. It was like he'd been avoiding her since they got back from the hike. But that's what she'd asked him to do, wasn't it? It's what she had wanted. So why was his lack of eye contact driving her mad right now?

"What kind of game?" Adrian asked. His hand had found its way to the small of Eleni's back when they'd all first circled around the fire and it hadn't left her skin since.

"I swear, if you say Truth or Dare..." Benny moaned.

"Never Have I Ever," she replied excitedly, flashing her eyes around the group. "Everyone know how to play?"

"Shit, I haven't played that since high school," Stevie chuckled softly before taking a sip of beer.

"Oh my God," Bec said, gripping Stevie's arm. Bec was already laughing as her words came out. "Remember when we played at Jason Young's party freshman year?"

Stevie's eyes lit up. "And...fuck what was that girl's name... Bethany? Remember how she wouldn't stop giving us dirty looks the whole night after we said we'd stolen a pack of cigarettes from the gas station?"

"We were such little criminals back then," Bec teased. "How could they even allow us in the same classroom as her?"

"I'm surprised she didn't get her daddy to buy the school and kick us out." Stevie rolled her eyes as she took another sip of beer. "Fucking rich assholes," she murmured into the bottle's neck.

Bec's body stiffened. She didn't dare look at Tyler who was sitting to her right. His arm was lightly draped around her waist as he sat silently, no doubt glaring at Stevie.

"So uhh....Eleni," Bec said. "Refresh my memory. How do you play?"

Eleni beamed. Bec had noticed that aside from Adrian, no one in the group really talked to her. Bec imagined that was the type of thing that chewed away at Eleni incessantly, like bed bugs infesting her ego. The girl needed attention like a fish needed water. But now, all eyes were on her.

"Whoever's turn it is says something—something they haven't done. Then if anyone in the group has done it, they have to drink."

"Easy enough," Benny chimed in. "And a good way to get all you criminals drunk." His eyes flashed to Stevie with drunken delight.

"I'll go first!" Eleni looked around the group with a clever grin. "Never have I ever stolen something."

"Really?" Stevie quipped. "Bec literally just told everyone we'd done that."

Eleni looked back at her with a sickly sweet smile. "No rule against me using what I know to win."

"No one wins Never Have I Ever," Bec stated. "The whole point is to get each other drunk."

"And reveal secrets." Eleni smiled.

Bec's stomach lurched. Her eyes darted to Stevie. She silently willed her to stop this whole thing before it got out of hand but all Stevie did was give her a shrug. It was nonchalant. A what-could-possibly-happen shrug, but Bec knew from past experiences that anything could happen. Life was unpredictable. She took a sip from her cup for losing the turn and downed an extra one for some courage.

Eleni looked around the circle. "No one else?" she teased.

Benny drank. So did Miles. Tyler gave her a disinterested look, refraining from lifting the cup in his hands. When Eleni looked at Monique, the woman's eyes were fixed rigidly on her.

"What about you?"

Eleni's jaw shuddered as she hid a flicker of emotion. "Please, me?" she laughed airily. "Honey, I could buy anything I want. I don't need to steal."

"No, but that doesn't mean you wouldn't want to."

Bec gave Stevie a sideways glance as Monique continued to burn her eyes into Eleni. Stevie's brow arched in response.

"You're being weird," Eleni stated, her face scrunching into a sneer.

"How about I have a turn?" Monique said flatly. She kept her eyes locked on Eleni as the corner of her mouth lifted into a scowl. "Never have I ever stolen something from a photoshoot and blamed it on someone else."

Bec's eyes went wide as she looked between the two women who were now locked in a death stare. "What the fuck is going on?" she whispered to Stevie.

Stevie shrugged happily. "I don't know," she said before throwing back her cup and taking a long sip. "But if Monique starts kicking Eleni's ass I'm going to need some popcorn."

Eleni gave Monique an exaggerated eye roll that Bec could tell was all for show. "Seriously, Monique?" She let out a puffy breath as she flipped her hair over her shoulder. "I told your assistant I forgot I was wearing it when I left." She averted her eyes and tossed her hands in the air. "It was an easy mistake. I don't know why you're still making a big deal about it."

"And what about telling the casting director that you saw me putting that $17,000 necklace into my bag, huh?" Monique leaned forward, the fire dancing shadows across her face. "That an easy mistake too?"

Bec watched Eleni's eyes tighten on Monique before she replaced the spiteful look with a friendlier, albeit faker, one. "Oh come on, Monique," she chattered. "I gave the necklace back, didn't I? It's all water under the bridge." She shook her plastic cup in the air pointedly before taking a sip. "Happy?"

"Hardly," Monique rasped.

Eleni noticed they were all staring at her and gave them an irritated glare. "Your turn," she said, patting Adrian on the arm before burying her face into her cup.

"Hmmm..." Adrian swirled the red wine around in his

cup. "Never have I ever gotten in a fight."

"This game is rigged," Stevie said as she drank.

Miles took a sip. Then Benny took a sip. Finally, Bec watched as Tyler drank from his cup.

"You've gotten in a fight?" She didn't mean for it to sound so condescending but it did. The desire to pull her words back into her mouth came as soon as she heard herself.

He looked at her steadily. "Yes."

"Like a legit, bloody fight?" Stevie probed.

Miles laughed. "Doubtful."

"I got into some fights in college," Tyler interjected. He locked eyes with Miles. "And yeah, some of them got a little bloody."

Benny cleared his throat uncomfortably. "My turn?"

Eleni nodded at him, careful to avoid eye contact with Monique.

"Fuck, let's see..." he started. "What haven't I done?" he laughed. He hesitated as he caught Bec's eye. His Adam's apple bobbed as he swallowed dryly, as if pushing down the thing that had come to his mind. It took him another minute. Finally, a moronic grin spread over his slightly sunburned face. "Never have I ever faked an orgasm."

All of the women drank, including Monique. Benny gave her a wild look. "You haven't—"

"Of course not, babe. Not with you," she consoled him before shooting a guilty look at Bec and Stevie. The girls exploded into laughter, only stopping when Miles spoke up.

"Never have I ever—" he began. Bec's eyes flashed to his, the light of the fire seemed to quiver against the glow in his eyes. It made her feel unsteady, unmoored. As he looked back at her, that feeling only grew worse. "Never have I ever been cheated on."

"I hate this game," Adrian muttered into his wine.

Bec pleaded silently with Miles, her eyes reaching across the fire with desperation. He ignored her and turned his gaze towards Tyler.

"Aw," Eleni cooed at Adrian. "It's okay. I bet she was a bitch anyways." Her brow knotted as a thought flitted through her mind. "Does it count if you were the one who cheated?"

Stevie slapped her hand against her forehead. "Obviously not."

Bec felt Tyler's eyes on her. She looked up at him hesitantly. The contents of her stomach felt like they were boiling in a vat of acid.

"It's just as traumatic being the one who cheats," Eleni argued. "I was so stressed that Georgio was going to catch me cheating on him with his roommate two summers ago that I lost like ten pounds."

It took Bec a second to realize that Tyler wasn't waiting for her to confess her sins. He was waiting for her to take a sip from her cup. Did he really think that the trauma her ex had put her through, the secret she'd been hiding all this time, had been nothing but infidelity? She was tempted to lift the cup to her lips, to let him think it was only that. She looked at him, the emotion in her eyes wavering as she considered it. No. She couldn't. The thought of doing that felt rancid. How could she portray Brennen as her undoing when it had been her that brought this on herself? She took a sharp breath as she set her cup down into the sand. Tyler pursed his lips curiously before looking back at the group.

"Uh, who wants to go next?" Worry had spread across Benny's face like chicken pox as he shifted uncomfortably in the sand.

"Never have I ever—" Eleni began. Her eyes wandered across the circle until her gaze landed on Tyler. "Never have I ever killed someone."

"Jesus," Adrian blurted out.

"I'd fucking hope not," Stevie laughed, shooting Bec a wild look.

Eleni kept her focus on Tyler, staring at him with a sinister sweetness dripping from her face. "No one?" she asked.

He glared back at her, keeping his cup in his lap. Bec watched the tension between them uncertainty. Why was Eleni looking at him like that?

"Never have I ever slept with someone in this circle."

Bec's focus ripped to Miles. Her eyes met his just as he took a long sip from his cup, draining it. Bec felt the warmth slip from her body as Eleni's voice shot to life like a referee's whistle.

"Who?" Her eyes locked onto him hungrily. "*Who?*" she prodded again. Her gaze danced across every face that sat in the circle, begging for the answer. "Who slept with Miles?"

Silence fell over the group, the only sound the pop of embers filling the cold air. Bec felt her chest tightening. Had the waves crashing against the beach gotten louder? The night brighter? Everything felt like it was bearing down on her. It was hard to breathe. Sweat mixed with anxiety pebbled on her forehead. Was this the moment? Was it over? Then relief and surprise washed over her like a bucket of ice cold water as Stevie raised her cup in the air and took a sip.

"You?" Eleni spat.

"Ha," Stevie interjected, the uncertainty pouring from her voice. "I guess the cat's out of the bag," she said before taking another big, dramatic sip.

Bec's eyes flickered across the group. Were people buying it? Benny was barely keeping it together. He looked like he might be sick. Monique looked at Stevie with a confused glare. Bec hoped Stevie saw it. It felt good to be on that side of jealousy—to know that the person you wanted couldn't stand to think of you with someone else. Bec finally looked at Miles. There was a heat behind his eyes that Bec felt on her skin. It seemed hotter than the fire that burned in front of her. Was he punishing her?

Eleni's face attempted to contort into confusion, the steady doses of Botox keeping the lines between her perfectly plucked brows from forming. "You're gay," she challenged

Stevie.

"Thank you, Captain Obvious," Stevie jeered.

"So why—"

"What? I can't get a little drunk and experiment from time to time?" Stevie chuckled and took another sip. "I mean, look at him. He's got that whole devil-may-care thing going for him."

Bec squeezed Stevie's hand as it rested in the sand—a silent thank you.

Eleni scoffed at Stevie. "Whatever." She quickly regained her composure, a fake smile plastered on her face mere seconds later. "Bec, you go."

Bec's hands tapped on her plastic cup nervously, mirroring the anxiety that swished and swayed in her chest.

"Never have I ever seen a dead body."

She didn't know why the statement came to her. It was morbid. But maybe that's why she had said it. Maybe she realized that only something so ridiculous, so obscene, could possibly move them away from what had just been done. Miles had opened Pandora's Box. Shifted the lid slightly, letting what was trapped inside slowly slither out. The others hadn't fully understood, but she had. He'd drawn a line in the sand. Without saying it, he'd told her enough was enough. He'd done something so definitive in her eyes, that the only way she could think to steer the conversation out of violent waters was by saying she'd never seen a dead body. Which was a lie. She had. As she looked up, Miles' head was cocked to the side, a curious look etched into his face.

"Ew, what?" Eleni commented.

Everyone chatted softly as Adrian took a sip, explaining that his grandfather's funeral, his abuelo, had been open casket. Bec hated herself for using that as her turn. It was sick. Wrong. She felt a different kind of guilt clamp down on her insides and twist hard. She took a quiet sip, looking up from the sand briefly—just long enough to see Tyler taking one as well.

As Stevie began to take her turn, Bec stood up from the sandy blanket she was sitting on. "I have to go to the bathroom," she announced.

"Want me to walk you back?"

She looked at Tyler. The glow of the fire lit up his face, revealing a soft gleam of care and concern. To Bec, it didn't feel like the loving look it was meant to be. It felt overbearing—suffocating. She tried to smile but it quickly faltered on her face. "No, it's okay," she said, shaking her head softly. "It's not too far. I'll be back in a bit."

She tried to distance herself from her thoughts with each barefoot step she took through the sand. She listened to her friends fade away into the distance as the darkness crept up on her. She should have grabbed her sandals. The sand molded between her toes, sinking her into the earth with every step. When she made it off the beach, her feet met the path, hard dirt mixed with coarse grains of sand. It felt firm against her skin, harsh. She kept walking, the occasional pebble digging into her flesh. The walk back to the house was dark. There were no lights leading up from the beach; only when you reached the first patio did the unnatural glow of manmade light show the way. But those lights were still a good distance away. They hung from their posts like small orbs, their radiance blurring out into the black of night and imposing vastness of the jungle.

Bec's awareness was pulled from the path in front of her as she heard movement. She stopped, her ears pricking up at the noise like a dog. A soft padding filled the air. Bec's brow furrowed, trying to place the noise. It grew louder, the repetitive momentum seeming to head towards her. It was then that she realized it was the sound of footsteps slapping against sand and dirt. Someone was running and they were heading for her. She turned quickly, a mass of shadow coming face to face with her as she did. It grabbed her by the waist and held her steadily.

"What the fuck, Miles?" she hissed, pulling his arms away

from her. "What the actual fuck?"

He relaxed back on his heels as he stuffed his hands in his pockets. "Hey."

"Hey?" She shoved him harshly, barely having any effect on his muscular frame. "What the fuck was that?" She tried to steady her breathing but she only felt her anger at him intensifying. "Why did you say all that shit?" she yelled. "Why did you admit you slept with someone?"

The way he looked back at her made Bec want to scream at him. She could see he wasn't ashamed of what had happened down at the beach. But that wasn't what made her irrationally angry. It was that for a brief moment, she had been ready. In those panic-filled seconds, she had accepted that her relationship was finally over. And she had been relieved.

"Maybe I wasn't talking about you."

A vicious laugh ripped through Bec's lungs. "Oh really? Who then?"

His eyes grew heavy as his smile deepened. "What's the problem? A little jealous?"

She shoved him again as her frustration boiled over. "Fuck you, Miles. This isn't a game."

"Then stop treating it like one."

She threw her hands up in the air, letting her emotions get the best of her. "I'm not the one treating this like a game," she stressed. "You're the one—fuck!" she raved, pressing her hand against her temple. "You're driving me crazy, Miles. I can't do this."

Miles moved towards her. As he sought to close the distance between them she fought to maintain it. With every step he took, she took one too until she had backed her way into the jungle that flanked the path. She stopped amid the vines and plants, halted by the delicate soles of her feet. He took two more steps into the undergrowth to reach her. He was close enough that she could see the softness that had grown in his eyes.

"I'm sorry."

For a second, Bec thought she'd misheard him. She studied his face but the confidence and cockiness that had been there moments ago had faded. "What did you say?"

"I'm sorry." Miles looked at her carefully. He reached up and gently brushed a strand of hair out of her face. "You're not the only one who's been going crazy during all of this. I mean—fuck." He let out a breathy laugh before his expression hardened again. "You don't know how much it kills me to see him with you, to see his hands all over you."

Bec considered it, the knot in her stomach growing. She thought about all of the times in the past two days that she'd caught Miles watching her and how many of those times Tyler had been wrapped around her. It was selfish, she knew, to lead Miles on like this. To lead Tyler on like this. So why was she? And why hadn't she stopped after the first time? She knew the answer but she wasn't ready to say it out loud.

"I'm sorry too," she said gently.

The devilish grin returned to his face in an instant. "Good," he stated. "Now that that's out of the way." He slid his hand around the small of Bec's back and pulled her towards him.

"Miles," she sighed, pushing him away as tenderly as she could. "We can't do this right now." Bec looked at him hopelessly and let out an exasperated breath. "This—" she said, gesturing between them, "—this is why we both feel like we're dying whenever we're around each other. We need to stop."

The lines between his brows strained together as confusion washed over his face. "What? No."

"I'm serious. We need to stop so I can figure out what to d—"

"You know what to do," Miles retorted. "You just won't do it."

"I'm with Tyler," she protested.

"Fuck Tyler," he laughed.

"I need time to figure this out," Bec argued. "I can't keep pretending like I'm not betraying him every time you touch me or I think about you touching me, or..."

"You think about me touching you?" He ran his tongue across his teeth as he stared at her with hungry eyes. "Do tell."

"That's not what I—"

The way he was looking at her made Bec want to take it all back. She wanted to forget it all. She wanted to forget Tyler. The pull towards him was so strong that Bec had to look away.

"This has to stop, Miles."

Bec took a step back towards the path. As she did, the vines around her fought to tangle up her legs. She fought through the vegetation but Miles stopped her.

"Tell me you don't want me."

Her heart skipped inside her chest. She opened her mouth to respond, to lie to him, but nothing came out. Instead she let out a helpless sigh and moved around him, trying to run away from him. The truth. All of it. His hands planted firmly on her waist as she did.

"Miles—"

Before she could finish her sentence, he was leading her backwards, deeper into the jungle. Bec yelped as a thorn ripped across the top of her foot.

"Ow—stop—I'm not wearing any shoes."

Miles ceased their descent into the dense greenery. From here, the lights from the patio had disappeared behind layers of palm fronds. The only glow of light was the moon peeking from the treetops above.

"You want me."

She tried to avert her gaze but he wrapped his hand around her chin and pulled her focus to him. His fingers curled up against her cheeks as he locked her in a steady gaze.

"You're supposed to be with me. Not him."

She let out a small laugh, trying to ignore the flutter of excitement in her stomach. "Oh, is that right?"

He took a step closer, pushing his body up against hers. Bec's heartbeat pounded through her. It felt like every part of her body was screaming to be uncaged. She looked at him cautiously. There was something about him that felt wrong but she couldn't help but feel an overwhelming familiarity too. He felt like home but not the one you grow up in—the one you search your whole life to find. Her breath hitched in her chest as he lifted her chin up until her eyes swam into his.

"Yes. You've always been mine."

She tried to roll her eyes but it was a pointless attempt. He had her right where he wanted her. All of her charades and excuses were quickly disappearing. She was here because she wanted to be. She couldn't lie to herself anymore. She didn't want to.

Miles trailed his fingers up her thigh slowly. "Be honest," he murmured.

She knew she should have stopped him right there, before it went any farther. But instead, she found herself welcoming the touch. The long sweater she was wearing over her bikini hoisted high on her hips as his fingers ventured up.

"You want me," he breathed.

Bec's heart rate rose as her body arched, anticipating the next touch.

"Say it."

Bec's eyes grew big, desperate. She had to stop this. They'd been playing this dangerous game for five months, ever since Miles had found her in Benny's kitchen. She'd been upset, fuming. She and Tyler had had another fight. She didn't even remember what it was about, just that she was done. She was done feeling like she was the problem, done trying to move at Tyler's pace, done trying to be the perfect girlfriend for him. When Miles had sauntered over to her with that warm smile of his and offered her a beer, for once, she didn't feel like the broken girl trying to live a normal life. She was Bec—just Bec. So, she'd fallen. Deep, deep into the pit of her own undoing she had fallen. And now, just as she was gripping the top of the well, about to step out into the sunlight, she uncurled her fingers and let herself fall again.

"I want you."

Miles was on her all at once. His hands snaked their way up her body as he tugged her closer.

"Say it again," he murmured into her ear hotly. His mouth sucked on the warm skin of her neck as he made his way down to her collarbone.

"I want—"

A twig snapped, causing them both to freeze. Bec held her breath, waiting for the noise to return. A shadow drifted up the path from the beach. She could barely make it out until it got closer. Tyler's form appeared in between the palm fronds as he passed by, causing her intestines to coil up tighter. He stopped momentarily, turning around. Bec's breath faltered. Had he seen them? It was only when a second figure appeared on the trail that Bec's panic was replaced with confusion. Tyler threw his hands up in front of him, halting the short figure's approach. He was angry. Very angry. Miles held Bec firmly in place as she strained to get a better look. Tyler was arguing with the person now but Bec couldn't make out any of the words. When the figure stepped closer to Tyler, no longer obscured by the dense jungle, Bec's brow furrowed.

"Eleni?" Bec whispered.

Eleni took another step closer, saying something to Tyler as she ran her hand up his arm. Tyler flicked her off and began yelling again. He stepped closer to her, his fist curling into a ball. Then he shoved her away, before turning and continuing up towards the house. Eleni stumbled slightly, whether from his aggression or her own inebriation Bec couldn't tell. As Eleni headed back down to the beach and disappeared from view, Bec let out the heavy breath she'd been holding in.

"Hey."

She was unwilling to pull her focus away from the empty path, her mind still reeling with questions.

"Forget him."

Bec seemed to hover there for a moment, stuck in a standstill while her body and her mind fought to get on the same page again.

Miles seemed to sense her hesitation. She felt his hands slip under her sweater and wrap roughly around her waist. She let her gaze meet his, the uncertainty still alight in her eyes. He brought his mouth to her ear as his fingers dug into her skin.

"Come back to me," he breathed. "I'm all you need."

"Is that right?" she teased, shoving him with feigned annoyance.

He pulled her in closer, his hands snatching her up with eagerness. She squealed a little as he grabbed her.

"I mean it."

His eyes were dark and heavy. They seemed to dig their way into Bec and find the darkest corners of her. Every glimmer pulled the puppet strings inside of her. Before she knew what she was doing, she was leaning into him. He cupped her face with both hands and brought his lips roughly to hers. She kissed him back, only stopping to tug at his bottom lip with her teeth. There was a fire inside of her that she hadn't felt for months—not since the last time she'd knocked on his door after the sun had sunk well below the horizon. Miles seemed to feel the return of that fire too, welcoming it back hungrily. He hoisted her up into his arms as he carried her further away from the path, stopping when her back pressed firmly against the trunk of a tree. Her fingers were already popping open the buttons of his shirt when he set her feet down among the thick, snake-like roots that covered the ground. Bec brought her lips to his chest, planting kissing slowly but with greed. She had been starving herself, trying to forget what she wanted, curbing her addiction. But now she had relapsed. Fully and completely. There was no turning back. Bec moaned breathlessly as Miles dipped his fingers underneath the fabric of her bikini. He watched her intensely, as if he couldn't bear to miss a single emotion that quivered across her face. Bec's eyes grew heavy and giddy, like he had shot her up with the most delicious drugs. She leaned towards him, desperate for more, her breathing sharp and shallow. His mouth met hers wolfishly.

Just as a soft moan escaped from her lips, footsteps echoed in the night. They both paused momentarily, alert. Miles turned back to look at the path. A figure had reappeared there, slowly heading back down towards the beach with heavy footfalls. A smug grin quickly replaced the caution on Miles' face. He placed his free hand on top of Bec's mouth and continued what he was doing. Her eyes widened in panic. She knew who was walking down from the house. They both did. Miles knew what he was doing. He didn't care that Tyler might catch them. He didn't care about the consequences. If anything, she was surprised he had covered her mouth instead of letting everyone on the island hear. Bec felt her guilt mix with bliss. This was a different kind of wrong. There were no excuses. There was no coming back from this.

She watched Tyler pass by the broken vines and leaves they'd trampled over in their frenzy as Miles strummed his fingers. A soft whimper slipped from Bec's lips as she began coming undone. Miles' eyes flashed wildly as he worked harder to make it happen. Bec's breath grew ragged, her eyes rolling back. Tyler was gone—from the path, from her mind. He didn't matter now. None of it mattered. A shudder ripped through Bec's body, thrilling and bittersweet. Miles removed his hand from her mouth and smiled down at her. She looked at him wildly, breathless, as she fought to understand what she'd just let happen.

"Good girl," he whispered, his voice low and husky. He

removed his other hand and sucked on one of his fingers before shooting her a wicked grin.

She shoved him as hard as she could despite the soft trembling in her body. "What were you thinking?" she seethed, her voice no more than a raspy whisper. "What if he had heard? What if he had found us?"

Miles just grinned. "So you didn't like that?" he prodded. "The thought of getting caught?" He ran his thumb across her bottom lip before she pulled away from him. "The thought of him finding you wrapped around my fingers?"

Bec was still trying to catch her breath. She glared at Miles with a dizzying frustration—frustration for what had almost happened, but more importantly frustration that he was right.

"God, you're unbelievable," she said, brushing him off of her. He could see right through her, she knew that. But still, she rolled her eyes and wrapped her arms across her chest. "Carry me back."

Without a second thought, Miles bent down and grabbed her legs. A soft shriek trickled from her lips as he threw her over his shoulder and walked them the twenty or so feet back to the path. When he finally set her down, she shot him a dirty look and adjusted her sweater.

Miles laughed softly, pulling a small leaf from her hair. "I can't wait until he's gone so you can stop the act."

She brushed her hands through her hair as she frowned at him. "What act?" she scoffed.

He gestured up and down her whole body. "This," he smirked. "This always being annoyed. Pretending you're not turned on. Pretending you don't like me."

She took a deep breath and sneered. "Maybe you're just annoying."

Tsk. Tsk. He clicked his tongue at her softly, then chuckled. "I missed that," he said, nodding his head back into the jungle.

Bec watched him carefully, trying not to lose herself in

the devilish grin on his face. "I did too," she finally admitted. She smoothed her sweater down once more before taking another deep breath. "Stay here," she told him. "Five minutes at least. Then you can follow, okay?"

"Seriously?" he laughed.

She shot him a sour look. "Yes, seriously," she stressed.

"Am—" Panic suddenly riddled his face and he stopped in his tracks. Uncertainty wavered in his eyes. "You're done with him. Right?"

The blissful, sinful feeling that had rushed over Bec minutes before left her with a vicious quickness. Emotions riddled lines onto her face as she shook her head at him. "What are you even—" Bec took a big shaky breath as guilt prickled inside of her. "Miles, I can't break up with Tyler on this trip."

He stared at her hotly, his expression steady and dark. "Then when?"

She chewed on the inside of her cheek, searching for the answer he wanted. But it was an answer she didn't have—not yet, anyways. "I don't know."

"If you don't do it in the next day or two, he's going to—" Miles stopped and wrung his hands together. "Please. I need you to do this before it's too late."

Bec's insides turned to soup. "Miles, I can't—"

"It's him or me."

He took a step closer but she kept her eyes low. She couldn't face him. Couldn't bear to see the look on his face when he realized she had slipped back into his arms only to abandon him—until the next time she revisited her bad habits.

"Wait five minutes. Then you can follow," she whispered.

As she stepped around him and headed back down to the beach, she hoped he would stop her. Just like the other night in the kitchen, she hoped he would make the decision for her. Because, she couldn't—not now. She wasn't strong enough. She ran a hand through her hair, her fingers trembling softly as she did. She was scared but of what, she wasn't quite sure. Was letting Miles in really that terrifying? She swallowed the lump in her throat. Yes, yes it was. She had barely let Tyler in. It had taken six months of dating to let Tyler make it official. Even then, she had struggled. She had fought the urge to run away at each and every moment. Nausea rumbled in Bec's stomach as she continued down the shadowed path. It was in both Tyler and Miles' best interests to let her keep them at arm's length. She had let Brennen in and he had paid for it severely. She couldn't risk that happening again. Even though she knew the demons of her past hadn't made the trip out, she couldn't help but feel them on her shoulder as she fumbled her way through the dark.

☖ BENNY ☖

Benny knew she'd fucked up the minute he saw her. She had that look in her eyes—the kind of look a teenager gets when they chuck the bag of weed into the bushes right before the cops come over. The restlessness was painted all over her face. Even in the dim glow of the fire he could see it. He just hoped no one else could.

Bec rejoined the group and sat back down in between Stevie and Tyler. She was silent, the guilty kind of silence. Tyler turned to look at her, his eyes lingering for longer than normal. Could he see what Benny saw? Benny took a long sip from his water bottle, starting to feel the heavy blanket of alcohol slipping off him. That was one benefit, or curse, of being a chunk of solid muscle—he was never drunk for long. He took another careful look at Bec. She didn't look like she'd been ravaged, but still, there was something different about her. It was like the guilt inside of her was leeching from her pores and filling the air around them all. She was toxic.

"Where'd you go?" Tyler asked.

Benny saw the flicker of panic on Bec's face.

"I—um went to the bathroom," she said.

Her eyes found Benny for a second, a kind of accidental glance that you wished had never happened. There was a feral quality to the unease in her eyes. Benny took it all in before she dropped her eyes to the sand. She knew she was fucked.

"I went up to the house. You weren't there."

Bec's hands fiddled with the plastic cup buried into the sand next to her. As her fingers pressed into it nervously, it let out a loud crinkle and pop.

"I decided to explore on my way back. I guess I uh—got a little lost," she replied to Tyler.

Benny felt Monique prod his side with a sharp elbow. When he looked at her, her eyes widened at him knowingly.

"I thought you said they stopped?"

He barely heard the whisper that left her lips but it still felt too loud.

"She told me they had," he muttered gruffly.

Benny and Monique both glanced across the fire. Bec was drinking now, no doubt trying to wash down the shame of being a slut and a cheater. Benny scoffed silently. He hoped she choked on it. The scowl that had grown on Benny's face slid clean off as Tyler caught his eye. He shot him a curious look over the flickering flames. Benny gave him a nod in return before snatching up the bottle of wine and taking a big gulp. This wasn't the time to be sober. He flickered his eyes back across the fire, but instead of seeing Tyler, all Benny could focus on was the figure that headed towards them across the sand. Benny watched Miles with tracker-like focus as he took his place around the fire. He searched his expression, expecting to find the shit-eating grin that would tell Benny everything he needed to know about what just happened. Instead, he saw a tension riddled between Miles' brows and locked in his jaw. There was a hooded brooding to his eyes and as Miles cast a look across the fire at Bec, Benny couldn't help but be surprised. Miles was looking at Bec with an anger so potent, Benny could have mistaken it for hate. Benny looked back and forth between the three of them— Bec with her silent shame, Miles with his burning gaze, and Tyler with a growing concern etched into his face. The last look was the one that worried Benny most of all.

"So," Stevie started, clearing the tension-filled air. "Anyone know any ghost stories?

No one said anything. The only people who hadn't seemed to notice the sudden shift in the air were Eleni and

Adrian. They had made their way closer to each other after Eleni had returned to the beach, wobbling drunkenly with a pouty sneer on her face. She had found one of the unopened wine bottles and nearly chugged half of it before snuggling up to Adrian. Now, the pair found themselves talking to each other in flirtatious, hushed tones, oblivious to what was going on around them.

"You get lost too?"

Tyler's eyes were fixed on Miles. Something had changed since Miles had rejoined the group. There was a building ire in Tyler's eyes that wasn't there before. Benny wondered if he was finally putting the pieces together. Miles slowly turned his head, pulling his focus from Bec and directing it at Tyler. As he did, amusement flickered onto his face.

"Is that what she called it?"

Tyler looked at him funny, his eyes briefly darting to Bec sitting next to him.

"What did you just say?"

Everyone was paying attention now. Eleni had pulled herself out of the tentacle-like snare of Adrian's arms. There was a dumb giddiness spread across her face that grew as she let the situation unfold around her. The corners of Miles' mouth slowly twitched up into a smirk. As the crackling fire lit up Miles' face, Benny watched the last lick of resentment disappear until all that was left was a nasty delight.

"You know, it's funny," Miles said, laughing to himself. "All this time I thought maybe you didn't care enough to see what was right in front of you." He titled his head at Tyler and flashed his eyes deviously. "Now I can see you were just too stupid to catch on."

Tyler stiffened.

"Miles," Bec snapped at him with a heavy breath.

It was a warning, but he seemed anything but concerned.

"Yes baby?" he cooed.

Tyler clenched his jaw. He looked down at Bec, a crude understanding slowly carving its way onto his face. She wouldn't look at him. She stayed focused on the figure across the fire who was now beaming from ear to ear with that shit-eating grin that Benny had known he'd see sooner or later.

"What's going on?" Tyler barked.

He was talking to Bec, but it was Miles who answered.

"Bec got lost." He grinned. "She's been getting lost all summer."

That was it. The night seemed to shudder as Benny watched bodies collide on the other side of the fire. He heard the yell before he realized what was happening.

♨ BEC ♨

"Tyler, stop!" Bec yelled as he lunged forward.

She was too late. Tyler's fist collided harshly into Miles' shoulder as he tackled him into the sand. The two wrestled, arms flailing, knuckles pounding against flesh. It was all a shadowed blur as the soft glow of the fire danced across them. Benny was on his feet now, looking at the fight with uncertainty.

"Do something!" Monique screamed at him.

Sand sprayed as the two men fought to gain control of the other. Bec sat in awe, not believing what was happening even though she'd foreseen it a thousand times. She knew this was her fault. But still, she was frozen in time, watching it play out frame by frame. All sound seemed to muffle as her eyes strained to follow the chaos. Who was winning? Who did she want to win? The questions made her head spin. The thud of bone against flesh and the sharp grunt of pain pulled her out of her stupor. Tyler's fist had slammed into Miles' mouth. As the blood began to pour from the crack of broken skin, Tyler wound his arm up, preparing to strike again.

"That's enough," Bec shouted, lunging towards them both.

Her fingers gripped the fabric of Tyler's shirt, giving it a hard yank. Her efforts did little against his strength, but nevertheless, he relented and pulled himself away from Miles. Tyler stood over him, as if admiring his work. When he finally looked at Bec, she took in his proud gaze with wide, uncertain eyes. She hadn't expected him to stop, for him to listen to her pleading. But now that he had, she wasn't sure what would happen next.

He brushed the sand from his linen pants and shirt casually. "Did I make my point?"

"That's it?" Miles laughed from down in the sand. Blood trickled from the cut in his lip as he shot Tyler a vicious smile. "She calls you off like a good little doggie and you leave it?"

Bec blinked a few times, trying to understand. All Tyler did was look back at her with a vicious heat in his eyes. "What?" she stammered, ignoring Miles.

From behind Tyler, Bec saw Miles stand up. His lip was swollen and bloody but other than that he looked intact. A few red drops flecked the sand as he spit the blood from his mouth. When he looked back up to meet her gaze, she felt relief and dread swarm over her. She couldn't explain it, but something about the moment felt like this was only the beginning.

"I said, did I make my point?"

Bec's focus ripped back to Tyler. He looked at her for a few still seconds before reaching for her.

She flinched, her movement slight but apparent. Her body eased out of its rigidity as she realized he was only tucking the hair behind her ear.

"I would do anything for you. For us," he said.

His fingers traced their way down her cheek until he reached her throat. His grip was light at first but as his eyes bore into hers, his fingers tightened around her throat. He held her there for a minute, locked in silence. Bec's heart flittered in her chest as she watched a glimmer of hate flash through Tyler. His fingers tightened further, constricting roughly against her windpipe. Her eyes went wide as she felt her breath slip from her lungs.

"Get off of her!" Miles yelled.

His hands yanked and pried at Tyler's shoulder but Tyler was determined. As Bec scratched her fingers against his arm, desperate for air, Tyler shoved her back by the neck.

"Don't fuck up again," he spat.

Bec stumbled in the sand, barely staying upright. Her head was pounding with a pressure that felt unbearable. Miles rushed to her, shoving Tyler aside on his way.

"Are you okay?" he whispered. "Did he hurt you?"

Bec let out a ripple of coughs as she forced deep breaths into her lungs.

"What the fuck is wrong with you?" Stevie snapped, joining Miles at Bec's side.

"Nothing," Tyler said flatly. "She made a mistake and now she knows not to do it again."

Stevie swore at Tyler under her breath as she pulled Bec away from both men. Bec rubbed the skin where his hand had been. There was a tenderness to her throat that made her wince. She stared Tyler down, trying to find an emotion on his face that made sense to her. Were they over? Had he just ended things? Did she care?

"You're fucking delusional, you know that?" Miles laughed cynically. His eyes gleamed as blood dripped from his lip. "You think all of this is because she made one little mistake?"

"Miles—shut up," Bec hissed. Her throat felt raw.

She watched him pace the sand outside the bonfire's circle. The light of the flames barely reached him, illuminating the anger on his face in patchy shadows.

"She doesn't want you," Miles rasped. "She never wanted you to begin with."

Tyler stood stoically, his eyes fixed on Miles.

"Stop," Bec said, her voice stronger this time.

Miles gave her a stern look but decided to listen. As he held his tongue, Bec swam in her thoughts. He had wanted this, she knew that. Some naive part of herself had thought he wouldn't do it. She had thought he wouldn't cause her the pain the truth would bring. But now she could see she had pushed him too far. Bec swallowed the pain in her throat and waited for something to happen. She knew she should say something, but she couldn't wrap her head around what would make the situation better. Her eyes darted around. Monique was looking at her with concern. It was a mix of pity and care that made Bec squirm in her skin but there was no shock there. Ah—Benny had told her after all. Benny was trying to look stoic but she knew he was savoring her downfall just a little. Adrian was looking at her with big pupils and a blank stare. She figured he was a few shots away from not knowing where the hell he even was, let alone what was going on. But Eleni, Eleni was smiling at her with a wickedness that ignited the deepest core of hate within Bec. Out of everyone, Eleni was enjoying her pain the most. The urge to run away from it all overtook Bec. She felt like her flesh was eating her from the inside out. The eyes she felt on her were heavy and overwhelming. She needed to get away from it all but her body held her firmly in place for fear of drawing any more attention.

"How many times?"

Bec felt her heart drop into her stomach. She looked at Tyler with panicked eyes but he wasn't asking her. He had turned to face Miles, who was spitting more blood from his mouth. Miles took a step towards Tyler, his tongue rolling across the bottom of his teeth like he was savoring every second of this. His eyes flashed to Bec, looking her up and down slowly.

"Including tonight?"

The two men hit the sand again with a heavy splash. Tyler was done holding back. Bec hadn't known he had been restraining himself to begin with but now, now she knew. Tyler's fists pummeled into Miles with rapid succession. She could hear the puffs of air releasing from Miles' lungs with every jab Tyler sent into his stomach. Bec didn't know when the tears had started flowing. She wiped them away quickly, the very existence of them feeling stupid now. As she took a step towards the thrashing sand, Stevie pulled her back firmly.

"Don't. You'll just get hurt," she rumbled in Bec's ear as she held her tightly. "Benny," she yelled across the fire. "Fucking break them up!"

Benny looked on with resignation, then gave Stevie and Bec a passive shrug. It was a look that told Bec he had every intention of waiting it out. He stood his ground on the other side of the fire, no doubt silently cheering Tyler on.

Miles had managed to bring his arms up in front of him, blocking the blows from Tyler that seemed to be unrelenting. Just as Bec was going to pull herself from Stevie's hold, everything changed. Miles squirmed against the sand and shifted his weight. Suddenly, he was on top of Tyler, pinning him down into the sand. Tyler's arms thrashed as he fought to gain back control but Miles had the upper hand now. As Miles pulled back his arm, the atmosphere seemed to change. Goosebumps prickled on Bec's skin as Miles drove a fist firmly into Tyler's face. Eleni shrieked as the blood seemed to be everywhere all at once. It gushed out of Tyler's nose in rivers of red, drowning his face. Finally, Benny acted. He was across the sand in seconds. His hands dug into Miles' collarbones, trying to yank him off of Tyler. Miles fought to stay put, his eyes beaming down at Tyler eagerly. Finally, Benny managed to toss him down to the sand and stood guard between the two men. Miles got up quickly, his adrenaline seeming to bounce him back. Instead of resuming his assault, he simply smiled down at the blood pooling into the sand. Bec broke away from Stevie's grip and ran to Tyler. She quickly kneeled in front of him, her eyes frantically taking in all of the damage.

"Fuck," she breathed as she fumbled for something to stop the bleeding.

The blood was flowing out his nose steadily, soaking the cream-colored fabric of his shirt. She hovered her hands in front of his face, unsure of how to make it stop.

"I don't want your help," Tyler seethed, swatting her hand away from him.

"Please let me just—"

"No. You've done enough."

The words seemed to take all of the air out of her chest. Her voice faltered as she tried to speak.

"Tyler—"

"Get the fuck out of my face!" he yelled.

Bec's eyes widened as she stared back at him blankly, unmoving. A few drops of red had found their way onto the plush fabric of her sweater and were now budding out through the threads like deadly blooms. Bec held Tyler's gaze, testing the gravity of his words. There was no respite there. His eyes bore into hers like claws. There was no disappointment or sadness behind his eyes—only fury.

"Come on," Stevie said softly, appearing behind Bec like a guardian angel. She wrapped her arm around her and pulled her away. "Let's go up to the house."

Bec said nothing but obliged, watching the scene in stunned silence as she moved away. Benny crouched down by Tyler, a few muttered words seeming to pass between them. Monique, Eleni, and Adrian were all wide-eyed as they processed what had just happened. Miles was standing on the outskirts of the group. Bec didn't think she could feel worse but somehow looking at him, she did. Tyler wasn't the only one who felt betrayed. That was clear to her now. Miles scoffed to himself as he broke his gaze from hers and then wandered off down the beach, away from the house and towards the jungle.

Bec pulled her eyes from his disappearing figure as Stevie led her away. This was her fault. Bec repeated the fact to herself as she and Stevie walked up to the house in silence. She had been greedy and confused and reckless. She realized they were passing the crumbled leaves and vines that signaled her earlier transgression and pulled her gaze away, trying to quiet the shame that was screaming inside of her. Stevie said nothing as they walked, only squeezed her arm. It was the only thing that seemed to be keeping Bec from breaking down. The simple touch signaled that what Stevie had said before still held true. No matter how badly or how many times Bec fucked up, Stevie would be there for her. The moment's comfort was fleeting as Bec's mind darted to Tyler. The way his hand had gripped her throat had scared her. There was an anger to him that she'd never seen before. It was calculated. Restrained. She doubted there was any coming back from this. As they reached the house, lit only by the few lights they'd left on in their bedrooms, a suffocating dread rose over Bec. They still had three full days in this house—on this island. As bad as tonight had been, she knew it wasn't going to get any better. Her stomach twisted inside of her. She had brought this on herself and whatever happened next, she deserved it.

♨ TYLER ♨

The bottle tilted back swiftly as the liquid slid down the back of his throat. Tyler didn't bother wiping the drops of tequila that dribbled down his chin. Instead, he took a breath and lifted the bottle again.

"Easy," Benny stressed as he snatched the bottle from his friend's grip.

"Fuck you," Tyler said, yanking the bottle back and taking another swig.

They continued walking down the beach, the glimmer of fire where they'd left Eleni and Adrian snuggled up slowly slipping away with every step. The waves crashed rhythmically against the shore, the only sound except for the occasional slosh of the tequila bottle.

It all seemed ridiculous to Tyler—unreal. Even now, as the blood dried on his shirt and his knuckles grew blotches of purple and red, he was waiting for the joke to be over. He was waiting for Bec to pop up behind him, a giant smile on her face as she announced it was all a prank. But she didn't and it wasn't. The more he thought about it all, the more it made him sick. Miles? *Miles.* He thought back to all of the times he'd seen Miles' eyes lingering on Bec. He had thought it was his overactive imagination, his jealousy. Obviously not.

His jaw clenched as he remembered the first time he'd met Miles. It had been at the gym. He'd seemed cool enough. They had struck up conversation between sets, quickly finding common ground in their love for the Lakers. It hadn't taken long for Tyler to consider him a close friend, someone that had his back. But now? Now he could see he was mistaken. Miles only wanted what belonged to Tyler. That wouldn't do. His anger gnawed at his insides like a starved rat. The feeling was feral and incessant.

"How long?" Tyler muttered between sips.

The blood had finally stopped pouring from his nose, the only reminder of it now was the constant throbbing that seemed to hit its peak when he leaned his head back to drink.

Benny stopped and looked at him cautiously. Tyler took one more pull of tequila before chucking the bottle into the sand. It landed with a muffled thud.

"How long did you know?" he repeated, louder this time. "You're too quiet for this to be news to you. So how long?"

Nothing came out of Benny's mouth for a long time. Tyler could see him struggling with his own thoughts, as if deciding whether he should tell the truth. When he finally spoke, it was worse than Tyler imagined.

"The whole time."

Tyler stared blankly at his best friend of over ten years. The anger that had ignited his eyes earlier dwindled to a sunken glow, like an ember fighting against the wind.

"How?"

Benny sighed and rubbed his face with the palms of his hands. He looked riddled with guilt, or shame, or both. Tyler didn't care. There was no excuse for this. Not for any of them.

"It happened at my place..." Benny paused, looking at Tyler hesitantly before he continued. "After you two got into that big fight at my party."

Pangs of emotion swelled up inside Tyler as he remembered that night in April. Even if it hadn't been Benny's birthday, he still would have recalled it clearly. They had gone over to Benny and Monique's apartment for the big surprise. Benny had been shocked as he'd opened the door to colorful streamers and all of his friends. Everything had been fine that night, until it wasn't. Tyler and Bec had been talking to a few friends when the conversation shifted to Benny and Monique's upcoming wedding. Everyone had been excited, especially Eleni. She had told them she loved weddings—that she couldn't wait for her own. Tyler remembered the way her eyes had flashed at him with obvious longing. Even now, the thought of it made him want to drink. As always, Eleni had done what she did best. She had been her snarky, conniving self and stirred the pot. She had asked Tyler if he and Bec were still planning on moving in together the following month. The comment might have seemed perfectly fine to everyone else, but Tyler knew it was a loaded gun. Bec was wary of moving too fast and it wasn't a secret. Tyler had let his frustrations slip out on more than a few, drunk occasions. It had been a mistake to let Eleni overhear it. But the biggest mistake had been telling his friends he wanted Bec to move in before he'd even asked her. He had been planning on waiting a few more months. He had barely convinced her to make their relationship official at that point. Eleni knew this—as she knew everything about everyone. So, she had lit the match and dropped it, smiling, into the barrel of gasoline that was his relationship.

Bec had said nothing at first, waiting until the conversation veered to a new topic before she finally turned to look at him. The panic in her eyes had been clear. The look had told him that she was not moving in anytime soon. The look had told him that she was going to pull away and put her walls up like she'd done many times before. But most importantly, the look had told him that he'd fucked up. She had excused both of them to the apartment's balcony where Bec had voiced her fear and frustration. It had poured out of her in a rush of jumbled words and wild gestures. He was moving too fast for her again—pressuring her. The way she had pushed him away that night triggered him. He had told her that he had been patient enough. He had told her that she was broken and he didn't know if he wanted to fix her anymore. The thought of it now drove a sharp pain through his chest. He hadn't meant to say it but his words had done their damage, just like Eleni's had. The arguing had raged on until finally his own emotions had overtaken him. He had left Bec at that party alone. He didn't know why. Maybe it was to teach her a lesson, to make her feel as alone as he'd felt. It had been impulsive but it had been easy—everything always seemed easier when rage pulsed through his veins. He had expected her to come back to his place that night, to admit she had overreacted. But she hadn't. He had assumed she had gone back to her apartment and hung out with Stevie for the rest of the night. Now he knew that he had assumed wrong.

His anger from earlier was gone. Now something different took its place—a new beast. It twisted and snarled inside of him, desperately trying to claw its way to the surface. His own voice rang in his ears as he finally put the puzzle pieces together. This was their fault, the people he called his friends. Eleni had driven a wedge between Tyler and Bec that night, just like she'd tried to numerous times before. Bec had sought comfort with Miles, the person who had been lying in wait, ready to offer it. And Benny had witnessed the whole thing, either as a cowardly bystander or an accomplice. Either way, they were all dead to him. In an instant, Tyler's rage broke through the surface. He lashed out at Benny, grabbing the collar of his shirt.

"Why the fuck didn't you stop it?" he snarled, getting up into his face.

"It was too late," Benny rumbled. He yanked himself out from Tyler's grip and shook his head. "By the time I saw what was going on they were already heading for the door."

Tyler shoved Benny harshly. "You could have fucking told me." Fury seeped from his mouth as he shoved Benny away from him. "You're my friend. You're supposed to have my fucking back."

Benny halted Tyler's advance as he gave him a heavy shove back, trying to create space between them. "Come on, man. This situation was fucked every way I looked at it," he raved. "He's my friend too."

Tyler stopped. He looked at Benny silently with a fire in

his eyes that he wished could burn the flesh from Benny's body. His gaze lingered before he finally turned and walked away, shaking his head as he did. He leaned over and pulled the tequila bottle out of the sand with a firm hand. He took a big swig before raising his eyes back towards Benny.

"Now Miles is your only friend."

Before Benny could protest, Tyler wandered off down the beach. Tequila slipped down his throat steadily as the darkness of the night swallowed him whole.

⚲ ELENI ⚲

Eleni felt giddy.

Part of it was the sheer quantity of alcohol swirling around her stomach, sure, but she couldn't help but be energized by what had happened. Something about seeing Bec's world come crashing down around her brought Eleni sweet bliss. It felt right. Bec didn't deserve Tyler, she never had. She was utterly normal, so normal it hurt. Why would he choose her? Eleni took a big sip of the drink Adrian had poured for her. It was bitter. Her face puckered as she smelled the wine. Had it gone bad? She shrugged before downing the rest of it. A bead of red wine slipped from the corner of her mouth, staining her top. *Bec. Bec. Bec.* Her mind spun. When Tyler had first started dating Bec, Eleni thought it was another 'fuck you' to his family. He'd had many of those over the years. He was the self-proclaimed black sheep after all. With all of the drinking and fighting and gallivanting off to South America, he had all but sent his parents to an early grave. He had always rebelled, so Eleni assumed Bec was just another part of that. A phase. But she wasn't. Tyler had never given his girlfriends, of which there had been many, this much care. It was like ever since Bec had come into his life, his only concern was being with her. Thinking of it now made an ugly thing scratch at Eleni's insides. It was only when she replayed tonight's events in her head that she found her way back to drunken bliss. The way Tyler had shoved Bec away brought a serene smile to Eleni's face.

Eleni felt Adrian's hand slip under her skirt. His touch felt hot against her skin as it moved with cautious excitement.

She allowed it, the rush in her bloodstream making her complacent. Was he her first choice? God, no. But he was cute enough. Plus, he was only a means to an end. Drinking always made her feel two things—horny and lonely. She knew she could solve both problems simultaneously, but her options were limited here. Benny was married, not that she'd give that brainless mound of muscle a chance. Miles had wandered off into the jungle and after last night's clear rejection, she wasn't interested anymore. Even in the state she was in, she had some dignity. Eleni had hoped that Tyler would come back to the bonfire looking to get back at Bec, but he hadn't. She had no idea where he'd wandered off to but she knew him well enough to know if he hadn't come back by now, they'd find him tucked away with a bottle of something strong in the morning. Tyler was off the menu tonight. So for now, Adrian would do.

His lips moved to her neck. She rolled her head back and welcomed the affection. She felt alive. Her fingers searched for her cup, eager for more wine. It tasted like shit but the feeling it left was divine. It reminded her of that time she'd rolled at Coachella. Was wine in Nicaragua laced with something? It wouldn't surprise her. The fire crackled weakly in front of them. The others had all deserted the bonfire. It had been gradual until suddenly it was just the two of them on the beach. She assumed that was why Adrian was making his move. There was no one here to witness his rejection. She knew she should be doling out that rejection now but she felt too good to spoil the fun. His excitement built as his lips pulled roughly against her skin. Eleni closed her eyes and pretended. She pretended it wasn't Adrian, but Tyler. She pretended he had chosen her all along. She pretended that they were married like they should have been years ago. God knows their parents had tried. She pretended he loved her. Eleni tugged at his shirt roughly, pulling him closer. Adrian moved his lips from her neck to the corner of her mouth. His kisses were soft and wet and she returned them hungrily. She was sloppy when she drank but she knew he wouldn't mind. Her tongue snaked inside his mouth, tasting him. The beach was still except for the soft panting that left their lips. His hand slid up her body and grazed her breast.

"You're so fucking hot," he said breathily against her mouth.

As his voice filled her ears, she was pulled out of her fantasy. It wasn't Tyler. It never had been. She fought to keep a scowl from forming on her face as she kissed him back. She let her mind wander as Adrian continued to mutter compliments against her lips. Miles and Bec? At first the thought had enraged her. However, the more she thought about it, the more Eleni realized Miles had just been a distraction for her. He was a temporary fix while what Eleni really wanted was out of reach. She didn't want Miles. She wondered if Bec really wanted him, but to be honest, she didn't care. The only thing that mattered was that Bec and Tyler were no more.

The realization made Eleni come to life. She swung her hips around so she was straddling Adrian. She felt him wrap his hand around her ass and give it a squeeze. He was getting bolder now. She found that amusing. Eleni wasn't paying attention though, not really. She was much more interested in where her mind was taking her—the future fantasy life with Tyler that was seeming more real with every second that passed.

Her lips pulled at Adrian's as her body went into autopilot. Bec and Tyler were over, for good. There was no way Tyler would forgive her after tonight. How could he? And if he did? Well, Eleni was prepared for that. She'd already threatened to tell his secret to Bec and he hadn't been happy about that. Not one bit. Tyler knew his options. He could tell Bec or Eleni would do it for him. If their relationship needed one more nail in the coffin, Eleni would be happy to provide it. Her head was spinning with tingling bliss now. Damn, that wine was good. Whatever happened this weekend, happened. She would be there for Tyler. She would help take his mind off Bec any way he pleased. A giddy smile slid onto Eleni's face. Tomorrow, her and Tyler's relationship would finally begin. But tonight? Tonight Eleni deserved to get laid. Just as her fingers wrapped around the hem of his shirt to peel it off, Adrian shoved her away from him.

"What the hell?" she said, her words slurring together into a jumble.

He pushed his way up out of the sand and threw a hand over his mouth. "Oh God." His eyes flickered unsteadily as his body swayed in the sand. "I think I'm gonna be sick," he murmured.

Repulsion erupted on Eleni's face. "Ew," she scoffed, wiggling herself away from him. "Don't do it here!"

Adrian gave her a helpless look before darting off up the path towards the house. Eleni lost sight of him in the dark as the fire burned dimly. The thought of Adrian's vomit cascading out over the sand made uneasiness rise in her own stomach. She forced out a few long, deep breaths, letting the crisp ocean air fill her nose. When she felt okay again, she groaned. She was all alone. She hated being alone. She tried to listen to the soft crackling of the dying flames and the hushed crash of waves onto the sand but it only made her more annoyed. Like always, everyone had left her. She rolled her eyes and hiccupped. She needed better friends. She wondered what Karli and Jessica were up to and considered texting them when she got back to LA. Had Karli forgiven her yet? In Eleni's eyes, she didn't need forgiveness but she knew Karli felt differently. Eleni didn't see what the big deal was. Karli had barely been in a relationship with that guy. Had they even made it official? It wasn't Eleni's fault that he had been more interested in sleeping with her. But that had been almost a year ago. Eleni was sure all was forgiven by now. If not, there were always the other girls from her agency. She was sure they'd be more fun than the weird trio she was stuck with now. Her lip curled up as she thought of how Monique had called her out earlier. How dare she. Eleni let the scowl on her face deepen. So what if Eleni had taken the necklace and blamed Monique for it? It was a stupid necklace and she'd given it back anyway. What a bitch. Eleni rolled her eyes one more time before pushing Monique from her mind.

She swished her hand through the sand until she found the bottle of wine. Empty. The night was over. Adrian wasn't coming back. Eleni pouted and whined. Her buzz had shifted. Her flurry of excitement and giddiness had morphed into a sleepy blur. She got up from the sand, swaying as she did. What was she doing again? She tightened her gaze on the bonfire in front of her, racking her brain for answers. Adrian had left her. She pouted again. It was time for bed. Just as she was about to head for the house, she heard footsteps pushing through the sand behind her.

"If you threw up," she slurred, popping the p, "we are done making out."

Silence.

She turned around, staggering in the sand. "Who's there?" she hiccupped, her words still slurring in her mouth.

The person across from her said nothing, only moved closer with steady footfalls.

"I'm tired," she whined. "Take me up to the house." She was met with more silence. She pouted and let out a drunken moan. "I said—"

Eleni's breath caught in her chest as she saw something glint against the dull embers of the fire. Her eyes widened as she realized what it was.

"Wha—"

Her voice stuttered as the person walked into her, filling her stomach with a heavy pressure. Eleni's eyes widened as she looked down at the handle sticking out from her tank top. Dark red spread out against the blue fabric like an oil spill. Her eyes blinked feverishly as she tried to understand. The hand that was still gripping the knife withdrew it with a heavy tug. She gasped hoarsely as the pain sprouted out like a dull ache. Eleni looked up and watched a vicious smile grow on the face in front of her before the blade was quickly shoved back inside. A cry for help gurgled up from her throat, only to be stifled by the knife being driven in and out of her gut for a third time. She convulsed, her breath expelling from her body with a heavy groan.

Eleni wobbled dizzily. Her hand reached out in front of her and caught nothing but air as she stumbled backwards into the sand. Her fingers clung to her stomach, the blood now drenching the front of her body in a sticky wetness. The shadow hovered over her, creeping close again. She tried to speak but she had somehow forgotten how. In and out. In and out. The knife slid through her shirt and into her abdomen twice more. Eleni gagged as the pain seared through her torso. A swell of bile rose into her mouth. She choked with desperation. Black patches dappled her vision as unconsciousness crept up on her. The last thing she saw was a nasty grin gleaming down at her as she floated away to the sound of the crashing waves. But the last thing she felt was the cold slice of metal against her skin. Something gushed hotly below her chin. It was everywhere, all over. Then there was silence. And finally, at last—the embrace of death.

SATURDAY

 BEC

She stared at the ceiling, listening to the house. Dishes clanked softly and voices murmured. The clock on the nightstand ticked with an unbearable consistency.

Tick, tick, tick.

It seemed to dig its way inside Bec's head, strengthening the headache that was already pounding there. She hadn't planned to drink that much last night but after what had happened, she'd come back to the house and attempted to find an ounce of comfort in a bottle of white wine. Wine drunk was the worst drunk. That's what Stevie had always told her. What Stevie failed to mention was the only thing worse than getting drunk off wine was being hungover from it. Bec pushed her fingers into her temple, feeling the light beading of sweat there. She shut her eyes against the stream of light coming in through the curtains.

Her mind started to wander to the night before but she slammed the lid on her thoughts quickly. She wasn't awake enough for that. Instead, she let her mind fixate once again on the sounds around her. There was the distant caw of birds outside, a persistent rumble and clang of activity in the kitchen, and the sound of soft breathing next to her. She tried to find the calm in those sounds but they only made her jittery and unsettled. She forced a glance at the clock. 9:52 a.m. She tried to remember when she had fallen asleep. Sometime after two, maybe? She couldn't remember, thanks to the wine. She reprimanded herself silently and made a promise not to drink anything today, no matter how uncomfortable it all got.

She sighed and rolled over to face Stevie. They'd both been awake for a while, she could tell by the typical sighs and groans that came from Stevie as she met the day earlier than she'd have liked. Bec always teased her about her grumpy disposition in the mornings. Late nights at work made Stevie the opposite of a morning person. Where Bec was typically up and about by 8 a.m. with a coffee in hand, Stevie would slumber until noon.

"On a scale of one to ten..." Bec blurted out in a sleepy monotone. "How fucked am I?"

A subtle, breathy laugh escaped Stevie's mouth. As she rolled over, Bec found the look on her face less than reassuring.

"Depends on who you're referring to."

Bec chewed on the idea for a minute, her fingers tracing circles on the bright-white sheets. Marta's voice drifted through the hallway and into the room like a ghost. She was bossing someone around, her voice raising and pitching in sharp bursts. If it wasn't for the women's odd disposition, Bec might have enjoyed having a conversation with her. How did she end up in Nicaragua? Did she own the island? There were so many questions, but the hungry smile that was permanently fixed on the woman's face kept Bec a stranger. She was glad this was her last day with the woman; Bec just wished it was also her own last day on the island.

Bec sat up in bed. The heat in the air was heavy and thick. She pushed the bedding away, desperate for a lick of cool air on her skin. They must have forgotten to turn the air conditioner on last night. Bec took a deep breath and ran her fingers through her hair. She wondered what would happen if she and Stevie hitched a ride back to the mainland. Stevie spoke some Spanish, maybe not enough to get by in any rural areas, but the city? Sure. There was at least cell reception there. Google Translate could fill in any gaps. Bec itched her arm as she thought about how much money was in her account. $1,800 maybe—give or take a hundred or two. The spark of hope she'd felt quickly dwindled as she remembered rent was due next week. There were some client invoices due soon but they were notoriously late, even the big companies. Ironically, those seemed to take longer to pay out than the small photoshoots she booked. Credit card. The idea popped into her head only briefly before she shook the idea away. Her balance was already dangerously high. How much was a plane ticket back home anyway? $800? $1,000? She had no clue. This had all been a surprise after all. Tyler had said nothing of cost, even though she'd asked. Maybe Tyler would pay for her to fly home early just to get her out of his face? The thought made her stomach tense up. No, he wouldn't do that. If anything, he'd spend the rest of the trip ignoring her. Last night replayed in her head slowly but this time she let it. The memory of him shoving her away, the hate in his eyes, everything made her feel like she couldn't take a full breath. Her lungs felt like they were being squeezed tighter and tighter. Finally, Bec came to terms with the fact that she was stuck here.

"Tyler," Bec finally replied. "One to ten, how fucked am I with him?"

"Eleven and a half," Stevie answered.

Bec let out a deep sigh, almost laughing as she did. "So not bad at all?" she said dryly.

"Last night was a shit show," Stevie replied. "There's no getting around it."

Bec let out a deep groan. "I'll be lucky if he ever speaks to me again."

Stevie got out of bed and grabbed a towel from where it was draped over the back of a chair. "Honestly, Becs. Is that really a problem?"

Bec shot her a look. "Seriously?"

"You said you were gonna keep going through this bullshit until it was no longer an option." She turned to Bec, her face contorting into something apologetic but honest. "Seems like it's no longer an option, yeah?"

Bec took a deep breath as she realized her friend was right. She no longer had the luxury of ignoring this mess she had created. There was no going back to how things were. She had to admit, she was a little relieved. The truth was finally out there. There was no more sneaking around, no more pretending. They had ripped off the Band-Aid—she just wished it'd hadn't taken some flesh and blood off with it. As Stevie headed for the shower, a nagging uncertainty raised another question from Bec's lips.

"And Miles?"

Stevie paused at the bathroom door, lingering there for a moment before shooting Bec a curious look over her shoulder.

"On a scale from one to ten?" Bec asked.

Stevie seemed to think about it for a minute. "Four," she said, before shutting the door behind her.

Four. Bec let the number swim in her mind as she lied back down against the mattress. It felt too hot against her skin. She shifted uncomfortably as her eyes found their way up to the ceiling. Bec's vision grew fuzzy, her eyes unfocused. Four. She could deal with four.

✹ MONIQUE ✹

Monique searched for a word to articulate the meal they were all sharing. Awkward didn't cut it. It was deeper than that, more visceral. It was ominous.

The group had meandered out to the large dining table on the patio one by one, silence riding on their shoulders like a plague. They had all sat down to eat the farewell brunch Ramon and Jamari had prepared for them—everyone except Adrian and Eleni. Benny had rapped his knuckles on Adrian's door after finding Eleni's open and empty. No one had answered. After some colorful commentary from Stevie and Benny, it had been clear to everyone that Adrian and Eleni would not be joining them for breakfast. The pair was obviously preoccupied with other things—things that no one wanted to interrupt by opening the door and calling them to the table. Did Eleni have no shame? After everything that had happened last night, the girl had somehow still prioritized her need for attention. Poor Adrian. Monique's gaze burned into the empty seat at the head of the table. Monique was sure Eleni would tease him until she had her fill. After that, she'd toss him aside, eager to dig her claws into the next one.

Monique's focus shifted to the elaborate meal in front of her. It was a true feast of eggs, sausage, rice, pastries, and even some pancakes that Ramon had shaped into perfect little circles. If it had been a normal morning, the spread in front of them would have no doubt energized them mentally and physically for the day. But it wasn't a normal morning. Monique picked up a sliver of pancake with her fork and chewed it slowly as her eyes did a gentle sweep across the table. It seemed empty without Eleni's voice resounding like a squawking bird. Monique gave a small smile, letting the image of Eleni as some obnoxious parrot play through her mind. Benny was next to Monique, his elbow bumping into hers lightly as he ate. His chewing seemed ravenous compared to her own. She didn't know if it was from growing up with four brothers or having so much muscle on his body, but Benny could eat. She shot him a cautious look which he met with a sleepy smile. He reached for her hand and gave it a quick, loving squeeze. If she could count on Benny for one thing, it was being blissfully naive at times like this. She had found it charming at first, how he would just roll with the punches and not let anything affect him. But sometimes she really wished he could read the room. Things might not have exploded for them on this trip quite like they had for Tyler and Bec, but the last few days hadn't been easy. For months, Monique had been feeling something deep in her gut. Now that she was on this trip, unable to find space away from Benny by taking a Pilates class or staying late at the office, she felt the roots of that thing grow stronger. She knew what it was, she just couldn't bear to name it. Naming it would make it real and she wasn't ready for that. Her older coworkers had warned her about the trials of marriage, how once the initial magic wore off everything slowly decayed until there was nothing left. That sentiment equally comforted and distressed Monique. They had barely been married for four months and already she felt it crumbling around her. Benny keeping the secret about Bec was merely a single brick falling from their marriage house. The true crumbling had begun the day Monique let him slip that engagement ring on her finger. Ever since then, she felt like she was desperately trying to keep it all from collapsing on top of her.

Monique forced herself to stop thinking and just eat. If she thought about her future with Benny for too long,

she might swipe her arm across the table and shove all of
the plates onto the ground. Her eyes crept passed Benny
and continued down the table. Stevie and Bec were eating
quietly, the only noise between them the soft clanking of
their silverware and the occasional hushed murmurs that
traveled between their lips. Monique wanted to talk to
them, to Bec especially. She had woken up that morning to
a quiet house—not even Jamari or Ramon had been in the
kitchen yet. As she had turned on the coffee pot, she'd heard
a sudden rustling behind her and turned to see Tyler, his
tall frame splayed out over one end of the couch, a blanket
halfway between him and the floor. The sight of it had made
Monique sick to her stomach. Tyler sleeping on the couch
meant one thing—he and Bec hadn't made up last night.
Tyler and Bec's lack of reconciliation meant that this trip was
going to get a whole lot messier. Sides would be taken. Lines
would be drawn in the sand. She knew the rest of the trip had
no chance of salvation once that started. And with the staff
leaving today, they didn't even have the benefit of a buffer.
They were on their own.

Monique shot both Stevie and Bec a sympathetic smile, a
quiet thing that barely lifted the corners of her mouth. It was
a look that told them—we're good, I'm Team Bec. At least,
she hoped it did. Only Stevie caught the glance but it was
returned with similar affection. Monique tried to ignore the
flutter in her stomach and the soft blushing of her cheeks
as Stevie's eyes hovered on her for longer than they should
have. Monique forced her eyes back on her plate, scooping
up a forkful of rice. Miles and Tyler were eating in silence
but the energy that came off of them was different than the
others. Theirs was a vicious silence that radiated out in heavy
waves. Ironically, they were sitting next to each other. There
was four feet of space between them, but the proximity
was enough to keep Monique on edge. The last thing today
needed was another fight.

A swift clap snapped through the air. Monique swore

quietly under her breath, the shock raising anger through her blood. She glared at Marta, who seemed overly awake and attentive as per usual. Monique thought she would be used to the woman by now, but every time she heard her hands slap together and looked up to see the wax-like grin on her face, it made a shiver run through her.

"Guests," Marta said, her voice booming across the patio. "We thank you for staying with us and wish you an enjoyable trip for your remaining days."

Her eyes flickered to Jamari and Ramon who stood on the edge of the patio. A silent command seemed to pass from the woman as the two men quickly stepped forward and began clearing the table. As plates and glassware disappeared, Marta continued.

"We shall be departing in one hour. We have left a note in the house with recommendations for the rest of your time here."

She looked over at Tyler, then to Miles as if picking up on the disturbed energy there. The corners of her eyes sharpened briefly before returning to her normal, cheerful facade.

"Snorkeling. Swimming. Hiking," she said. "Many options for you to choose."

With a quick nod, she was finished. Her departure was as abrupt as her clap had been and before Monique could think about what they all might or might not do today, the woman was gone. Everything happened quickly after that. Tyler stood up from his chair, the legs scraping back harshly across the patio. He gave Bec a steady look from across the table, the first one he'd managed all morning. If silence could be loud, his was deafening. Monique's heart began thumping wildly in her chest as Tyler turned to look at Miles. She felt Benny's body tense next to her. He was finally paying attention, seeming to sense the fight lingering in the air. Nothing happened for a few seconds. Their apprehension faded as Tyler stepped away from the table without a word. As he stormed off towards the house, Bec and Stevie turned to each other. A quiet conversation passed between them. Stevie shrugged and the pair stayed seated. Miles stared down at the table cloth, as if debating if he wanted to stay at the table and deal with Bec or head inside and face Tyler. He ultimately decided against both, getting up and heading for the jungle. Monique felt Benny touch her side gently. As she looked up at him, he gestured his head towards the house. She chewed over the decision for a minute. Bec was facing away from them all now, her eyes fixed on the horizon. Monique could tell it wasn't the right time to talk to Bec. She wouldn't want to answer the questions Monique was dying to ask. With a dreadful hesitation, Monique nodded to Benny and got up from the table.

"Let's talk later?" she offered to both Stevie and Bec. "Yeah?"

Bec only nodded, her focus not wavering from the endless expanse of blue in the distance.

"Yeah," Stevie answered, looking at Bec with a worry that Monique had rarely seen cross her face. "Later."

❋ STEVIE ❋

The wake spilled out from underneath the boat as it pulled away from the dock.

Stevie could see Marta standing on the deck, her hands clutching the railing. A weird feeling washed over Stevie as the uncanny presence of the woman blurred into the distance. They were finally alone. Where Stevie expected to feel relief and freedom with that realization, she was met with a small ball of ants scurrying around her stomach. They were all alone on a remote island, surrounded by miles and miles of empty ocean. She wasn't normally one to be spooked about these kinds of things, but something about the trip had felt off to her from the start. Why an island so far away? Why Nicaragua? Couldn't Tyler have booked some yacht in San Diego for them to party on and call it good? Her eyes tightened on the boat as it grew smaller and smaller on the horizon. She had considered trying to convince Bec to leave with the staff. She didn't have much cash and she doubted Bec did either, but they could have figured it out. Stevie wasn't opposed to lifting a wallet from some wealthy, oblivious tourist when they got into the city. But she'd held her tongue all morning. She could tell her friend was wrestling with her own thoughts. The last thing Bec needed was more uncertainty thrown her way.

As Stevie looked at Bec lying next to her on a colorful beach towel, she wondered how she was going to fix things for her. Stevie figured Miles would be the easy part. Yes, he was upset now, but he'd come around. She could tell by the way he looked at Bec that he was wrapped up in her.

That wasn't going to change overnight. And as stupidly as he'd acted last night, Stevie couldn't blame him for feeling burned. Bec had a way of always slinking back to Tyler after succumbing to her temptations. Stevie had seen the texts Miles had sent over the summer. Message after message asking Bec to figure it out, to finally break up with Tyler and be with him instead. Stevie had tried to offer her advice but Bec hadn't wanted it. She'd said she couldn't break up with Tyler. She'd said it wasn't the right time. Stevie had called bullshit. It wasn't about time. It wasn't even about sparing Tyler's feelings. Stevie knew her friend well enough to know she simply didn't want to face her actions and the resulting consequences. Bec had always evaded conflict and after what had happened with Brennen, it had only gotten worse. On the other hand, Stevie had always run headfirst into conflict, whether it involved her or not. When some girls in junior high called Bec a slut for getting to second base with Danny Miller, Stevie had been the one who'd given one of them a black eye. When a client of Bec's had refused to pay their invoice, Stevie had been the one who had shaken them down on the phone, pretending to be a lawyer with a bunch of legal bullshit she'd found on Google. Stevie always fought Bec's battles, not because Bec couldn't, but because she wouldn't. Bec seemed to just let the world kick her down. So now, as Bec lay tanning on her stomach next to her, Stevie knew it was her responsibility to make sure Bec came out of this weekend alive.

"What are you gonna do?" Stevie said, breaking the peaceful silence that had found them almost thirty minutes ago when they'd camped out on the beach with towels, sunscreen, and beers.

Bec lifted her head off the towel and shot her friend a playful look. "I was just going to lay here like nothing happened until the boat came back. Is that not an option?"

Stevie laughed and cracked open two beers. The bottles were coated in beads of condensation, growing warm under the sun as it grew higher in the sky.

"Here," Stevie said, pushing one of the beers against Bec's arm. "To help you think." She smirked.

Bec sat up and shook her head. "Nah, I'm not drinking today."

"Yeah, right," Stevie scoffed. "Come on, it'll help your hangover."

Bec rolled her eyes but inevitably took the beer from Stevie. As she crossed her legs and got comfortable, sand crept onto the corners of her towel. Her fingers tapped against the brown bottle, deep in thought like she'd been all morning. Stevie watched her patiently. There was no getting Bec to open up when she didn't want to. She had to make the decision on her own. Bec took a long sip before resting the bottle between her thighs.

"I hate this," Bec finally mumbled, her eyes fixed out onto the waves crashing gently against the beach.

Stevie took a deep breath and let it out in a ragged sigh. "I know. But you can't just ignore them both."

"I know."

The defeat in Bec's voice made Stevie's stomach roll. She nudged her friend and gave her a supportive smile. "You're not alone in this, remember?"

Bec shot a soft smile back at her. "I know. Thanks."

"Good," Stevie nodded, taking a sip of beer. "Now let's figure this shit out."

The skin around Bec's nose scrunched up as she made a face. "Fine."

"Do you want Tyler back?"

Silence drifted between them as Bec considered the question.

"Do you?" Stevie prodded.

Bec let out a heavy breath and shook her head. She gulped down some beer before responding, "I don't know."

Stevie swallowed the impatience on her tongue but it came right back up. "If you don't know, that pretty much tells me it's a no."

Bec swirled the beer around the bottle. Stevie thought she might actually be honest for a moment before a conflicted look washed over her face.

"Fuck, Stevie. I don't know. Okay?" She laid back down on the towel and held her beer on top of her stomach. "It's all...confusing. If I think about it any more I'm going to explode." She let out a frustrated groan as she pressed her hand into her forehead. "And this hangover isn't helping."

Stevie shot her a stern look but Bec wasn't looking. She was staring up into the clear blue sky as her fingers picked at the beer bottle's label.

"Okay," Stevie sighed. "Explain the feelings to me."

Bec looked at her sideways. "Did you really just ask me to share my feelings like I'm some sort of toddler?"

"Yeah, I did. Because if you're going to act like a toddler, you might as well—"

Bec swatted a bit of sand toward her. "Funny," she said sarcastically. A minute went by before Bec finally gave in. "Fine," she muttered.

She sat up, twisting her beer bottle down into the sand like it was a cupholder. She took a heavy breath, running her hands through her hair. Stevie sat quietly, waiting for something, anything.

"I like Tyler." Her mouth hung on the word 'like,' stretching it out as if she was considering its weight. "I know you don't," she added before her voice softened again. "But I like him."

"Okay," Stevie said carefully. "And what about Miles?"

Bec chewed at the inside of her cheek. "Miles is different."

The corner of her mouth twitched. It was only when she looked at Stevie that she saw the true conflict on her friend's face.

"How is he different?" Stevie prodded.

"Tyler..." She took a moment to find the words. "Tyler

does all of the things you would expect," she started. "He goes out of his way to make me feel special and safe and loved and all of that." She tossed her hand dismissively before dropping her eyes down to the beach towel. "But Miles…"

Without her saying anything else, Stevie knew. It was etched across Bec's face, in every quiver of her lip and hesitant flicker in her eyes. Bec was in deep.

"It's more than that," Stevie offered. "He feels right."

Relief relaxed the pitted space between Bec's brows. "Exactly," she breathed. "There's just something about him… It's like he knows me better than anyone. I feel like I've known him for years. He can see through all of my bullshit but somehow it doesn't scare him away. He still chooses me. I know—I know what I did was shitty…"

Stevie stifled the urge to interject as Bec struggled to find the right words.

"I've tried to forget him, Stevie. You know I have. But every time I tried I just felt myself being pulled back. Like he was supposed to be in my life." Bec blew the air out from her lungs before she laughed at herself. "Jesus, that sounded corny."

"No." A pause hung on Stevie's breath. "I know what you mean."

Stevie closed her eyes as she took a long sip of beer. She tried not to think of Monique but like always, it was hard not to. She knew what Bec meant because she'd felt it. Every time she was in the same room with Monique, every time someone brought her name up in conversation, every time she saw that old t-shirt of hers she refused to throw away or give back in the dresser drawer—Stevie felt it. Call it an infatuation or soulmates or whatever you wanted but it was a hard thing to ignore.

"Okay, well…it sounds to me like you've made your decision," Stevie remarked, shoving Bec lightly with the beer bottle in her hand. "Now you gotta do something about it."

Bec cracked open two more beers. She offered one to Stevie, who polished off hers before taking the fresh one. They both drank silently for a few minutes. Stevie leaned her head back, letting the sun melt away the last of her morning drowsiness. The warmth of it seemed to revitalize her and for a second, she felt as though things might be okay. So what if Tyler was a little pissy for a few days? He'd get over what Bec had done. And so what if Stevie had to watch the love of her life frolic around an island with her dumb jock of a husband? At least there was free booze and an endless jungle to explore. How bad could the rest of this trip be?

"Can I ask you something?"

Stevie shrugged. "Course." She watched the reluctance pool in Bec's eyes as she drank her beer. "Come on, ask me," Stevie prodded.

Bec closed her eyes and took in a long, unsteady breath. "Do you think it's my fault that Brennen's dead?"

Stevie's eyes went wide. When she tried to speak, all that came out at first was a jumble of air.

"Do you?" Bec asked.

"Jesus," Stevie finally managed. "Of course not." Stevie rubbed her eyes with her hands, not believing what had just come out of Bec's mouth. She let out a breathy rumble of curse words before speaking again. "Do you honestly think that?"

Bec's mouth was a rigged line. Stevie could tell that she was trying to keep the emotions from bursting out of her. There was a flicker in Bec's eyes that worried Stevie. It was more than pain or guilt or grief. It was acceptance. Stevie took a deep breath. She really wished she'd brought something stronger than beer down to the beach.

"That was not your fault," Stevie stated harshly. "Why is this coming up now?"

She shook her head as she looked away from Stevie. "It's nothing. Forget I said anything."

"Hey," Stevie quipped. "What happened that night was

not your fault. Despite what those fucking assholes online have to say about it."

Bec's mouth formed into a small smile but it was all for show. Stevie could see it in her eyes that Bec didn't believe her.

"Thanks."

Stevie held Bec's gaze firmly as she nodded in response. There was still a glimmer of something in her eyes that she found unsettling. Stevie's brow furrowed as she watched Bec finish her beer. It had been four years since Brennen died and almost two since Bec had brought up anything related to that night. So why now? Bec looked back towards the house. Stevie followed her gaze, half expecting to see Eleni or Monique heading down to join them. But there was no one, only the sand and endless green behind it. She could barely see a sliver of the roof over the sand dune and wall of palm trees that guarded the beach.

"You know how I said I wasn't drinking today?"

Stevie smirked and nodded to the two empty beer bottles in Bec's lap. "Yeah?"

"Well," Bec started, "I've decided I need a lot more to get through the day."

"Is this your way of asking me to go back to the house and restock so you don't have to face anyone yet?"

Bec gave her a sheepish smile. "I would literally love you forever."

"Oh please," Stevie jested as she hoisted herself up off the beach towel. "We're already locked in for life. You're stuck with me whether you want to be or not."

"You're the best." Bec beamed.

As Stevie brushed some rogue grains of sand from her legs, she paused. Her eyes drifted a short distance down the beach. "Do you think anyone left any alcohol down here?"

Bec followed the direction of Stevie's outstretched hand and shrugged. "Maybe?"

As Stevie started walking, Bec hurried to join her.

"So about last night..."

Stevie waited for her to catch up, throwing a devilish smirk her way when she did. "You mean the total smackdown for Bec's love and affection?" she laughed.

Bec scoffed as she and Stevie continued walking toward the bonfire pit. "You and your jokes."

"So what about it?"

"How obvious was it that Miles and I—"

"Fucked in the jungle?" Stevie snorted.

"We didn't—" Bec stopped herself and let out a deep sigh. "So, obvious?"

As they reached the empty bonfire, Stevie gave her a comical look. "Very."

Stevie began sifting through the sand with her bare foot, lazily searching for a bottle that may have been buried amidst the previous night's skirmish. As she kicked a pile of sand away, something dark made her do a double take. She squinted against the harsh glare of the sun and crouched down to get a better look. Her hands sifted through the red-hued grains, expecting to find the remains of the wine bottle Monique and Eleni had been nursing all night. Stevie wasn't a fan of wine, but it would serve Bec's needs. As her fingers reached deeper into the sand, her skin was teased by a heavy dampness. She pulled her hand away and made a face at the spilled wine and sand that caked her fingertips. Before she wiped her hand clean on her shorts, something in her brain clicked on. She held her fingers closer to her face and let her eyes roam over them. It wasn't wine. Her brow furrowed as she tapped her fingertips together, feeling the slight stickiness of them. A sudden realization drove disgust onto her face.

"Oh fuck," she yelled, quickly raking her hands against the sand.

"What is it?"

"The boys bled all over the sand and I fucking touched it," she groaned as she continued to rub her hands clean.

"That doesn't make sense," Bec stated.

Stevie gave her hands one last scrub against the gritty sand before clapping them together. When she was satisfied that they were somewhat clean, she turned to Bec. "Were you even watching the fight?" she questioned her. "Tyler's nose exploded like a bloody fire hydrant."

Bec shook her head slowly. "They didn't fight there."

"What?"

Stevie watched as Bec walked ten or so feet across the fire pit and stopped. When Bec finally looked back at her, the uncertainty on her face made Stevie nervous.

"They fought here."

Stevie looked at the fading blood stain at her feet and then to where Bec stood. It was too far from the fight. It didn't make sense.

"Did they fight again? After we went back to the house?"

Stevie heard Bec's question but didn't register it. She was too focused on the dark red patches of sand in front of her. Her eyes moved from her blood stain to the one she assumed Bec was staring at. "How much blood is over there?"

Bec looked at her strangely. "What? I don't know." Her eyes traced the red beads of sand in front of her before she shrugged. "Like a few splotches? It's pretty dried up."

Stevie's eyes drifted down to her feet. The blood here was wet and hadn't fully absorbed into the sand, which meant there had been a lot of it. But why was it buried under the surface?

"Stevie."

She blinked, her focus coming back to Bec.

"What's up with you?"

Stevie flashed her a forced smile. "Uh, nothing."

Bec gave her a weird look before continuing to search for leftover booze. Stevie's gaze drifted out to the waves. They had gotten bigger since they'd first come down to the beach, as high as four, maybe five feet now. As they broke against the shore, Stevie couldn't help but feel something slinking up her spine. She'd had this feeling on a few occasions before. The most recent had been at work. She had been watching two guys chatting in front of the bar when an unsettling feeling had crept over her. She'd trusted her gut and nodded to one of the security guards who always stayed close by. It had only taken a few seconds for the man to draw his gun and point it at his companion. The rest had been a blur. The man had managed to fire one shot in the air before the security guard had tackled him down. After that, Stevie had promised herself she wouldn't ignore any gut feelings. But now as she pulled her gaze from the sand and walked away, she did just that.

"There's nothing here to drink," Stevie called to Bec. She motioned up towards the path. "Come on, let's go back. I'm sick of all this sand."

"Already?" Bec challenged. She let out something between a laugh and a whiny moan. "Fine, but don't expect me to go fix all my problems right now. I'm way too hungover for that."

Stevie gave one last, lingering look to the bonfire as she and Bec grabbed their things and headed back to the house. If her gut was right, something bad had happened here. She just hoped that whatever it was, it'd stay far away from her and her friends.

 BEC

Bec blinked her eyes slowly. The fuzziness of sleep dissipated until finally she got a clear picture. As the room came into focus, confusion rippled through her mind. What was she doing in here?

Her elbow dug into the cushion of the mattress as she propped herself up. She paused for a brief second, letting her senses activate. Her fingers gently grazed the bedsheets beside her. No cool spots. No blood wetting the tips of her fingers. She managed to take a deep breath and look around the room. She had come back to the house to take a nap, but she didn't remember falling asleep in here. Her eyes continued to roam Tyler's room—the one that had briefly been hers, up until last night. When Bec had dragged her suitcase to Stevie's room at one in the morning, it had been clear to her that she wouldn't be returning. So how had she ended up in his bed?

As Bec swung her legs over the edge of the mattress, her reflection in the full-length mirror across the room made her pause. She was wearing one of Tyler's old college t-shirts, and nothing else. She mouthed a silent curse word as she got up and began searching for her clothes. How much had she had to drink on the beach? She thought she'd only had a couple beers but questions and uncertainty flooded her mind as she swept her eyes across the floor. There was a pile of clothes by Tyler's suitcase, everything there his. She couldn't find any of the clothes that she'd been wearing earlier. A crash came from outside the door. Bec's heart dropped into her stomach as she froze in place. She turned her head slowly towards the noise and listened. Something felt wrong. She waited for one of her friends to laugh or swear at their own clumsiness, likely to have let a glass or plate slip to the floor and shatter. No sound came. What was going on? Another crash. Bec's heart was thumping loudly in her chest now. She took a step towards the door, still listening for an explanation for it all. She waited there, ear to the door, for a full minute. It was only when the doorknob rattled that she lurched backwards.

"Tyler?" she called out.

The doorknob stopped rattling. Everything went silent.

"Tyler?" Bec whispered.

"Yes?"

A gasp sprung from her lips as she reeled to look behind her. Tyler stepped forward out of the shadows of the room, head hung low.

"What...what am I doing here?" Bec's voice wavered.

Tyler's head rose slowly. His face was covered with the soft speckling of dirt and blood. The sight of it made Bec's heart flutter.

"What happened?" She stepped towards him hesitantly. "Did you and Miles get into another fight?"

He wrapped his hand around her waist, holding her close now. His breath was steady, calm. Bec furrowed her brow as she looked at him.

"Are you hurt?"

"No," he said quietly. He brought his other hand up to her waist and smiled. "But you are."

The knife slid into Bec's side like he was slicing butter. She gasped, the air already feeling thin in her lungs. Her eyes pleaded with him as the blood started to trickle from her flesh. Her hand reached for the gash instinctively, only to be yanked away by Tyler's grip.

"No. Let it happen," he cooed.

Numbness crept over her. She could feel it crawling up, like she was sliding deep into the bath.

"Why?" she rasped.

"Why do you think?" Tyler smirked as he raised the knife high above his head before bringing it down onto Bec's skull with a heavy crack.

Breath ripped through Bec, the ferocity of it sending her into a coughing fit. She rolled over in bed, letting the air expel from her lungs in ragged bouts. She lifted a hand wildly towards the bedside table and grabbed the glass of water she'd set there. She drank in big, eager gulps, only forcing herself to stop at the threat of another coughing fit. She set the glass down roughly and pushed her hair out of her face. The sheets underneath her were coated in sweat. She took a deep breath and rubbed her face in her hands.

"Fuck," she muttered.

Nightmares weren't a stranger to Bec. Maybe before Brennen, but certainly not after. Whenever she had nasty bouts of them, she remembered what a doctor had told her years ago. Stress and alcohol was a curious mix. The doctor had advised her to cut out the booze and find healthier ways to cope. She'd bought a bottle of tequila on the way home from the doctor's office. Now it seemed the nightmares had returned, but just like before, Bec had no intention of being sober. She forced another deep breath from her lungs before pushing herself out of bed. There was a brief pause as she looked at herself in the standing mirror that rested in the corner. It was identical to the one in Tyler's room but relief washed over her as she saw she was still dressed in the bikini she'd slipped on for the beach. No old college t-shirt. No dread creeping up on her. Her nerves settled more as she looked around the room and saw Stevie's things strewn about the dresser and floor. There was a touch of nostalgia to it. It reminded Bec of three years ago when she and Stevie had first moved to LA. They hadn't been able to afford a two-bedroom apartment so they had decided to rent out a studio instead and make do. They had hung floor-to-ceiling drapes in the middle of the loft in an attempt to create some privacy. But the pretend walls hadn't stopped Stevie's mess from slipping its way to Bec's side of the apartment. Bec took one last look around before grabbing the clean towel that Stevie had set out for her and heading for the shower. As she reached for the doorknob, she was back in her dream. The malicious smile that had spread across Tyler's face floated in her mind. She could almost hear the crack her head had made against the force on the blade slamming into her skull. The thought sent a chill across her already sweat-slicked skin.

"It was just a dream," she breathed as she turned the knob and stepped into the bathroom. "It was just a dream."

✹ TYLER ✹

Tyler tapped his fingers impatiently. He'd been sitting on the patio for an hour, building himself up to this moment. Now, just as he felt ready, it seemed like the moment would never come.

The scrape of the sliding glass door against the jamb pulled at his attention expectantly. When it was only Benny, annoyance swelled inside of him. Tyler shot him a quick glare before looking away. Benny hesitated at the edge of the patio. The cowardice of it only set Tyler more on edge.

"If you're gonna come outside, do it already," Tyler barked. "You're letting the cold air out and the girls have already been blasting that shit all morning."

He fixed his eyes back on the view, refusing to look at his best friend as he closed the door and headed over. Benny quietly sat down in one of the big wicker chairs next to Tyler. He scratched a sunburned patch of skin on his shoulder before clearing his throat.

"Still hate me?"

Tyler mulled the question over in his head. Did he hate Benny? Hate was a strong word. He only reserved that word for a few people, two of those being his father and his older brother. But Benny? No, he didn't hate Benny. But disgust was a word that came to mind when he looked at the hungover face whose eyes were almost pleading for forgiveness.

"No," Tyler finally muttered. "But that doesn't mean we're good either."

Benny sighed and nodded his head. "I'm fucking sorry, bro. I really am."

Tyler looked at his friend carefully. He seemed genuine, but Tyler didn't care about that. Didn't give two shits. Something had changed in Benny over the course of their friendship. The life-of-the-party, NFL-bound freshman he'd met during a game of beer pong had slowly morphed into someone else. Sure, his football career had changed him a little after they'd graduated, but if anything it had been for the better. Benny had developed a self-assured, albeit cocky at times, personality over the years. He was never one to back down from a fight or let anyone walk over him. All of that had changed when Benny met Monique. Tyler thought she would be good for him. She was a good woman, after all. She was educated and beautiful. She could cook. She had established herself in a successful career and was independent. While Tyler had ultimately seen that as a good sign, a sign that she wasn't after Benny's then three million dollar NFL contract, it had ultimately been her deadliest trait.

It had only taken her five months to turn Benny into a spineless yes-man. She'd housebroken him before Tyler had even realized what was happening. So when he looked at Benny now, sitting across from him with a slightly sunburned nose that peeled at the tip, he could only feel pity. Pity and disgust. Benny didn't even have the balls to look Tyler in the eyes and tell him Bec was the one at fault here, not him. Didn't even have the spine to tell him what a slut she was. Or to tell him that Miles had always been a shitty friend, maybe never even a friend at all. But no. Instead Benny could only slink back into submission and ask for forgiveness. It was almost too much for Tyler to bear.

"Come on," Benny said, chewing at Tyler's calculated silence. "I'm sorry." He let out a big breath and rubbed his forehead. "She told me it wasn't going to happen again. She promised me that shit was over."

Tyler's gaze tightened on Benny. "And what about him?"

Benny looked confused at first. "Miles?" He scoffed and brushed the air away with his hand. "He told me it was none of my fucking business."

"It wasn't," Tyler retorted. "But it was mine."

"I know, man. I fucked up."

The sliding door creaked open with a whine. Both of the men paused and lifted their gaze to the house. Bec slipped out onto the patio, hair wet from the shower. She looked at both of them hesitantly as she slid the patio door shut behind her.

Tyler turned back to Benny abruptly. "You did fuck up," he muttered. He shot him a hardened stare, aware of Bec moving through his peripheral vision. "Prove to me that you won't do it again. That you have my back," he urged.

Benny nodded. "Of course," he said quickly. "Just tell me what you need me to do."

Tyler's eyes flashed back to Bec, who had slowly begun to head down one of the paths that lead into the jungle. He could still catch her if he hurried.

"For now," he said, looking back at Benny. "Fuck off."

Without another word Tyler left Benny and headed across the lawn.

BEC

Bec's heart rate grew steadily as she hiked along the path. Even as she ventured further into the jungle, it still didn't seem far enough away.

The house felt stifling. She felt her anxiety bundle in her chest. The tension reminded her of those few months back in Reno after Brennen had died. The lingering stares. The gossip. How people who had once been her friends kept themselves at a safe distance from her. Bec didn't think her friends now would be as cruel—it was a different situation, after all. But still, Bec could feel an uncomfortable thickness in the air, so she'd slipped on her tennis shoes and headed for the jungle. Stevie had offered to join her but Bec had politely declined. She needed time to herself. Time to think.

She'd only been walking along the path for a few, solitary minutes when another set of footfalls added to the rhythmic padding of her own. She whipped her head over her shoulder, expecting to see Stevie running after her with a pair of beers in hand. But instead, Bec felt everything inside of her drop into emptiness as Tyler's face appeared from behind a patch of ferns. She searched his eyes for any emotion, any sign of where his head was at. He was blank, guarded. It made her nervous. She would have preferred to see a glimmer of hurt or anger on his face. That way, she would know what to expect out here, alone with him in the jungle. She tried to stop the flashes of her nightmare from playing in her head as he stepped onto the trail.

"Hey," he said, coming to a halt a few feet from her.

"Hi," she replied quietly.

Her eyes roamed the dizzying green of the jungle around her, unable to hold his gaze. She chewed at the inside of her cheek as they stood there for a minute, saying nothing. Bec took a deep breath, filling her lungs until there wasn't any space left.

"Tyler, I really don't want to talk about everything right —"

"I just have one question."

She looked at him cautiously as she played out the next minute in her head. *How could you? Why did you do it? What does he have that I don't?* They were all questions she didn't want to answer. Her mind darted back to her nightmare. She imagined what it would feel like to have that knife jammed inside of her, scraping against her ribs. Would it be more or less painful than what was coming? As Tyler opened his mouth to speak, Bec felt her entire body constricting into a giant knot of anticipation.

"How stupid do you think I am?"

Bec's panic seemed to swallow her like a tsunami wave. It left her without breath and any sense of direction. Her eyes searched his face frantically for the emotions she'd expected to be there. All she saw staring back at her was a cruel certainty. There was a dash of resentment, too, like icing on top of a poisoned cake.

"What?" she said, fumbling her words.

He gave her a slick, bitter smile as he stepped closer. "How long did you think you could let him fuck you before I found out?"

She was frozen. Her thoughts tripped and stumbled as she struggled to answer him. Even her tongue seemed to fumble in her mouth.

"How long did you think you could make a fool out of me?" he breathed.

Bec pulled away as his fingers began to trace the outline of her jaw. "What? I—" Bec took a step away from him, alarm darting across her face. "Tyler, I didn't mean to..."

The contents of her stomach seemed to curdle as she digested the calm hatred on his face. He wasn't sad. He wasn't devastated. He was sure. But sure of what? The question left Bec reeling. If there wasn't any grief there, what was left? Her eyes flickered to the left and right. She was surrounded by dense vegetation on both sides. She could either go deeper down the path, into the jungle, or head back to the house. The only thing that stood in her way was the thing that worried her most. She looked over her shoulder, considering what seemed like her best option.

"Walking away now is only putting off the inevitable," Tyler uttered, as if reading her mind. He took a step closer to her, cracking a few small twigs under his shoe as he did. "Answer me."

Bec took a quick breath in. All of her life, she'd run from her problems. She made little messes and quickly fled, leaving tiny smoldering fires in the rearview mirror. But she was all out of options now. Do not collect $200. Do not pass Go.

"I didn't mean to hurt you, Tyler," she said as steadily as she could. "I made a mistake. I fucked up." Bec took a deep breath. It caught in the back of her throat, as if unwilling to break the surface. "I'm sorry," she said, her voice wavering.

"Thank you."

The look on his face was void of any emotion. His face held a deadpan stare that only mounted the unsteadiness inside of Bec.

"But if anything, this is my fault."

Bec's head cocked to the side. "What?"

"I should have known better."

"Tyler this isn't your faul—"

"It's in your nature, Bec," he said, a soft smile that felt anything but comforting now growing on his face. "This is just who you are."

"What are you talking ab—"

"You're a mess, Bec. You barely get by. You treat your life

like a joke. You have no sense of what's good for you. You just fuck your life up for the momentary thrill of it..."

Bec's eyes grew wide with disbelief. A sick feeling rumbled inside her stomach. Did he really think so little of her? Bec wondered if this was merely a result of her actions—her betrayal. Maybe what she and Miles had done had pushed him over the edge, ruptured something inside of him that now leaked and spewed. Or maybe, just maybe, this was who Tyler was all along. Maybe this was the person Stevie had always seen. Maybe Bec just hadn't paid enough attention to notice. Bec shoved her thoughts away as Tyler took a step closer, cutting the distance between them once more.

"You're like a dog. Desperate for whoever will give you the most attention, to whoever will scratch that itch—"

Bec's hand struck Tyler's cheek with a swift slap. The action startled her as much as it did him. She withdrew her hand quickly, as if she'd touched something hot, and took a step back. She stood there silently, mouth slightly agape. Her heart beat loudly in her chest, seeming to sync with the thrum of the wild jungle around her. Tyler's eyes flashed as he raised a hand to his cheek and brushed the flushed skin. He let out a breathy laugh.

"Didn't think you had that in you."

"I'm sorry," she breathed. She stared at him in shock, both for his actions and her own. "Fuck. I'm sorry, Tyler." The space between her brows knitted with distress. "You can be angry. I get it. I deserve it." She caught the breath that hitched in her throat. "But you don't get to talk to me like that. Ever."

"Don't spread your legs for him again and I won't."

Everything seemed to engulf Bec at once. The violent thrumming of her heart in her chest. The buzz of mosquitoes in her ear. The humidity that seeped in and out of her pores. The sick pleasure that seemed to drift from Tyler's face and taint the air around her. It was too much. Once again, her body seemed to take over while her mind stayed frozen in time. She pushed past Tyler roughly. The smell of campfire and tequila that wafted off of him welled into her nostrils. The smell tugged at the uneasiness in her gut and she quickened her pace. It reminded her of last night and everything that she had done. Was Tyler right? She ignored the question as she let her feet drive her forward, away from what had just happened. Her ears honed in on every noise around her. Would he give her space or would he follow her?

Bec saw a flicker of something dart through a tangle of tree branches and vines. The flash of black and white hair was quickly followed by a shrill screeching that fired up Bec's fried nerves more. She glimpsed up at the small monkey that watched her with big, worried eyes from high in the tree. It let out one final, primal screech as she passed. Bec couldn't stop the shiver from raking down her spine as the sound echoed through the jungle. When the echo of the sound finally left her, it was quickly replaced by the incessant thought of Tyler's voice in her head. A dog. He'd said she was no better than a dog. She swallowed harshly as she continued forward down the trail, biting back a quiver of emotion that threatened to spill from her throat. Whatever dark, filthy thing that had slithered out of Tyler last night, she hoped it would go back to where it came from. Maybe when he calmed down, when the shock and pain of what she'd done finally left him, he'd return to his normal self. But Bec knew if this sliver of his soul, if this thing covered in tar and filth and hate, didn't slink back to where it belonged, then what had just happened would only be the beginning.

✱ ADRIAN ✱

The door opened with a lingering creak.

It took him a while to make it down the hall, his body aching as unsteady steps carried him to the kitchen. Adrian had been in bed too long. He could practically feel where the bed's lumpy mattress had molded against his spine. Sleep's sweet fog began to slowly lift as the babble of conversation and the smell of food drifted towards him. His stomach knotted and curled into him with an empty sickness. He hadn't eaten since dinner last night, unless he counted the liquor. There had been plenty of that. What time was it even? How long had he slept? He let out a burp, unleashing the stale, vile taste of last night's mistakes. The tang of it made him shiver. Curious eyes met him when he finally emerged from the shadowed hall and into the kitchen. Monique and Stevie were cutting up vegetables as the soft twang of pop music played from a speaker.

"Well, look who finally woke up," Stevie teased, her mouth curling into a smirk.

Adrian mumbled something as he shuffled along. His eyes drifted past the two women, searching for the smell that was teasing his nose. He stopped at the open sliding glass door and took in a savoring whiff. The charred, sweet smell of meat wafted towards him and made his stomach awaken hungrily. He eyed Benny, who was towering over the little barbeque grill on the patio. Benny turned and met Adrian's sleepy gaze with an impish grin.

"So big man," Benny teased, taking a few steps away from the grill so he could slap Adrian on the shoulder. "How'd it go?"

Adrian's forehead furrowed as he stared back at Benny.

"You know..." Benny nudged, "with Eleni...?"

He gave him a wink and suddenly, it all started coming back to Adrian.

Shit. Fuck. He had completely forgotten. Adrian closed his eyes as he dragged his hand across his face.

"I'm an idiot," he muttered. He looked up at Benny, humiliation drenching his face. "She's never going to give me another shot after that."

Benny seemed both amused and confused at Adrian's apparent anguish. "It couldn't have been that bad," he laughed. "You guys were at it all day."

"What are you talking about?"

"Fuck, how hungover are you?" Benny said, turning back towards the grill and flipping the steaks over.

The aroma glided up Adrian's nostrils and provided a brief moment of salivation before the roll of nausea tumbled in his barren stomach. He clenched a hand to his mouth and forced the sick feeling down with a series of steady breaths.

"Where's Eleni? I need to apologize," he mumbled through clenched teeth, fighting back a series of sickening burps.

Benny stopped what he was doing. He stared at the grill for a minute before turning towards Adrian. "What do you mean, where's Eleni?"

"Did all that football turn your brain to mush?" Adrian scoffed. "Where is she?"

"First of all, fuck you," he snorted. "And I haven't seen her. She's been laid up in bed with you all day."

"Come on, Benny. Stop fucking with me. I need to talk to her."

The two men stared at each other blankly. In their silence, Stevie and Monique sauntered out onto the patio, carrying plates of vegetables for Benny to grill. As they set them down, Adrian turned to Monique.

"Have you seen Eleni today?"

She scrunched her face up. "No…"

Stevie let out a breathy laugh behind them. "Damn, dude. How bad are you in the sack that she's already run off?"

An absurd chuckle drummed from the back of Adrian's throat. "What the hell are you talking about? Eleni and I didn't hook up last night." He paused and reconsidered for a minute. "Okay, well yeah we started to on the beach but it didn't get that far." He scoffed to himself and ran his hand through his hair. "Thanks to my drunk ass."

"Wait, you didn't spend the night with Eleni?" Monique questioned.

Adrian hesitated as he registered the growing concern on her face. "What's the deal?" he asked. "Why is everyone so concerned if Eleni and I slept together last night?"

Stevie and Monique exchanged an uneasy look.

"What is going on?" Adrian spat. "Where's Eleni?"

The snap of branches and heavy footfalls pulled everyone's attention. Adrian turned towards the jungle, anticipation seeming to hang on his every breath.

"Eleni?" he called.

Through the dense mass of fronds and vines, Bec emerged. She trampled down the path towards them, her pace short of a jog. The closer she got to the group, the more agitation was visible on her face.

"Bec?" Stevie called. "What's wrong?"

The sliding glass door closed behind them all with a solid thump. Miles took a minute to look at the group before his gaze fixed on Bec.

"What's going on?" he asked.

The jungle rustled once again but this time it was Tyler who appeared from the trail Bec had exited moments earlier. His footfalls were heavy and determined. His face was tense, his mouth pulled into a taunt grimace.

Stevie's eyes darted between the two as they approached. "What the fuck happened?"

"It's nothing. He just—" Bec started.

"What happened? Did he hurt you again?" Miles demanded, stepping in front of Stevie and reaching out for Bec's hand. She pulled away from him instantly.

"He fucking hates me," Bec snapped at him. "You wanna know why, Miles?" She took a step closer, getting in his face. "He hates me because I cheated on him. With you. I fucked up. And now Tyler thinks I'm a degenerate piece of shit—"

"He said that to you?"

Bec looked at Miles with utter bewilderment. "I ruined my relationship and you're worried about what names he called me?"

"Was Eleni with you?"

Bec ignored Adrian. She was now arguing with Miles but Adrian wasn't listening. Whatever mess Bec had gotten herself into last night, although amusing at the time, he no longer cared. He looked past Bec and Miles and their lover's quarrel. He looked past Tyler who was now heading across the lawn with fury in his eyes. Adrian looked past them all until he was staring at the mouth of the jungle, waiting for Eleni to saunter down the path, smiling that toothy grin of hers that she rarely expressed. When she didn't show up, panic filled his chest. What happened last night? He racked his brain but it was all a choppy blur. He had been drinking on the beach. Eleni was there. She'd looked so hot last night. He'd given her some wine and then... Fuck.

"Where the hell is Eleni?" he yelled.

Miles hesitated for a minute. "You should know," he muttered, his eyes not leaving Bec. "She was with you."

"Why does everyone keep saying that?" Adrian protested.

Everyone continued to ignore him as Tyler pushed his way through the group, bumping Miles' shoulder as he did. "What? Suddenly have nothing to say?" Miles barked. "You'll take it out on her but not me?"

"Miles, stay out of it," Bec said.

Tyler turned back, already halfway inside the house.

"Yeah, Miles," he replied in a snarky tone. "Maybe you should learn not to stick yourself into other people's lives." He looked him up and down coolly, the only emotion on his face coming from the vicious glare in his eyes. "Or their girlfriends."

Benny stifled a laugh, the sound quickly faltering as Monique's elbow dug into his ribs.

"What?" he whispered to her. "That was kinda funny."

Monique rolled her eyes at her husband and said something about his comment being in poor taste. Adrian didn't quite catch it, he was too focused on the way his head felt like it would split open at any minute. His stomach did another vicious roll. He clenched his teeth as he waited for it to pass. He should have made himself throw up earlier, maybe that would have saved him from the agony he was enduring now. Monique's voice rang in his ear like a shrill bell.

"Adrian, did Eleni sleep in your room last night?"

His skin itched but it wasn't from the heat. This was bad. He turned to her, restlessness slipping down the back of his throat. "No," he mumbled.

Monique pursed her lips as she looked at the rest of the group. "Has anyone seen Eleni since last night?"

Head shakes passed amongst them as did the lingering silence.

"When was the last time you saw her?" she asked Adrian.

"The bonfire," he stated carefully. "We were..." he paused and licked his lips. His mouth went dry. "We started making out and I was feeling sick. I ran back to the house to throw up and I guess I passed out on my bed or something. I don't know."

"You don't know?" Stevie quipped.

"I was drunk," he argued. "I don't remember much else."

Bec's brow furrowed. "So you left her out there by herself?"

Adrian didn't like the way she had said it. It sounded

accusatory, like Eleni's absence was his fault. His mind shot alive like a house alarm. Shit. Shit. Shit. Panic blared and flashed inside of him as he replayed the night—at least, what he could remember. And he'd just remembered something that made his insides go runny. He stammered, trying to find his voice.

"I mean—" Adrian said. "It's not like we're at some sketchy resort. It's just us." He felt their eyes on him. Did they know? They couldn't know. His gaze darted around the group, careful not to look anyone in the eyes for too long. "We're all adults here, right?" he emphasized, his voice cracking. "If Eleni wanted to get drunk and fall asleep on the beach, that's her business."

"She's not on the beach," Stevie interjected. "Bec and I were there earlier."

"Where could she have gone?" Monique asked.

Adrian heard the worry in her voice. He looked out across the patio where the ocean now shined a deep hue of blue against the slowly falling sun. It would be dark in a few hours. Would they find Eleni by then?

"She didn't get on the boat, did she?" Monique asked.

"No," Stevie said. "We would have seen her getting ready this morning if she had. Plus, we saw the boat leave. It was just the staff."

A funny feeling grew inside of Adrian. It wasn't the waves of nausea he'd been fighting off all day. No, this felt more profound. It was like a bottomless pit was forming inside his gut, growing deeper by the second. It was the feeling that whatever had happened to Eleni, it was all his fault.

✶ MONIQUE ✶

"What do you think?"

Monique breathed heavily as she trudged up the hill. When Benny had asked her which way she wanted to go in search of Eleni, she had picked the trail right behind the house. It was a path none of them had explored yet, dusty and slightly overgrown with plants that tickled Monique's ankles every few steps. It had seemed like a simple trek but now Monique could see that it was anything but. After the first fifteen minutes, the trail had grown steep and rocky. And now, almost forty five minutes in, it felt like they were climbing a mountain. Monique wondered if the trail led to the top of the cliffs that they had seen on their hike the day before. No, it couldn't be. They were heading in the opposite direction. The more she thought about it, the more Monique realized she had no idea how big the island actually was. Tyler had never showed them a map or even an Airbnb listing. For all she knew, the island was as big as LA county and here they were, exploring it on foot in a futile attempt to find one person. And as much as she hated that person, she couldn't help but feel dread creeping up her skin. Benny's heavy breathing filled the air close behind her. It sounded worse than hers.

"What do I think about what?" Benny huffed.

Monique's eyebrows shot high on her face as she gestured around the jungle. "This," she stressed. "We're hiking through the jungle in Nicaragua looking for Eleni. This is bad, Benny. What else could I be talking about?"

He shrugged, finally catching up to her. "Eleni wandering

off isn't the only thing that's gone down lately." He pushed a fallen palm frond out of their way and motioned for Monique to go ahead. "Bec and Tyler's relationship finally imploded. Miles is a smug bastard. And I'm gonna spend the rest of this trip begging my best friend to forgive me. I can sure as hell forget about getting that hundred grand from him now..."

Monique stopped in her tracks, whipping her head back toward him. "What hundred grand?"

She watched as Benny's mind did backflips, trying to find a way out of the mistake he'd just made. At the same time, her own thoughts ricocheted through her head.

"Did you ask Tyler for money again?" she asked. Her voice boomed through the jungle, causing a few birds to quickly take flight from their perches amongst the canopy.

"Can we talk about this later?" Benny said as he stepped around Monique and continued the climb. "We need to find Eleni."

"Oh," Monique ranted. "So now you give a shit about finding Eleni? And here I thought just a second ago you were talking about your own problems."

"Babe..." Benny stopped and wiped a trickle of sweat from where it slid down the side of his face. "Can we please not do this now? It's too fucking hot to argu—"

"What is your problem lately?" she spat. "First you don't tell me about Bec and Miles and now you're going behind my back and asking Tyler for what? A loan? After you pissed it away that last time he bailed us out?" She mumbled obscenities under her breath, trying to contain her frustration. "Why do you need money, Benjamin? You said things were going well at the barber shop."

He hesitated, his eyes fidgety and unsure. "Everything's fine, I was just trying to...you know, trying to do my own thing."

"Your own thing?" Monique squinted as she looked at him, her eyes fighting against the glare of the sun that beat down on them harshly. "And that means what exactly?"

"I'm going to open my own barber shop."

She stared at him, the lines in her face growing deeper and more pronounced as she tried to understand what was happening. "Benny, you've been a barber for three months."

"Yeah, so?"

"So?" Monique let out a breathy laugh that was anything but amused. "So how are you going to go off on your own when you barely know what you're doing?"

"Wow," Benny replied. "You know, this is exactly why I didn't want to tell you yet."

Monique shook her head and closed her eyes. He was unbelievable. Yet again, she was the bad guy. When she had told him to get a job after he had lost his NFL contract and sat on the couch for two months, she had been the nagging wife. When she had suggested they spend a year being engaged instead of getting married four months later, she had been the one with cold feet. And now when he went behind her back to ask their friend for money, she was somehow the villain again. What the hell? Monique felt her cheeks burn with anger. After their first month of being married, she had learned that Benny had all but spent everything he had. His NFL salary. Savings. And for what? To play big boss man off the field? Now, yet again, he had asked Tyler to help them out. But $100k? That was too much, even for Tyler. He wouldn't let it go without some sort of plan, some sort of deal. Monique forced a deep breath from her lungs. Priorities. They had more important things to worry about than Benny's latest impulsive decision. She tried to give her best attempt at a supportive smile, but she could feel it fading fast.

"At least tell me you're going to keep working at Broadway Fades until you get a business plan and a client list built up and all of that."

There it was again—that hesitant look on his face. After four months of marriage, Monique was beginning to understand exactly what that look meant. It meant Benny had done something she wasn't going to like. She let out a sigh, trying to keep her frustration in check.

"Can you go back and tell them you want to work part-time until you get things worked out? I'm sure they haven't had time to replace you yet. When did you quit?"

"Nah, I don't wanna go back. They were a bunch of douchebags."

A slow simmering of irritation rose up inside Monique as she looked carefully at Benny. Equally to her relief and dismay, he was a shit liar.

"You didn't quit, did you?"

He said nothing. She shook her head and ran her tongue along the inside of her cheek, trying to restrain the violent chatter of words that threatened to spill out of her.

"What did you do to get fired?"

Benny scoffed and looked away. "Nothing," he grumbled. "Like I said, they were a bunch of douchebags."

"And you didn't think to tell me that once again we're going to be living off of my income and savings? Jesus, Benny. We haven't even paid off everything from the wedding."

He mumbled something under his breath.

"Please. Speak up," Monique snarked, her eyes boring into him relentlessly.

Finally, he turned to look at her. "You're being a real bitch, you know that?"

Monique tried to settle the rage that was flowing through her body but she couldn't. Like lava, it seemed to incinerate everything it touched as it slugged through her veins. She didn't even want to look at Benny and his stupid face but she did. With a dark, nasty glare, she took it all in. This was her husband, the person she had tied herself to for the end of time. She sucked on her teeth, pushing past him.

"You think I'm being a bitch now?" she laughed. "Just you wait til I make you sell your G-Wagon because your stupid little barber shop has eaten up all of our money."

"Monique."

She could already hear his regret. But instead of being

relieved, it only angered her more. She wanted to scream at him, yell until she was blue in the face. She wanted to expel a years' worth of regret and fear. She wanted to let loose the truth she stifled like a muzzle. The only thing stopping her was the thought of Eleni somewhere out in the jungle: alone, terrified, hungry, maybe worse.

"I'm going back to the house," Monique snapped. "Eleni didn't come up here last night. If she was as drunk as Adrian said she would have rolled an ankle a mile back."

She started heading back down the trail, leaving Benny standing in silence.

"And if you keep this bullshit up—the lies and all of your shit—you're going to be out a job and a wife," she yelled back.

BEC

Bec's heart felt like it was going to jump out of her throat. It thumped wildly as the heat bore down on her. Would she ever get used to this heat? She wasn't sure how long they'd been walking but it felt like forever. If the circumstances had been different—and if the humidity hadn't been so intense that her clothes stuck to her like papier-mâché—Bec might have actually enjoyed the scenic walk through the jungle. But, the circumstances were what they were and the walk was anything but pleasant.

The decision to search for Eleni had been a quick one. Dinner had been taken off the grill and left half cooked on the counter. Timelines and events had been shared and retold again and again. The group determined that Adrian had been the last person to see Eleni. He couldn't remember when he'd left the beach. They all guessed it had to be close to 1 or 2 a.m.

Tyler had been the one who suggested they all pair up to go search for her. Bec had looped her arm into Stevie's as soon as the words had left his mouth. She wasn't going to risk getting stuck with anyone else, especially since Benny and Monique were an obvious pair. Before Bec knew it the couple was already heading out the door, Monique leading the way at a brisk pace. Her urgency surprised Bec. They all had an uneasiness about them but Monique's distress was elevated. Monique didn't like Eleni. After last night's bonfire game, Bec thought Monique might actually hate her. But that didn't seem to matter now. Monique had asked all sorts of panicked questions before she'd headed out to search.

Did anyone remember what Eleni was wearing last night? Did Eleni speak Spanish? Did she say anything weird to Adrian before he left her? The more Bec thought about it, the more she began to understand. It wasn't about Eleni at all. It was the idea of being out there all alone, lost among the dense vines and shadowed canopy, without a soul searching for you. How much time had they wasted simply because no one had cared enough to check for Eleni? The thought sent a shiver down Bec's spine despite the 90 degree heat.

With Monique and Benny off before the rest of the group could delay them with questions and Bec and Stevie paired up, the three remaining men were left out. Ultimately, they had decided to each go alone. Adrian hadn't seemed too fond of the idea, but Tyler proposed that they'd cover more ground that way. Although it was true, Bec knew it was bullshit. Tyler had barely shown concern when Benny knocked on his bedroom door and announced that Eleni was missing. He'd dismissed it at first, claiming she had probably wandered off for the attention. It was only when Monique had told him that Eleni had already been missing for over twelve hours that Tyler conceded. So no, Bec knew he wasn't concerned about covering more ground. He just couldn't bear to breathe the same air as Miles. Bec had refrained from looking at both Tyler and Miles as she left the kitchen with Stevie. But as she had stepped onto the patio, a light grip around her wrist had stopped her. 'Be careful', Miles had whispered, before giving her wrist a squeeze. Bec might have acknowledged the moment with a soft smile if it hadn't been for Tyler's eyes searing into her. She had quickly pulled herself away from Miles, headed off after Stevie, and disappeared into the jungle.

Now, as the jungle passed by with each heavy step, Bec couldn't help but let her mind drift away from the trouble she'd gotten herself into. After last night, she'd thought the trip's demise would be petty drama. In what seemed like the blink of an eye, bigger problems had found them. No one had a good answer for what might have happened to Eleni. The fact that they had gone the entire day without noticing her absence stirred a sickly brew inside Bec. If Eleni had only been missing to get attention as Tyler suggested, she would have given up by now. Bec had kept herself from building a list of potential catastrophes in her head, but now as the steady path put her body into autopilot, it was hard not to. More crocodiles. Deadly spider bites. Elaborate booby traps set by a long-lost indigenous tribe, like in the movies. A swarm of terrible outcomes crossed Bec's mind. It was only when Stevie pulled her from the dregs of her thoughts that Bec realized they'd reached the beach.

"Now what do we do?" Stevie asked, the slightest bit of hopelessness slipping from her tongue.

Bec stopped next to Stevie at the mouth of the trail and put her hands on her hips. She took a few deep breaths to steady her heart rate as she looked around. The path had opened up onto the beach, nothing but sand and waves ahead of them now. It was difficult to tell how far they were from the bonfire, but Bec had a gut feeling that they weren't that far at all.

"What if she drank too much, started walking up the beach, and passed out or something?"

It was one of twenty explanations Bec had come up with in the last thirty minutes. Although it seemed unlikely that a nasty hangover would have kept Eleni from hobbling up to the house, it was one of her less morbid thoughts.

Stevie shrugged and stepped out onto the sand. "I guess it's possible."

Bec could tell that Stevie was growing more unsettled by the minute. It was rare for Bec to see her worried. Stevie was the one who usually kept her cool in the myriad of situations she and Bec seemed to get themselves into. When they'd been detained by mall security in junior high under the assumption of having stolen from one of the department stores—which they definitely had—Stevie had been the one who'd looked the plump man in the face and bluffed. It had been Stevie who snuck them out the back of a grimy Las Vegas club in their early twenties when it had been raided by police for a drug bust. And it had been Stevie who picked Bec up from Miles' apartment the morning after she'd made her fatal mistake. Stone-cold Stevie was the joke that had followed her around since high school. Nothing seemed to shake her. So when she turned around and gave Bec a look that chilled her to her core, Bec knew whatever it was—it wasn't good.

"Bec, go back."

"What is it?"

"Don't." Stevie pushed her back gently but Bec's stubbornness was stronger.

"What are you doing?" she protested. "Whatever it is, I can—"

Bec's words caught in her throat as she stepped past Stevie. It was the flies her brain processed first. Buzzing around wildly—feasting. Next was the blood. It was dry, whether from the sun or time, Bec didn't know. It seemed to crust around the tatters of the blue tank top. Bec guessed there had been a lot of it. It was obvious in the way the dark red smears ran down her skirt and onto her bare legs. The trails stopped just short of her shin bones, the red seeming to taper off. Blood had a funny way of flowing. It rushed and gushed until it decided not to. Until the body said, *that's enough. Why don't we stop for a bit?* Bec knew there was science behind it. Coagulation. Blood loss. It made sense. But looking at it now, the whole thing felt unreal.

The smell hit her next. Foul by itself, ungodly in the heat. It was a putrid sweetness of decay and defecation that soured every bit of food in Bec's stomach. The eyes were the last thing Bec saw before she puked. Big. Bulging. The eyes that had once graced fashion campaigns and endless Instagram posts were now as lifeless as a doll's. Sweat prickled Bec's forehead and vomit dripped from her bottom lip as Eleni's cold, dead eyes gaped out at her. A fly buzzed around Bec, finally veering away from her to land in the dark, gaping hole of Eleni's mouth. Bec dropped her eyes away from the girl's face. It felt wrong, looking at her like that. She tried to look away completely but her focus snagged on the brutal cuts riddled into Eleni's flesh. She began to count.

One. Two. Three.

Stevie was next to her. Bec could hear the muffle of her words but the meaning of them was lost on her.

Four.

Bec felt a light grip on her arm. It slowly tugged at her but she didn't budge.

Five.

Bec blinked slowly, hoping the picture would change every time the black washed over her lids. The nightmare in front of her was clearer with every curtain raise.

An overwhelming rush of fear raced up Bec's spine and erected itself like a flag pole. Bec's eyes raised to Eleni's face once again but it wasn't her face that stole every bit of heat from Bec's skin. It was what was underneath it. Hidden amidst a bloody tangle of long, black hair was a four inch gash, sliced into Eleni's neck so deep that Bec expected the girl's head to slide off into the sand at any moment. In an instant, nausea heaved from inside of Bec once more. It spilled out onto the sand in hot, vicious chokes. She felt Stevie's hand on her back as she dropped to the ground. It was no use—she was long past being consoled. Bec's fingers dug into the sand harshly as her gagging turned into uncontrollable sobs. She kept her eyes low, unable to look at what was in front of her anymore, unable to accept what she already knew to be true. Eleni was dead. Eleni was dead and it was her fault.

✹ TYLER ✹

No one said anything for a while.

It had been ten minutes since they'd followed Stevie and Bec down to the beach. Disbelief and grief had already settled into the group before they'd even laid eyes on the body. Monique had been the most upset. She had yelled at Stevie, told her not to joke about something so horrible. But when they had gotten to the body, nestled up against the tree line, they had all seen that what Stevie said was true. Now, an eerie silence had fallen over them. Tyler understood. As he stood quietly and watched with sharp eyes, he could tell his group of liars and backstabbers was going through all sorts of emotions. Monique was sobbing softly into Benny's shoulder. Benny seemed to be ignoring Eleni's body completely, his attention fixed on his wife. Tyler wondered if he was unconcerned about the butchered girl in front of him or scared to look for too long. Adrian and Stevie were both staring into the sand. Stevie looked lost in thought whereas Adrian was harder to read. Tyler thought he saw a glimmer of a tear but wasn't sure. He hoped he didn't. Any tears Adrian shed for Eleni were wasted. Eleni didn't give a shit about Adrian, which he would have seen if he was honest with himself. But it didn't matter much now. Then there was Bec. Tyler's gaze hovered on her. She wasn't looking away like the others. No, Bec was staring straight at Eleni, her eyes almost glazed over with too much focus. Curiosity flickered inside of Tyler. He doubted many of his friends had ever seen a dead body—a real dead body. Not a peek at a cleaned up corpse at a funeral. A real mess like the one that was in front of them now. The memory of Bec's cup tipping back stealthily during Eleni's childish bonfire game invaded Tyler's thoughts. Bec had seen a dead body. Whose? Her parents? He knew she'd grown up with her aunt. He'd assumed her parents were dead but she'd never told him one way or the other. Had it been someone else? This was the type of thing he should know as her boyfriend.

Was he still her boyfriend? He hadn't exactly cleared the air during their jungle walk like he'd hoped. If anything, he'd made things worse. As he'd sat on the patio that morning, drinking his coffee, the goal had been simple: talk to Bec, get her to apologize, start fresh. It hadn't seemed like that difficult a task but in the heat of the moment, his intentions had shifted. It wasn't his fault that he lost his temper sometimes. People couldn't get away with making a fool out of him. And that's exactly what he'd allowed Bec to do. For that, Bec deserved to be a little hurt. She deserved more than what she'd received. He'd gone easy on her. He hadn't hit her, which he'd greatly considered last night in his frenzied rage, before redirecting it to the person who deserved it more. Even today when she'd given him that childish slap, he'd considered sending one across her face to return the favor. But, he hadn't. He had shown restraint. Despite the betrayal that was still devouring his heart, he knew his words were enough. Bec had learned her lesson. The slap she'd given him was all emotion and reflex. He knew she didn't mean anything by it. All he had to do was wait until she was ready to apologize, which could take a day or two due to her unbelievable stubbornness. Until she did, he'd remind her what was good for her—him.

He looked at Eleni's flaccid body in front of him. Her back was rested up against the trunk of a palm tree, her hands resting lifelessly at her sides. Even in death, Eleni had to cause problems for him. He couldn't propose now. The whole weekend was ruined—tainted. Fucking hell. He never should have invited Eleni. He hadn't had an option though. She had too many of his secrets rolled up her sleeves. He couldn't get on her bad side. Better to keep your enemies close. But Eleni was gone now. His secrets were safe. He only had one thing to worry about—Bec. If anything could push her back towards him, it would be this. Fear was a great motivator.

Sniffles filled the void of silence. Tyler threw a sideways look at Adrian. He had been right. Those were tears brewing under Adrian's eyes. It seemed pitiful to Tyler but then again, Adrian deserved no sympathy from him. Adrian wasn't as innocent as he let on. If he wanted to cry for the woman who had strung him along—let him. Tyler felt his nerves prickling under his skin the longer he stood in the hot sun. The patience he'd graciously offered the group was growing thin. He knew this was only the beginning of an uncomfortable situation for them all. No one else was going to step up. It had to be him. There were things to be done and the most important one needed to happen now. Eleni had to be dealt with before the real decay set in. Yes, her body was growing as stiff as a board now but if they didn't do something with her before she bloated like a balloon, they'd be fucked. If the stench of her organs shutting down and rotting didn't overwhelm his friends, he knew the sight of her skin sliding off her bones like chicken wings sure would. He'd relish seeing the terror light up in some of their eyes, sure, but he'd prefer to save Bec that nightmare.

"We have a few options," Tyler announced, his voice jerking the group's focus away from the corpse in front of them. When none of them responded, he continued. "We can bury her or we can burn her."

Monique's eyes seared into Tyler with a mortified fury. She released her clutch of Benny's arm and marched towards him. "Did you really just suggest we burn her?"

Tyler could no longer hide his disdain. There was no need to save face and pretend that Monique didn't irritate him. Tyler knew as long as Benny was busy begging for forgiveness, decorum was off the table. Tyler glared at his best friend's wife before addressing everyone.

"That body is decaying," he said, gesturing down to the sand. "The heat out here isn't going to do us any favors. We can do something about it now or we can have the rot waft up to the house and hope animals don't come out of the jungle for a nice meal."

It was now Adrian's turn to look at Tyler with shock and disgust. "Her body," he corrected him. He wiped away the salted tears from where they had welled under his eyes. "Eleni."

Tyler scoffed. "That stopped being Eleni the minute her blood went cold."

"Oh, fuck you, Tyler!" Adrian snapped, squaring up to him. "How about pretending you have some fucking empathy for just a minute, huh?"

"I'll make sure to have some empathy tonight when you're puking your guts out because the entire island smells like death."

"Tyler."

Tyler met Bec's gaze quickly.

"Please," she said quietly. "Just stop."

A shiver of regret raced up his spine as he saw the terror on her face. But it wasn't just that. It was the way she was looking at him, or really, through him. She seemed only halfway present, like her mind was a million miles away. The look concerned him more than anything. Was she strong enough for this? Was what they were about to go through going to break her? His mind began to backpedal. He couldn't lose her before he'd even had a chance to get her back.

"Listen—" he began. "I know this is hard."

His eyes flashed to Miles, losing his train of thought for a minute. Miles was standing next to Bec. His presence was innocent enough but Tyler felt his chest tighten. In an instant, he pictured him all over Bec—his hands, his mouth. He imagined Bec's head rolling back in ecstasy, panting Miles' name. Tyler pushed the image away with a splitting bitterness. His jaw tightened as Miles looked back at him plainly, unaware of the movie that Tyler's mind had just played. Tyler tried to steady his building rage but it was hard when reality was so clearly painted in front of him. Bec hadn't made up her mind. If she had, she wouldn't have been standing there between them. She would have distanced herself from one and fallen into the arms of the other. Bec was still weighing her options. And Tyler couldn't help but feel that right now, Miles was in the lead.

"It's awful," Tyler continued, feeling the tinge of artificial sweetness on his tongue. "But we have to deal with this before it gets worse."

No one said anything. He realized he wasn't going to sway the group with logic alone.

"Think of Eleni."

A few eyes raised from the sand to meet his steady gaze. Tyler felt like he was giving a sales pitch. He just had to convince a few of them to convince them all.

"She wouldn't want to be like this—on display. She would want us to give her a proper burial."

Monique cocked her head at Tyler, an absurd look splashing across her face. "We're not burying her here," she scoffed. "What about her family?"

"You think they want her to rot on a beach?"

"We need to call the cops, man," Benny chimed in.

"Your phone working?" Tyler mocked him.

Benny grew silent, finding his way back next to Monique.

"I didn't think so," Tyler said. He addressed the group, his voice booming a little louder over the crash of waves. "And what do you think is going to happen? The Nicaraguan police are just going to handle it, no questions asked?"

"Wait, they're going to question us?" All the tears were gone from Adrian's eyes. He seemed jittery—panicked, even.

"How's everyone Spanish?" Tyler taunted him. Despite his parents being from Cuba, Tyler knew that Adrian didn't know a lick of Spanish other than: dos más cervezas, por favor. Adrian would be as fucked as the rest of his so-called friends. "Ready to be interrogated in a foreign country?"

Adrian seemed to shrink into himself. "Why would we be interrogated? We didn't do anything."

"That's a fucking dead body," Tyler scoffed, pointing to Eleni's brutalized corpse. "Look at her. She's been slaughtered like an animal."

Silence. The conversation hovered in a quiet limbo as Tyler's words were digested. The stillness seemed unbreakable the longer it went on.

"You think someone killed her?" Benny asked.

Adrian stepped up in front of the group. Tyler noticed his hand had a slight shake to it. "Eleni wasn't murdered."

"No?" Tyler quipped. "Then what happened, Adrian. Huh?"

"I don't—"

"Come on, look at her." Tyler shoved Adrian towards the body. It took everything in him not to force Adrian's head down to the ground to get up close and personal with it. "Really look at her. What do you think happened?"

Adrian's eyes barely glanced at the body. For a minute, Tyler thought he might puke all over the sand. "I don't know," his voice wavered.

"How could she have been murdered? We're the only ones here," Benny stated.

"And the staff," Stevie spoke up.

Tyler glanced at her curiously. The shock of what was happening seemed to be slowly shedding from her. Tyler didn't care for Stevie, not more than he needed to considering she was basically family to Bec. Regardless, he was glad to see at least one other person was capable of thinking critically.

"You've got to be kidding me?" Benny let an uncertain laugh loose from the back of his throat.

Stevie turned her gaze on him harshly. "Does this look like a joke to you?" she seethed, gesturing down at Eleni's body.

The amount of flies had doubled now, the smell drawing them in. Tyler noticed that everyone seemed to shift their weight every so often, slowly moving themselves farther from the dead thing that used to be their friend.

"How can you think she was murdered?" Benny argued. "That's ridiculous."

"Oh yeah, Einstein?" Stevie snapped, seeming to grow just as impatient with everyone's denial as Tyler was. "How do you think those stab wounds got there, then?"

Benny's eyes flashed between Stevie and the body but he refrained from saying anything more. It was like he was fighting the reality in front of him, desperate to deny it all. Tyler kept a sneer from slipping across his face. As of late, Benny seemed to be finding more and more ways to disappoint him.

"Let's say someone did kill her," Monique ventured cautiously. She looked around the group, meeting everyone's eyes one by one before continuing. "Who could have done this?"

"Why don't you tell us, Adrian?" Tyler probed. "You were the last one to see her, right?"

"I mean... You can't honestly think that I—"

"What if Stevie's right?"

Tyler glared at Miles. "You think the staff did it?"

Up until now, Miles had been silent, simply hovering at the back of the conversation like a vulture. Now that he'd spoken up, Tyler resented his presence. It wasn't just the fact that he'd managed to pry Bec away from him once. It was the fact that even now, Tyler knew he was eager to do it again.

"You have any better theories?"

"The staff couldn't have done this."

"Why?" Miles persisted. He took a step towards Tyler, his eyes gleaming now. "Because you paid them too much to disrupt your perfect little trip?"

Tyler fought to hold back his anger as Miles came toe to

toe with him. He could easily punch him in the face, make his nose gush red just like Miles had done to him last night. It was tempting but Tyler knew now wasn't the time. He'd find a way to even the score later.

"Because I vetted them. This place. Everything."

"And what?"

Tyler could see in the way Miles' eyes were lit up that he was purposely egging him on. Last night had changed things between them. There was no need for pretending anymore. They both wanted the same thing. Tyler knew what he was willing to do to keep Bec. But what would Miles be willing to do?

"You think a background check is enough proof that someone on this island didn't snap and take one of us out?" Miles continued.

"Maybe it wasn't the staff who snapped."

Miles sucked his teeth, considering it. "That's a fair point." He walked around Tyler until he was back next to Bec. Tyler didn't miss the way Miles' hand brushed up against hers. "Maybe someone got some bad news last night. So bad that they took it out on someone else."

"You fucking—"

"Stop."

Everyone looked at Bec. Her face was haunted as she glared at them. "Eleni is dead."

Tyler balled his hands into fists before forcing himself to take a step back. He shot her an apologetic look and offered his hands up peacefully.

"The sun is going down," Bec continued. Her eyes lingered on the painted glow of oranges and pinks that was setting above the ocean. "We need to do something."

Monique's brow furrowed as she followed Bec's gaze towards the horizon. "Bec's right. We can't just wait here for something to happen."

"Not to make this situation worse..." Stevie said as she crossed her arms in front of her chest. A breeze had picked up, sending a chill into the air, a prelude to the arrival of night that quickly approached. "But let's just say it wasn't the staff..."

Everyone seemed to cling to each word as it left her mouth.

"What if someone else did it," Stevie's eyes flickered nervously. "And what if that someone is still here, on the island?"

Tyler watched a few of them process what Stevie had just said. Monique's eyes darted around, searching the tree line while Benny stepped closer to her.

"We need to go," Miles' voice came out a little more than a whisper but pulled attention from the whole group. The concern on his face seemed to seep into everyone around him.

"Get back to the house. Now," Tyler commanded.

"What about Elen—"

"Leave it." Tyler's words pounced on Adrian. "Whether there's someone out here or not we need to get back to the house before it gets dark."

Without saying a word, Benny grabbed Monique's hand. He started walking up the beach, forcefully leading her towards the house. Tyler could hear her protesting but Benny kept tugging her hand along. Monique shot them all a look over her shoulder, a silent plea to join and follow them to safety. Tyler looked at Bec earnestly. An instinctual urge to protect her swelled inside him as he saw the apprehension in her eyes. He'd never seen her truly scared before and the sight of it now seemed to wash away all of the hurt and pain that had sunk into him like fangs.

"Come on," he said, gesturing to where Benny and Monique were already halfway up the beach. "We need to go."

She gave him a faint nod before complying. She walked past him quickly and coldly. Whether she still cared for him after their earlier altercation, he couldn't tell. The only sound of her retreat towards the house was the swish of her footsteps against the sand. The rest of the group followed quickly. The potential danger of their situation had seemed to still any opposing opinions for the time being. Even Miles walked past Tyler in silence. As the group trekked through the sand and headed towards the house, Tyler felt an uneasy feeling creep up the back of his neck. He turned to look back and in the fading light, he swore Eleni had turned her head to watch them go, the over-eager smile he knew so well plastered on her face.

✹ STEVIE ✹

"Locked. All of them," Stevie said to Tyler as she made her way back into the kitchen.

"Good," he replied curtly. His focus seemed to be everywhere all at once.

Stevie eyed the room. There were too many windows in the living room. It felt too open, too accessible. All it took was one rock through any of them and the house was no longer secure. They were safe for now, but she still felt on edge. Unknown to the others, Stevie had slipped a small paring knife from the kitchen into her pocket before inspecting all of the rooms. Even now, she grazed the edge of it with her fingers, making sure it was still there. Call it paranoia, but something about the house had seemed off when they'd returned. There was a tainted feeling in the air. So when she'd walked through all of the rooms, double checking the window locks, she'd clutched the little knife. Part of her kept expecting someone to burst from a dark closet or bathroom. No one had. As far as she could tell, the house was safe. Her gut clenched. Safe for now, at least. She watched Benny pace around the kitchen. He wasn't handling the situation like she'd expected him to. He'd practically bolted from the beach when she'd implied that there was a killer on the loose. And now that they were back at the house, it seemed like he might do something just as frantic. She wouldn't be surprised if he suggested they barricade all of the doors and windows with furniture. Stevie supposed that wouldn't be too bad. At least whoever killed Eleni couldn't get in through a broken window then.

Someone. Killed. Eleni.

That phrase had been swimming in her head since they'd found the body. The truth had been clear to her from the jump. She'd seen the aftermath of enough bar brawls to know what stab wounds looked like. She'd just never seen them on a dead body. When she and Bec had gathered the group, she'd tried to look at Eleni with ignorant eyes. Maybe it was an accident. Maybe it was suicide. Try as she might, she couldn't feign that much ignorance. There were four, maybe five stab wounds. The slit throat didn't make matters any better. And even if Stevie ignored the fact that Eleni had been brutalized, other evidence was harder to explain. There were deep trails in the sand around her body. Stevie wasn't sure if anyone else had realized their implications, but she had. Someone had dragged Eleni under that palm tree and propped her up to be found like that. It was no suicide. Which only left one answer.

"I can't believe we just left her out there."

Monique's voice was quiet, almost not making its way across the room to Stevie's ears. Stevie's chest tightened as she looked at her. Her eyes were glued to the kitchen tile floor, her presence as timid and lost as her voice. It was clear to Stevie that Monique was trying her best to keep it together but the fear swimming around her hazel eyes drove a hollow ache into Stevie's heart. She knew Monique was strong, but she also knew that Monique had a softer side that was just as powerful. She wasn't built for this—for death. Looking at her now, all Stevie wanted to do was hold her. If she could tell her everything would be all right, maybe she could stop the tears that were softly spilling from Monique's eyes. Stevie could comfort her, not just because she so desperately wanted to, but because she knew she was the only one who could truly do it. Did anyone here really know Monique better than she did? No—not in the slightest. Stevie doubted Benny knew half of the things that she knew. Hell, he didn't even know that she and Monique had been together. He was clueless. Stevie didn't know how much of that was truly Benny's fault. She could see in the way that Monique and he interacted that he had barely scratched the surface of who she truly was. Monique, the loving wife, seemed to be nothing but a role she was playing now. So many parts of her seemed to be missing when she was around Benny, parts Stevie knew intimately. Maybe if Stevie walked across the room and pulled her close, maybe—just maybe—she'd get a glimpse of the woman who had slipped out of the apartment to bring back coffee and bagels so many mornings. Just as Stevie moved her body forward, Benny stopped his pacing and draped his arm around Monique's shoulders.

"We didn't have a choice, babe."

Resentment prickled inside Stevie as she watched Benny kiss the side of Monique's head. Benny held his wife closely but Stevie wasn't watching him. She was watching the way Monique had shifted ever so slightly, creating the tiniest bit of space between them. As Monique raised her gaze from the floor, her eyes locked with Stevie's. Whether it was on purpose or an accident she wasn't sure, but the look in Monique's eyes caused her to swallow her anger. In its place, a vicious flicker of hope warmed Stevie's heart. There was a hesitancy in Monique's gaze, but it was more than that. Was it longing that lingered in her eyes? Stevie curbed the smile that threatened to dance across her face as she remembered what was happening. This wasn't about her and Monique. There would be time for that—after. She would make sure of it. Right now, this was about Eleni.

Stevie glanced across the room, feeling the dread and hesitation wash over her again as her eyes landed on Bec. Bec was leaning against the kitchen's island, staring off into space. There was a severe heaviness in her gaze that worried Stevie. Bec had barely spoken since they'd gotten back. She'd simply walked into the house and stood silently as everyone shuffled in. Even when Tyler had begun barking orders, she'd stayed fixed in place. Bec was like a ghost, there but not. Stevie knew this would happen. She had tried to stop Bec from seeing the body but Bec had been stubborn—so stupidly stubborn. Unlike Monique, Bec didn't meet Stevie's gaze. Instead, she seemed to let the stillness swallow her. Stevie hoped Bec wasn't repelling into the deep recesses of her mind where her nightmares lived. Stevie could protect Bec from a lot, but her past wasn't one of those things.

"We'll handle it in the morning," Tyler assured Monique.

"Her. Not it," Adrian said, raising his voice. "Why do you keep doing that? Dehumanizing her like that?"

"In case you haven't noticed, someone killed Eleni. We have bigger problems now..."

There it was—that phrase again. Except this time, it wasn't just stuck on a loop in Stevie's head. Someone had finally said it out loud. Stevie's eyes flashed to the sliding glass door. They'd turned on all of the outside lights. A soft glow was cast across the patio, daring to illuminate anything that might seek to sneak up on them. It was both comforting and chilling. But now as the sun fell lower beneath the horizon, the darkness seemed to creep closer to the house, slowly suffocating their visibility.

"...so stop worrying about what words I'm using and start worrying about what that means for us."

"This is ridiculous." Benny gave Tyler a dubious look, still embracing Monique in a gesture that looked more protective than romantic. "Is this a prank? Is this one of those old school murder mystery parties and we're supposed to figure out who 'killed' Eleni?"

Stevie's brow furrowed as his fingers motioned for air quotes. Did he really think this was a joke? If Benny didn't snap out of his denial soon, he'd just be deadweight for whatever came next. The thought sent a shudder through Stevie. What was coming next? She swallowed the thought like a lump in her throat but as she looked at the rest of the group, the pit in her stomach held steady. She didn't know when Bec would find her way back to them, but Stevie hoped it would be soon. Monique seemed to be coping better than Benny, but she had a nervous edge to her. Tyler had taken over as unappointed leader as soon as he'd seen the body. For now, he seemed to be playing that role well but what happened when he was all out of ideas? Stevie wasn't sure about Adrian. She'd been watching him closely ever since the beach. He'd seemed upset enough, but something about it bugged Stevie. It was like he was waiting for moments to be upset and lash out. But once those moments passed, he was nervous and jumpy. Stevie knew grief was different for everyone but she couldn't help but feel that he was hiding something behind the glimmer of fear in his eyes. But what was it? She watched him carefully as he sat on the kitchen counter, his legs fidgeting in the air like a child waiting at the doctor's office.

"She's dead," Tyler stressed. He had the same concerned look on his face that Stevie imagined was currently on her own. "This isn't a fucking game."

"So what?" Benny bellowed. "The more rational explanation is that one of us killed her?"

"Woah," Monique looked at Benny like he'd suggested she'd killed Eleni herself. "No one said that."

Stevie's gaze flashed back to Adrian as an uninvited thought popped into her mind.

"The staff left this morning," Benny rambled. "We're the only ones on this fucking island. And there's no boogeyman out there creeping around the jungle. We're off the coast, hours away from anyone else. No one is sailing out to a remote island to kill some random American."

"You didn't seem to think that theory was out of the question when you practically ran back to the house earlier," Miles added.

"I was thinking of my wife," Benny protested. "You'd understand that if you got a girl of your own instead of fucking someone else's."

Miles glared back at Benny silently. Stevie had to admit,

his restraint was impressive.

"What if they killed her last night?" Monique interjected. "Before they left."

"Could be," Tyler sighed.

"But?" Stevie prodded, sensing his disbelief.

Tyler ran a hand through his hair. "It just doesn't make sense to me."

"Why not?" Monique asked. "I can't be the only one that was a little afraid of Jamari...or Marta."

"What about the butler?" Stevie added, flashing her eyebrows at Monique. "It was the butler in the kitchen with a candlestick."

Monique shot her an annoyed look. "Seriously? This is a joke to you too now?"

"Sorry, sorry," Stevie offered, putting her hands up in front of her. "Just couldn't stand to see you sad for another second." Stevie looked at Monique, her eyes burning into her dangerously. She knew she was playing with fire, but she didn't care. Not anymore.

"For fuck's sake," Tyler said, shaking his head at them all.

This was killing him—Stevie could tell. He wanted to talk down to all of them, to tell them that they didn't know shit. But Stevie knew he wouldn't, not with Bec here. He would end up faking some sort of compassion and humanity like he'd done at the beach. He couldn't show his true colors anymore without looking like a heartless piece of shit. He'd already made that mistake when he'd suggested they burn Eleni's body. *Burn her?* Seriously? Stevie knew he wouldn't make a mistake like that again.

Tyler sighed, deep and heavy. "Let's say it was the staff," he conceded. "They're gone. We saw them leave."

Everyone seemed to agree on that as a silence floated through the room.

"So if they did it, there's no threat anymore."

"Until they come back." Stevie didn't mean for it to come out argumentative but she couldn't help it. The situation wasn't as simple as Tyler was making it out to be. Plus, she'd be damned if he was the voice of reason in all of this.

"Okay," Tyler grumbled. "So we make sure we're prepared for anything when they come back." He rubbed his hand along his jaw, tracing the stubble there as he thought. "But don't you think they would have stayed on the island and chopped us all up last night if they did kill her?"

He gave Stevie a subtle look that may as well have told her she was an idiot. Their distaste for each other had always been muted, pushed aside for the best interest of Bec. But now as that bridge between them had begun to crumble, their mutual animosity spit out from them like venom. Stevie's eyes tightened on him as he molded a look of concern on his face before turning back towards the group.

"Who knows what kind of headspace Eleni was in last night. For all we know she could have taken a knife for the kitchen and done that to—"

"No," Adrian spat harshly. "Fuck you, Tyler." He was off the counter now, storming over to the man who towered nine inches above him.

"Eleni didn't kill herself. She was fine when I left her. She was having a good time. She was okay. I mean—she was…" He'd started crying now, his emotions ripping through his body like water from a faucet. "Oh God, how did I let this happen?"

Monique stepped forward and wrapped her arm around him. "I agree with Adrian," she said. Her eyes seemed to dare Tyler to stand against her. "Eleni wouldn't have done that and looking at her body, that doesn't seem possible."

"I didn't know you had a medical degree," Tyler taunted.

"Have you ever heard of someone stabbing themself in the stomach?" Stevie retorted. "There's a reason it isn't common for suicide. Do you know how bad that would hurt? Let alone that strength and mental willpower it would take to do it multiple times? And what about the fucking slit in her throat?" Stevie let out a loud scoff before shaking her head at him. "No one is doing that to themselves. Especially not drunk."

"Fine," Tyler seethed. "Then what the fuck happened?"

"We're back where we started," Stevie snapped back. "Someone is on this island with us."

The group fell silent, considering what she had just said. Benny mumbled something to Monique. Tyler's jaw was clenched tightly as he chewed on Stevie's suggestion. She couldn't blame him for his skepticism, she didn't want to believe it either. She didn't want to believe that their vacation had turned into a nightmare. She didn't want to believe that there was some psycho out in the jungle, either fully satiated by his kill or plotting his next move. But when Stevie thought about it, that was better than the alternative. And the alternative wasn't something she was ready to give a voice to just yet.

"It makes sense," Monique said, breaking the silence. "Maybe someone was camping out on the island, living off the land or something. Someone isolated—not right in the head. They came across Eleni all alone, and..." She couldn't finish. She took a deep breath and looked at all of them with a grave steadiness. "It's the best explanation we've got."

"Okay," Tyler said crossly. "Let's pretend someone is on this island with us."

Stevie let her gaze drift back outside, into the dark of the night. It was crazy how in just a few hours, everything had changed. The energy of the very island had seemed to shift. Last night, she would have looked out at the jungle, draped in darkness, and been hit with a shudder of excitement. Now, a different feeling gripped her. It was the hesitation you got going through a haunted house. You didn't know what was coming but you knew it wasn't good.

"Adrian, Benny, Miles—" Tyler paused, looking at the three of them firmly. "We'll each take shifts tonight. Two hours each. We'll post ourselves in the kitchen and make sure nobody gets in this house. Agreed?"

"Totally," Benny replied quickly.

Adrian and Miles nodded in agreement.

"Then tomorrow we'll figure out what to do next."

Stevie wanted to argue with Tyler and ask why it was only the men who were keeping watch but she bit her tongue. They were past the time for arguments and petty differences. They needed to be united.

Tyler looked at Miles, a glimmer of hatred shining in his eyes. "Think you can manage to stand guard for a few hours without luring Bec to your bed?"

"Tyler!" Bec's focus ripped from her daze as shock and anger spread across her face.

"Yeah," Miles said steadily. He locked his eyes on Bec before stalking past Tyler. "But it's not my willpower I would worry about."

 BEC

The little food Bec had managed to eat sat unsteadily in her stomach.

For the past hour, they had all gone through the motions, trying to act normal but painfully aware of the missing presence in their group and the potential presence outside. Monique had taken the lead on cooking dinner since their half-cooked meal had wasted away on the counter. Breakfast for dinner was the consensus, with Stevie and Bec assisting Monique in the kitchen. While they cooked, the room stayed silent. Benny had stood at the counter, carefully watching over Monique as she scrambled eggs in a pan. Miles had sat on the sofa, his eyes occasionally meeting Bec's with their usual urgency and longing. Bec knew he wanted to talk but now wasn't the time. Her mind was spiraling, reeling back in on itself. So every time their gazes had crossed, she'd averted her eyes and busied herself with the task at hand. Tyler had stared out the window the entire time, his eyes fixed steadily on the black night that lied beyond the patio's border. And Adrian? Bec wasn't quite sure where he had been until dinner was served and he had shuffled out of the hallway.

Now as they ate, forks scraped plates lifelessly and collided with the dull sounds of steady chewing. Bec didn't know if everyone was still in shock or if they simply didn't know what to say. Whatever the cause, she welcomed the silence. It gave her an excuse to stay adrift in her thoughts. She didn't know what to say to the others, didn't know how to explain it all to them. Stevie would understand because she knew. She had been there to help Bec pick up the pieces when this had happened the first time. But the others? Bec found herself grinding her teeth tightly as she chewed. The others wouldn't understand. And if they did, they would understand one thing only—that Bec had brought this on all of them. Bec let her eyes glaze over as she stared down at her plate.

One. Two. Three. Four.

She stopped her train of thought but not before Eleni's beady, lifeless eyes flashed in her mind. She swallowed quickly. The desire to spit the food back up on the plate tugged at Bec's stomach. She closed her eyes, hoping the darkness would ground her, but it only made it worse. Five. Five stab wounds. Her mind flashed with images but they weren't of Eleni. They were of Brennen. Five wounds to the abdomen. Stab wounds. Brutal, gaping things. One slit across the throat. Deep. Fatal. Four words texted to her phone from a number she still knew by heart. *He can't have you.* Bec forced her eyes open as she felt her chest constricting in panic. She took a sharp breath, louder than she meant to.

"You good?"

Bec looked at Stevie, really looked at her. Bec searched her eyes for any sense of knowing, any sign that Stevie had come to the same conclusion after seeing Eleni's body. Bec looked, but didn't find anything but concern splayed across her friend's face.

"Yeah," Bec mumbled. "I'm fine."

Stevie's gaze hovered on Bec even after Bec turned away. For a minute, Bec thought Stevie had put it together. She was waiting for the murmured 'aha' moment, the fearful whisper that asked: is this happening again? But it didn't come. Stevie simply turned away and began eating once more. Bec had missed her opportunity and she felt a wave of regret wash over her. If this was happening, she couldn't get through it alone. She'd tried that last time and it hadn't worked. It had cost her everything. Bec stabbed a bite of scrambled egg with her fork as her mind spun dangerous webs. She swirled the fork in her hand, desperately hungry but also plagued by sickness. Would it stop with Eleni? She forced the bite of food to her mouth, chewing numbly, trying not to taste it. Why had he chosen Eleni? He. The thought of him perched in her mind like a gargoyle. He had done this. Right?

"What are we going to do?"

No one said anything.

"We can't just pretend something isn't happening," Monique continued.

Tyler wiped his mouth on a napkin and looked down the kitchen's island to face her. "We're not pretending anything," he said coolly. "We're taking shifts tonight. You'll be safe and then in the morning we can figure out what—"

"Fuck that," Stevie argued. "Eleni is dead. *Dead*," she stressed, as if trying to convince herself just as much as everyone else. "You can't expect us to go to bed without some sort of plan for what the fuck we're going to do next."

"I know today has been a lot, but if you just trust m—"

"Trust you?" Stevie laughed. "Your dream vacation has taken a turn, my guy. I don't trust you for shit." Stevie murmured something unsavory under her breath as she snatched a piece of toast off her plate.

As she chewed furiously, Bec slipped back into her thoughts. Eleni was dead. Was it really her fault or was she seeing ghosts where there weren't any?

"She's right."

Bec threw her eyes across the kitchen at Miles. He was leaning with his back against the fridge, his dinner plate balancing in his hand. He met her gaze expectantly.

"Oh yeah?" Tyler sniped.

"We need to do something."

"And what do you suggest, huh?"

"Anyone's phone working?" Miles asked.

Mumbles and head shakes around the kitchen confirmed that no one had gotten any service since they'd left the marina. A quick breath drew into Stevie's lungs, causing Bec to flinch in surprise.

"Holy shit!" Stevie gestured her hands wildly. "The phone."

"What are you on about?" Tyler said, gawking at her with annoyance.

"The fucking satellite phone!" she exclaimed. "Didn't Marta tell us there was someone else on the island who had a satellite phone in case something happened?"

Electricity seemed to pulse through the group as the same unspoken question flitted through their minds.

"The security guard," Miles murmured.

"Felix?" Adrian stated uncertainly.

"Do you think..." Monique began. "What if it was him?"

There was a pause that permeated the air like poison. The silence ticked away as they all considered it fully.

"If it was, I'll take care of him."

Bec's eyes flickered to Tyler. What did he mean exactly? Take care of him? It sounded like something out of an old mafia movie. She didn't like the heaviness that seemed to flow off of Tyler at that moment. Something had been off about him since last night. Different. Darker.

"We should go there tomorrow," Tyler stated.

"You want to go visit the killer?" Benny blew a long breath out of his mouth and chuckled softly. "This is some vacation."

"I don't think we all should go," Tyler said, throwing a glance at Bec. "The girls should stay here."

"Wow," Stevie sneered. "That doesn't seem misogynistic at all."

"Because I want you all to be safe?" Tyler snapped back.

"Because you think we need to be kept safe just because we're women."

Tyler gave her an incredulous laugh. "I didn't say that." He moved his eyes between Stevie and Bec. "I just don't want anything to happen to you. That's all."

Bec knew the comment was directed at her. She found

a sliver of comfort in Tyler's concern. Adrian had just lost Eleni so maybe Tyler was truly fearful of what might happen to her. But the words Tyler had spat at her in the jungle hung in the back of her mind like a vulture waiting to scavenge. He'd seemed to think so little of her then. Had all that hatred really left him in a few hours?

"How sweet," Stevie chimed in with a mocking tone. "And what if the killer comes here and butchers us all while you're off playing King of the Jungle?"

He seemed to consider it for a minute. "Fine." Tyler took a forkful of egg and pointed it at Stevie before taking the bite. "You, Miles, and Adrian will go." He chewed casually and swallowed. "Benny, Monique, Bec, and I will stay here and watch the house.

"Fine." Stevie leaned back in her chair and rested her hands behind her head. She dropped her voice to a breathy grumble that only made its way to Bec's ears. "I'll gladly risk running into a psycho if that means getting away from your narcissistic ass for a few hours."

Bec took a deep breath and shook her head softly. Stevie coped with humor, she knew that. But the thought of Stevie walking out into the jungle with a potential killer on the loose made Bec's skin prickle. She didn't like the idea of any of them going off into the jungle. If she was right, everyone was in danger—especially those she cared about most.

"Are we sure that's a good idea?" Bec pipped up. She chewed the inside of her cheek nervously as everyone's eyes flashed to her.

"She speaks," Benny teased.

"We need to try to get the satellite phone," Tyler stated. "It's the only way we're going to get help. Or else we're stuck here 'til Monday."

Bec nodded as she dropped her gaze. Once again, opportunity slipped by. It would have only taken ten seconds of courage to speak up, to let them know there was something they needed to know. But fear kept her silent.

"I'm going to take a lap around the house to make sure everything is good," Tyler announced, getting up from his seat.

"I'll come," Benny offered.

Tyler nodded to him and the two wandered out the patio door. Bec saw a small beam of light spark out from Tyler's phone as he turned on the flashlight function. It was good to know there was still some use they could get out of their phones. As the two men disappeared into the darkness, Bec felt a knot tighten in her gut. She might not know exactly how she felt about Tyler but the thought of him getting hurt made her stomach curdle. Everyone started moving around the kitchen, washing dishes and picking at leftovers in the pan. It was unsettling how normal it all seemed. Bec carried her plate to the sink but as she handed it to Stevie her focus was drawn away. Miles gestured for her to follow him before slinking down the hallway. Bec took a deep breath and fell into step behind him. As soon as they reached the privacy of the hallway, his hands were on her waist.

"Are you okay?"

Bec fought the urge to brush him away before Tyler saw. Did she even need to do that anymore? She hadn't told them, but she had made her decision. Hadn't she? Bec brushed the thought away and let herself melt into his touch. After everything that happened today, she needed a lick of comfort. She needed someone to help her feel like the world wasn't crumbling beneath her feet again.

"What do you think?" she said, no louder than a whisper. Bec kept her eyes low but felt the heat of his stare on her.

"Hey." His fingers traced the skin under her chin lightly before pushing it up and forcing her eyes to him. "It's going to be okay. I'm not going to let anything happen to you."

She offered up a half-hearted smile. She believed that he believed it, but it wasn't something he could really promise. He didn't know what was going on. None of them did. Even Bec, who was desperately trying to fit puzzle pieces from the past into the blurry array in front of her, didn't truly know what was going on.

"I can't do this ag—" Bec forced a calm breath from her lungs and wrapped her fingers into the fabric of Miles' shirt. "I'm scared, Miles."

"I know, baby. It's okay." He looked at her steadily, an almost peaceful look forming on his face. "Nothing bad is going to happen to you, not while I'm here."

He moved closer to her, pressing his body up against hers so that his breath was hot against her skin. Bec lifted her lips up to his but hesitated as the image of Eleni's bloodied tank top flashed through her mind. She tried to shake off the thought but the flakey, dried blood and the early stretch of death was all she could think about. She gave Miles' shirt a soft tug before stepping away from him.

"Thank you," she said softly.

She noted the flicker of uncertainty in his eyes as she headed back into the kitchen. Part of her wished she could stay in that hall with him, let him comfort her. She wished she wasn't on this island, in the middle of the mess she'd made. But more than anything, she wished she didn't carry the weight of Brennen's death on her back with every step she took. The weight of her guilt had lightened more and more as the years had passed but now she felt its weight again in full. It seemed to ache in her bones. As Eleni's body flashed in and out of her mind, Bec felt the weight of her too.

"Can I talk to you?"

Bec looked up, forcing herself from her thoughts. Tyler stood in front of her, hesitation riddled on his face. She furrowed her brow softly.

"Okay."

Tyler nodded before guiding her back into the hallway. Miles was gone now, hopefully in his room. Bec didn't want him to see Tyler leading her into the bedroom. She couldn't bear to see the look that would wash over his face. She took a deep breath as Tyler closed the door behind them.

He hesitated, his body seeming to float by the door. As Bec turned around to look at him, she felt his uneasiness cling to her.

"What did you want to talk about?"

"Our fight earlier."

Bec nodded softly but the rest of her body grew rigid with anticipation. "Yeah, we should probably talk about that."

"I'm sorry."

She tilted her head as she looked up at him. Gone was the Tyler that had belittled and provoked her. In its place was the Tyler she had fallen for. The fiery playfulness in his eyes had returned. There was even a quiver of a smile perched in the corner of his mouth. He was himself again, at least for now.

"Me too," she agreed.

"No," he continued. "You don't have anything to be sorry for. I was out of line."

Bec chewed on the inside of her cheek. "We both did things we regret."

He nodded, his hesitation quickly returning. It took a second before he stepped towards her. Slowly. Warily. His hand raised with the same caution. Bec watched him, her body tensing as he reached for her. She tried not to think about the knife slamming into her skull or the way the nightmare version of him had grinned wickedly while doing it. It was only when his fingers grazed her cheek tenderly that her body relaxed again.

"I don't know what's going to happen or if there's really someone out there, but I'd feel better if you slept here tonight."

"What?"

"It doesn't have to be—" He let out a deep sigh. "I'm going to worry the whole night if you're not next to me."

"You want me to stay here? With you?"

A quiet smile drifted out across his face. "Yes, with me."

Bec considered it. She knew she shouldn't give it a second thought. She had already made her decision. But when she looked into his eyes, she saw the offer of comfort—a comfort she still desperately needed. Fuck. She was going to regret this.

"Okay," she agreed.

The smile deepened on Tyler's face, causing his eyes to grow heavy with eagerness. "Good. Go get your stuff from Stevie's room. I have the first shift tonight but I'll be back in a few hours." He pulled her in close and kissed the top of her head before leaving the room.

Bec felt the regret sooner than expected. Miles. Shit. Miles was going to hate her after this. But nothing had to happen—nothing was going to happen. It was just a place to sleep. Nothing more. Just sleeping. She sat down on the bed with a heavy plop and dropped her head into her hands.

Bec, you idiot.

✻ BENNY ✻

2:37 a.m.

Benny gave the little glowing clock on the microwave a scowl like it felt like he'd been doing every ten minutes for the past hour and a half. He still had another twenty minutes of keeping watch over the house. The two hours he'd slept during Adrian's shift had done nothing but left his nerves fried and his body desperate for more. He blew a silent puff of air out from his lungs as he got up from where he was sitting in the kitchen and walked over to the living room. As he paced back and forth, careful to keep his footsteps quiet on the carpet so as to not wake everyone up, he felt foolish. Ever since they'd found Eleni, something had changed inside of him. He felt something gnawing at him, like one of the maggots that would soon be feasting on her body. He had been shoving it deeper and deeper into the recesses of his mind all night, but with nothing but his thoughts to keep him company now, he had to face that feeling. There was no mistaking it. It was fear.

It wasn't a feeling he was familiar with. All his life, he had been the type of guy others were wary of. He had grown almost a foot in eighth grade, towering over his classmates at 6'5". When he'd begun playing football in junior high, he'd slowly started packing on muscle. By college, he was built like the NFL player he'd come to be. Benny was, by all accounts, a force to be reckoned with. But he wasn't sick with worry about the possibility of a psycho hiding out in the jungle for his own safety. No, it was hers. Monique had seemed to float into his life like an angel when he'd needed her the most. She'd arrived just after his mom had passed and as the NFL career he'd dreamed about for so many years had begun to slip from his grasp. His world had started to gray at the edges. A few more months and the depression might have consumed him whole. Then Monique had arrived.

It had been before Bec introduced Benny to any of her friends—pure coincidence. He was on a plane back to LA when a woman had beamed a beautiful smile at him and gestured to the window seat beside him. He had gotten up quickly, eager to let her slide into her seat and—unbeknownst to him—change his life. It had only taken a few minutes for the conversation to flow between them. It was natural with Monique. Easy, even. It was like she was the piece of his soul he'd been missing. Now, he didn't know if he could survive without that piece.

He cast a look down the hallway that led to the bedrooms. He'd considered slipping back into their room about a dozen times. His mind drifted constantly to the window by the bed. What if it was open? He'd checked it before he'd started his shift but what if it wasn't locked anymore? What if someone smashed the window to get to her? The constant siege of thoughts left him more on edge than he had been the second before. If anything happened to her, he just might burn the entire island down to catch the fucker who did it.

Creak.

Benny froze. He turned around slowly, his eyes locking on the door on the back wall between the living room and kitchen. It was technically the front door, but with the way the house had been positioned in the clearing of the jungle, the sliding glass door was the one everyone had been using to get in and out. Benny had completely forgotten that the other door even existed until now. He took a few careful steps towards it, his eyes fighting through the darkness of the room until they arrived at their destination. The brass lock on the door was flipped to the right. Locked. The tight feeling of panic in his chest loosened, but only for a second.

Creak.

He stopped moving again. Benny did nothing but listen for a full minute, the soft rustling of the jungle outside filling his ears. He thought he could hear the muffled screams of monkeys in the distance. It sounded like they were being hunted—but by what? He tried to still his heavy breathing in order to hear the noise again. It sounded like someone was on the back porch. He'd noticed it on his perimeter walk with Tyler. The porch was connected to the back house by a short path. The back house was where Marta, Ramon, and Jamari had been staying. He leaned forward on the balls of his feet. What if they were out there now? What if they had come back? He knew it wasn't a rational thought but the stress of the day tugged at his tired brain incessantly. Benny stepped forward silently until his feet rested at the base of the door. In a haze of panic and curiosity, his body took over. He didn't even know what he was doing until his hand had already flipped the lock and turned the knob. As he pulled the door open, his heart leapt into his stomach. The flash of black against the dark of the night was quick. He almost missed the small animal scurry off the porch, frightened by his looming figure. Goddamnit. He had been ready to chase down and tackle a fucking—*What had that even been?* A monkey? Benny let out a breathy laugh as he rested against the doorframe.

"Looking for the killer?"

Benny flinched and whipped around just in time to see the wicked grin slide onto Miles' face.

"Fuck," he muttered.

He closed the door and flipped the lock with a solid click. As he turned back towards Miles, his heart was still pounding through his veins.

"Don't tell me I scared you?"

Benny ignored him and instead looked at the blue glow of

the microwave. It was 2:49 a.m.

"You're early."

Miles slid onto one of the kitchen barstools and shrugged.

"Didn't want to be late. Like you said, I have someone else's girlfriend to worry about." He cracked his neck, the tension releasing with a quiet pop. "Can't expect Tyler to look out for her when he doesn't even know whose bed she's in half the time."

Heat rose inside Benny's chest as he glared at Miles. He clenched his teeth together, trying to stave off the chain of insults and fury that was beading on his tongue. It took him a second and a deep breath to regain his composure.

"You know what, man? I was really hoping this was going to work out differently. The whole Bec thing..." He shook his head, not able to keep the distaste from slipping onto his face. "I was ready to cut you some slack and chalk it up to bad decisions. I wanted to be your friend. I really did. But now?" Benny chuckled. It came out in a sick and tired puff of air. "You're still trying to fuck his girl. It's pathetic. Really, man it is. I feel bad for you."

The muscles in Miles' jaw clenched oh-so-slightly. "Feel bad for me?" he quipped, trying to laugh it off. "And why's that?"

"Because you're just a mistake she made." Benny said smugly as he walked past him. "Even now, you're out here by yourself and she's back where she belongs—in bed with him."

No response. Benny glanced back, happy to see a prickle of confusion across Miles' face.

"Oh, you didn't know?" he smirked, relishing the moment. "Sounds like you're the one who doesn't know whose bed she's in."

SUNDAY

⚔ TYLER ⚔

The smell of vanilla and plums wafted into Tyler's nose as he woke up. It took him a minute to understand where it was coming from. When he finally emerged from the fog of sleep, a smile drifted across his face.

His hand snaked around Bec's hips and he pulled her towards him. Her body fit into his perfectly. Every curve molded against him with its soft warmth. He still couldn't believe he had convinced her to sleep in their room last night. But, like he'd anticipated, fear was convincing. He felt her slowly wake, her body stirring against his. He dug his fingers into her skin greedily as he nuzzled his face into the crook of her neck.

"Good morning," he cooed.

She didn't say anything, but her body stilled against his voice. Tyler imagined her drifting back to sleep, safe and secure in his arms. He closed his eyes and let himself relish the moment. He took in another breath. Sweet. Warm. He'd recognize her blind. The perfume she wore everyday never seemed to leave her pores. He pulled her in tighter. He could feel her heartbeat now. It pounded lightly through her veins, growing steadier. Faster. If he had it his way, they'd stay in bed like this all day. They'd forget everything: the cheating, the fighting, Miles, Eleni. None of it mattered. All that mattered was getting back to the way things were. The way they were supposed to be.

The stir of bedsheets jerked him back to reality. The peace he'd felt was snatched too soon as Bec began to disconnect her body from his. He reached after her desperately, pulling her back towards him before shifting his weight so he was on top of her.

"What are you doing?"

She looked at him blankly, almost confused. Tyler looked back at her with nothing but need.

"What does it look like I'm doing?" Tyler smirked before planting kisses from Bec's neck down to her collarbones.

He felt her body arch into his as he slipped a hand under her shirt. She still wanted him. He could tell. The realization seemed to wake him up like a cup of coffee. He looked down at her with hungry eyes before moving his mouth to hers. She returned the kiss softly at first, almost hesitantly. Tyler wrapped his hand around her throat as he kissed her. His mind flickered back to the other night on the beach. The anger he'd felt when he gripped her neck. The way she'd looked at him with fearful eyes. He knew it was wrong, but it had felt so good. The power. The control. Even now, as he gripped her throat tighter, he felt that power wash over him. He'd make her forget Miles. Whatever had caused her to stray, he'd make sure it never happened again. Tyler felt her pulse thump under her skin. A fleeting look of fear filled her eyes. *Too tight.* He loosened his grip on her throat as he planted heavy kisses on her neck. He tugged at her pajama shorts feverishly. He wanted her more than he wanted anything else right now. Wanted to claim what was his. His fingers slid under the waistband of her shorts.

"Tyler, stop."

The words seemed to slice into him. He was wrong. She didn't want him.

"What do you mean, stop?"

He sounded angrier than he wanted to, but only because he knew exactly what she meant. Tyler rolled off of her, letting her go. She scooted out from under him and got out of bed, readjusting her tank top. She refused to look him in the eyes.

"We can't."

Tyler let out a less-than-enthused laugh in a huff as he got out of bed. "Why the fuck not?"

He was truly angry now. He didn't care if she knew it. After all of the bullshit she'd thrown his way, he couldn't take this too. He watched her fumble for the answer. It didn't matter though, he knew what it was—who it was.

"Because of him, right?" Tyler spat. He didn't wait for her response. Instead, he stomped over to her and placed both hands on the side of her face.

"You're a fucking idiot, Bec." His words seemed to spray from his lips like fire. "You think Miles is a good guy? That he'll treat you better than me?" He let out a snarky laugh and pushed her face away from him. "He can't offer you half of what I can. If you pick him, you'll continue to live a miserable fucking existence and regret it your whole life."

She looked back at him in shock, her face growing pale. He knew he should stop. He knew he should walk away right now. He should give himself time to calm down before he truly fucked this up for good. Judging by the alarm in her eyes, the same flash of fear he'd seen in the jungle yesterday, he was only moments away from that. But it was hard to stop—especially when all he could think about was whether Bec ever told Miles no. Tyler threw his hand up in the air as he paced around the room.

"Why are you doing this to me, Bec? Huh? Do you enjoy torturing me?"

He leaned his hand against the dresser and dropped his head down. His jaw was clenched so tightly he thought it might shatter. "Get out."

"Tyler, I—"

"Get out," he yelled, louder this time. His voice carried across the room with a vicious boom. He heard her moving quickly behind him. He hoped she would cry. He wanted her to get down on her knees in front of him and beg for his forgiveness. Then maybe the rancid part of his heart would start to heal. When he heard the sound of the door shimmying open, he felt his insides continue to rot. As Bec shut the door behind her, a wave of fury and regret ripped through Tyler.

"Fuck!"

He slammed his fist on top of the dresser with a violent thud. The skin scraped off his knuckles, causing tiny drops of blood to pepper the broken skin. He closed his eyes and tried to calm his breathing. Forget her. Forget him. The more he tried, the harder it seemed. Bec was burrowed deep in his mind. He gave the dresser a heavy shove, rattling it against the wall. This wasn't over. Somehow, he was going to get what he wanted. And more importantly, he was going to make sure that when this trip was over, Bec wanted nothing to do with Miles.

✒ BEC ✒

Bec heard the bang behind her as she closed the door. She knew he was pissed, that much was obvious. She couldn't even blame him. If she had just broken things off with him the other night—or better yet, months ago—she would have undoubtedly lessened the amount of pain Tyler was being forced to go through now. But no, she had been selfish—stupid, even. And now, she knew she was only doing more damage.

Bec hurried down the hallway as another loud noise came from behind the bedroom door. It sounded like he was tearing the place apart. She tried not to think about it as she stepped out into the kitchen. *You've got to be kidding me.* She thought about retreating to Stevie's room but it was too late. He had already seen her. Miles looked her up and down slowly before a gruff laugh left his throat.

"I see he didn't even give you a chance to get dressed before he threw his first tantrum of the day."

Bec looked down at herself, suddenly feeling exposed. The tank top she'd slept in was slightly stretched out from Tyler's greedy hands. Her shorts weren't any better. The tiny cotton pair hung high on her hips, failing to cover much. She wrapped her arms across her chest as the chill of the morning and her embarrassment snaked up her skin.

A smile flickered at the edge of Miles' mouth. "Nothing I haven't seen before."

"Thanks for reminding me," she muttered as she made her way across the kitchen. As she reached her hand out towards the fridge, his voice stopped her.

"You don't deserve it, you know."

Bec hesitated, taking in his words before looking over her shoulder.

"To be treated like that," he said, gesturing towards the bedrooms. "You don't deserve it."

She tried to read the emotions on his face but all she could see was quiet composure. He was the opposite of everything Tyler had just displayed in the bedroom.

"How much did you hear?"

"Enough."

Discomfort rocked in the basin of Bec's stomach. If Miles had heard, that meant everyone in the house probably had too. If Eleni were here, she'd be having a field day with everything she'd just overheard. Bec's stomach dropped further when she realized she was speaking about the dead.

"I'm pretty sure I'm getting exactly what I deserve," she mumbled.

Bec bit down hard on the inside of her cheek. She let her eyes wander through the contents of the fridge as she fought back tears. She did deserve it. All of it. More than Miles or anyone else even understood.

"Why are you still with him?"

The question caught Bec off guard. Her brow furrowed slightly as she turned to look at him. "I'm not. I was just..." She drew in a wobbly breath through her lungs, suddenly dropping all of the tension from her face. "I'm not with him anymore."

"Does he know that?" He stared her down, his eyes growing darker as he spoke. "Probably not, since you decided to sleep with him again."

"I didn't sle—" Bec stopped herself. "You know what—I don't need to explain myself."

"So what, then?" he challenged her. "I'm just supposed to believe nothing has changed? That I'm back to being the thing you play with when you're bored?"

"What? No. I—"

"Then tell me. Help me understand."

He held her gaze steadily. His eyes seemed to eat at every inch of her with contempt. It flared something delirious inside of Bec. He couldn't be mad at her, not after everything she'd already fucked up to have him.

"You want me to explain myself?" she retorted. "Fine." She shot back the same hateful look he was still boring into her. "In the past 48 hours, my boyfriend has found out we slept together, you two literally beat the shit out of each other, and now our friend is dead. *Killed.* And you want to know why I'm making dumb decisions?" Her nails dug into her palms as she tried to contain herself. "What would make you feel better, Miles? To hear that I didn't have sex with him? If it wasn't made obvious by Tyler screaming at me this morning—I didn't."

She raised her eyebrows at him, forcing the point home. The anger had slipped from his face but Bec didn't care. Hers was still squirming under her skin. "I know everyone thinks all I seem to do is ruin my life but we have bigger problems now," she scoffed. Bec turned away and snatched a water bottle out of the fridge. "So give me a fucking break."

As Bec snapped the cap off the bottle she heard Miles move. The barstool scooted against the tile floor harshly. She kept her gaze on the inside of the fridge as she drank. She thought he had gone back to his room when she set the half-drunk water back in the fridge and closed the door. Her body jolted as she turned around and found his face inches from her own.

"Fuck, you scared me," she grumbled. She waited for him to move around her but he didn't.

"I'm sorry."

She rolled her eyes and stared him down. He'd have to do better than that.

"I know—" He took a moment and ran a hand through his messy curls. "I know this is a lot. I know this isn't the time for any of this but I'm dying here. Seeing you with him?"

His jaw clenched but he shook the anger away. "It's fucking killing me."

Bec's breath caught in her throat as she saw the anguish in his eyes. She had told herself Miles would always be all right. He was a guy. Guys didn't really care. She swallowed the lump of emotions at the back of her throat.

"I don't want to hurt you," she mumbled.

"Then don't."

Miles wrapped his fingers around her waist, bringing her closer. He looked at her before dropping his gaze to her lips. She silently pleaded for him to kiss her, to take the fear and hesitation away from her. But as he leaned in, Bec's mind slipped into the dark. She thought of Eleni, then Brennen, then the person who had caused all of that suffering. Her body tensed. She pressed her hand against Miles' chest and pushed him away as softly as she could.

"It's inevitable," she said. "Being with me, getting hurt." She blinked back frustrated tears and pulled away from him. "Nothing good comes from loving me."

His brow furrowed as she turned to walk away. Before she could retreat into the living room, he reached out and tugged her wrist back gently.

"I know you think that, but it's not true."

She couldn't bear to look at him anymore, not when he met her gaze with such certainty. He had no idea what he was saying. No idea the pain she had caused long before Miles or Tyler ever showed up into her life. She was broken, cursed, fucked up. She had come to terms with it a long time ago. She hadn't been able to save Brennen, but she could save Miles.

"Let me go."

His hand had already left her wrist but that wasn't what they were talking about.

"No."

"Goddamnit, Miles," she huffed. "I can't lose you, too."

"You won't."

"You really want to bet your life on that?"

He looked at her curiously but his faith didn't waver. He looked too sure of himself, ready to risk it all. It drove Bec mad. He was being an idiot. He didn't know what he was saying—what fate he was sealing himself to. She wanted to yell at him and demand he leave her alone but she couldn't. All she could manage to do was wrap her fingers up into his hair. She played with a rogue curl as her breath released unsteadily from her lungs.

"Please—don't let me lose you."

He smiled, both hands wrapping around her waist and holding her tight. "You couldn't lose me if you tried."

"Maybe talk a little louder so Eleni can hear you."

Bec whipped her head towards the hallway. Tyler was leaned up against the wall, the fury in his eyes venomous.

"What is wrong with you?" she breathed.

The words were meant for Tyler but she couldn't help but feel the pressure of the question inside her own chest. When would she stop hurting people? Bec shook her head as she stepped away from Miles. She headed for the patio, stopping at the locked sliding glass door. She hovered there, eyes fixed on the grass that was still fresh with dew. She shouldn't go outside. None of them knew what was going on. It was better to be safe, to stay inside and endure the unbearable situation she had created for herself. No, fuck that. She flipped the lock and gripped the door handle firmly, then she stepped out onto the patio and into the soft, morning light that filtered across the island. As she turned to shut the door behind her, both men eyed her restlessly. Before either of them could stop her, she turned on her heels and headed across the lawn.

⸗ MONIQUE ⸗

A small waft of smoke drifted from the stove. She needed more oil.

Monique pushed the pieces of potato around the pan. They quickly absorbed the fresh oil that glistened and sizzled against the heat. Her stomach growled loudly. She'd barely eaten anything last night, she'd been too on edge. Even now, she felt as though her stomach might slide up and out her mouth at any minute. But as much as the thought of filling her stomach made her queasy, she knew she'd need the energy for today—whatever today brought. She began cracking eggs in a separate pan.

Crack. Sizzle. Crack. Sizzle.

The repetition almost seemed to lull her into a trance. For a second, she was far away. She forgot what was happening and stopped thinking about what might happen. She was safe. It was only when Benny's hand threaded around her waist that she was quickly pulled from peaceful disassociation. Her hand flinched, tossing some pieces of scrambled egg onto the cooktop.

"Christ, Benjamin! You scared me." Monique swatted Benny's hand lightly with the spatula as he snuck a piece of potato out of the pan. "Get out of here and wait for everything to be done cooking."

Benny dug his fingers into her side playfully. "Oh come on," he teased. "Feed me a bite of those eggs. No one's looking."

She ignored him and continued stirring the food around the pan.

Benny sighed and dropped his hands from her waist. "Fine. At least let me help with something."

"Grab those vegetables and cut them into little pieces," she said, nodding her head back towards the counter.

"Yes, ma'am," Benny said.

He planted a quick kiss on Monique's cheek before getting to work. Monique smiled but kept her focus on cooking. They needed food, but even more than that they needed something familiar, something ordinary. She might not be able to take down some psycho, if there was one, but she could at least make sure everyone was properly fed.

"Uhhh…"

She barely registered the tone of confusion from Benny.

"Babe, are you using one of the knives?"

She barely turned, her hands still busy in the pan. "No, why?"

Benny took a small step to the side and gestured to the blocky wooden knife holder that sat on the kitchen counter. "There's one missing."

A chill seemed to wind its way up Monique's spine until it teased the base of her neck. She stared at the knives for a few seconds before pulling her eyes away. She shook her head lightly and she added some shredded cheese to the eggs.

"It was probably missing this whole time."

She could taste the lie as the words left her mouth. If there was anything she'd learned about Marta in the past few days, it was that the woman ran an orderly house. There was no way she would have let one of the knives be misplaced. Monique threw a quick look back at Benny. He had started chopping mushrooms and green onions into somewhat uniform pieces. Her eyes hovered on the knife in his hand as the blade cut through the vegetables one after the other.

Chop. Chop. Chop.

She wondered if the blade had slid into Eleni that easily. The thought overtook her for a second, startling her. She dropped the spatula in the pan and pushed her hands over her eyes. Disgust wound tightly around her insides as the image of Eleni's blood-stained tank top flooded her mind. She had been stabbed so many times. How does someone do that to another person? Nausea rolled in Monique's stomach again. She forced a few quiet breaths through her nose as she tried to repel it. The smell of burning plastic made her eyes shoot open.

"Goddamn," she cursed as she pulled the half-melted spatula handle away from the pan's lip.

She tossed it in the sink as a few more curse words dripped from her lips in a hushed babble. Her mother would have called on Jesus Christ himself if she heard half of them. The smell hovered in the air, despite Monique's best attempt to dissipate the lingering stretch by waving around a kitchen towel. Lord, what a morning. Benny dropped the veggies he'd cut into the pan and watched while Monique stirred them in with the potatoes.

"Babe," he said softly into her ear.

She kept her eyes on the pan. "Hmm?"

"You know we're gonna be okay, right?"

Her head nodded up and down slowly, like a seesaw. She truly didn't know if she believed it, but she knew any objection would only wake up the distress she'd witnessed in him yesterday.

"Call everyone to eat, yeah?"

"Hey, everyon—"

Monique's gaze burned into him playfully as he yelled across the kitchen. "Seriously?"

"Come eat," he continued, beaming down at his wife with a mischievous grin. "It's hot and ready."

He slapped her on the ass and dashed away before she could raise the spatula up to smack him. She let out a small laugh but quickly stifled it as she watched the others gather. It felt too out of place. Too normal. A few words passed between Adrian, Stevie and Miles as they got up and headed towards the wafting smell of food.

Monique's eyes flickered past the patio door. Tyler was sitting in one of the wicker chairs, his eyes fixed stoically on the jungle. Uneasiness bubbled in Monique's stomach as she watched him.

"She's not back yet?" Monique asked Stevie, who'd sat down at the counter.

Stevie shook her head softly. "No."

"This is stupid," Monique replied as she began scooping heaps of food onto plates. "She shouldn't have gone off by herself, not with..." She couldn't get the rest of the words out. She took a sharp breath as she slammed a pile of eggs onto Stevie's plate. "Someone needs to go find her."

"She's fine," Miles said as he took a plate from Monique.

Monique locked eyes with him as the plate left her hand. "How do you know?"

He gave her a heavy look. Was he as worried as she was? "Because she just is. Okay?"

"Wow, I feel so much better now. Thanks." Monique stopped herself from rolling her eyes, settling for a scornful glare instead.

"Look—" Miles sighed. "She's smart. I'm sure she didn't wander off too far."

Monique cocked her head at him as she handed a plate to Adrian. "So what? You got her and now you don't care?" She huffed, tossing the spatula into the pan after plating the rest of the food. "Who cares if some freak is out there killing Bec, at least you got to fuck her, right?"

"Don't you ever—"

"Woah, let's just take it easy, okay?" Stevie said.

They both ignored her. Miles' jaw clenched as he looked at Monique.

"She is the only person I give a shit about on this island," he quipped. "I would never let anything happen to her." He forced out a deep breath, dropping the tension riddled in his face. "Look—we don't know what's going on, or if there even is anybody out there. I'm not going to treat her like a child just because we're all on edge. If she's not back in ten minutes, I'll go get her. Okay?"

The statement drove a mumble from Stevie's lips that Monique didn't quite catch. Monique wanted to argue with Miles. Not because she didn't agree with what he'd just said but because she needed to let out the apprehension she was currently bottling up. She felt like any more of it and she might throw up. Instead, she merely nodded at him.

"Come on, babe. Don't stress about it, okay?" Benny said, leaning into her. "It's daytime. There are no shadows to lurk in. I'm sure she's fine."

Benny patted Monique on the back. The gesture felt like he was trying to reign her in more than comfort her. She shook her head as she grabbed a plate for herself and began eating where she stood. The truth was Bec could walk through the door at any minute, having taken nothing more than a leisurely stroll. Except Monique knew it hadn't just been that. She'd heard the yelling from Tyler and Bec's room this morning. While most of the words had been muffled, the general sentiment had been clear. Tyler was still angry. She couldn't blame him for being angry. Lord knows she would yell until her head popped off if Benny ever cheated on her. But, even if Eleni's death was a freak accident, which felt foolishly naive, Monique knew there was a time and place to handle indiscretions such as Bec's. And now wasn't the time to work through relationship issues. Monique cast a look outside. Tyler was still sitting in the chair, eyes glued to the jungle. She nudged Benny with her elbow.

"Go get him, please."

"He's not going to come in until she's back. I already tried."

Her eyes widened at him impatiently. "Then tell him to get in the jungle and find her," she ordered.

Just as Benny began to walk across the kitchen to do as Monique asked, Tyler stirred in his seat. He got up quickly but stayed where he was on the patio. Monique caught sight of Bec as soon as she stepped onto the lawn. A sigh of relief left her chest. She quickly grabbed Bec's plate and set it in the microwave for thirty seconds. The humming from the appliance drowned out the short conversation between Tyler and Bec. As Tyler threw his hands up in the air, the microwave beeped loudly.

"You don't want to listen..." Bec's voice drifted into the house as she stepped through the threshold.

"I'm fucking listening," Tyler snapped as he followed her inside.

Bec's eyes swept through the room. Monique could tell she was overwhelmed. She held the plate out to her with a soft smile.

"Careful, it's hot."

A wave of gratitude filled Bec's red-rimmed eyes. "Thank you," she said with a soft breath. She took the plate and sat down next to Stevie who punched her arm playfully.

"Maybe don't run off into the jungle next time these guys are being jackasses. Okay?"

"Sorry," Bec whispered, giving her best friend a guilty look. "This whole thing is just—I needed a walk."

"We'll go with you next time, yeah?" Monique offered.

Bec smiled back at her and nodded.

Tyler walked around the kitchen's island and grabbed his plate off the counter.

"When are you two leaving?" he asked harshly, gesturing towards Miles and Adrian with a forkful of food.

"Hello?" Stevie said, wavering her hand in front of her. "Three, remember?"

"Yeah," Tyler rolled his eyes. "So?"

"Once we're done eating we'll head out," Miles said steadily.

"Are we sure this is a good idea?"

Everyone's attention pulled towards Monique.

"I don't like the idea of us splitting up."

"What if we all wen—" Adrian stated.

"No," Tyler barked, casting a heavy look over all of them. "If someone else is on this island, we can't give up the house."

Monique thought the notion was dramatic. Why would someone take the house while they were gone? This wasn't some game of capture the flag. If someone was out there, she was sure they'd rather trap them in the house to pick them off one by one rather than kick them out of it. The idea set her teeth on edge. Maybe they shouldn't be in the house at all. They were like sitting ducks here. She bit her tongue and kept her thoughts to herself. There was no convincing Tyler of anything. All she could do now was try to be helpful.

"Do you want me to pack up some food really quick? In case the walk is farther than you think?"

"They'll be fine," Tyler said dismissively. "You should leave now." His focus was solely on Miles now. "Before it gets too hot."

Monique knew Tyler couldn't care less if the trio baked in the heat. With Miles out of the picture for a few hours, Tyler would have all of the alone time he needed to fight with Bec. Monique took a deep breath and looked at Stevie and the two men.

"Be careful, okay?"

"We'll be back before you know it." Stevie grinned before stuffing one last bite into her mouth.

/ ADRIAN /

Adrian hated everything about this recon mission he'd been tasked with. He would have much rather stayed back at the house to play babysitter while Tyler sweated his ass off instead. But no—like always, Tyler had convinced everyone that he knew best.

As beads of sweat grew on Adrian's chest and bled through his shirt, he wondered why Tyler had picked him and Miles to head off into the jungle. If there was a satellite phone at the guard shack, wouldn't Tyler want to be the one to retrieve it and play the hero? Adrian scowled as he imagined Tyler on some stupid podcast, talking about how he'd saved his friends from a killer. God, Adrian hated him. Not just because Tyler was an arrogant piece of shit. He hated Tyler for everything that he had. Money. Women. Power. Adrian just wanted a nibble of it. He deserved it. He hadn't worked his ass off, balancing multiple jobs all throughout high school and college, just to watch some spoon-fed asshole be handed everything he wanted. He clenched his teeth and wiped a hefty bead of sweat from his forehead. Adrian wasn't asking for much. Money. He could check that off the list. He had stashed away a good deal of money thanks to Tyler's lack of awareness for his own. Power. That would be the last thing to come to him, the hardest to achieve. Women? A deep breath rattled from his lungs as the trail steepened. He had almost had Eleni. His stomach lurched as he replayed the other night in his head. The thought of her wrapped around him drove a toxic mixture of horniness and guilt through him. The guilt was stronger and spread over him like hives. He shouldn't have done it. No matter how badly he had wanted her, he shouldn't have done it. A patch of mud squelched under Adrian's sneaker. Maybe if he hadn't, she would still be alive. Guilt itched at his swollen, hot skin. How long had he been walking for? An hour? It didn't matter. He couldn't take it anymore.

"How much further?" he called up ahead.

"How the fuck should we know?" Stevie laughed. "The shitty map that Marta left said it was a little over three and a half miles to the guard shack." She looked back at Adrian and gestured to his wrist. "That fancy watch of yours tell you how fast we're walking?"

Adrian wiped a bead of sweat off of his brow just before it dripped into his eye. He scowled at Stevie as she turned back around. She was treating all of this like some sort of adventure. Even now, she bounded up the trail to catch up to Miles. It was like she was barely fazed, by the heat or their circumstances. Angry grunts erupted from Adrian as he walked into a spider web. He thrashed around wildly, tearing the thin strands of web from his body.

"Fuck!" he yelled, his frustration boiling over.

Stevie shot a look back, a smile curling on her face. "You don't make it outside a lot, do you?"

"What's that supposed to mean?"

She shrugged and kept walking. "You just seem like the type who would rather we vacationed at a club in Dubai."

He wanted to hurl a retort her way but he couldn't think of one in time. Besides, she was exactly right. He would have much rather been drinking his bodyweight in vodka at a beach club than bushwalking his way through the jungle in search of some shack. This whole trip was seriously fucked. He was fucked. If only he had been the man he wished he could be, then this trip might not have been the absolute pit of misery it was turning into. Adrian's mind drifted as the path leveled out and his strides grew less strenuous. He thought about the first time he'd seen Eleni. It had been at one of Bec's art shows last year. Tyler had dragged all of them out in support of Bec. Adrian even remembered when Tyler had invited him. He'd come in for his usual appointment, wanting to chat about next year's investments. The art show was later that night and Tyler had insisted that Adrian go. Adrian knew it wasn't about who went, it was about appearances. Bec was dating Tyler, therefore everything she did was now attached to him. Tyler cared about his own image, nothing more. Before Adrian knew it, Tyler had meandered through the office, chatting up anyone he saw to invite them to the show. An unsightly bout of jealousy had struck Adrian then. As he had watched Tyler socialize with his coworkers and even his boss, he realized that Tyler was everything Adrian wished he could be. Wealthy, confident, a magnet for women. There seemed to be nothing Tyler wanted that he couldn't get.

That had been the day that Adrian decided to steal from his friend. Nothing major, just a little here and a little there. A little doctoring of the reports, no more than losses from trades that proved a little too risky. It had been easy to convince Tyler that not every investment turned out how they hoped. Tyler had so much money, it was barely a ripple in an ocean. The hardest part had been keeping the books clean. But now, after a few months of planning and seven of lining his own pockets, no one was the wiser. Aside from the disdain that had grown to new heights since then, Adrian did owe Tyler one thing—that art show. Adrian had been annoyed to be there at first. He'd grabbed a glass of red wine and roamed around the gallery aimlessly. It was only when he'd walked up to a certain print that everything had changed. It was a black and white photograph, striking in its detail and composition. But even more striking was the woman in the picture herself. He had stared at it, awestruck, until someone eventually joined him. "Pretty, huh?" the voice had said. When he had turned around, his stomach had dropped what felt like thirteen stories. The woman from the photo had stared back at him, a sultry look glazing her angelic face. That had been it. After that night, Adrian was completely and utterly in love with Eleni. For better or for worse, he had been hooked.

As his feet snagged on a thick path of vines that snaked across the trail, Adrian's mind shot out of its dreamy reminiscence. Eleni was gone. Eleni was gone and he had played a part in that. Pain and guilt rose up inside of him, but so did something else. He let his mind play out all of the times that Eleni had rejected him in front of the group only to flirt with him in private. Or the times where she had wandered away from their conversation at a bar, only to reappear minutes later with her tongue down someone else's throat. The memories flooded into Adrian's mind like a plague of locusts. Had he loved Eleni? Yes. But had she really deserved that love? His eyes narrowed as another thought fluttered through him. He regretted how the other night had turned out, but what if things had happened for a reason? He chewed on his tongue, swollen from the heat, like he was chewing on the questions that racked his mind. Was he not better off? Released from her grasp? He swatted at a swarm of gnats that cloaked a patch of air around him, and then picked up his pace, trying to catch up with Stevie and Miles. Now that she was gone, he was free. Right? The snap of fallen branches and fronds crunched under his feet.

"Hey," he said, finally side by side with Stevie. "I gotta take a leak."

Stevie looked at him plainly. "Okay, and?"

Adrian wondered if she was a bitch to all men or just the ones she was friends with. He dismissed her attitude with an obvious look. "Let's take a break."

"Yeah, okay. But hurry up. I'd prefer to make it there before tomorrow."

Miles laughed quietly next to her. Adrian ignored them both as he stepped off the path and into the tangle of the jungle. He walked about thirty feet before deciding it was enough. He glanced back at the trail, just to check. Miles and Stevie were barely visible through the dense wall of green. He paused as his fingers grazed the fly of his shorts. His already-high heart rate ticked higher as he realized something. If they got the satellite phone, they'd call for help. Someone would come to deal with Eleni's body. They'd do an autopsy. His eyes flickered back and forth between Stevie and Miles. If they did that, they'd find out. They'd ask questions. They'd know what he'd done. His life would be over. Everything he'd managed to build would be gone. Poof. No money. No future. He started to sweat more than he already was. Eleni's body couldn't make it off the island. He couldn't let it.

⚔ BENNY ⚔

Benny and Monique sat on the patio in silence.

Tyler and Bec had started yelling at each other thirty minutes ago. It had only taken a few of those minutes before Monique shot a look at Benny, signaling their need to escape. Benny had hoped that his and Monique's departure would wake Tyler up to the fact that he was having a full on screaming match in front of his friends. It hadn't. The privacy had only egged Tyler on more. Now, Benny heard the slam of a door. Judging by the pitch of Tyler's voice, Benny could only assume that he was trying to yell through the door Bec had just slammed in his face. A deep breath left Benny's lungs as he leaned further back into the wicker chair. Could this trip get any worse?

"He's an ass," Monique said, breaking the silence.

"He's hurt."

"Boo hoo," Monique chittered. "He should know how to handle his emotions better." She threw her hand back towards the house and let a *tsk* smack the back of her teeth. "He's acting like a child."

"So you don't think she did anything wrong?"

She shot a look at Benny that told him he was on thin ice. "Now when did I say that?"

Her eyes widened at him, as if waiting for a response. He knew her well enough to know it was a rhetorical question. Answering would only annoy her more.

"Bec made a bad decision, I will admit that..."

Benny watched her carefully. There was a hesitation behind her eyes. "But what?"

She took a deep breath in and held it there for a second, as if she wasn't sure whether to release the words on the tip of her tongue.

"Doesn't it bother you that Eleni is..." She struggled to finish the sentence but finally spit it out. "That she's gone and all Tyler cares about is his relationship?"

"I don't know," Benny shrugged. Was Tyler acting rationally? No. But if Monique cheated on him, Benny was pretty sure he'd be going on a rampage right now too.

Monique looked back towards the house, as if checking to see if anyone was listening to her. When she was sure no one was, she leaned in towards Benny and dropped her voice. "Tyler took charge the moment we found Eleni. But now when there's a chance to find the satellite phone and call for help, he would rather stay behind and yell at Bec?" She shook her head. "It's weird."

Benny considered it. Tyler had taken charge, but Benny was used to it. All throughout college, Tyler had been the leader of their friend group. He was the one who got them invites to all of the parties. He was the one who decided what house they were going to rent. He was that guy. So should it surprise him that Tyler was taking on that role again? No. But still, Monique had a point. A loud slam rumbled the house behind him. Benny turned his head to see Tyler, silently fuming as he stalked away. Benny was surprised he hadn't shattered the glass door on his way out.

"You good, man?" Benny called to him.

"Fine," he replied harshly as he headed across the grass.

"Where are you going?" Monique called.

"To check on the body," he yelled back, not even bothering to look their way.

Benny shook his head as he watched his friend disappear down the path. "Fuck this trip," he muttered.

"I should go check on Bec."

Benny gave her a long look, considering it. "You know what we should really do?" he started. "Check out the house behind ours."

"The staff house?"

Benny nodded. "Yeah. I've been thinking about it all morning" He got up from the chair and gave his back a long stretch. "What if they have a phone or something in there?"

Monique's eyes widened. "So you're saying you thought there might be a phone 50 yards from where we're sitting and you let them go out into the jungle without saying anything?"

He let out a deep sigh. Fucking hell. He should have seen this coming. He was always doing something wrong. Could he have one day without Monique riding his ass about something? "They're going to be fine," he rambled. "If there is someone out there, it's three against one."

She didn't seem pleased with that answer.

"I'm sorry I didn't mention it sooner, okay? Now let's go check it out."

Monique chewed on her bottom lip. Benny knew that look well. She was nervous.

"What?"

"What if whoever..." She flashed her eyes towards the house before continuing. "What if someone's in there?"

"No one is in there," he laughed. He reached out and gave her hand a squeeze. "But you can go inside and hang out with Bec. I'll just go check it out for a second."

"No," Monique blurted out. "No, it's better if we don't split up."

An excited grin spread across Benny's face. "Good. Let's go."

⚔ MONIQUE ⚔

"I have a bad feeling about this…"

Monique watched as Benny strained and pulled at the door, trying to pry it open.

"We shouldn't be breaking into their house like this."

"Seriously?" Benny chuckled as he turned around to face her. "There could be some freak out there killing people and you're worried about breaking and entering?"

She glared at him before waving him along. "Fine, keep doing whatever you're doing then."

A pleased look danced across his face. His fingers fumbled with the credit card he'd pulled from his wallet. He slid the thing in the sliver of space between the door and the jamb and began moving it up and down. It was almost comical to watch but Monique kept her mouth shut. After another minute, she could tell the door wasn't going to budge despite Benny's best efforts.

"Kick it."

Benny let out an unbelievable sigh as he turned around. A bead of sweat was forming around the collar of his tank top. It was already hot as hell outside.

"If you want to get in, you need to kick it."

"A second ago you were hassling me and now you want to bust down the door?"

Monique rolled her eyes. He could be a real pain in the ass sometimes.

"Just do it," she coaxed him.

It took three heavy kicks for the door to come crashing in. It dangled off the wall by a few screws that clung desperately to the top hinge. Monique waited for Benny to flip on the lights before stepping through the threshold. Something about the house already creeped her out.

"No wonder that one guy was always in a shit mood."

Monique followed Benny's gaze. The space seemed more like a studio apartment than an actual house. It was barely the size of the main house's kitchen and living room combined, minus all of the windows. The only natural light that seemed to creep into the small space, aside from the broken front door, was a tiny window in the kitchen. Benny stepped deeper inside and began pulling drawers open with reckless abandon. She wanted to scold him for making a mess but she stopped herself. She couldn't deal with any more bickering. It was too hot. Monique watched him silently from the doorway. She found herself stuck, an unsteady feeling in her gut seeming to keep her there. A small kitchen lined the wall across from her. It was pitiful compared to the elaborate setup in the main house. Next to it was a small bathroom; Monique could see the faint outline of a toilet and shower through the ajar door. Against the back wall were three beds, more like cots, with white bed sheets tucked perfectly at the corners and a blanket hanging off the end of each.

"It's like fucking military bootcamp in here."

Monique tried to laugh off the comment but Benny was right. It seemed like it wasn't just the main house that Marta kept in perfect order. In the room they were standing in now, there didn't seem to be a speck of dust or an item out of place. As Benny continued rummaging through the drawers, Monique felt the disturbance of the space. Her skin prickled as she watched Benny dump things all over the desk. There was no hiding the fact that they'd been in here.

"Did you find anything?"

He shook his head as he opened another drawer. "No, there's noth—" His words cut out as he pulled a stack of papers from the desk. "What the fuck?"

Monique hovered by the door, craning her neck to get a look at what was in Benny's hands. "What is it?"

He nodded for her to come over. "See for yourself."

Her feet took her across the house quickly, not wanting to spend a second longer than she needed to in this weird place. Benny pressed the stack of papers into Monique's hands.

"Why would they need to know this?"

Monique furrowed her brow as she thumbed through the pages. "It makes sense, I guess." Her voice was distant as her focus stayed on the papers. "If I had a private island in another country, I'd probably run background checks on all my guests too."

"Don't you think it's messed up?" Benny gestured to the papers and let out a breathy laugh. "...that they have all this private information on us?"

"Of course I do," Monique answered. "But I'm just saying—it makes sense."

She flipped through the papers until she found one that wasn't like the others. She held the obituary out in front of her to get a better look.

"Why is this in here?" Her eyes flickered to Benny uncertainly before returning back to the page. "Brennen Jeremy Mills, passed away at age 27 in his hometown of Reno, Nevada on Friday, April 23rd. Beloved son, brother and friend. Brennen is survived by his loved ones, who are determined to see justice brought in his name..." Monique stopped reading, her eyes frozen to the page. "Do you know a Brennen?" she asked Benny.

"No." He scooted closer to look over Monique's shoulder. "That's creepy as hell."

Benny was right—it was creepy. Why was there an obituary in their pile of background checks? She tried to shrug it off as she stuffed the page at the bottom of the pile. As she read the next page, her brow knotted.

"Okay, I think they just mixed other things into our pile..."

She scanned her eyes over the printed news article. It seemed more like gossip than journalism but the more she read, the more familiar everything seemed. She dug the obituary out from the bottom of the pile and compared the two pages.

"What is it?" Benny prodded.

"It's like a—" As Monique read more, her face became riddled with concern. "It's like some sort of gossip site for true crime lovers."

"Huh?"

"It's about the guy from the obituary. Listen." Monique's fingers gripped the new article tightly in front of her as she began to read out loud. "Home invasion gone wrong or shady domestic dispute? Brennen Mills, age 27, was found dead in his girlfriend's apartment by police. Police have ruled it a home invasion turned bloody but many have speculated online that things aren't adding up. Girlfriend to the deceased, Amelia Owens, age 25, told detectives that she had fallen asleep next to her boyfriend that night. She had supposedly woken up around 2 a.m. after feeling sick from a night of drinking. She claims to have fallen asleep in the bathroom only to be woken up by a loud noise coming from the bedroom. When she returned, she found the room in disarray and Brennen stabbed to death. After multiple holes in her story have surfaced, people are left wondering..."

"What the fuck?" Benny huffed.

Monique stared at the piece of paper in her hands as Benny let out a hesitant laugh.

"So what? Some girl went crazy and killed her boyfriend and blamed it on burglars?"

Monique's heart fluttered in her chest as she shuffled the page back to the bottom of the stack. She didn't know who had stayed here before them, but she didn't want to read about it anymore. Not with what was already going on. Just as she was about to put the papers back in Benny's hands, something caught her attention.

"Hold on—"

"What is it?" Benny said.

Wrinkles formed at the outer edges of Monique's eyes as she tightened her gaze on the top page. "It's Tyler's background check. It says that he—"

"Wait—"

Benny popped over her shoulder, trying to snatch the paper from her grasp. Monique glared at him as she held the paper at a distance where they both could read it.

"This can't be right, can it?" Monique asked, flipping to the second page.

Benny said nothing as his eyes darted across the page along with hers. A sickly feeling crept into Monique's chest as her eyes devoured every word. It was like someone was wrapping their arms around her: squeezing tighter and tighter, crushing her chest, snapping her bones.

"Did you know about this?" she breathed. She looked up at Benny, her eyes full of distress.

"I—" Benny looked at her blankly for a few moments before he found his words again. "Uh, no—of course not."

Monique flipped back to the first page and stared at the small black and white photo in the top left corner. She tried to think of a reason why the information in the background check she held in her hands wasn't a big deal. She tried and tried but every excuse left a nagging feeling in the base of her chest. As she stood in the small house, Benny's breath hot on her neck, that feeling only seemed to grow deeper. She didn't believe in coincidences. Something was either related or it wasn't. When she looked at the information in front of her, it was hard not to jump to conclusions.

"We need to tell them."

Benny's face contorted in immediate panic. "What? No."

"Seriously, Benjamin?" she argued. "This says that—"

"I'll talk to him, okay?"

She eyed him carefully as she weighed his words against the feeling inside of her.

"Please, babe. Let me talk to him first and get the whole story. Okay?"

There was a nervousness about him that Monique found less than comforting.

"What if he—"

"Don't be ridiculous. Tyler didn't do anything," Benny laughed. It sounded forced, like he was trying to convince himself as much as he was her.

She took the pages from Tyler's background check and chucked the rest on top of the desk.

"I think we should at least tell the others that—"

"I'll talk to him," he blurted out. "Let me just talk to him and then we figure out the rest. Okay?"

"Fine," she said, folding the papers and stuffing them into her pocket. "But I don't trust him."

⚔ BEC ⚔

Bec hadn't heard any noise come from outside the room in almost an hour.

After Tyler stormed out, swearing and slamming things as he went, she had sequestered herself in Stevie's room. She knew she should go talk to Monique but she couldn't find the courage. She didn't want to deal with the things that would come up. She didn't want to talk about her and Tyler. Or her and Miles. And she definitely didn't want to talk about Eleni. She couldn't. That topic was like a loaded gun. It wouldn't take much for Bec to break down and tell her friends the truth. She could feel it scratching at the back of her throat. It wanted to come out. So she'd stayed in the room, setting the air conditioning unit on full blast and trying not to think about anything. Not thinking had proved trickier than she hoped. The silence that had fallen over the house made her think that maybe Tyler was off sulking on the patio. But for all she knew, he was sitting at the kitchen counter, waiting for the chance to berate her with more insults and questions.

She took a deep breath before shimmying the door open. She peeked her head out, checking to see if the coast was clear, before taking a few steps down the hall. As the entire kitchen and living room came into view, her body relaxed. No Tyler. As she wandered further into the room and peered outside, confusion rippled across her face. No Monique and Benny. She slid the door open and stepped out onto the patio. The surface was hot against the bare soles of her feet. She moved gingerly across the concrete, sweeping her gaze from the lower patio to the jungle as she went. No one was there. An eerie feeling crept over Bec. Why was no one there? She stared out into the jungle, waiting for someone to come into focus. Had they found the satellite phone and called for help? Why hadn't they knocked on her door? Had they left her? Panic prickled across Bec's skin until it was all she could feel. No, they wouldn't have done that. Something was wrong. Something had happened. She needed to get back inside, find something to protect herself with. As she turned back towards the house, the crack of palm fronds made her freeze. Her head swiveled slowly until she was staring into the jungle. Silence. Then the soft chattering of birds. A bug buzzed in her ear. She didn't bother swatting it away. Bec felt every nerve in her body come alive as she waited, breathless. The sound of heavy trampling reached her. Her eyes flickered across the wall of green. Nothing. No one. Just plants. It was only when she started to look away that a shadow slithered across her peripheral vision. Her stomach rolled. She fixed her gaze on where the jungle opened up to one of the paths. Her eyes widened, unblinking. It took her brain a minute to put the pieces together. She watched silently, until a gut wrenching yell ripped through her lungs.

"Stevie!"

Panic hit her like a bullet train. *Stevie.* Bec raced across the grass and onto the path, rocks digging into the flesh of her feet. As she rushed over to her friend, the world seemed to slow. Blood. There was blood. Bec held Stevie's face in her hands as her eyes scoured over her. Red dripped down from Stevie's scalp, streaming in bloody rivers. Bec dabbed at the blood with shaky fingers, failing to stop it as it leaked from the gash in her head. Stevie blinked feebly as a drop dripped over her eyelid.

"Holy shit," Bec stammered, her voice wavering as tears began blurring her vision. "What happened?"

"I don—"

Stevie's body crumpled into Bec's like a limp bag of potatoes.

"Shit. Shit," Bec whispered in ragged breaths as she hoisted Stevie up and began carrying her back to the house. "Help!" she screamed, her voice seeming to echo through the silence. "Somebody help us!"

TYLER

The first thing that concerned him was the blood. There was a small trail of it leading across the patio and through the door. The next thing that concerned him was the thump against his chest as he walked into the kitchen.

"This is your fault!" Bec yelled, as she shoved Tyler over and over again.

She was hysterical. He looked down at her as he grabbed her wrists, stopping her feeble attempts to hit him.

"Calm down," he demanded. His eyes darted passed her and took in the scene. Benny was standing by the fridge, looking at him with panicked eyes. Stevie was sitting on a barstool at the counter. She kept her focus straight ahead as Monique pressed a wet towel to her head.

"It was your idea for them to go into the jungle."

Tyler sighed as Bec thrashed under his grip. Monique stepped away to get a clean towel, giving Tyler the chance to survey the damage and cause for Bec's hysteria. A two inch gash glistened at the top of Stevie's forehead. It was just along her hairline, outlined by a swollen bump.

"It was Stevie's choice to go into the jungle. I didn't tell her to go."

Bec stilled at the comment. She let out a shaky breath before ripping her hands free of Tyler's grasp. "You brought us here," she retorted. "Fuck this trip, Tyler. We're leaving. Now."

"Oh yeah?" Tyler sneered. "And how the fuck are you going to do that Bec? Gonna swim home?"

She held her hands out in front of her in frustration and

gestured like she was going to start beating her tiny fists against his chest again. She let out an angry grunt before walking over to Stevie. He knew he should find the situation more concerning but if he was honest, it was only amusing. He'd specifically chosen Adrian and Miles to go get the satellite phone. Stevie's ego was to blame for this. Stevie turned to look at him. It was a long, hard look. He noticed the slight wavering in her eyes. Whatever had happened, she was still a little out of it.

"Where the fuck have you been?"

"Hello to you too," he scoffed. Tyler took a minute to read the emotions on her face. This was more than the typical Stevie attitude. This was distrust. "I walked down to the beach," he finally answered.

"Oh yeah?" Stevie prodded. She winced as Monique touched the new towel to her wound. "Why?"

"Went to check on the body." Tyler squeezed past Benny and opened the fridge. It was still packed with water bottles, alcohol, and food. At least they wouldn't starve.

"Why? It's not like she's going to get up and walk away."

"Hey," Monique scolded her. "Don't make jokes about the dead."

"What happened?" Tyler asked.

"What does it look like happened?" Stevie snapped at him. "Someone smashed a fucking rock into my skull."

Tyler considered what she was saying as he poked through the contents of the fridge.

"Did you see who did it?"

"No."

He popped the cap off his beer and took a big swig before responding. "And the others?"

"Like I already told everyone else," Stevie sassed. "Miles and Adrian were gone when I woke up."

The conversation paused as Tyler's mind raced.

"Did you burn the body?" Stevie asked.

Tyler lowered the bottle from his lips mid sip. "What?"

"When you were down at the beach. Did you burn the body?"

"No."

"Then what were you doing?"

The day Stevie learned to shut up would be the day he finally got along with her. Tyler turned around and watched the dazed look on her face come and go in waves. He wondered if she had a concussion.

"I told you. I was taking a walk."

"I thought you went to check on the body. Now it was a walk?"

"Come on, you guys," Bec uttered. "Cut it out."

"I'm asking simple questions here." Stevie stared Tyler down. She flinched as Monique tapped gauze against her head. "I thought you were going to stay at the house to keep Bec safe."

"I was—"

"What if the asshole who jumped me had come here next while you were off dicking around on the beach? What if Bec had gotten hurt—or worse?"

"For fuck's sake," Tyler snarled. "I wasn't gone for long. Nothing happened."

"Nothing happened?" Stevie argued, pointing at her forehead.

"Yeah, you got a bump on your head. Get a grip, would you?"

"That's rich coming from someone who's been losing their temper every five minutes."

"Everyone stop," Monique snapped, her voice commanding the full attention of the room. "Drop the personal shit and focus. Fighting amongst ourselves is only going to make things worse."

She met Tyler's gaze briefly before she quickly pulled her focus away. There was something in her eyes that pulled Tyler from his standoff with Stevie. Was that fear he'd seen briefly flash across her face? Fear for what? Or who? He watched her curiously but she avoided his gaze.

"She's right."

Tyler looked at Bec. The tears had dried on her cheeks. The only remnant left of her distress was her flushed red skin. He watched her walk over to the door and stare out through the glass. Now, there was something else there. Focus. Maybe it was the obvious fact that, besides having a big bump on her head for the next few days, Stevie would be fine. But Tyler realized it was something else. Bec had remembered that it hadn't just been Stevie who'd gone out into the jungle. She'd remembered that Miles was still out there. Tyler's jaw clenched as he considered what he was about to do. Miles could rot out in the jungle for all he cared, but there was something he wanted more than to see Miles suffer. He locked eyes with Bec as she turned back towards the kitchen. If there was ever a time to be the good guy, he guessed this was it.

"We need to go find them," he muttered through clenched teeth.

⚔ ADRIAN ⚔

Shit. *Oh fuck.*

He slipped and let out a throaty groan that Benny would have called him a pussy for. Pain shot through his abdomen like fireworks. Adrian clawed at the ground, stumbling forward on hands and knees.

"Help," he screamed, though his voice came out choked and raw.

He yanked on some vines and managed to pull himself up before they snapped in his hands. He stumbled again. His body slammed against a tree trunk and drove another groan from his lips. With every move he made, his flesh felt like it was ripping apart. He reached for his stomach, his hands shaking as the blood trickled across his skin. He patted the deep slashes that marred his flesh with stifled moans.

Snap.

Adrian lurched at the sound before shoving himself away from the tree and venturing deeper into the jungle. Fuck. Fuck. Fuck. He tried to listen to the sounds around him but he was breathing too heavily to hear anything. How long had he been running? He lifted his wrist but his watch face was coated with blood and dirt. He was pretty sure it was cracked, too. Shit. Adrian staggered forward on shaky legs. His head was pounding. He could literally feel his insides weeping into the muddied fabric of his shirt. What the fuck was happening? Why was—

Terror filled his heart as more bramble snapped around him. He felt like he was being hunted. But wasn't he? Suddenly, the jungle around him stilled. No birds called out from above. No insects buzzed incessantly in the air. Silence floated heavily around him. He stopped and listened. There was an unnatural stillness to it all, the kind that made you feel anything but alone. Adrian was sick with fear. God was taunting him—punishing him. He should never have done it. Sneaking it into the country had been stupid enough. But giving it to Eleni? Fuck, he knew better than that. He wasn't some predatory frat guy. He had just wanted to loosen her up. She was always so fixated on how people perceived her. He just wanted her to give him a chance. It was just Molly. Eleni wasn't shy about drugs. He was sure if he would have offered it to her, she would have taken it willingly. He hadn't meant for anything to happen to her. But something had. Fuck. Karma was a bitch.

Adrian groaned in pain as he continued through the jungle, paying no mind to the branches and thorns that slapped and tore into his skin. They were nothing compared to the gaping wounds still dripping with blood. Every inch forward seemed to spark them alive like the knife was revisiting his flesh. It was agony.

"God, please save me."

Adrian was crying now. His shoe hit a rock, sending him flying into the ground once more. His eyes flickered wearily until they finally closed. There was no salvation for him here. For his sins, he was in hell. He listened to the jungle and prayed until it all blurred into nothingness.

✎ STEVIE ✎

The pounding in Stevie's head had lulled to a dull ache thanks to the three ibuprofen Bec had given her. It had taken some coaxing for Bec and Monique to even agree to let her tag along, but the alternative had reluctantly won them over. If Stevie stayed at the house alone, who was to say whoever had attacked her in the jungle wouldn't come back to finish her off? So they had all agreed—everyone was going.

Tyler had made Stevie recount her story several times since they'd begun the hike. It had been annoying the first two times. But now? Now she was ready to find a rock of her own and give him a live-action replay.

"How did you not see them?"

"He was fucking behind me," Stevie explained. "I don't have eyes in the back of my head."

"So it was a man? Or are you making assumptions again?"

Stevie groaned. It was like the more time she spent with Tyler, the more she resented Bec for bringing him into her life in the first place. She couldn't blame Bec too much though. She was sure there had been some deceit on Tyler's part to win her over. How else could her best friend have been charmed by such an asshole?

"I don't know." Stevie rolled her eyes and picked up her pace so she could be side by side with Bec. "The point is, someone was behind me and hit me over the head. When I woke up, Adrian and Miles were gone. I figured I better get back to the house before whoever attacked me came back to finish the job."

"Hmmm."

The murmuring between Tyler and Benny at the front of the group irked Stevie.

"What?" she sassed.

"Where did you say Miles and Adrian were when this happened?"

"I told you." Stevie shot a look at Bec who gave her an apologetic look in response. Bec had already tried to get Tyler to stop pestering Stevie with questions. The reprieve had only lasted five minutes before the questions had begun again.

"Adrian went off to take a leak. Miles and I were waiting for him back on the trail."

"I see…"

Stevie's blood boiled. "This is the last time I tell him this story," she mumbled to Bec. "If he asks again, I'm gonna kill him."

"He's just trying to get to the bottom of all this," Bec offered. "We're all freaked out here."

Stevie motioned up ahead. "Does he look freaked out to you?"

Bec chewed on the inside of her cheek. "You know Tyler isn't exactly great with his emotions."

A snarky laugh left Stevie's throat. "No shit. He made that clear when he almost choked you out the other night."

"He—"

"No," Stevie retorted. "You don't get to make excuses for him anymore. I'm sick of you acting like he isn't a shit human being."

Bec quieted instantly. Stevie felt a pang of regret and shot her sideways glance.

"Sorry."

"It's fine," Bec mumbled.

"No, I'm being a bitch. I'm just on edge, you know? I mean someone hit me with a rock. A fucking rock. Honestly, I'm more pissed at myself. Someone killed Eleni and here I was traipsing off into the jungle like a fucking—"

"I said it's fine, Stevs."

Stevie tilted her head at Bec, surprised at the sharpness in Bec's tone. She waited for her to say something else, to laugh it off and apologize for her own freak out. But Bec said nothing. She continued walking in stride with Stevie, her eyes lowered to the trail. For a moment, there was only the sound of the jungle. Birds cawed overhead from treetops, alerting the world to the trespassers that stalked the jungle floor below. Stevie saw a few small creatures scurry off the trail. Aside from nature's beasts, there didn't seem to be anything else out here—let alone anyone else. Stevie's body grew tense as the group came up to a bend.

"Wait," she called.

Benny was the first to turn around, followed by Monique. Finally, Tyler reared his head around, a miffed expression on his face.

"We gotta keep moving. The sooner we get that satellite phone the better."

Just as he turned to continue, Stevie's voice stopped him. "This is where it happened."

Stevie took a few steps around, searching. As she stepped off the trail, her eyes caught something. Holy shit. She held up a large rock, her eyes glued to the streak of dried blood smeared across it. Bec let out a soft gasp which caused Tyler to head over with heavy footfalls. He snatched the rock from Stevie's grasp and admired it for a second. When he was done, he hurled the rock into the jungle. It struck palm fronds and tree trucks on its arching descent.

"What the fuck?" Stevie yelled.

Tyler glared at her before addressing the group. "Now that show and tell is over, can we go?"

He started a brisk pace forward, leaving the others as he took the curve in the path. Monique mumbled something to Benny. He wrapped an arm around her shoulders before leading her after Tyler. Stevie stifled her flicker of jealousy and redirected it into the anger that still pulsed through her.

"Your boyfriend's a dick," Stevie stated as she stood there and watched the trio ahead disappear from sight.

"He's not my—" Bec gave up and let out a deep sigh. "Yeah," she breathed. "Yeah, he is a dick."

A weird feeling pulled at Stevie. It was the type of feeling that struck you in a crowded train, only to realize that someone was staring at you. She whipped her head around, letting her eyes search through the thick green flora that flanked the trail. She strained to see something, anything. The distant sounds of animals and birds seemed to dampen amidst her focus. The jungle was alive but all that found her was an eerie stillness. It was like nature was holding its breath, waiting for the perfect moment to strike.

"Stevs."

Stevie flinched as Bec's voice snapped through the air.

"Sorry..." Bec gave her an unsettled look before darting her eyes up the trail. "But I think we should catch up with the others."

Their solitude suddenly blared at Stevie like a horn in traffic. She'd just been attacked in the jungle, on this very path, and now she'd just separated her and Bec from the group. She cursed herself silently before nudging Bec forward.

"Come on," she said, starting up the trail. "Let's go before I get another rock to the skull."

✐ BEC ✐

Bec didn't know what she'd expected, but it certainly wasn't this. The guard shack was just that—a shack.

It was the size of a large tool shed and had one tiny window in the front. From where she stood the window was so caked with dirt and age that seeing in or out of it seemed impossible. She rocked on her heels unsteadily. They were all standing a good fifty feet from it, keeping their distance like they would from a rabid dog on an old, rusty chain. Bec knew she was being paranoid. It was nothing more than a building, a seemingly empty one at that. Nothing or no one had stirred from inside when Benny yelled towards it a minute ago. Still, she was nervous. The hike had done little to quell the jitteriness swimming inside her gut. Standing in the clearing in front of the shack, something told her not to take a step closer. So she didn't.

"Benny," Tyler called, motioning for his friend to join him.

Benny mumbled something to Monique and kissed her cheek before moving towards the shack. Bec knew it should strike her as sweet but something about it felt like a dead man's farewell. As Tyler rattled the knob and shoved the door open with his shoulder, Bec sucked in a sharp breath. She watched them step inside, noting Tyler's lack of caution and Benny's overabundance of it. Her mind spun, wondering which of the two would prove the wiser. The men stepped inside. The shack was still. Bec's face tensed, causing the two little lines between her eyebrows to form like tallies carved into a stone wall. She took a step forward, then another. She paused. Waited. Listened. Nothing happened. Bec knew only a few seconds had passed but time seemed to tick by with a heavy dread.

"Tyler?"

No response.

"Benny?"

Bec's stomach curdled. It was just a shack, right? Clearly if someone was inside she would have heard something. The guard was probably patrolling the island. Or stalking them. She pushed the thought away quickly, ignoring the urge to look at the jungle behind her. Tyler and Benny were probably busy searching for supplies. That's why they weren't responding. That's why they hadn't come out yet. Bec let her mind create a flurry of probablys as she moved closer. The sun beat down heavily from above, causing her to squint against the glare. She had forgotten her sunglasses. She heard Monique and Stevie's voices flittering in the background. Her heart thumped in her chest like a drum, building in tempo the closer she got.

Lub-dub. Lub-dub. Lub-dub-lub-dub-lubdublubdub.

As she reached the threshold, anxiety lurched inside of her. Why hadn't they responded? The skin on the back of her neck prickled, a silent warning provided by her body. She didn't listen. Her foot lifted to step inside but she didn't move forward. She found herself at a standstill, suspended, then slammed into the earth by a force she didn't recognize. In seconds, she was on her back. It took a few more for her to understand what had happened. She was on her ass, in the dirt, air stolen from her lungs. As she fought to breathe, a wet, squelching gag erupted next to her. She turned to find Benny on his hands and knees, heaving the contents of his stomach into the glistening dirt.

She tore her eyes from the vile chunks that coughed out of him. She tried to close her ears to the sound of it but she couldn't. Just as she considered scrambling away to a safe distance, the smell found her but it wasn't coming from

Benny. She covered her mouth with her hand as she searched for the culprit. It smelled bitter—stifling. She knew that smell. Terror swam up her throat and choked her. When she finally saw the blood dripping down the floor of the shack and into the earth, she froze. Her eyes stared at the vibrant red as it dripped, splashing slowly into a tiny puddle in the dirt. If it wasn't for Stevie's hurried hands pulling her up from the ground, she could have stayed there for a lifetime, unable to move towards the reality that had seemed to have found her once again.

"What the fuck, dude?" Stevie hissed at Benny. "Maybe don't tackle someone half your size, huh?"

Stevie helped Bec up to her feet but let go of her arm when she met Bec's gaze.

"What's wrong? Did he hurt you?"

Just as Stevie turned to look at the shack, Tyler barreled out. He ushered Bec and Stevie away, coughing. Once he'd walked them a good fifteen feet back, he bent over and forced a few deep breaths of fresh air into his lungs.

"Shit," he coughed. "I didn't find the phone yet but I'll go back in as soon as my stomach settles."

"What's up with the shack?" Stevie protested, peering over his shoulder.

Bec's mind worked slowly, putting the pieces together. As she did, the haze of it all slipped away. The disorientation and dread she felt was replaced by a new fear. It reared up inside of her wild and erratic, forcing words from her lips in a panic.

"Who is it?"

Tyler looked up at her from the corner of his eye. She tried to read his expression but couldn't. The ambiguity only heightened her panic.

"Oh, fuck," Stevie raved. "Someone's in there?"

"Tyler, please. Who is it?" Bec urged. Her face paled when he hesitated. Then, she moved.

"Bec, don't—"

His voice faded as Bec launched herself forward. She was racing into the shack now, the tears already spilling from her eyes. She felt the tug of Tyler's hand on her arm but fought it off. She needed to get inside, needed to see for herself. She needed to know it wasn't him. She needed to know it wasn't Miles' blood she'd glimpsed pooling on the concrete floor. By the time she made it through the door, Tyler's arms were wrapped around her tightly. They did nothing to stop her eyes from taking in the scene.

She blinked steadily as she absorbed every piece of information, every color. There was so much. How could there be so much? The walls were splattered in red. Some spots were faint while others had big, dark splotches, already seeping into the wooden planks that lined the walls. It was all over the floor too. It dripped off the table in the center of the room. Slow, heavy, thick globs of red. What it dripped from should have caused the most alarm in Bec. Instead, it was a fleeting comfort. Not Miles. That was the only thing she could think of as she stared at the mutilated body of who she assumed was the island's guard. Felix. That had been his name, hadn't it? She felt it was only right to call him by his name. After all, this was her fault, wasn't it?

At first, she was looking at him without actually looking, her brain glossing over the parts that seemed too disturbing, too real, to commit to memory. But her naïveté didn't last long. It was when she started counting that the floodgates opened.

One.

The eyes. Like Eleni's eyes had been. Wide, glossy orbs, void of light—void of life. They seemed to reach into her soul, find the darkest parts and burrow there. It felt like they'd reveal her secrets if she wasn't careful.

Two.

The dark speckles of red dried against the paleness of his lips.

Three.

The way his head flopped to the side, resting against the table lifelessly.

Four.

Bec's eyes burned with mascara and tears. She couldn't turn away. She hadn't finished counting yet.

Five.

Deep cuts. His stomach was riddled with them. Oozing. Bec's eyes snaked back up to his throat, just like she had done with Eleni. She had to double check, had to be sure. Yep. Now she was sure. She felt her body teeter against Tyler's hold. She swiveled her eyes across the room wildly. She needed to look at something else, anything else. But what she found brought her no comfort. Painted across the wall behind the body, dripping in messy, hand-drawn streaks of red was a message. She didn't need to read it twice. She understood loud and clear. Her breath left her. Her mouth was gaping, gasping. She felt her body slipping down into the depths, into the darkness where she didn't want to go again. Bec would have slumped to the floor, sinking into the pools of blood underneath her if it weren't for Tyler's tight embrace that held her to the spot.

"Holy shit." Stevie stepped up next to Tyler and Bec. She gagged before putting her hand up, covering her nose and mouth. "How..."

"Knife," Tyler said flatly.

Stevie went to take a step closer but stopped when her sneaker squelched against the puddle of gore. No one said anything for a minute. Bec wanted to scream, to confess amidst the silence. She had lied before. She had lied about Brennen. Now, she was facing the consequences. She knew who was doing this. She had always known.

"His wounds," Tyler murmured. "They look like Eleni's but worse...a lot worse."

Bec couldn't bear the smell or sight of it anymore. She wiggled out of Tyler's arms, fighting her own dizziness, and pushed her way out the door. Benny was still kneeling in the dirt, trying to catch his breath. Monique was trying to comfort him, her hand gently stroking his back. Bec kept her gaze straight ahead as she passed them both. From the periphery, she saw Monique's head turn to follow her.

"Is it…"

"No," Bec replied quickly. "It's neither of them."

Bec kept walking until she reached a large rock at the edge of the clearing. She sat down with a heavy sag. Her body was ready to give up. Her adrenaline was crashing. It threatened to break her open like a dam. Her teeth dug into the tender flesh of her cheek. How was this happening again? Her eyes blurred as she stared into the ground. Bec watched a troop of fire ants march across the dirt. They journeyed past her sneaker and into the fauna beyond. She watched with a distant numbness until the urge to pick one of them up hit her with desperation. She knew their bite was brutal, agonizing even. But that was the point. The scared part of her brain craved the pain—needed it. She needed something to ground her. As much as she didn't want it, she needed a reminder that this was real. She fought against dissociation's tempting call. Her mind was screaming at her to let go, to shut down and give up. She watched the last ant scurry away. Another missed opportunity.

Her gut jerked her back to reality. She needed to tell them. Her eyes flickered up to the group. They were talking now. She could tell they were worried, scared. She didn't blame them. They had every right to be. They didn't know what was happening. She did. She did and she was scared as hell. She swallowed harshly as she got up from the rock, her body feeling woozy from the heat cand the fear that spiked her blood. She needed to tell them. Her body guided her across the clearing despite the flailing panic of her mind. Everything would change once she told them. There was no going back after that. The truth would not set her free. It would only damn her. As she reached them, their words broke through the cloudy haze that had swallowed her. Bits and pieces slowly turned to sentences and meaning.

"We have to get back to the house."

"We can't just abandon them," Stevie bellowed. "I don't give a fuck how much you hate him. We can't just leave Miles out there. Or Adrian."

"And what do you suggest?" Tyler spat. "We're unarmed. Unprepared. We don't stand a chance against whoever—"

Bec didn't hear anything else. She was awake now. She had missed something so obvious, so critical, it was almost enough to send a vicious laugh from her throat. Adrian and Miles were still out there. Miles was still out there. The realization anchored her. It sobered her. She eyed the bloody trail that was leaking out of the shack's door. She could wait to tell the group. Now wasn't the time. Right now, she needed to find Miles.

⚔ MONIQUE ⚔

"This is fucking crazy, Benjamin." Monique hissed as they hurried down the trail.

He pulled her in close, whispering in her ear. "What do you want me to do? Summon a helicopter to whisk us away?"

He was rattled, she could hear it in the strain of his voice.

"I want to tell them."

"What?"

"Eleni is dead," she stressed. "Stevie was attacked. That fucking shack was like a scene from Texas Chainsaw Massacre. Miles and Adrian are both missing."

She fixed her eyes on the back of Tyler's head as he led the group. Something twitched nervously inside of her. Ever since they'd left the house, she'd searched his mannerisms and expression for anything. A flicker of guilt. A hint of malice. She hadn't discovered anything so far but regardless, Tyler wasn't who she thought he was. And given their circumstances, that worried her.

"I want everyone to look at the same piece of paper we did and understand that maybe Tyl—"

Benny tugged at her arm quickly. "No."

She staggered backwards as he stopped them both in their tracks. Monique shook his hand off of her. "What do you mean, no?"

"We agreed earlier that I would talk to him." Benny peered around nervously before lowering his voice "We don't know if this has anything to do with Tyler."

The rest of the group was far ahead of them now. There was no way they could hear what was being discussed behind them. And if they could, Monique didn't care. They should know. They needed to know.

"Even if he's not, everyone else deserves to know," Monique argued, "Him being your friend doesn't change the fact that he—"

"No," he rasped, his voice overtaking her own. "After what we just saw, it would only freak everyone—"

"Everyone is already freaked out," Monique all but yelled. "This isn't about them. This is about you trying to salvage your friendship with that sociopa—"

Movement up ahead stilled Monique's rant. It was a blur at first, dashing through the dense green with a swiftness that she couldn't follow. Branches snapped as it barreled closer. Benny tensed. He seemed as unsure as she did.

"What is—"

Monique screamed as a brown mass of hair broke through the bramble. It charged towards them, grunting and squealing with a feral hostility that made Monique cling to Benny. She found herself stumbling backward, desperately trying to flee the impending assault of tusks and fury. Benny stood his ground, raising his arms high above his head as he stepped in front of Monique.

"Hey, hey, hey!" he shouted, waving his arms in a craved frenzy.

The boar came to an abrupt halt a few feet in front of Benny, its beady black eyes seeming to assess the giant in front of it. Monique watched with trembling limbs as the animal grunted and pawed at the earth. She saw the rest of the group at the top of the trail. She wanted to yell for help but feared it would only draw the beast's attention towards her. She focused on Benny. He was holding steady in front of the animal as it paced back and forth. Monique couldn't help but stare at its tusks. They were stubby, the color of bone, jutting out from its snout. She knew they were deadlier than they looked. Her eyes flashed towards Tyler as he began to jog back towards them. In an instant, the boar let out a shrill squeal. Monique's body tensed as it reared its head towards the sky before galloping back into the jungle. She watched with wide eyes until the last flash of fur was out of sight.

"Jesus," Tyler breathed as he reached them. "You guys okay?"

Monique tried to hold back the hysteria that bubbled inside her. She had been scared, she could admit that. But behind that fear was something else. Anger. What kind of place had Tyler chosen for Bec's birthday? Crocodiles? Wild pigs? What was next? Her apprehension shifted to terror as she realized the answer. More dead bodies. That was what was next.

"Yeah, man," Benny breathed. "Fuck, that thing was pretty big, huh?"

"Come on, let's get back to the house and then—"

"What the hell is going on, Tyler?"

He gave Monique a funny look. "What?"

"You heard me. Why are we on this godforsaken island?"

Bec and Stevie had made their way back down the trail to join them.

"Is everything okay?" Stevie asked, her eyes darting between Tyler and Monique.

"No. Everything is not okay. I'm trying to understand why Tyler brought us all to an island in the middle of nowhere with wild animals and no cell service and no one to help us," she sputtered. "Oh yeah, and don't forget that someone is out there killing people!" She took a step towards Tyler, ignoring the murmured protest from Benny. "Know anything about that?"

He closed the distance between them quickly, getting up in her face and matching her hostility. "Are you suggesting that I—"

The jungle came alive. The entire group froze as branches cracked and leaves rustled.

"It's coming back," Benny stated.

Monique's gaze darted out among the thicket of

leaves and vines. Her body stiffened in preparation. Her heart pounded in her chest. The rustling quieted but only long enough for Monique to catch her breath. The noise reemerged from the jungle again and as it did, she felt the intensity of her pulse rise into her eardrums.

Lub dub. Lub dub.

The thrumming grew louder and louder until it was all Monique could seem to hear. Her eyes scoured the maze of greenery in front of her, desperate to see what her ears failed to place.

Lub dub. Lub dub.

All seemed still until once again the sound of something crashing through the jungle resumed. It built and built until finally she could place it. Benny's body had moved in front of her again. She could see the veins in his neck straining under tension as he braced himself for what was coming. Her eyes grew wide as she looked to her right at the leaves and branches that snapped and shuddered. A scream slipped from her throat. Benny lunged forward. Bec's voice rang out in panic. Monique finally saw it. A mass of dark, curly hair. Monique felt her blood run cold as a familiar face emerged from behind a palm frond. Miles stumbled onto the trail with slow, staggered movements, blood splattered across his face.

"Oh my God," Bec cried out as she pushed past Benny and Monique. As she reached him, he seemed to collapse into her arms. "Miles—Miles, look at me."

A strained groan left his throat as he pulled away from her slowly.

"Shit," Bec whispered as she looked him over quickly. She'd started to shake. "Miles, talk to me. Are you okay?"

Monique's stomach twisted as she looked at him. Miles' shirt was covered in blood and slashed in multiple places.

"Shit," Bec repeated as she tried to hold him upright and assess his injuries at the same time. Miles mumbled something to Bec, staggering as he tried to stand on his own.

Benny stepped forward to help, tossing Miles' arm over

his shoulder roughly. Miles let out another groan as he shifted his weight against Benny. The urge to jump in and help tugged Monique but the unsteady buzz of fear kept her where she stood. She was desperately trying to make sense of it all.

"It's going to be okay," Monique uttered. "Everything's going to be fine." Her voice tapered off into nothing as uncertainty snaked around her vocal chords. Things were not going to be fine. Nothing about this was fine. As Bec pulled at Miles' shirt, he winced again.

"Fuck, sorry," she breathed, moving her hands at an even slower pace.

Bec managed to roll Miles' t-shirt up despite the thick coating of blood that had dried against the sun's heat. Monique looked away as soon as she saw the first cut on Miles' skin. What was happening to them? The thought ran around her brain in a tortured loop, like a twisted merry-go-round. First Eleni, then Stevie, and now Miles? And the guard. She couldn't forget the guard. A mound of dread had been forming in Monique's stomach all day, but now it was too big to ignore. She looked away, trying to block out Miles' muffled groans. For a second, she thought Tyler was looking at her. She offered him a weary smile, caught off guard in the moment. When he didn't react, she saw that he wasn't looking at her at all. She swept her gaze across the path and furrowed her brow. Bec was still fussing over Miles, using Benny as a sort of crutch to hold him up as she tried to stop the bleeding with her t-shirt. She was standing in her sports bra, back towards Tyler. Was Tyler that jealous? Bec was just trying to help. Monique realized that Tyler wasn't looking at Bec. He was looking at Miles.

Bec stepped back, blood-soaked shirt in hand. "I don't know what I'm doing," she breathed.

"Here—let me help," Monique offered as she stepped towards them.

"It's okay," Miles said, reaching out and giving Bec's hand

a squeeze. "Everything is going to be okay."

Monique ignored him and turned her focus towards the bleeding. Beneath Miles' shirt were three gashes. They weren't deep but had been big enough to make a mess. The blood oozed slowly now; Bec's attempt to stop the bleeding seemed to have worked temporarily. Monique had taken a few first aid classes growing up, before her childhood ambitions of being a nurse had been squashed by her squeamishness when it came to needles. Looking at him now she could tell that Miles would need stitches. She bent down to get a better look, careful not to get her fingers and any dirt she had on them into the wounds. They seemed to be superficial, having only broken the skin and not pierced muscle or anything deeper. He was lucky. She moved her eyes up his face. There was a light trickle of blood pooling from the thick curls of his black hair. A head injury. Like Stevie? Monique's brow furrowed as she looked at the specs of blood that were splattered across his face and neck.

"What happened?"

Monique could hear the hostility coming off of Tyler.

"We were hiking to the shack and we stopped." Miles winced as he adjusted himself against Benny's support. "Something hit me in the head out of nowhere. I was out of it and then something cut me. A knife, maybe."

Bec's eyes were dripping with silent tears.

"I tried to fight him off but I was out of it. I passed out."

"Welcome to the club, man," Stevie chuckled darkly.

"We need to go."

"What about—"

Tyler shot Bec an irritated look, eyeing her up and down. "You want to wait around for whoever did that," Tyler said, gesturing to Miles' bloodied torso, "to come back?"

Bec went a few shades paler and shook her head no.

"Can you walk?" Tyler asked Miles.

Miles pulled himself away from Benny and nodded.

"Then let's fucking go."

✎ MILES ✎

Bec ran her fingers through his curls, gingerly pulling them away from his forehead. It felt heavenly.

"This might sting a bit."

Miles sat still as she wiped the blood from his face with a damp cloth. He let his eyes melt over her. Bec's brow was furrowed with focus. She had makeup lightly smudged around her eyes. Her skin was sticky from sweat. Miles loved every bit of it. Fuck, she was beautiful. As she began dabbing at the small cut on his forehead, he pulled away suddenly, wincing with pain.

"Shit," Bec whispered. "I'm sorry."

He shot her a devilish grin that only took her a second to understand. "I'm just messing with you."

"Cut it out," she protested, smacking his chest playfully. "I'm freaking out enough as it is."

He wrapped his hand around her lower back, teasing her bare skin with his fingers. "Sorry." He wasn't sorry. She was cute when she was annoyed. He looked her up and down before pulling her closer to him. "I just like seeing that look on your face."

Bec pursed her lips, her head tilting slightly. "What look?"

"The look on your face when you're worried about me. The one that lets everyone know that you actually do care about me."

Bec paused. He could tell there was something there behind her eyes, something that was fighting to get to the surface. His fingers traced her skin delicately, trying to coax it out of her.

"I do, you know," she said quietly. "Care about you."

"I know, baby."

He watched her chew on the inside of her cheek. She was nervous.

"This is all just so..." She struggled to find the words and let her frustration out with a quivering breath. "You and Stevie were attacked out there and it's my—"

"Hey," he said, bringing her focus back to him. "You're going to be fine."

"No, it's not that. It's..." She held his gaze without saying anything for a while. The wet towel in her hand dripped down her wrist and onto the floor, splaying small drops of watery blood against the tile. "If anything happens to you or Stevie, or..." She shook her head softly. "I won't be able to forgive myself."

Miles closed his eyes and took a deep breath. He wished he could promise her that nothing else would happen. He wished he could promise her that they'd gotten through the worst of it. But how could he promise that? He let his breath out through his nose slowly and met her gaze. There was so much hurt and fear in those soft eyes of hers. She needed to be comforted—so a lie would have to do.

"Nothing is going to happen."

"You don't know that," she stressed, her voice wavering with emotion. "You don't know what—"

"I know you're not going to lose me. Ever."

Her eyes pleaded with him. She wanted an escape from it all but he didn't have one for her. There was so much pain woven in that pretty face of hers that it crushed him. It made him want to take back every mistake he'd ever made or would make. It made him want to be better. It made him weak and desperate. He wanted to be everything she needed—everything she deserved. Right now, he didn't know how to do any of that.

Bec grew quiet and resumed tending to his wounds. Miles tried to catch her eye but she was avoiding his gaze now. The moment was gone but the closeness they had now wasn't wasted on him. Miles let his eyes roam across her face, searching every inch for the love he craved. She needed him. She wanted him. He knew that. He could feel it in the way her pulse quickened whenever he touched her. But did she still want and need someone else too? His eyes darted to Tyler. He was sitting on the couch. He'd been sitting silently ever since they'd gotten back to the house. He was tense— more so than usual. Miles could tell that he was thinking things through. Planning. What erratic thing would come out of Tyler's mouth next and how would Miles have to deal with it?

"There," Bec said carefully, setting the towel down on the counter. It was sporadically splotched with dark red throughout the fibers. Miles reached up to touch his head but Bec swatted his hand away.

"Hey," she scolded him. "You heard Monique. You have to keep your cuts clean."

She took a step back, looking over his shirtless torso. "We're lucky Monique knew how to stitch you up," Bec stated, gesturing to the tiny stitches that had been sewn across Miles' abdomen. It had been a hack job done with the sewing kit they'd found under one of the bathroom sinks. "Even if she did almost throw up on you," Bec teased.

"So tell us..." Tyler said, raising his voice across the room as he got up from the couch.

He walked into the kitchen, glaring at both Bec and Miles as he made his way over to them. Miles could sense Bec's unease as she pulled away from him. As she did, a vicious resentment flared inside him. If Tyler wasn't there, Bec wouldn't feel the need to distance herself. She would have stayed where she belonged—next to Miles. As Bec wandered into the kitchen and Tyler came face to face with Miles, Miles couldn't help but hate the man even more.

"What?" Miles quipped.

"What really happened out there?"

"You seriously want to hear it again?"

"Maybe I just can't believe someone got the best of you like that."

A twitch rippled through Miles' jaw as he stared Tyler down. "Like I said," he spat. "He tried to hit me over the head before coming at me with a knife. I tried to fight him off but I passed out. I was bleeding pretty bad when I came to so I didn't stick around. I took off into the jungle and tried to find my way back here."

"So you ran."

Miles felt his skin grow hot, peppering with malice as Tyler shot a cocky glance his way.

"You ran like a coward."

"God, you're an asshole," Stevie interjected. She was sitting up on the back counter with an ice pack against her head. "Let's have someone hit you over the head and shish kabob your insides and see what you do."

"I'm just glad Bec wasn't there." Tyler sucked his teeth and gave his head a shake. "Seems like you would have easily left her for dead like you did with Stevie and Adrian."

"Tyler, stop," Bec urged.

"Stop, what?" he said, faking naivety as he shrugged. "I'm only trying to figure out how one person bested these two. Must be a real killer."

Bec quieted instantly. Miles watched her shrink back and grow small. Her eyes dropped to the floor before she seemingly retreated into her thoughts. Miles wanted to pull her towards him and bring her back to the surface.

"We need to find Adrian," Monique piped up.

"No," Tyler argued. "We need to find whoever did this."

Miles turned to Tyler, his brow raised high. "Oh, yeah?" he challenged. "And how do you plan to do that?"

"Hunt him down. Tie him up. Wait for the staff to come back so the coast guard or the police can take him into custody."

"That easy, huh?"

"Yeah," Tyler said, letting out a breathy laugh as he crossed his arms across his chest. "That easy."

Heat grew in Miles' eyes. "You think you can take him?"

"Yeah," Tyler repeated. "And I'm not gonna run."

Miles got off the barstool in an instant, stepping up to Tyler. "I hope you do find him," he taunted. "I'd love to see how—"

"Enough."

Monique's voice ripped through the room with the shrill force of a school teacher's. She eyed everyone carefully until her gaze finally landed on Miles and Tyler.

"We don't have time for your macho bullshit," Monique continued. "We have to get out of here."

"How many times do I have to tell you," Tyler shot back. "There's no getting off this island until Monday."

"We can't stay here until Monday," Stevie laughed sickly. "There's some psycho out there killing people and leaving creepy messages in blood."

Everyone grew quiet, everyone except for Benny.

"That shit was super weird," Benny mumbled. "*'You belong to me.'*" He tried to laugh but it came out uneasy. "What the fuck was that about?"

"They're obviously out of their fucking mind," Stevie uttered.

Miles flickered his eyes to Bec. She was still quiet but the fear that had slipped across her face was new.

"What is it?" he asked her.

Everyone turned their focus on her. Miles watched her eyes grow flighty and unsteady. He took a step towards her but it seemed to make her more nervous that she already was.

"I—I'm sorry."

"What?" Stevie asked. "Bec, why are you sorry?"

Miles watched the way the panic bled into Bec's eyes as the words caught in her throat. He saw it all like a hunter stalking a deer. It played out slowly, in vivid detail. She was terrified.

"This is my fault."

Her fault? Miles cocked his head and watched the confusion pass from Benny's face to Monique's to Tyler's and finally to Stevie's.

"Oh, come on," Stevie chuckled, though he could tell she was growing uneasy. "Just because we're here for your birthday doesn't mean that this—"

"It's him." Bec locked her gaze on Stevie. "He did this."

Miles leaned forward, clinging onto Bec's every word.

Benny let out a nervous laugh. "What do you mean it's him? Who?"

Silence hovered around them all as Stevie stared back at Bec. Finally, Stevie's eyes went wide. The air in the room shifted. Miles felt all the hairs on his arms stand up.

Stevie shook her head softly. "You can't think that..."

Bec's hands were trembling now. A single tear had slipped from her eyes and was trailing down her cheek slowly.

"Tyler," Stevie blurted. "How many times was Eleni stabbed?"

Tyler shot her a weird look. "I don't know. Five? Six if you count..." He gestured to his neck.

"What about the guard?"

Tyler grew silent. Miles knew they were all counting in their heads.

"What's going on?" Monique asked.

"I—"

"Bec, you don't know that it's him," Stevie insisted.

Miles felt anticipation spike his nerves. It was potent and laced with fire. "Who?" he echoed.

"What are you talking about?" Tyler barked.

Bec swallowed harshly. The shakiness hadn't left her. She pressed her hands against the counter, as if trying to steady herself.

"Four years ago," she started.

"Stop," Stevie demanded. "You don't have to—"

"I had a stalker."

Stalker? Miles' teeth clenched down tightly but he stayed silent.

"I thought it was harmless. I—I didn't tell anyone about him." Bec shot a wary look at Stevie. "Not my aunt, not Stevie, not my boyfriend, not the cops."

The room seemed to be balancing on the edge of a cliff. It was as if one breath or word out of place would push them all over the edge.

"He was possessive," she breathed. "He didn't want me dating anyone else but I thought if I ignored it, he would finally leave me alone."

"So what are you saying?" Benny laughed. "You think your stalker killed the guard?"

Monique glared at him and quieted his amusement. "Bec, I'm so sorry you went through that." She stepped towards her carefully like she was a ticking bomb. "But what does that have to do with what happened here? To the guard? To Eleni?"

Bec dug her nails into the counter as she dropped her gaze. "He killed my boyfriend." Her voice wavered as emotion filled her throat. "Ex-boyfriend."

The room went silent again. Stevie was rocking on the balls of her feet, ready to race over to Bec at any second.

"Why didn't you tell me?" Tyler said, his voice more unsure than Miles had ever heard it.

Miles watched a tear splash against the kitchen counter. Bec wiped the rest away quickly.

"Really?" Stevie snapped. "That's what you're concerned about right now?"

Benny cleared his throat. "How did he...?"

"He broke into my house while we were sleeping, and..." Bec didn't finish her sentence, her voice slipping away into nothing.

"Oh my God," Monique breathed.

Miles watched her shoot a panicked look at Benny.

She leaned up into his ear, whispering something that drove an equally concerned look onto Benny's own face.

"And you're sure this is him?" Tyler paced softly against the carpet in the living room. "Why? What makes you think it's the same person?"

He moved towards her too quickly. Bec retreated deeper into the kitchen until her back bumped against the fridge.

"I—"

"Can't you see she's freaked out here?" Stevie shot him a death stare. "Give her some space."

"You have to admit," he chided her. "It's pretty extreme to assume that some guy, from what? Four years ago? Followed her here, to a foreign country, to go on a killing spree." He paused, waiting for an answer that didn't seem to be coming. "I just want to understand it all." He moved towards Bec again.

"Shut up, Tyler. Leave her be."

"You shut up, Stevie," he snipped. "I just want Bec to tell me why—"

"My ex was stabbed five times and his throat was slit," Bec said, her voice hitching.

Tyler stepped back abruptly like she'd shot a loaded gun. Miles watched the glistening tears fall from Bec's eyes. The group had grown quiet again. Everyone was lost in their own thoughts but Miles couldn't take his eyes off Bec. The shaking in her hands had reached its way up to her chest. She was visibly holding back her own panic and fear with every shuddered breath she took. Miles cut the distance between them quickly. He wrapped his arms around her, wincing softly as his stitches pulled at his skin. It was like little fractures of electricity shooting into his nerves.

"It's okay," he whispered, his lips pressing against her hair. "I'm here. It's okay."

He took a deep breath and rode through the pain in his stomach as he steadied the silent sobs that rocked through Bec. The slices hurt more than expected. He'd take some painkillers later. They would take the edge off nicely, but not completely. He needed to stay sharp for what came next. And looking across the room, he figured things were about to get a lot more interesting.

"So who is h—"

Stop," Stevie raged at Tyler. "No more questions. Not now." She ran a hand through her hair. Miles noticed some pieces were caked with dried blood. "Bec needs a drink." Stevie swore under her breath. "And so do I."

✎ BENNY ✎

It was muggy, too muggy. The air stuck to Benny like a second skin, trapping the moisture in his pores. He felt overheated and sticky—two things he thought he was done with when he'd been kicked out of the NFL. Had it been like this the entire trip? He didn't think so. It had been hot but not this hot. Maybe it was the stifled panic working its way up the collar of his tank top. He panted lightly as he stood on the patio with Tyler.

Benny took a puff of the cigar Tyler had given him. He had said they were for Bec's birthday but now? Now there wasn't much to celebrate. As Benny blew the smoke out, savoring it, he felt like he was at a funeral. There was a gloom in the air, full of unspoken mourning and uncertainty. He could feel it as heavy as the damned climate.

"Fuck, man," he croaked. "Is it just me or is the humidity getting worse?"

Ash dropped to the ground as Tyler flicked his cigar. "A storm's coming," he stated, his eyes fixed on the horizon.

Benny squinted his eyes against the glare of the day and took a few steps forward to get a better look. "Seriously?" he asked. "How can you tell?"

"See those small gray clouds over there?" Tyler pointed to his left. "Rain."

Benny followed his gesture and could barely catch the glimmer of gray on the horizon. "Really?" he laughed. "What are you, like a weatherman now?"

"I grew up sailing," Tyler said smoothly, puffing on his cigar. "You learn to read the skies."

"Well, shit. Look at you."

Benny kept his eyes on the horizon, but his interest in the storm that was rolling in dwindled quickly. Another day was ending. The sun sank lower on the horizon with every cloud of smoke he sent from his mouth up into the air. They had spent three nights on the island. So far, two people had died. What would happen tonight? And what about the night after that? He thought back to Monique, who was somewhere in the house. She was safe for now. They all were. But the possibility of that safety not lasting forever chewed at his insides like a sewer rat. No one knew exactly what they were up against—no one except maybe Bec.

She had divulged a bit more of her past, after much prying from Tyler. Stevie had snapped at him like a guard dog the entire time. But even after many questions and multiple drinks, Benny still couldn't help but feel like Bec had left some parts out. She had told them that she had woken up to find her ex, Brennen, dead. Benny didn't know if he would have put two and two together if Monique hadn't reminded him about the obituary they'd found. The name had been different—Bec's name. He'd wanted to question her about it but Monique had stopped him. The trauma was painted all over Bec's face. Monique didn't want to risk pushing her over the edge. She had looked close enough to it already. Bec hadn't stopped trembling the entire time she answered their questions. Her story had followed the general narrative of the article they'd found amidst the stack of background checks. Except for one, critical part. Bec had never shuffled off to the bathroom to throw up that night. She had stayed in bed and woken up next to him—next to his body. The bed had been soaked in his blood. She had slept in a drunken daze as his life seeped its way out of him, lapping at her skin, and woken up to a crime scene. The details got fuzzy after that. It was hard to get much else out of her after she'd started crying again and Stevie had told them all to back off. Even with all he'd learned in the past hour, Benny still felt unprepared. He dabbed the sweat off the back of his neck. For fuck's sake. He'd never sweat more in his life than on this goddamn trip.

"So what do you think?" he muttered, before taking another puff of his cigar.

"About what?" Tyler replied coolly.

"About what?" he repeated wildly. "About your girlfriend having a psychotic stalker who murders her boyfriends."

Tyler titled his chin to the sky as he let out a puff of smoke. "Not just boyfriends, apparently."

"Thanks, that makes me feel a lot better," Benny said gruffly.

Silence passed between them. Benny was waiting for Tyler to say something. Wasn't he upset that Bec hadn't told him any of this before now? Wasn't he scared? If Bec was right, Tyler had a target on his back. He was America's Most Wanted, if America was some stalker freak. Benny watched Tyler ash more of his cigar, seemingly unconcerned by the reality they'd found themselves in, until Benny couldn't hold back his curiosity anymore.

"Do you think she's right? That some guy followed her all the way to Nicaragua to what? Kill off her friends?"

"I don't know," Tyler said flatly.

Benny wiped some sweat from his brow before taking another drag of his cigar. Tyler still wouldn't meet his gaze. "Pretty crazy we didn't know this huge thing about her life."

Benny could feel himself heading into dangerous territory. He could feel the words crawling across his tongue. He wanted to swallow them but he knew it would only make things worse. Bec's theory about her stalker hadn't changed anything for Monique. She had given him an ultimatum before he'd stepped outside with Tyler. Either Benny convinced Tyler to tell everyone what he'd done or she would. Benny's eyes flickered to Tyler nervously as the words choked from his mouth.

"But I guess you can't be too mad. Bec's not the only one with secrets."

Tyler said nothing.

Benny cleared his throat. "Does she know yours?"

Tyler's eyes flashed with instant recognition before his expression grew vacant again. "No."

Benny knew this was his out, his chance to drop it before the conversation went further. But he also knew that wasn't an option.

"Monique knows."

Tyler's jaw clenched. "What?"

"I didn't tell her, man. I swear," Benny said, raising his hands up in front of him defensively.

Tyler took a deep, steady breath. "How, then?"

Benny puffed on his cigar nervously, coughing out a bit of smoke as he did. His voice sputtered as he tried to suck in a breath to respond.

"We searched the staff's house for a phone earlier." He shook his head as Tyler's face lit up. "There wasn't one," Benny said before he could ask. "But we were looking through all of their stuff and found background checks they'd done on us."

Tyler let out a mumbled grunt of understanding in between puffs of smoke.

"She read it before I could swipe it from her. I told her I didn't know. That I'd talk to you about it."

"Okay," Tyler said coldly. "So you talked to me about it. End of story."

Benny felt a nervous buzz of dread inside him. "Not exactly."

Tyler shot him an irritated look. "What do you mean, not exactly?"

"Monique said she's going to tell everyone if I don't convince you to tell them yourself."

Tyler stopped smoking. He dropped his cigar to the ground, snuffing it out with one heavy twist of his shoe. "Fucking pathetic."

"What?'

"You," Tyler said. "You're pathetic."

Benny's brow furrowed but before he could respond, Tyler was in his face.

"You let her tell you what to do and now you think, what? I'm going to do the same?" He scoffed and looked at Benny with a disdain so fierce that Benny almost took a step back. "She's neutered you. Turned you into nothing more than her bitch," Tyler seethed. "Which makes sense, considering her history."

"What the fuck is that supposed to mean?"

"Oh, you don't know?" Tyler smirked, taking his time with his words. "Monique plays for both teams."

"What?" Benny's face contorted into utter confusion. "What are you saying?" A big chunk of ash fell onto Benny's slides, barely missing his toe, but he didn't notice. "Monique isn't bi. She would have told me."

"Trust me, she is." Tyler stifled a laugh as he shook his head at him. "Fuck, that means you don't know about Stevie, either."

Benny looked at him. His head spun with questions and it took him a second to find the words. "What about Stevie?"

Tyler flashed his eyes at Benny cruelly, arming the truth he held hostage with his silence. It didn't matter. Benny pieced it together quickly enough. He didn't want to believe it, but Tyler made it real.

"Our good friend Stevie was piping your wife way before you were."

Benny's stomach dropped with a clenching panic. "You're full of shit."

"Not about this," Tyler said, raising his eyebrows at him wickedly. "Who knows, maybe she still is. Stevie might be an annoying little fuck but at least she has the balls to do whatever she wants."

"Fuck you, man," Benny blurted out.

Tyler smiled. "So what now, huh?" He laughed as he stepped away from Benny to look out at the storm that was growing darker on the horizon. "Going to betray your friend again for another whore?"

Rage burned inside Benny's chest. It was hollow and deep, seeming to ache against his ribs. "You're a fucking asshole, you know that?"

Tyler said nothing but the flicker of a smile that hovered at the corner of his mouth was enough to turn the flames inside of Benny into an inferno.

"How do you think Bec's gonna feel when she learns your secret, huh? You still going to be a smug son-of-a-bitch then?"

Benny saw the smile on Tyler's face twitch into something else.

"How safe do you think she's going to feel with you when she learns you killed someone?"

Tyler's hands were on Benny's throat before he could blink. Benny thrashed against his grip but Tyler was strong—stronger than he looked. Benny began to feel lightheaded, the blood flow to his brain slowing as Tyler's fingers dug into his carotid artery.

"If you tell her, I'll kill you."

In an instant, Tyler released his grip and pushed Benny away. Benny coughed and sputtered. He bent over, his hands resting on his knees as he struggled to take in the dense air around him. He had never said it out loud—that Tyler had killed someone. But it was the truth. Now that he had said it, a weight seemed to lift from him. His friend had killed someone and gotten away with it. That was the plain, simple truth. Benny had always let himself believe that it was more complicated than that. After what had just happened, he realized it wasn't. It didn't matter if Tyler hadn't meant to beat that kid to death. It didn't matter if Tyler had been blackout drunk or in total control of his actions. None of it mattered. All that mattered was that Tyler had killed someone and he'd just threatened to do it again. As much as Benny wanted to laugh it off, he knew Tyler wasn't kidding.

For the first time in his life, Benny looked at his best friend with truly hateful eyes.

"Maybe it's not her stalker we should be worried about."

"Fuck you," Tyler spat, gesturing him away with his hand.

⚔ MONIQUE ⚔

Sizzle. Flip. Sizzle. Flip.

Monique went through the motions over and over, thankful to let her body settle into habit once again. She had resumed her self-appointed role in the kitchen and was frying up some fresh fish that Ramon had caught before he left. She couldn't remember what he had called it. Dorado? Her brain was too preoccupied with other things. Regardless of what it was, Monique figured the group would be happy to eat something other than eggs. As she stood over the stove and watched the tiny particles of oil sizzle and pop, she let her mind slip away. It slipped away to her parent's house. The cottage-style home was tucked away on the edge of Lake Champlain in northern Vermont. Her parents had lived there ever since they'd retired. It was a dreamy place, storybook, even. She wondered what her parents were doing right now. Maybe her father was out on the deck, reading one of the mystery novels he loved so much. She pictured her mother in that big, sunny window in the living room, painting abstracts with oil. Monique had already bought her and Benny's plane tickets out there for Christmas. It was something she had been looking forward to for months. She imagined cozying up in the big armchair of her father's that looked out over the lake, the rich smells of Nigerian food wafting out of the kitchen as her mother cooked. And the snow. It had been so long since she'd had a Christmas with snow. Now, she wondered if she'd get the chance to see it again.

The patio door slid open, causing her to jump. Her body relaxed as she saw it was only Benny. He was quiet as he closed the door behind him. Monique resumed cooking, pulled unwillingly out of her far-away thoughts. She could feel Benny's presence hovering behind her, like a little kid who wanted to ask a question. She looked over her shoulder briefly, acknowledging him.

"It should be ready in about ten minutes."

She leaned over the stove to peek inside a small pot. The rice looked like it still needed more time. She turned her attention back to the fish and turned the heat down.

"Maybe twenty," she joked.

Monique paused what she was doing, finally aware of the unusual silence seeming to rise off of Benny, like the heat coming off the food. She eyed him carefully as she turned to face him.

"Are you okay?"

He didn't say anything, just held her gaze with a harsh uneasiness she hadn't seen before.

"What?" she prodded. She flashed her eyes outside. Tyler was standing at the edge of the patio, looking out at the ocean. "Did something happen? Did you talk to him?"

His silence held strong.

"Benjamin, say something to me."

His eyes avoided her, his mouth rigid. Monique felt her heart patter softly in her chest. This wasn't like him. He could barely keep quiet during a movie, let alone a conversation.

"Hey," she coaxed. "What is it?"

He swallowed harshly before turning his gaze to her. "Did you sleep with Stevie?"

Monique felt her heart drop through the floor. She had thought this moment had eluded her. After so much time, she had convinced herself it would never come—that she had outsmarted it. She had been vague, evaded questions about her exes, played coy. In the grand scheme of things, she knew it shouldn't be that big of a deal. It was before they met. There was no overlap. It was just a fling. It meant nothing. Monique opened her mouth but the lies circling her mind wrapped around her vocal chords and squeezed. She could already anticipate his response. If it had meant nothing, why hadn't she told him? Why had she hidden it away like a trinket in an old jewelry box? She knew the answer. She'd known the answer for a while. She'd known before the wedding. She'd known before he got down on his knee. She'd known before she'd even met him. Monique had known the truth when Stevie had slipped out that morning, leaving nothing but a note and a coffee on the counter. As soon as she'd read those words, scrawled sloppily on a napkin, and felt her heart lurch in anguish, she had known. It hadn't been nothing. It had been everything.

"So it's true?"

Monique fought to find the right words but what left her mouth was far from that. "It was before we met."

"Jesus," Benny breathed.

He took a small step away from her, running a hand over his buzzed head. Dirty blonde hairs prickled out against his scalp, his skin slightly red from the sun.

"It wasn't serious." She almost choked on the lie.

"Why didn't you tell me?"

"I didn't think you would care."

He looked back at her, turmoil slapped across his face. "Have you done anything since we—"

"No," Monique answered quickly. "No. It was over before we started dating."

Benny seemed content with that answer, dropping some of the tension from his shoulders. A few seconds passed in silence. Just as Monique thought it might be over, he spoke again.

"Did you love her?"

A sharpness sliced into her chest like a cold blade. She gritted her teeth, trying to control the flicker of something fierce inside of her. Stevie's smile flashed in her mind. Bright, stupidly cheerful, mischievous. Monique thought about the way Stevie's hand felt in her own. She thought about the way

Stevie talked in her sleep but adamantly refused to admit it. The last thing Monique remembered before she tuned into the man in front of her was the look on Stevie's face at the wedding. Tough, but broken—like Monique's own heart.

"No," she said, forcing the words out as steadily as she could. "No, I didn't love her."

Whether Benny believed her or not, he didn't show it on his face. "Okay."

"Is it?"

He forced a deep breath from his lungs. "It's shitty you didn't tell me. But it's not like I can really be mad. It's old news. Right?"

"Right," she repeated slowly.

A breathy laugh left Benny's throat, though it sounded more relieved than amused. "Fuck, Tyler's a dick."

Monique scrunched her nose at him. "What does Tyler have to do with this?"

"He just told me you and Stevie had something going on."

"What?" she snapped.

Benny hesitated. "We got into it a little out there."

"Why?" Monique's eyes lit up as she realized. "Did you talk to him about the background check?" She stared at him, waiting for his response. He'd gotten sunburned again on the hike. If the circumstances were different she would have scolded him about wearing sunscreen, but now wasn't the time.

"What happened?"

"Nothing."

"Nothing?"

He stayed silent, driving a scoff from her lips. "You accused him of murder and nothing happened?" She watched his eyes go wide. She knew she was talking louder than she should be but she didn't care. "No more secrets," she said, ignoring her own dishonesty, and pressed further. "Tell me."

"He didn't mean to do it. It was an accident."

"What?"

"I said it was an accident."

Benny hesitated, setting Monique's face into a stern glare. He rubbed his face with his hands.

"What aren't you telling me?"

Silence.

"Tell me."

He looked up at her, guilt etched across his face.

"I already knew."

Monique felt the breath leave her lungs. In one quick whoosh, it seemed to suck out of her and lodge in the back of her throat. A million thoughts raced through her head. Each one ricocheted inside of her, desperate to leave her tongue. But before she could yell at him, a thin waft of smoke rose from out of the corner of her eye.

"Shit," she muttered, quickly racing to flip the fish in the pan. As Benny stood silently next to her, she scraped a small patch of burnt fish off with the spatula. She flicked it into the sink and turned the heat down before boring her eyes into him. "What do you mean, you already knew?"

His focus darted around the room. Monique's followed. It was just them. She had no idea where everyone else was. She assumed in their rooms, seeking solace amidst the nightmare.

"Fuck, I'm sorry. You started reading the background checks and I didn't know what to—"

"Explain. Now—or so help me Benjamin—"

"Okay, okay," he uttered. He took a deep breath, his face growing serious. "Back in college, Tyler was a bit of a hothead."

Monique's brow furrowed but she stayed silent, waiting for him to continue.

"He would drink and pick fights with people at parties—stupid shit." Benny closed his eyes and shook his head. "Just typical stupid shit. You know? Some guys get drunk and think they need to prove themselves."

"It doesn't surprise me," Monique quipped. "Tyler has a big enough ego for both of you."

She didn't mean it as an insult but she saw a flicker of shame drift across Benny's face.

"Yeah, well, he was worse in college," he continued. "One night, we all went to a frat party. It wasn't Tyler's fraternity, it was this guy we all knew from class."

Monique nodded quickly.

"It was after a football game," Benny went on. "We'd won. Barely—in the last few moments. It was crazy. Everyone was partying hard."

"What happened?" Monique snapped, her patience wavering.

"We all drank a lot. A lot of that night was pretty fuzzy. But I remember all of a sudden, someone was yelling my name from the backyard." His eyes went wide as if he'd been taken back to that night. "One of my teammates was screaming at me to help him. I got closer and he was trying to pull Tyler off of somebody."

Everything around them seemed to blur as Monique was pulled into the story.

"Tyler elbowed Darius, my teammate, in the face. I don't know if it was an accident or if he was trying to keep him away. Darius was leaking blood everywhere so I stepped in. I had no idea what Tyler was doing but Darius kept yelling at me to stop him. So I did. I yanked him back over and over again until finally I got him off the guy."

Benny paused, looking away from Monique.

"God, he looked so small. He wasn't a small guy but on the ground, crumpled up like that? Fuck I couldn't even tell who he was, his face was so messed up."

His voice hitched. It was slight, but suddenly, Monique understood. A sick feeling crept up into her throat and across her skin, crawling over her like ants. Suddenly, she didn't know if she wanted to know any more.

"I tried to wake him up."

Monique saw the pain in Benny's eyes. She wanted to reach out and comfort him. She wanted to tell him it wasn't his fault, that everything was okay. But she didn't, because she needed him to finish the story.

"We left the party. Tyler said we had to go home. We were drunk," he urged, grief and guilt seeping from his face. "I didn't really know what had happened, at least, I hadn't processed what I'd seen yet. You know?"

"What happened to Tyler?"

The emotion fell from Benny's face. "Nothing."

Monique's brow furrowed as her voice raised a little higher than it should. "What do you mean, nothing?"

Benny motioned for her to keep quiet. He leaned in closely. "I mean nothing," he whispered. "The cops came and brought Tyler down to the station a few days later because someone had snitched. His dad got him a lawyer and it never went further than that."

"What do you mean, it didn't go further?" Monique hissed. "You just told me that Tyler beat someone to death. Why didn't he get charged?"

"I think Tyler's dad paid off the cops and the family. He had to do community service for like a year but that was all."

"When did this happen?"

"Junior year."

"Does Bec know?"

"No," Benny snapped. He took a second to regain his composure. "No," he said, softer this time. "And we can't tell her. Tyler said he'd kill me if I did and with the kind of mood he's in now...I'm not gonna test my luck."

Finally, the question that burned inside of Monique the strongest raced from her lips. "Why didn't you tell me?"

Whereas Benny's other answers had been quick, this one took time. He looked at her hesitantly. There was no good answer but they both knew he had to give her something.

"I didn't want you to hold it against him."

A shrill laugh exploded from Monique. She held her gaze

on him steadily for a minute, waiting for him to offer another excuse.

"Please tell me you're joking."

He wasn't. She gritted her teeth, wrapping her fingers tightly around the spatula.

"You brought a murderer into my life and didn't tell me because, what?" She laughed and slapped the spatula on the counter. "You wanted me to think he was a nice guy?"

"He's my friend," Benny said. "I wanted you two to get along."

Another vicious laugh escaped from her lungs. "This marriage is a joke."

"What did you just say?"

Monique closed her eyes and tried to steady the rage inside of her. Her father had told her that marriages were work. There would always be things that upset or hurt you. She went into hers expecting there to be good days and bad days. But this? A vile repulsion curled around her heart like barbed wire. This was too much.

"I said this marriage is a joke," she said flatly. "In the past four days, I've learned that you've been lying to me and keeping secrets."

"And you've done nothing wrong?" he snapped back. "I just learned that one of our friends has fucked you. You don't think that counts?"

Monique pressed her fingers into her temples roughly, trying to rid herself of the resentment that swelled inside of her. "You just said you were okay with that. But apparently that was a lie, too."

"So if I'd slept with Bec before I met you, you wouldn't care?"

"No."

"Yeah?" His jaw tightened but his focus on her didn't waver. "And what if Stevie slept with Bec?"

Monique tried to keep her expression flat despite the heat that burned in her cheeks. "What does that have to do with us?" she raved.

"Just wondering if you care more about Stevie than you do about me."

"What the fuck are you talking about?"

"You've been acting weird since the wedding," Benny started. He took a step towards her. "I thought it was stress. I thought you were upset that I quit football, but now I think it was something else."

She gave him a wild, unbelievable look. "You didn't quit football," she screamed. "You were kicked out after you acted like an idiot and picked up Tyler's coke habit."

"I was on a fucking boy's trip in Miami," he shot back. "I was just trying to let loose a little."

"You were trying to be like him!"

He paused. Monique had never said it out loud, but it had always been clear to her why Benny did some of the things he did. It was like a teenager drinking at a party for the first time. They just wanted the coolest, most popular kid to like them.

"I'm not trying to be like him," Benny argued. "I wanted to do it, so I did. I liked it. I wanted to keep doing it, so I did. I can make my own decisions, Monique."

"Obviously you can't—not like an adult. You lost your job, you're too proud to get another one and you're best friends with someone who should be in jail," she spat. Her fury was at its breaking point. She felt her head pounding against the emotions she couldn't contain. Like a latch tearing from a door, they broke free. "How the fuck do you expect me to want to raise a child with you when you're a child yourself?"

He recoiled instantly. She watched her words splinter through him. She knew she should take it back. She had gone too far. But it was too late, and it was the truth. She had meant every word. Benny left the kitchen with a miserable silence. By the time he had slipped out the patio door, Monique had already turned her focus back on cooking. More burnt fish flakes coated the pan. She wanted to scream and cry and throw it all in the garbage. She wanted to hug her mother. She wanted Stevie to walk into the kitchen and kiss her and tell her everything was going to be okay. But most of all, Monique wanted off this fucking island.

✦ BEC ✦

Bec ate in silence, alone in the kitchen.

She'd left Stevie resting in the bedroom, nursing a headache with a frozen bag of hash browns and two ibuprofen. As Bec mindlessly plopped bites of overdone fish into her mouth, her thoughts consumed her. At first, she thought about Adrian. He was still out there. Tyler refused to allow anyone to go look for him, not when it would be dark in a couple of hours. Not when he didn't know what was going on. Bec knew what was going on but Tyler had been too stubborn to believe her story. He'd asked question after question but he still didn't get it. Everyone was in danger. He was in danger.

Her mind drifted to him. Not Tyler—*him*. He was like a shadowy figure in her mind. Faceless. Haunting, like a flicker in the corner of your eye. Always there but never caught in the light. The idea of him had latched itself to Bec's mind like an octopus, its tentacles strong and unrelenting. He was out there. He had found her. Her stomach churned as the realization fully set in. Moving to California hadn't stopped him. Changing her name had only seemed to buy her time. He was inevitable.

Bec pushed the idea of him away like the remaining food she scraped across her plate. She looked around the room, eager for something, anything, to keep her out of her own thoughts. Everyone had slinked away over the past hour. It was like they were hiding from her and the horrors she'd introduced them to. She didn't blame them, she just wished she didn't feel death clinging to her like a contagion.

Monique was the only one around but she wasn't really around—not in any way that felt comforting. Aside from letting her know that dinner was ready, Monique had barely said a word to her. Now she sat on the couch, her plate of food balancing on her lap. Bec expected to see Benny nearby, guarding her like a lovesick watchdog, but he was gone too. Judging by the argument she'd overheard earlier, she guessed he was licking his wounds. She would never have told Tyler about Stevie and Monique if she'd known he'd use it so brutally. It hadn't been Bec's secret to tell and it definitely hadn't been Tyler's. Bec had briefly seen Tyler as she'd sat down at the kitchen counter to eat. He had been on the patio, doing nothing but staring at the horizon. Now, he had disappeared too. Even Miles had seemed to retreat from her. She hadn't seen him since he'd headed to his room. He had taken a bottle of whiskey with him, likely to curb the pain of his freshly sliced skin—or maybe to forget everything he'd just learned about her.

Bec felt a dull ache growing inside of her. She felt so alone. She wondered if he wanted it that way. She could already feel the isolation drifting towards her like a misty fog. It was a feeling she remembered well. It started with shame and fear. Next came denial. Pretty soon she'd be standing alone in its haze. Breathless. Waiting for him to punish her like he'd punished her before. Bec closed her eyes and dug her teeth into the inner flesh of her cheek. The pain held her in place until she was able to think straight. Last time she had tried to wish it all away. This time, she knew better. She opened her eyes and shot a look over her shoulder. Monique was still staring out the window, food barely touched. Bec forced herself off the barstool. If her past came for her, it wasn't just Bec who would suffer. She knew how he worked, how he thought. If she had any doubts, what he did in the guard shack had erased them.

"Hey Monique," Bec said softly. "You okay?"

The question felt stupid as soon as Bec said it. Still, she

sat down on the couch next to Monique and waited for a reply. There was a long pause before Monique slowly turned her head.

"Hell no."

Bec chewed at the inside of her cheek, the flesh tender now. "I'm sorry."

Monique looked at Bec sternly. "Don't do that. Don't apologize for this," she chided. "This is not your fault."

Bec felt a wave of emotion crash down onto her. It was deep and cold. Monique was wrong, but still, Bec let her words lift the weight of her guilt for a few seconds.

"Thank you."

Silence passed between them. Bec noticed the way Monique's hands fidgeted in her lap as she turned back to stare out the window.

"Where's Benny?"

Monique's breath spilled out in a big sigh.

"I don't know. Gone."

Bec tried to keep her expression as neutral as possible. She didn't need Monique to know she had been eavesdropping. "Gone?"

"We had a fight," she stated. The distance in her tone made Bec's heart wrench.

"Oh," Bec said softly.

Bec sat next to her silently, restlessly, trying to figure out how she could possibly help until she realized she couldn't. She leaned in towards Monique, tucking her head onto her shoulder and let out a deep sigh. Monique leaned her head against Bec's, nestling the two of them together.

"Some birthday, huh?" Monique muttered.

Bec let out a cynical laugh. "Fuck," she breathed. "I totally forgot."

A comfortable silence settled between the two women as they leaned against each other. Bec closed her eyes, letting the tranquillity of her friend's presence balance out the unending chaos that had seemed to find her so quickly.

"Can I ask you something?" Monique said, her voice breaking the stillness.

Bec leaned away to meet her gaze. "Of course."

"Why did you cheat on Tyler?"

The question caught Bec off guard. She pried at the inside of her cheek with her teeth. Why had she done it? Had the fight really pushed her to Miles? She had told herself it had, but now she wasn't sure. It had been obvious to her, months before the fight, that Miles was interested. It was the way his eyes lingered on her. The way he always seemed to find subtle ways to brush against her arm or the small of her back when he passed by. The flirty banter. She had noticed it and done nothing to stop it until finally the buildup of tension had boiled over. She had done it because it had felt right. He felt right.

She sighed, knowing there was no good explanation. "I don't know," she told Monique. "It was stupid."

Monique nodded her head, seemingly wrapped up in her own thoughts.

"Did you know I almost didn't even come on this trip?"

Monique gave her a ridiculous look. "For real?" she insisted. "You almost missed your own surprise birthday?"

"Yeah," Bec laughed, although it wasn't really funny—at least, not to her.

The conversation she'd had with Tyler a few days before the trip flashed through her mind like a scene from a bad sitcom—petty comments and shouting and slammed doors. It was a lot like the past few days. She was at fault for most of it, she could admit that now. The worst part was, she didn't even have a good excuse. It was just more of her typical bullshit—her self-sabotaging, as Tyler called it. Now she realized that she'd been trying to end things with him. In her own cowardly way, she had been looking for an out. She had tried to push Tyler far enough past his breaking point so that he'd end things himself. But he hadn't. He'd only rooted himself deeper in their relationship, promising to do better.

Out of naivety or cowardice or both, Bec had complied. Things would have been so different if she had only had the guts to end it then. No more back and forth. No revealing her betrayal. No trip. If she had ended it, none of them would be here. Tyler would have gotten them all reimbursements for their plane tickets. She would have spent the weekend in LA drinking at Riptide, the shitty little bar Stevie worked at. Or in typical breakup fashion, she would have had a movie marathon with ice cream and her favorite takeout. Miles would have called her nonstop, eager to replace Tyler. And Eleni—*Eleni would be alive*. The realization hit Bec's heart like a skewer. Eleni would be alive if only Bec hadn't been so weak. All of a sudden the room felt too small. Bec felt her guilt tighten around her inch by inch until its suffocating squeeze was too much to bear. She reeled up from the couch, her haste startling Monique.

"I need some air," Bec stammered, already tugging open the sliding glass door before Monique could voice her concern.

The humidity hit Bec like a wall, knocking her out of her thoughts and back into the world. She didn't mind the heat or weight of it on her skin. It felt overpowering yet grounding. The further she got from the house, the better she felt. She took a deep breath, letting it seep into every nook and cranny of her lungs. Her breath raced in and out of her like an overworked train engine. She was beginning to hyperventilate. She closed her eyes and pressed her fingers into her temples. She needed to calm down. It was only when she heard the squeak of a chair behind her that Bec snapped out of it.

"You okay?"

Bec kept her focus on the jungle in front of her. "Fantastic," she muttered.

A soft chuckle left Tyler's throat. "Yeah, not exactly the vacation I had hoped for."

Rage crawled up her spine. She knew it was misplaced.

She knew none of this was Tyler's fault. If anything, it was her fault. But she had to get it out—the rage, the fear, the grief. Tyler was just in the wrong place at the perfect time.

"Why exactly did you bring us here?" Bec snapped. "Why drag us all the way down to Central America for a fucking surprise party? Couldn't you have planned dinner like a normal person?"

The words were a sweet release but left the tang of poison on her tongue. She couldn't turn to face him, didn't want to see the suffering on his face. This whole trip, she'd done nothing but act out. She didn't know who she was trying to run away from anymore, him or her own failures.

"I wanted this weekend to be special."

If she'd struck a nerve, he wasn't letting it show. His voice seemed almost calm. The feeling of it unnerved Bec enough to force her to turn around.

"Why?"

He let out a breathy laugh. "Oh, Bec," he sighed.

She stared at him steadily, the lines on her face furrowing deeper as he smiled back at her.

"I was going to propose this weekend."

Shit. Her skin grew clammy as his words settled into the crevices of her mind. For the first time all weekend, everything made sense. The trip. The way Tyler had been pressuring her for months to meet his mom. How he wouldn't give up on her no matter how many times she fucked up.

"I've wanted to do it for a while," he continued. "But I wanted it to be special."

She wanted him to shut up. She didn't want to hear the story. She didn't want to hear how he'd shopped for the perfect ring, one that matched her personality. Or how he'd spent months planning this trip as the perfect proposal. Or maybe how he'd thrown the ring into the ocean when he learned that Miles' hands had been all over her. She didn't want to hear any of it, because it might kill her.

"Wow," she finally blurted out. "I'm sorry."

"I know."

Her head tilted, caught off guard by the continued coolness of his tone. She expected more yelling, more insults, more disappointment. All that Tyler shot her way was a look full of understanding.

"You messed up," he said. "It happens."

The confusion etched deeper into Bec's face as he continued. Was Tyler actually being understanding?

"The last year hasn't been easy. I've made my own mistakes. That's just how life goes."

"I—" Bec stuttered, unsure what was happening.

"Bec, I love you. And I want to spend the rest of my life with you."

Panic stirred inside of her. This wasn't happening, was it? Was he really doing this now?

"I want to start over. Can we do that?"

Her flaring panic settled but only slightly. Bec stared at him like an animal caught in a snare. The delay in her answer only made him more eager.

"Can we?"

Her breath caught in her throat. In its place, something else climbed to the surface. She tried to stop herself. She tried to fight the nagging voice in her head that wouldn't rest. It was an itching feeling that made her restless. It was the fear that despite any feelings she'd had for the man in front of her, she truly didn't know who he was or what he was capable of. So instead of answering him, she kicked open a door she knew she couldn't shut again.

"Tell me about the person you killed."

He flinched back. For a moment, she thought he might walk away, leaving her with unanswered questions and prickling nerves. She knew she should have eased into the conversation but his declaration had shaken her. So, she had deflected. She dropped her words dead at his feet like an outdoor cat with its latest trophy.

"Who told you?"

"No one told me, I—"

"I swear, I'm going to make Benny regret he ever—"

"Tyler, stop," Bec urged. "No one told me. I overheard Monique and Benny talking."

He was quiet for a moment. Bec waited, her heart pounding steadily in her chest. She had only overheard bits and pieces earlier. Beat someone unconscious. Background check. He killed him. They were wild, untethered phrases floating around her mind. She needed Tyler to catch them like loose balloons floating away from a child's hand. She needed to hear him give some sort of explanation or excuse. She needed it not to be true.

"I have a past," Tyler said flatly. He looked her up and down. The flecks of resentment in his eyes made Bec shift. "And from the sound of it, you do too."

"Yes, I do," she said carefully. "But I told my story." She bit the inside of her cheek as she forged courage into her words. "Now I need you to tell me yours."

"Why, Bec? Tell me why it matters? It has nothing to do with you and me."

"Because—"

"Admit it. You just want another excuse to run away from this."

"Tyler this isn't ab—"

"Why can't you accept what's good for you? I'm offering you a future any other girl would die for but for some reason you're too focused on some fucking thing that happened in college."

Bec let out a vicious laugh. "So you'd rather just pretend it didn't happen? Is taking someone's life really that insignificant to you?"

"It was a mistake," Tyler yelled, his face flushing a violent shade of red. "I was young and drunk and stupid. I'm not proud of what I did. But talking about it isn't going to change anything, Bec. He died. I killed him. End of story. I can't undo that."

She stood across from him silently, trying to process what he'd finally admitted. Tyler killed someone. It wasn't an exaggeration. It wasn't a miscommunication. He had done it.

"I need you to—"

She backed away from him as he moved towards her. The reaction stopped him entirely, his mouth hanging open against the words that failed to come out. He swallowed harshly, the tension in his jaw returning as he stared at her with steady, shark-like eyes.

"So what? You're afraid of me now?"

She tried to deny it but her words were lost to her. He quickly stepped closer until her personal space was his. She fought against every urge in her body to stay still. She felt sick. She wanted to run. He laced his hand up through her hair. As his fingers rested against her jawline, she felt her heart beating in her ears. The loud, dull thumps only grew more overwhelming as Tyler looked down at her with an unwavering focus.

"Do you really think I would hurt you?"

Her eyes darted across his face, searching for something to steady her nerves. Instead, she only saw someone she didn't know. She wrapped her hand on top of Tyler's. A smile drifted across his mouth but only for a second. As she pulled his hand away from her face, she watched the last drop of hope leave him.

"I want to believe you wouldn't but I don't know anymore."

"I see," he breathed gruffly. He turned to walk away but something stopped him. "Tell me one thing."

Bec stared at him as dread wrapped its way around her insides.

"Is this really about me?"

"What?"

"I mean is this really about my past? Or is this about him?"

"What?" she repeated. Bec pulled a harsh breath into her lungs in an attempt to steady herself. It didn't work. Her frustration ran up her throat in a vicious spout. "I'm so fucking sick of you blaming everything on him," she spat. "I just learned you killed someone and you're still thinking about Miles? Miles isn't the problem here, Tyler. Miles isn't the reason our relationship is over."

"Over?"

He looked at her curiously, but it was the dark severity of his eyes that froze Bec to the spot. Her words had left her in such a rush that she hadn't realized what she had said until he repeated it back to her. She had finally said it. Relief washed over her, but only momentarily.

"Bec, this isn't over." He studied her carefully, as if trying to dig his way inside her head. "You fucked up when you cheated. I fucked up in college. We both kept things from each other. We've even. From here, we move on. We do better."

Her words felt like they were stuck to the roof of her mouth but she needed to get them out. "I don't want to do this anymore."

"Of course you do," he replied.

"I think it's time we both realized this isn't going to work out the way you want."

He let out a breathy laugh but his face changed when he realized she was being serious. "No," he stated flatly. "It's going to work out exactly how I want."

"Tyler—"

"You do this all the time. You get cold feet and act like it's over and then eventually you come around. You know why that is?"

She refrained from answering, his condescending tone telling her that there was no point. He was going to tell her exactly what she thought, as if he knew her better than she did herself.

"You know you'll never do better than me," he spat,

stepping closer. "I'm the best you've got."

"Is that so?" she snapped back. "Wow, how truly lucky I am to have bagged such a great guy. Deluxe boyfriend package..." she said, gesturing her hands in front of her dramatically. "Now including homicide."

"You can be a real cunt. You know that?"

"Maybe you should let Miles have me then."

"How long do you think it'll take for him to get tired of your shit, huh?" he said, his fingers curling tightly against her arm. "I give it a month until you're crawling back to me."

"Fuck you," she spat, yanking herself away from him.

"I'm running out of patience here, Bec," he shouted after her. "If you walk away, we're done. There's no coming back."

She didn't say anything. Instead, she raised her middle finger over her head as she walked through the patio door. Rage thrashed inside her as she made her way through the kitchen and down the hall. It wasn't until she came to a rest in front of Stevie's door that she took a full breath. She stared at the wooden door, her eyes burning into the grains. She was tired of the yelling, tired of feeling so destructive. She was tired of Tyler's bullshit. He viewed her as something to round out his perfectly curated life, something to collect and hang up on the wall like a hunting trophy. She didn't belong to him. But now, it didn't matter. She was done. She was free of him. That freedom pulled at her like a bad smoking habit.

She shouldn't. She knew it would only make everything worse. But still, she found herself walking a little further down the hall until she rested in front of a different door. She raised her hand, hovering inches away from the worn wood surface. When she finally rapped her knuckles on it, the instinct to slip into Stevie's room before another mistake could be made swelled inside of her. Was it a mistake? It didn't matter. She couldn't stop. It was like dropping a match in a field and ignoring the regret long enough to reach for another. As she stood in front of Miles' door, waiting for him to open it and flash her that devilish smile, she felt herself drop the second match. She knocked again.

"Miles, it's me," she said softly.

Her brow furrowed as no noise came from inside the room. She waited in silence, anxiety teasing her heart. What if he was finally done with her? What if it was too late? Panic thickened in her throat and made her pull her hand away from the door. Miles had been quiet earlier. He hadn't berated her with questions like Tyler and Benny had. Why? Bec could guess why. It was the same reason so many of her friends from Reno had seemed to disappear from her life after it had happened. It was too much to deal with. She was damaged goods.

Rejection pierced Bec's heart.

He was done. It was over. She knew she was being irrational, hasty, but the sting of his silence latched onto her like a leech. She retreated to Stevie's door. As she turned the knob, she shot a glance back, staring at the door, hoping it would swing open and shake loose the pain that was burrowing inside of her. His door didn't budge and the pain took hold. Bec closed Stevie's door behind her.

✦ STEVIE ✦

"Are you feeling any better?"

Stevie rolled over in bed as Bec closed the door behind her. "Eh," she muttered, rubbing sleep from her eyes. "I don't feel terrible. But this headache sucks."

"Do you want me to get you anything?" Bec sat on the edge of the bed. "Do you need more ibuprofen?"

"Nah, I think I'm capped out for the next few hours." Stevie propped herself up in bed, getting a better look at the careful way Bec kept her eyes low to the ground. "What about you? Are you okay?"

"Fine."

"You're fine?" Stevie prodded.

"Yeah," Bec muttered, tracing circles on the bedspread with the tips of her fingers. "I'm fine."

"Yeah and I like men," Stevie replied snarkily. "Cut the shit." She scooted closer and gave Bec a stern look. "None of this is fine. Don't pretend it is."

Bec let out a deep breath that quickly turned into a lone, desperate laugh. "Everything is fucked." She shook her head softly, dropping her voice to a whisper. "Again."

"I'm sorry," Stevie offered. "I know it's not helpful, but I'm sorry this is happening."

"Thanks."

Bec continued tracing her fingers along the floral pattern of the bedspread. Stevie watched her do it as she tried to figure out what to say next. What could she even say? If Bec was right, some freak was out in the jungle waiting to—what, exactly? Kill them? Kill Bec? There was no good outcome here, not one that Stevie could see.

"Do you really think it's him?" Stevie said, finally mustering the strength to get the words out her mouth.

Bec stopped tracing circles. She picked at a loose thread, the tug of her fingers unraveling it. "Yes," she said softly. "I know it's him."

Stevie reached out and squeezed Bec's shoulder. "We'll be okay," she said. She pulled her gaze away before Bec could look at her. Stevie didn't want her to see the doubt that flooded her eyes. The likelihood of them being okay at the end of this was slim. But panic and fear weren't going to help. They needed to be strong. Stevie needed to be strong. If not for herself, for her friends.

"We'll be getting drunk at Riptide before we know it."

Stevie waited for a flicker of a smile to dance across Bec's face. Instead, all that she saw was her friend slowly slipping away into her thoughts.

"Hey," Stevie said, wrapping her arm around Bec's shoulders. "Fuck that guy. Whatever sick game he's playing, whatever he wants—we're not gonna let him win."

"You don't understand," Bec huffed, abruptly shrugging Stevie's arm off of her as she got up from the bed. "Him getting what he wants is the only way this ends."

"What are you talking about?"

Bec ran her hands through her hair and paced softly across the room.

"Seriously, Bec. What is it?"

"I lied to you."

Stevie felt her heart beat a little faster as Bec's pacing continued. "What the fuck are you talking about?"

"When Brennen—" Bec's breath caught in her throat. She stopped pacing and wrung her hands together. "When it happened before, I told you that I had been getting messages from this random guy, that he got obsessed with me and was jealous of Brennen."

Stevie's brow furrowed as she stared at Bec. "Yeah?"

"Only some of that is true."

"Excuse me?"

"He was jealous of Brennen. But he wasn't random."

Stevie's body stiffened. She felt something dreadful creeping over her, like a scratchy blanket on a hot day.

"I've known him since I was 15."

"Bec…" she muttered, a flurry of panic in her chest. "You know who's doing this? Who did that to Brennen?"

"I mean, no, I've never met him in person," Bec said, casting her eyes away from Stevie. "We met in a chat room."

Stevie just stared. She didn't know what else to do. Bec began pacing again.

"It was fine for the first few years," Bec continued. "We'd talk every day after school, tell each other secrets, complain about our lives. You know, typical depressed teenager shit." Bec took a breath. "And then we grew up and things changed."

"What do you mean things changed?"

Bec chewed her bottom lip nervously. "Remember when I drove out to California with my aunt right before we moved into our first apartment?"

Stevie's face scrunched together. "The trip to visit your extended family? When we were like 21?" Bec nodded softly. As she did, Stevie began to understand. "There was no trip."

"There was, just not with my aunt." Bec shot a hesitant look at Stevie. "I went to meet him by myself."

"For fuck's sake," Stevie scolded her. "You could have been kidnapped by some creepy, online predator. Why didn't you tell me? I would have gone with you."

"I'm sorry," Bec said. "I don't know. I mean when we first started talking I was embarrassed. I was one of those people with an online friend. Then we'd been talking for so long it was weirder that I hadn't met him or even seen his face. I didn't want to be judged."

"I wouldn't have judged you," Stevie shouted. "Goddamnit, Bec, you should have told me. I'm your fucking best friend."

Bec's voice grew quiet as she sat back down on the bed. "I know, I'm sorry."

Stevie let out a deep sigh. Her stomach was in knots now. Somehow, the fact that Bec knew exactly who was doing this made it worse. So much worse.

"Fuck. Okay. Tell me the rest of it. What happened when you met him?"

"I didn't," Bec answered. "I chickened out. I left the place we were supposed to meet before he got there. After that, he wanted to come visit me. He asked all the time but I always made up excuses."

"Why?"

"I don't know. After all that time, I was scared to meet him, I guess. What if he wasn't the same in real life?"

Stevie bit back the flurry of horribly-timed jokes about psychopaths that popped into her head. "Okay well, what happened after that?"

Bec shook her head. "We kept talking. I guess you could have said we were dating at one point."

Stevie really wished Bec would stop talking. Every time she thought it couldn't get worse, it did.

"I don't understand how you could date someone without knowing who they were. And you just kept all this from me?" Stevie lectured. "This feels like some messed up Catfish-Dateline crossover."

Bec seemed to shrink into herself, and Stevie put her hands up in front of her defensively. "Shit, sorry. I didn't mean to be all judgey. I just don't understand how you let all that happen."

"It was just one of those things. When we were younger, we were both a little shy. Then we got comfortable with each other and I was honestly more nervous to find out who he was. It was easier not knowing. It didn't feel as real. He was a major part of my life and I didn't want that to go away."

"Okay," Stevie breathed, trying to understand it all. "So

you two were in some sort of online relationship and then what? He snapped?"

"I met Brennen."

"Shit."

"Yeah," Bec replied, letting a sick, fearful laugh rip from her throat. "Shit." Bec's hands shook softly. "It was all my fault."

"No. What happened wasn't your fault."

"Yes," Bec said. "Yes it was."

"How?" Stevie argued. "How could you have possibly known he wou—"

"He told me."

Stevie quieted instantly.

"He warned me what would happen if I didn't break up with Brennen," Bec said quickly. "He told me and I thought he was being dramatic. I didn't believe him."

"Jesus..." A sick feeling sloshed around Stevie's stomach. All these years, she'd tried to play the big sister role, protecting Bec from whatever came her way. But as Stevie had been watching the outside world for problems, Bec had let trouble slither up closer than Stevie could have ever imagined. "When was the last time you heard from him?"

Bec hesitated. It made Stevie physically ill.

"Bec..."

"When we moved I got a new number. I changed my name. It was supposed to be ove—"

"Tell me—"

"Two weeks ago."

Stevie's blood seemed to turn to ice in her veins. She sat there, mouth slightly agape, fighting the urge to yell at her friend for her stupidity. Instead she forced a deep breath from her lungs and spoke as calmly as possible.

"What does he want?"

"Me."

A bloodcurdling scream erupted from behind the bedroom door. As Stevie met Bec's gaze, she felt adrenaline explode through her. By the time the second scream filled her eardrums, reverberating like an alarm, Stevie was halfway out the door. She clutched the ceramic sculpture she'd snagged off the dresser as she stepped into the hallway and prepared to meet Bec's secret friend.

✦ MONIQUE ✦

Her throat felt scratchy and raw as the third scream ripped from her lungs. No matter how much it hurt, she couldn't stop. She couldn't believe what was in front of her eyes. It had to be a dream. It couldn't be real. It wasn't until Stevie appeared at Monique's side that reality started setting in.

"Holy shit," Stevie muttered under her breath as she stared out onto the patio.

A sharp crash erupted at Monique's feet as the sculpture Stevie had been holding slipped from her grasp. Little shards of ceramic grazed Monique's legs. She barely noticed; all Monique could focus on was the blood. Stevie raced out the door and caught Benny as he stumbled forward, his bodyweight almost knocking her to the ground as she struggled to keep him upright.

"A towel," Stevie screamed. "Bec, get me a towel."

It all went by too quickly. Bec pushed past Monique, a towel swinging in her hand as she scrambled out onto the patio. Monique watched Benny's eyes grow wider and wider as Bec held the towel firmly against the slit that ran horizontally across his throat. She would never be able to get the blood out of that shirt. That was his favorite shirt. She watched the blood rush and gush down Benny, her own body motionless and hollow. She blinked a few times, as if she was waiting for the picture in front of her to change. Benny was on his knees now, his burly build too much for Stevie to hold up for any longer. Monique took a few steps forward until her feet grazed the harsh concrete of the patio. Her body hovered in the doorway, unable to go any further. Bec was yelling at her, but Monique couldn't hear a thing. Stevie yelled something at Bec, frantically adding the weight of her hands on top of Bec's as they held the towel in place. It grew dark and soon the plush white fabric was soaked from the slick of red that flowed from Benny's throat.

Monique staggered out onto the patio as Miles pushed past her and ran toward Benny. Benny jerked away, causing the towel to slip from its position. Red splatters hit the ground in thick drops. Bec was crying now, the tears rushing down her face as the blood guzzled out of Benny. He was still pulling away from them, his eyes growing frantic and his mouth letting loose an indistinguishable gurgle of blood and half-formed words. Stevie tried to contain Benny's flailing, panicked arms to press the towel against his wound but it was too late. Benny let out one final gurgle before collapsing onto the patio with a thud. A delirious scream ripped from Monique's lungs. She wrapped her hands around her mouth tightly and stared wide-eyed at the limp body. She waited for him to move, to pull a ragged breath back into his lungs. When he didn't, everything slowed down. He was dead. Her husband had bled out in front of her. She had watched, silently and helplessly. Why had she just stood there? Her chest tightened. The wail that left Monique's throat was animalistic. It came from the depths of her soul and refused to finish, even when her voice cracked. Her feet carried her in heavy, staggering steps. She dropped to her knees in front of him, babbling incoherent noises as she buried her face into his chest.

"This can't be happening. This can't be really happening."

She felt the warm trickle of blood pooling down her front as she pressed against him. Hands pulled at her carefully but she shook them off.

"No," she screamed, clinging to Benny harder. "Get off of me!" Her sobs rocked her body. "Benny, wake up. Please wake up."

Her fingers pulled at him, shaking him, desperate for him

to spring to life as if nothing had happened. She wailed and cried until finally, there was nothing left in her. Her voice was gone, burning in her throat. She leaned against him, hyperventilating until she felt the taste of bile in the back of her mouth. It was only when she realized she was covered in his blood, soaked to the bone with it, that she let Stevie and Bec pull her away. Her eyes flickered up to his face. The bright goofiness that she'd fallen for was drained from Benny. All that remained was the panicked look in his dead eyes. His body was slumped against the ground, looking smaller than she'd ever seen it. A pool of blood flowed around him, like an ocean surrounding an island. Their island. She rolled her head back and screamed again, grief ripping through her body in one final, desperate howl.

✄ BEC ✄

Bec's eyes slipped outside to the patio once more.

Benny's body was long gone; Miles and Tyler had carried it to the back house. All that remained was a dark circle of blood. Bec couldn't seem to pull her eyes from it. Even as chaos unfurled around her, she found her focus wandering outside just to check and see if the stain was still there. It always was. She forced her attention back towards the group as Tyler's voice rose through the room.

"Everyone calm down. We'll figure this out."

"Calm down?" Stevie laughed bitterly. "Three people are dead. Dead. We can't dick around anymore. We need to find a way to defend ourselves. We need to get out of here."

Tyler's frustration seeped out as the open palm of his hand slapped the countertop harshly. "There's no way off this island until tomorrow. Have you been listening to me at all?"

Stevie pulled a medium-sized knife out of the kitchen's wood block and held it up in front of her. It unsheathed from the holder with a sharp twang. "Well I'm not dying on this fucking island."

"Put that away," Tyler scolded her. "Have you ever used a knife on someone? You're going to hurt yourself."

"Do you ever get tired of being a know-it-all piece of—"

"You did this."

The argument stopped as everyone turned to look at Monique, but Monique was looking at her—Bec.

"Benny's dead because of you."

"Monique," Stevie snapped. "This isn't Bec's—"

"Benny and I read the story. You know the one that said

your boyfriend's death was a little suspicious?"

Bec felt panic strike her heart. She tried to speak but guilt seemed to swell her tongue.

"What are you talking about?" Stevie asked.

"Marta did background checks on us," Monique said matter-of-factly. "They had some interesting information on Bec. But that's not even your real name, is it?"

Bec felt the room bearing down on her, suffocating her. "I can ex—"

"Did you do it?" Monique snarled. "Did you kill your boyfriend?" She was off the couch and up in Bec's face now, shoving her. "Do you even have a stalker?"

"Monique, what the fuck!" Stevie yelled, pulling her off Bec. "She didn't kill anyone."

Monique swatted Stevie's hand away. "Then why do a bunch of people on the internet think she did?"

"Because people are assholes," Stevie retorted. "They need something to talk about. They sit behind their keyboards and go on their little true crime podcasts and pretend to be detectives. It's a bunch of bullshit."

"It doesn't sound like bullshit to me," Monique snapped back. "Funny how there wasn't any mention of a stalker in what I read. Wonder why that is..."

"It's because officially there was no stalker." Bec felt all eyes on her as soon as the words left her lips. Anxiety began to kick her heart into overdrive but she managed to get her next words out before it paralyzed her. "I didn't tell the cops about him."

"What?" Tyler questioned. "Why wouldn't you tell the cops?"

Bec looked away from him. The look he was giving her seemed to eat its way under her skin. It was all confusion and disappointment and doubt. It was too much. Her gaze drifted, eager to find someone who didn't look at her like a caged animal. She found what she was looking for in Miles. He stood there, leaning against the wall, with eyes filled with something much different than Tyler's.

Monique was pacing back and forth in wild agitation. "Because she obviously killed him!" she yelled.

"Jesus Christ, Monique," Stevie yelled back. "Bec didn't do it."

Bec took a shaky breath. Monique was one of her closest friends in LA. Over the years, she'd considered confiding in her multiple times. Every time, a gut instinct had stopped her from divulging her past. Bec knew it was too much for anyone—too complicated, too messy. Hell, she hadn't even told Stevie the whole truth until now. But as Bec watched Benny's death rip Monique apart inside, she wondered if things would have gone differently if she had told Monique earlier. Or maybe the hatred Monique spat at her now was unavoidable.

"I didn't tell the cops because he was my friend."

Miles tilted his head at her. His eyes seemed to pry at her, desperate for answers. Bec looked away quickly. Whatever he thought of her now, she couldn't bear to know.

"What are you saying?" Tyler asked. "Your friend killed your boyfriend?"

"It's complicated," Bec started, feeling her stomach squirm nervously. "We met in a chatroom when we were younger. We never met in person."

"I don't believe you," Monique said flatly. She had stopped pacing and was standing in the middle of the living room, eyes still blazing. "You really think we're buying any of this bullshit?"

"Monique," Stevie snapped. "I know you're going through a lot right now but calm the fuck down. This isn't her fault."

"No, Monique's right," Bec said quietly. "It's my fault Benny is dead."

"Stop," Stevie pleaded. "It's not, though. You have no control over what some fucked up guy on the internet does."

"Don't I?"

Stevie was silent at that. Bec chewed on the inside of

her cheek until it drew blood. She let the metallic twang of it melt onto her tongue before sucking in a deep breath and preparing for everything to end.

"I told you he contacted me two weeks ago but I didn't tell you what he said."

Bec was only talking to Stevie now. She couldn't bear to see the look on anyone else's face as she admitted how selfish and cowardly she had been. She prayed that Stevie would understand, that she would forgive her. But Bec knew that was foolish. She couldn't even forgive herself. How could she expect anyone else to? As Tyler moved towards her, Bec felt the words tumble out of her.

"He texted me asking who made me happier. My boyfriend, or my..." Her eyes flickered to Miles.

Miles looked at her carefully, his brow raising in contemplation.

"He said I had to choose. I had to choose one of them to..." Bec's voice slipped away.

"To what?" Tyler spat.

Bec dropped her gaze to the floor and didn't let it budge. "Make it right."

"Oh fuck," Stevie sighed.

"Are you hearing her?" Monique shrieked, looking at everyone with big, bulging eyes. "You sound insane," she spat at Bec. "There's no stalker. You killed your ex. You probably killed Benny. You did this. You did!" Monique had started crying again, ragged fits of shuddering breath ripping through her. She slumped onto the couch as she lost control of the torrent of emotions plaguing her.

"She has a point."

It felt like Miles had slapped Bec from across the room. His words gutted her. She met his gaze and found his curiosity replaced with doubt.

"Not about you killing people," he clarified quickly. "I'm just saying, how did your friend know about this trip if you didn't?"

Bec thought about it for a minute. Could he have stalked Tyler too? Hacked into his email somehow and gotten the details for their trip? She felt like there was a brick in her stomach. Yes—yes he could have. She knew what this was, even if no one else believed her.

"So what?" Stevie prodded. "You think it's someone else?"

"I do," Miles stated. "Someone with motive. Someone who could get on the island. Someone who knows us."

"The fuck are you saying?" Tyler scoffed. "You think one of us did this?"

Miles looked at him with cold calculation. Bec's body tensed as she watched his eyes grow dark.

"That's exactly what I'm saying."

"Come on, Miles," Stevie laughed but Bec could hear the uneasiness in her voice. "You know it wasn't any of us."

"Do I?" he quipped. "It seems like anytime something happens, one of us is always nowhere to be found."

Bec watched Monique's focus snap to Miles. She fidgeted on the couch, as if a snake was slithering across her lap.

"Where were you when we were attacked in the jungle?" Miles asked carefully as he stepped towards Tyler.

"You're a fucking idiot," Tyler scoffed. "I don't need to answer that because I didn't do anything wrong."

"And what about when Benny was killed?" Miles continued. "You were the only one not in the house. Well, except for Benny..."

"I was down at the beach."

"Convenient," Miles replied. He had made his way across the kitchen and was now standing in between Bec and Tyler. "What were you doing this time? Checking on Eleni again?"

Bec felt her head spin. She tried to steady her thoughts. What had Tyler been doing when Benny died? He'd shown up after it had happened. Bec and Stevie had led Monique to the sink to clean up. Bec had watched Tyler carefully through the window. He seemed distraught at the sight of his best friend slumped to the ground like a sack of potatoes. He had yelled and shoved Miles away. After what felt like an eternity of him just sitting there on the patio, he had mumbled something to Miles before the two of them had carried the body away. When Tyler returned, it was like he was made of stone. He had barely looked at any of them. But now, now his face was alight with emotion.

"I needed some space. That's all," he rasped, the corner of his lip turning up into a scowl.

"Space, huh? Couldn't have gone to your room?"

"I needed to get out of this house," he snapped. "I needed to get away from Bec."

Bec flinched at that.

"Why?" Miles prodded.

"Why?" Tyler taunted. "Because you fucking ruined her."

"Ruined?" Miles was toe to toe with Tyler now, his gaze searing into him. "If you think that then you never deserved her in the first place."

Bec saw the whole scene play out in her mind. Tyler would leap across the room, his fist colliding with Miles' jaw, resulting in a loud crack. The two men would wrestle to the ground, each trying to get the upper hand. Stevie and Bec would desperately try to pry them off one another. None of that happened. Instead, all Bec saw was a dark gleam fill Tyler's eyes. He stayed where he was and nodded.

"You're right," Tyler said flatly. "She's all yours."

Miles seemed taken aback for a second, as if he'd been expecting the same scenario that Bec had imagined. He held Tyler's gaze steadily for a moment before smirking. "Hey, baby," he called behind him. He gestured towards the hallway but his eyes stayed fixed on Tyler. "Go grab your stuff and toss it in my room."

Bec stayed put and avoided eye contact with the both of them. This was stupid, childish. She wanted to tell them both to fuck off. But something held her tongue. It was a nagging thought that seemed to charge her nerves like a live wire. While they were all arguing, where was he?

"But Miles—I want you to know something."

Miles scowled at Tyler and raised his eyebrows. "Oh yeah? What's that?"

"When Bec decides she's bored with you—and she will—you'll know where to find her."

Miles let out a sickly laugh as he headed for Tyler. "The only thing that's going to ha—"

"Where were you when Eleni died?"

Monique's voice jetted across the room and seemed to push the two men out of their egos. In seconds, Monique sprang into action. She stormed across the room, only stopping when she was face to face with Tyler. Something had cracked behind her eyes. It danced wildly as she stared at him.

"Benny came back that night and said you were getting shitfaced on the beach. He said that you were pissed and now that I think about it...I don't remember seeing you at the house until the morning."

"You've got to be kidding me," Tyler said, the anger picking up in his voice.

"We all know what happens when you get drunk and angry, Tyler," Monique spat, fighting back fresh tears as her face contorted in anger and pain. "And I know you threatened him..."

Bec's stomach dropped. Her eyes flashed to Tyler, trying to study his face as he argued with Monique, claiming his innocence and her insanity. But as Bec watched, a memory of Eleni and Tyler on the darkened path flickered in her mind like an old movie. Tyler and Eleni had been arguing the night Eleni died. Tyler had shoved her. He had been angry. Waves of deep-seated dread crashed into Bec as she tried to understand.

"...you don't know what you're talking about," Tyler argued. "It was fucking college. I was drunk. It was a mistake."

"That doesn't make you any less of a murderer," Monique

screamed. "You killed that boy just like you killed Benny. You gutless motherf—"

Monique's hands pummeled against Tyler's forearms as he tried to fend off her assault. All Bec could think about was how Tyler had acted over the past few days. Angry. Volatile. Cruel. He seemed capable of anything in those moments of fury—moments like the one she had witnessed alone in the jungle. She swallowed harshly.

"Stop," Bec yelled, pulling their focus to her. "Tyler, what were you and Eleni doing—"

Her words cut off into a scream as something smacked against the sliding glass door. It took her a second to take it all in.

"What the fuck? Is that..." Stevie murmured as they all stared through the patio door.

"Adrian," Miles said quietly.

Bec watched Adrian's body slide down the glass, his hand leaving a bloody print. Words slurred from his mouth, muffled by the glass and the weakness in his voice. Bec started for the door but Miles stopped her, griping her wrist tightly. She could feel his fear digging into her skin.

"Wait," Miles said firmly. "What if it's a trap?"

They all looked at each other, considering it.

"Didn't finish the job?" Monique chided Tyler. "Seems like a rookie mistake. Especially for you."

Bec shot a look at her and the look on Monique's face scared Bec more than Adrian's bloodied body outside. When she looked at Monique, all she could see was the grief that had ruptured something inside of her. She wasn't thinking clearly. She had thrown blame at both her and Tyler. Who was next? Miles? Stevie? As Bec pulled her focus back to the door, she met Tyler's gaze. There was a fear in his sharp blue eyes that raised the hairs on her arm. He was scared, too. But of what, exactly? Adrian's hand rapped on the glass unsteadily. Bec's heart jumped in her chest as he raised his head to look at them. Blood had dried down his neck in messy streaks. Bec noticed the small nick in the middle of his throat and felt her blood chill. Her eyes shifted to his torso where a series of slashes scored the fabric of his shirt.

"Let him in," she urged everyone. "We have to let him in."

Tyler and Miles eyed each other uncertainly, their hostility temporarily sidelined. Fuck this. Bec pushed past them both before yanking the door open. As she did, Adrian's body collapsed at her feet.

⚔ MILES ⚔

Miles gritted his teeth as he watched Adrian. He was no more than a lump on the bed, his legs and arms splayed out weakly. He barely reacted as Bec pressed an alcohol-soaked towel to the deep lacerations that were carved through his abdomen.

"Why won't it stop?" Bec muttered as fresh blood poured from the dirty cuts. "Stevie, where's that sewing kit?"

Her voice rang past where Miles was stationed by the door and down to where Stevie was frantically digging through the junk, liquor bottles, and leftover food that was starting to pile on the kitchen counter.

"Gimme a second!" Stevie shot back.

"We don't have a second."

"Here, let me help," Tyler said, heading across the room towards Bec.

"Stay the hell away from him," Monique roared, blocking Tyler's path.

"Are you serious right now?"

"Deadly." Monique crossed her arms in front of her chest. "Until Adrian wakes up and tells us that you didn't do that to him," she continued, "you're not so much as breathing on him."

"Fucking unreal," Tyler snapped. "You honestly think I did this?"

"Yeah. I do."

"Give me one good reason why I would have done this."

Adrian stirred, his eyes flickering open for a second. Miles' heart skipped a few beats. Adrian hadn't said anything when they'd brought him inside and carried him to his room, only let out a pained murmur before slipping into unconsciousness. Monique said it was due to blood loss and dehydration. Whatever the reason, he didn't look good. Miles forced out a deep breath as he watched Adrian's eyelids flutter shut again. How did this happen?

"I'll give you multiple," Monique quipped. "You have anger issues. You've killed someone before—"

Stevie walked back in, her eyes flashing wildly as the information was thrust on her.

"Oh yeah, in case you missed it earlier..." Monique raged on. "Tyler got drunk and beat someone to death in college. So you could say he's got some practice at this."

"You're unstable," Tyler said. "I think Benny's death has seriously—"

"Don't you fucking talk about him," Monique seethed, cutting him off. "Benny confronted you earlier and you fucking snapped. And we all know what happens when someone does something you don't like."

"You've seriously lost your mind. Benny and I were fi—"

"Fine?" she chided him. "Benny told me earlier that you threatened to kill him if he told Bec about your past."

Everything in the room stopped. Bec pulled her hand away from Adrian's wounds. Stevie dropped the needle and thread on the bedspread. Even Miles ripped his focus from the unsteady, shallow rising and falling of Adrian's chest. Tyler had gone pale.

"Funny that you seemed to keep that promise," Monique said with a vicious twang before choking back a fresh batch of tears.

Tyler started to shake his head at her but stopped. He clenched his jaw, swallowing harshly before taking a step away from her slowly. "I didn't kill Benny," he said harshly. "He was my best friend."

"We'll just see what Adrian has to say," Monique stated, staying firmly planted between Tyler and the bed.

Tyler shook his head softly. There was a hesitation to him

now that Miles had never seen before. His typical arrogance had left him. Tyler was no longer in charge. Desperation seemed to hike its way up his face. Miles could tell by the way everyone was looking at Tyler that he was done for. He looked guilty.

"Fuck this," Tyler muttered, pushing passed Miles and leaving the room. "You can all think whatever the fuck you want. I'm going to figure out a way to keep us safe until the boat comes tomorrow. You can thank me later."

Monique seemed to watch the door like a mother bear protecting her cubs. Her body was tense until the sound of Tyler's bedroom door slamming shut reverberated through the room. Miles watched grief and anger play tug-of-war on her face as she stared off into the empty hallway. He felt bad for her, he really did. He couldn't imagine what it would feel like to lose the love of your life. His eyes flickered over to Bec. She was working with Stevie to stitch up Adrian's wounds. There were lines of tension forming around her eyes as she repeatedly wiped Adrian's blood away so Stevie could slide the needle under his skin. Breathy grunts slipped from Adrian's lips as his eyes darted back and forth under the lids. He was out of it, but he could obviously still feel pain. Miles returned his focus to Bec. She looked so worried but there was still determination there. She was a fighter. She took a shallow breath as one of Adrian's cuts wouldn't stop bleeding. Her lips quivered slightly. She was breathtaking in her fear. Miles could watch her for hours. At that moment, she looked up at him, catching his gaze. He smiled, hoping to bring her some comfort. She shot something back that was almost a smile before turning her attention to the task at hand. The gesture was enough to fill Miles with warmth.

"I have to take a shower," Monique muttered feebly.

She was looking down at herself, her husband's blood still all over her clothes. It was dried and caked into the fabric now. Miles saw the fierce protectiveness leave Monique's face all at once, like she was taking off a mask. It was replaced by exhaustion and misery. Whatever adrenaline Monique had earlier, it was gone now.

She stopped by Miles as she headed for her room. "Make sure Tyler doesn't come back in here. Yeah?"

Miles nodded. "Of course."

He turned, his eyes following her down the hall until she slipped into her room. He stared at the closed door for a second before bringing his attention back to Bec. Her hands were shaking again. She was clutching the bloody towel, watching Stevie finish up the last few stitches. The patch-up job was anything but pretty. Adrian had jagged lines of thread woven across his abdomen. Blood leaked from the small crevices, dyeing the beige threads sutured through his skin a bright crimson color. He looked like Frankenstein.

As Bec tended to him, her gaze seemed to lose its way. Her eyes grew distant and glassy as she stared at the sewn-up stab wounds. She was still sitting on the edge of the bed, eyes glued to Adrian, by the time Stevie packed up the sewing kit and scooted off the bed.

"Hey," Miles murmured.

Bec pulled herself out of the trance, numbness slipping from her eyes as she looked back at him.

"You okay?"

"What do you think?" Stevie quipped.

He shot her a side-eyed look which she returned with a tired groan. "Don't," she sighed. "I'm covered in blood. I think I'm allowed to be a little bitchy. Okay?"

Miles let out a breathy laugh before turning back to Bec. Her eyes hadn't left him.

"Come here," he said softly.

"Okay..." Stevie said, exaggerating the word. "I think I'm gonna go clean up before I see something I can't unsee." She raised her eyebrows at Bec before slipping into the hall.

Bec stayed on the end of the bed with the inside of her cheek buried in her teeth.

"Come here," he repeated, not able to keep the smile off

his face this time. She was too stubborn for her own good.

She walked across the room slowly, too slowly. It took everything in him not to meet her halfway and snatch her up into his arms. He took a deep breath and waited. She hovered a few feet away from him. He could see the uncertainty and hesitation on her face. He pushed himself off the doorframe he'd been leaning on and closed the distance between them. Her pupils dilated oh-so-slightly as he weaved his hand around her waist. She still wanted him. Good. He pulled her closer, feeling the quickening of her pulse against his skin. Just as he brushed his thumb against her cheek, thunder rumbled overhead. She jumped slightly.

"Easy. I've got you," Miles teased. He held her tightly. He didn't want to let her go. He wanted to keep her safe with him always. "I'm not going to let anything happen to you."

A flicker of annoyance danced across her face before she smiled at him. "If you say that one more time I'm going to punch you."

He brushed his thumb along her jawline until his hand rested on the back of her neck. He held his focus on her, letting everything else drift away. She had a few beauty marks on her cheek, peppering her skin in soft brown hues. His eyes trailed down the few on her neck. He'd let his mouth trace the patterns they drew on her skin on more than one occasion. Now, he felt his body yearning to do it again. Something interrupted his train of thought, though—something he needed to know.

"Tell me about him."

Bec looked at him, her face softly reddening.

"What?"

Thunder boomed overhead, seeming to shake the house.

"Your friend. The one you think is doing this."

Bec pulled away from him. It was subtle but he noticed. Her eyes drifted along the floor.

"I don't want to talk abo—"

"Did you love him?"

Her focus shot up to his face immediately. "What?"

He took his time answering, desperate to read any flicker of emotion that her face gave away. But all he could see was panic.

"You said you didn't turn him in because he was your friend." Miles swallowed harshly, trying to keep his own emotions at bay. "You must have cared for him a lot."

"I did."

Miles felt her words run over every inch of his chest like tires in the mud. In that moment, the room felt too loud. Rain pounded down onto the roof heavily. Bec's silence was louder than anything that brewed above them. It seemed to drown out Miles' thoughts for a minute. All he could do was stare into her eyes, clinging to her presence like a buoy keeping him afloat. Another roll of thunder erupted over the house. Miles' brow furrowed, rogue thoughts pulling him into the violent current of his mind once again.

"Why?"

Bec broke eye contact, but not before Miles saw something flicker in her eyes.

"You can tell me. I would never judge you."

She took a steady breath but kept her gaze away from him. "Two of our friends are dead, Miles. And the guard. Adrian needs to get to a hospital."

Her voice wavered. Miles wrapped both hands around the sides of her face and pulled her gaze to him softly.

"Hey, don't worry about that now," he whispered.

She had tears in her eyes. She tried to shake him off but he held her face firmly in place.

"I'm going to get us both out of here. Okay?"

She stayed quiet but he could feel her breathing begin to settle. He smiled down at her as he brushed a rogue tear off her cheek.

"Remember when you didn't make the volleyball team junior year and you thought the world was ending?"

She tilted her head, her eyes reaching him curiously.

"Yeah, but—"

"You thought your life was over. But it wasn't. You joined the art club instead and everything worked out."

"Miles, this isn't the sa—"

"Everything worked out." He leaned in closer, his mouth hovering inches from hers. "This will work out too."

Miles moved in towards her, ignoring the hesitation woven into her eyes. She was still scared, but he'd make things better.

A moan from behind them ripped his focus. He pulled back, shooting a worried glance over Bec's shoulder. Adrian's eyes were still closed but he was squirming against the bed, his hands slapping at his raw, exposed skin.

"Shit," Bec muttered. "What if he rips out his stitch—"

Miles grabbed Bec's arm quickly, stopping her as she tried to head towards Adrian. She turned around, confused. He quickly released his tight grip on her, letting the concern on his face loosen up into a smile.

"Don't. You need to rest. I'll take care of it."

Thunder boomed overhead. Bec's body tensed as the house shook lightly. A dash of lighting danced behind the rain-streaked window. The storm was getting closer. Miles smiled as he brushed a piece of hair behind Bec's ear.

"Seriously. I got it. I promised Monique I'd stand guard anyways. Go clean up and we'll talk later, okay?"

Bec nodded. She reached out and squeezed his hand before leaving the room.

Miles watched her leave, locking eyes with her one final time before she slipped behind the door to Stevie's room. He should have kissed her. He shook his head at himself as he stepped back in Adrian's room and closed the door behind him. A muffled groan of pain left Adrian's throat. It sounded about as bad as Adrian looked. Miles watched from across the room as Adrian raised his eyelids slowly, mumbling in pain until finally his eyes opened. As he blinked away the haze, he looked panicked.

"Hey, man. It's okay," Miles offered. "You're okay now."

Adrian's eyes went wide as he thrashed around. It only lasted a few seconds until he slipped back into unconsciousness. Miles swore under his breath as he leaned over Adrian to get a better look at him. The cuts were deep. As deep as they needed to be to do damage. How had he managed to even get back to the house? He was tougher than he looked. He'd been left for dead and somehow found his way out of the jungle. Even Miles had to admit it was impressive.

Miles tried not to laugh as he eyed the bloodied strands of thread that looked like the work of a child trying to patch a hole in their favorite sweater. They were worse than the ones Monique had stitched into him. Adrian would be lucky if he didn't get an infection from Stevie's ill attempt at playing doctor. Adrian's breathing was ragged. He twitched slightly but didn't wake again. As Miles kept watch over Adrian, he let his mind wander. Adrian wasn't the only one who was surprising him. Tyler wasn't who Miles thought he was. Acting aggressively with Bec. Killing someone in college. Miles stared out the window, watching the storm rage outside. With every day that passed on this island, it seemed more and more likely that Tyler was capable of anything.

⚔ MONIQUE ⚔

The mirror fogged over and Monique disappeared.

She wiped the sleeve of her sweatshirt against the glass until her reflection stared back at her. She looked awful. But not as awful as she felt. Stray curls were popping out of her braid and mascara was smeared down her cheeks, leaving long trails of black. The sight startled her. She had a haunted look. She felt haunted. Every time she closed her eyes, all she could see was that gaping slice across Benny's throat. The thought of it now made her tremble.

She reached past the shower curtain and checked the water temperature. It was hot but not hot enough. She wanted it to burn when she stepped underneath it. She needed her mind to be occupied by other things, physical things. A chill had swept through the house as soon as the rain had begun beating into the ground. Now, the harsh rumble of the storm outside seemed to rock the emptiness inside of her. Monique's focus drifted from the storm to the soft whooshing of the showerhead as it unleashed steady sprays of water onto the tile. Her mother had always told her not to take a shower during a storm. She let the warning drift away. A deep, desolate feeling was spreading through her chest. It had started earlier but now it seemed to ache with every breath she took. There was a piece of her missing and the lack of its presence was hitting her harder than she expected. Benny wasn't perfect. Their marriage was in shambles. But she didn't care. She just wanted him back. Monique looked back into the mirror, her eyes only visible for a second before she disappeared into the steamy hot mist once again. She almost laughed. She never imagined the world could be this cruel.

Something shot Monique awake. A noise. She turned her head towards the bathroom door and waited there for a moment. The storm raged outside, but had it gotten louder? Her brow furrowed as she reached for the door knob and turned. Stepping into the bedroom, a fresh chill hit her instantly. Why was the window open? Her eyes stared into the darkness that filled the open windowsill. Her bare feet shuffled across the floor quickly, then shot up onto her tip toes as she stepped on something wet. Sprays of rain blew in through the open window, sliding down her face like tears. The sun had disappeared underneath the horizon, only leaving the eerie glow of the moon. It illuminated the palm trees that swayed violently against the wind. She struggled to shut the window. Finally she pulled it closed with a hard thud. All at once, the noise and chaos of the room diminished. All was still except for the murmured roar of the storm outside.

She headed back towards the bathroom but then stopped, turning to stare at the window once more. Had she left it unlocked earlier? Had the wind blown it open? Was that even possible? She fought her own mind to make sense of it. The last hour seemed like a blur—a living nightmare. She didn't know up from down. All she could seem to think about was the way Benny had fallen to his knees on the patio, his eyes yearning for her to help him. Why hadn't she gone to him before it was too late? Her gut wrenched and she sucked in a sharp breath to keep the tears at bay. She'd cried enough today. She'd cry again at the funeral—if there was a funeral.

Her feet carried her back across the room numbly. As she began to strip off her shorts, the crinkle of something pulled her focus. She took the wadded-up papers out of her pocket, almost ripping them in her haste. Her eyes burned into the pages, reading line by line until she couldn't take it anymore. She scoffed and tossed Tyler's background check onto the dresser. Why was she even bothering? She knew what was on the pages, knew what Benny had told her. Tyler had admitted it. He was a murderer, no matter how he spun it. Monique's grief turned to rage as she stripped off her sweatshirt, now damp with rain and stained beyond help with dark, dried blood. She stood in front of the dresser in her underwear and bra but something kept her from heading to the shower. Her eyes glared down at the background check one last time. She stared at Tyler's picture. He had a look in his eyes, a dark thing that lacked remorse. The look of a killer. The chill that had found her earlier lingered and spread across her bare skin until goosebumps rippled her flesh. She knew it was Tyler. It had to be. She'd convince the others. She'd lock Tyler out of the house until tomorrow if that's what it took.

She heard a soft thump behind her. Monique's heart leapt into her chest as her eyes flickered to the window. She stood there, frozen in place, waiting for something to appear. Her mother's words echoed in her mind. *Be stronger than your fear.* She swallowed her fear and took a step closer. Then another. She peered through the window, her vision distorted by large flecks of rain on the glass. She jumped as palm fronds blew against the bottom corner of the window. It was just the storm. She forced a deep breath from her lungs. But just as she turned around to head for the shower's warm, numbing embrace, she paused. Her eyes flickered back to the window. Something nagged at her, a feeling that she was missing something. A feeling that something wasn't right but she couldn't think clearly enough to know what it was. Grief had a funny way of shaking your brain like a snow globe.

Monique stepped forward and flipped the lock on the window. She wished Benny were here. He was tough. Her mind went to the back house. The image almost dropped her to her knees. She steadied herself on the wall, trying not to think of how he was lying on the floor in that prisonlike room. Cold. Alone. Dead. Benny was dead. At 34 years old, Monique was a widow. She took a deep, shaky breath as she pushed herself forward. She needed to clear her head, get herself right. The soft hiss of the shower and the hot steam that drifted from the bathroom door carried her forward. A shower would help, it had too.

She closed the bathroom door tightly behind her. The warmth of the steam that filled the room caressed her skin with a comforting embrace. Everything was going to be okay. She didn't believe it but she forced a nasty glimmer of hope to root inside her anyways. She knew who was doing this. There was no maniac out there stalking them. The danger was inside the house. And while the thought brought a sick ache to her stomach, somehow she was less scared. She'd rally everyone when she got cleaned up. Miles would help her restrain Tyler. Stevie would be overjoyed to help. The staff would come back in the morning. They'd call the police. It all seemed reasonable to Monique. Doable. Survivable. Everything was going to be okay. But when she wiped the steam from the mirror and saw an extra pair of eyes looking back at her, she knew she was anything but okay.

Monique tried to scream but hands wrapped around her mouth too quickly, trapping any sound that tried to burst from her lips.

"Surprise," he said softly in her ear. The mirror had already fogged over but she could tell by the zeal in his voice that he was smiling. "Easy," he whispered.

Monique's body fought against him but he was strong, holding her in place with what seemed like little effort.

"We can do this your way or my way."

Monique felt the cool touch of something against her skin. She froze as the pressure of it grew sharp. Her eyes drifted down to her stomach. A kitchen knife rested against her skin, remnants of blood flaked on the handle. The moisture in the air seemed to make the blade glimmer in the light. Fear licked at Monique's throat as she stood there breathlessly. She stopped struggling.

"Good," he breathed into her ear. "Now I want you to

know there's no hard feelings, okay?"

The air came out of Monique's mouth in harsh, ragged breaths. Was this how Benny had felt? Had he been held in this twisted limbo where she was now? Knowing he was about to die before it even happened?

"You're just caught in the middle. Collateral damage."

Something in his voice slipped just then, the calmness momentarily replaced by his suffering.

"An unfortunate consequence of knowing Amelia—of loving her."

Monique struggled to understand as her panic swarmed her like a hive of bees. Amelia? *Right, of course. Amelia. Bec.* Suddenly, everything made sense.

"Wrong place, wrong time."

He pressed the tip of the knife against Monique's skin, teasing the flesh. It didn't draw blood but her heart didn't care. It pounded inside of her with unbridled fear. She stared at the tip of the blade, anticipating the second it would finally pierce her skin.

"Out of all of them, I hate you the least," he continued. "You and Adrian."

He let out a soft laugh, pulling the blade away from her. Monique's eyes darted around, desperately trying to find something, anything, that would save her.

"Damn, could that fucker run. I went easy on him, though. I shouldn't have done that."

Hair dryer. Toothbrush. Benny's electric razor. Monique's breath quivered in her throat as she realized there was nothing.

"But like I said," he continued. "I don't hate you. You and Adrian wouldn't have gotten in my way. You would have let me have her. That's why I almost feel bad about this."

Monique released the breath she'd been holding but it was short lived.

"But not bad enough."

The knife went in and out of her stomach so quickly that

Monique barely knew it had happened. A sharp gasp left her lips. The sound slipped between his fingers as his hand loosened from her mouth. Her eyes dropped and watched the blood as it slowly oozed from her. Everything seemed to come alive inside her all at once. *Get out*, her mind screamed at her. *Get out of this bathroom. Get away from him.* She staggered forward, using the bathroom sink to hold her up as the pain in her stomach radiated out in violent pangs. In and out. In and out. Her body dropped to the floor as the knife glided into her back not once, but twice more. She let out a soft grunt as her hand groped at the doorknob.

"Help," she moaned.

Her vision grew splotchy as she felt the knife sink into her side, only to be yanked free a few seconds later. She drew in a sharp breath and let it out in a soft cry. The storm thundered against the house, blurring into the rhythmic sound of the shower and muffling her pleas.

"Help." She cried out a little louder this time but it still wasn't enough.

The knife slipped in between her back ribs, meeting resistance as he yanked the blade out of her. Everything was growing cold. Wetness seemed to run down her in streaks. The bathroom light beamed at her like the heavens above, calling her to come upstairs. She felt her head being pulled back slowly. Even in her fading mind, she knew what was coming. A white hot pain seared from her scalp as he gripped her hair and dragged her backwards until she was crumpled against the tub. She reached up and pawed at the shower curtain and he smiled at her, a wide, sickly grin that made her want to close her eyes and never see anything ever again. It was the face of the devil. She pushed her fingers into the ground as she tried to get up but slipped against the slick flow of blood.

"Stop" she breathed, the act of speaking shooting pain through every slice in her body. "Please."

"It's a little late for that."

He smirked as he crouched down next to her and ran his fingers across the blade. Smears of blood ran down his fingertips and dripped onto the floor to join the rest of the damage he'd done. Monique blinked weakly, trying to see the picture in front of her. His eyes glowed dark like a deep pit that would consume her. He looked like a rabid dog, too far gone to be saved. It needed to be put down. Monique tried to back away as he brought the blade to her neck. He let out a deep breath, as if savoring the moment.

"Tell Benny I said hi."

⚔ BEC ⚔

Bec paced the room. The rain outside pattered harshly against the window.

Tap-tap-tap-tap-tap-tap-tap.

She took a deep breath and stopped, placing her hands on top of the dresser, and stared into the mirror that hung over it. The look of turmoil and fear woven into the contours of her face was all too familiar. She dropped her gaze and rested her head in her hands. She needed to leave. That's the only thing she could think of. Every time she had tried to come up with a different solution, that one had swung back around like a boomerang.

She needed to leave.

Her eyes flickered to the bathroom door. Stevie was still in there, seemingly taking the world's longest shower. She was probably realizing that it took a while to get the feeling of blood off your skin. It never really left, though. Bec looked down at herself. She'd done nothing to clean herself up. Adrian's blood dappled the hem of her tank top in light splotches. Benny's blood was there too, darkening the collar. It was under her fingernails too, in little flakes of red that made her stomach queasy. It didn't matter. She needed to leave. If she left now, Stevie wouldn't be able to stop her. She'd be deep in the jungle before anyone realized she was gone.

She didn't give herself a chance to reconsider. She opened the bedroom door but hesitated as she stepped into the hall. She should grab a jacket, try to find a flashlight, get something to protect herself... She should be prepared—

just in case. As she contemplated it all, the door across the hall squeaked open. Shit. Bec shut Stevie's door behind her quickly and began walking.

"What are you doing?"

Bec stopped, teetering on the edge of her sneakers. Miles would stop her if he knew what she was planning. She should be sprinting down the hall and out the patio door right now. She needed to leave. Instead, she found herself turning around to face him. He shook a few drops of rain from his hair as he stepped out of his room.

"What's going on?"

"Nothing," Bec stated with a shaky breath. She dug her teeth into her cheek before turning on her heels. If she looked at him any longer, she wouldn't be able to go through with it.

"Wait," he said, snatching her wrist. He tugged her to a stop. "What are you doing?"

She said nothing. She couldn't. How could she explain? As he stepped closer, she pulled her wrist away.

"I need to leave."

"What are you talking about?"

"I have to go, Miles," she said, her words jumbling together in urgency. "I need to go now before—"

"You're not going anywhere," he stated flatly. "Just take a deep breath. Okay? Have you seen the storm outside? And where would you go? There's no way off this island—"

"I'm not trying to leave the island."

He looked at her carefully. "Then where are you going?"

Her answer settled on the tip of her tongue but the words wouldn't come. She tried to walk away but he pulled her back again, this time by the waist so she couldn't escape.

"Stop," he scolded her. "What's going on?"

"I need to go, Miles," she argued, twisting away from him the best she could.

"Go where?"

"To find him!"

His face went flat, frustration seeming to run off of it like the water that spilled down the roof. "You're going to look for him?" The question came out slowly, carefully. "Why?

"No one else is going to die because of me."

His dark eyes grew solemn. It was the type of look someone gave you when a family member passed away. It was the look Stevie had given her for months after Brennen had died. Sympathy. Sorrow. Pity. She didn't need any of it right now.

"If I go to him, he'll stop. He just wants me. When he gets me, it'll be over."

Miles pulled her in tightly before she could attempt another retreat. His skin was chilled but it felt like fire to her. For a moment she forgot what was happening and why she needed to leave.

"You know it's too late for that."

His words ripped her back to reality. There was a severity about his expression that made Bec want to fall into his arms and weep. He didn't think they were going to make it off this island alive. She could see it in his face. Bec felt her hands begin to shake. She curled them into fists, staving away the torrent of emotions building like a crescendo inside of her.

"I don't have time for this," she said, yanking herself free of him. She turned away and set her eyes on the end of the hall. Her pace quickened. She needed to go before he convinced her it was a death sentence. It was, but she still had to go. "I have to try. I can't let—"

The words were snatched from her breath as her feet left the safety of the ground. She hit the floor with a loud smack. Pain radiated from the base of her skull. It was fire in her nerves. She stared up at the ceiling, watching the splattering of stars and black spots dissipate from her vision. Miles was leaning over her. He was talking but she didn't hear him. The world seemed to warp and echo around her. Nausea curled inside of her as her senses fought to straighten themselves out. She pushed her hand into the floor to get up, but as she did, her hand slipped. Her vision tunneled as she lifted a red stained palm in front of her face. Long drips ran down her hand, only to plop back down into the gory puddle from which they had come. She blinked a few times, trying to understand. Voices shot through the air harshly. They were loud and frantic but it all seemed too far away to understand. All at once, Bec felt cold. She cast her eyes away from her hand and stared at the floor. Blood pooled around her, soaking into the fabric of her shorts and coating her skin wherever it touched. She tried to push away the throbbing in her skull and focus. She was hurt. She needed to find the source of the bleeding. She felt the base of her skull. It was tender but otherwise intact. She felt her stomach. Her gut clenched as she did, expecting to find slashes in her skin. She didn't. Finally, she raised a shaky hand to her throat. Her fingers left red streaks across her skin as she felt around. Nothing. Her eyes swam in the pool of red in front of her. Her mind screamed at her to stop but she didn't. Her eyes followed the red until it took her to the base of a door. Trails of it slipped from under the crack, over the baseboard, and into the pool that flowed around her. Bec looked up. She stared at the large slab of wood and the old brassy doorknob. As the floodgates of reality seemed to open on her, Stevie's panicked voice called out nearby. Bec felt the soft touch of someone's hand on her elbow as they tried to help her up. It was Miles. Stevie was yelling now. Bec felt the cool wetness slip from her skin as she found her footing. The entire time, all she could do was stare. Something bad had happened behind that door. As she had paced around Stevie's room, debating if she should go find him, he had been just down the hall. Miles steadied her, grabbing her by her shoulders. He was asking if she was okay. Was she? She didn't respond, lost in the depths of her mind. She stared at Monique and Benny's door. She had been wrong. There was no finding him first and there was no stopping this. There was only waiting—and death.

✒ STEVIE ✒

"Fuck!"

Stevie slammed her hand against the wall.

"Fucking fuck. This is fucking bullshit!"

Tears prickled at the corners of her eyes but she blinked them away. Stevie stomped through the kitchen, her hand swiping against everything on the counter. Plastic cups tumbled to the ground with an empty rattle. Stevie made contact with a tequila bottle, sending it crashing into the sink where it shattered into jagged pieces.

"Calm down," Miles demanded.

"Calm down?" Stevie snapped. "Monique was just killed in the fucking house! He came into the fucking house and—"

Her breath pounded in and out of her lungs. Her pulse raged through her. Every part of her was alive and agitated. She was hyperventilating now, her breath seeming to put her body in a chokehold. She stopped trashing the kitchen and put her hands on her knees as she bent over. Was she having a panic attack? Stevie tried to take steady, deep breaths but it was pointless. She felt like she was underwater, flailing wildly as she struggled to breach the surface. Her skin was hot and flushed. She felt her chest grow tighter with every frenzied breath. It was paired with a searing pain that throbbed from the center of her chest. Monique. Monique was gone. Stevie's throat constricted painfully. Ever since Benny had proposed, Stevie thought Monique was lost to her. But now—now, she realized that Monique had merely been out of reach. Stevie could have gotten Monique back if she tried hard enough, if she had gotten out of her own way. Now it was too late.

Monique wasn't lost to her, she was dead.

Lightning flashed, illuminating the patio in a quick strobe. Stevie's gaze flickered outside, and she held her gaze there long after the lightning had disappeared. Darkness stared back at her, unfriendly and uninviting. As her eyes unfocused, grief turned back to anger. Monique was gone before Stevie had ever told her the truth. Monique would never know that Stevie ended things because that was it for her—that she would have married Monique if it went any further. She hadn't been ready for that. She still didn't know if she was ready for that. So, out of fear, Stevie had left. Her teeth clenched as she staved off tears. Monique didn't deserve to die. None of them did.

"I'm gonna kill him."

"Stevie."

Stevie snapped her focus towards Bec. Fear had seeped into her pupils, the dark circles having grown slightly larger. Stevie could see the vacant haze still swimming around her eyes. How hard had she hit her head? Miles was at her side, holding a frozen bag of something to the back of her skull. His other hand was lightly draped against Bec's thigh. Stevie stared wildly, her anger circling back around. But she wasn't staring at Miles' hand. No, Stevie was staring at Bec's thighs. The back of them was lightly stained, faded red streaks splotching the skin. Stevie had watched Miles pull every towel from his bathroom to try to clean up. The floor. Bec. Everything. Stevie had wanted to help but couldn't. She had been paralyzed. Shocked. Devastated. Miles hadn't gotten it all off Bec. How could he have? There had been too much of it. Stevie turned away from Bec. She couldn't look at the final traces of Monique's life dried on her legs anymore.

"I'm gonna kill him," Stevie repeated, her voice stronger this time.

"We need to come up with a plan," Miles said. "We need to think rationally here."

Stevie glared at him. She knew he was right but that only

pissed her off more. She didn't want to be rational. She wanted to run into the jungle like a banshee and hunt down the fucker who did this.

"No," Stevie snarked back. "We need to do something. Now."

Miles set the frozen bag of corn on the counter. "I agree we need to do something but we need to be smart about it. I'm not going to risk anyone getting hurt because you want revenge."

"Fuck you," Stevie spat, tossing her hands in the air. "I'm sick of men calling all the shots here. Tyler didn't have any fucking clue how to handle this and neither do you." Stevie's eyes widened as soon as the words left her mouth. "Hold up—where the hell is Tyler?"

"No. No, please, no."

The words tumbled out of Bec's mouth as she stumbled off the barstool. Miles tried to stop her but she was already across the kitchen, heading for the halfway. She stopped at the first door, yanking it open quickly.

"Tyler!"

Stevie rushed in after her, expecting the worst. Her eyes scanned the room as Bec's voice grew panicked. Stevie felt her stomach drop. It was like she was at the top of a rollercoaster but when she looked down, the tracks below were rusted and broken. She was headed for a vicious freefall, something unforeseen yet inescapable. Stevie felt Miles slide into the room behind her. The mumbled curse word that came out of his mouth only made her feel worse. She let her eyes take in the empty room one last time. It was only when she saw the open window that she felt the roller coaster car move forward, sliding down to the depths of her demise. Tyler's window was open, just like Monique's had been when they found her.

"Where is he?" Bec said.

Stevie eyed Miles cautiously. When he looked back at her, she knew he had the exact same thought running through his mind.

"We need to secure the house," he stated. "Every door and window. And we need to do it now."

One thought repeated through Stevie's mind in a loop. Finally, she found the courage to say it out loud. "What if he's still here?"

"Grab a knife from the kitchen. You check your room and Monique and Benny's. I'll check mine and Eleni's. Do it quick."

Bec stared at both of them. Stevie could see the fear clouding her mind. She didn't understand—not yet.

"We need to find Tyler!"

"Adrian," Stevie realized, her eyes flashing wide. "What if—"

"I'll check on him first, then sweep the rooms," Miles said. "Meet me back in the kitchen when you're done. If you see Tyler..." He paused and gave her a stern look. "Don't hesitate."

"Oh, I won't," she laughed dryly.

"What are you talking about?" Bec asked before the realization lit up her face. "Wait, no—"

"Go check the rooms now," Miles instructed Stevie.

"Stop," Bec yelled, her voice quivering. "Everything that happened earlier, everything we said...we were in shock, upset." Her eyes darted between the two of them. "You don't actually think Tyler did all of this."

"Bec..."

"No," she yelled at Stevie. "It can't be Tyler. It doesn't make sense."

Miles shot Stevie a look before turning towards Bec. "Yes, it does." Bec went to argue but Miles' continued. "He has motive. He has a past. He has the means." He let out a breathy laugh and shook his head as he gestured around them. "Look where we are. Tyler brought us to a private island in the middle of nowhere and sent everyone else home. It's too much of a coincidence."

"He—he was going to propose," she blurted out.

"What?" Stevie almost choked.

"Have you seen the ring?"

"Wha—"

"Did he show you the ring?" Miles prodded.

"No but—"

"So you don't know if it's real."

Conflict etched its way across Bec's face as she seemed to fight her own thoughts. "No. No, this doesn't make sense. Why would he—"

"Where's your stalker from?"

Bec stared at Miles before her voice shot out weakly. "What?"

"Where is your—"

"California," she said carefully, the lines between her brows growing deeper.

"And where did Tyler grow up?"

"Hold the fuck up," Stevie said sharply.

Bec's hands were shaking now.

Stevie let out an unbelievable laugh. "You think that—"

"That's exactly what I think."

Stevie watched the life drain from Bec's face slowly.

"He's obsessed with you," Miles stated carefully. "He won't let you go." His face softened as he took a step towards Bec. "I'm sorry. But we need to face facts here."

Bec was staring at Miles, shaking her head softly. Her hand darted across her mouth seconds before she bolted towards the bathroom. Stevie heard her emptying the contents of her stomach into the toilet bowl. As Bec choked and coughed, Miles crossed the room and pulled the window tightly shut. The lock flipped with a click before he turned back towards Stevie.

"Take her to the kitchen and stay with her. I'll check the whole house and meet you there."

Stevie nodded at Miles but grew distracted by the lightly speckled red on his t-shirt. There was so much blood on all of them. Even if it wasn't there, Stevie could feel it dried into her skin. How would she ever be free of it?

"Hey," he said, snapping her focus back. "Don't let Bec out of your sight. If anything happens to her…"

"I got it," Stevie replied. "Just go."

Her mind was reeling now. Tyler? *Fucking Tyler.* She had always gotten a bad vibe from him. But this? This was too much.

"Don't forget to make sure Adrian is—"

Darkness. Stevie blinked feverishly, trying to get her eyes to adjust. The lack of light kicked Stevie's other senses into high gear. She heard the storm raging outside. Heard the harsh downpour of rain on the roof. She could even hear the quick whip of wind against the trees. The floor creaked and her stomach lurched.

"Guys?" Bec called out.

"We're okay," Stevie called back. She tapped her pocket for her phone before realizing it was sitting on the dresser in her room.

A harsh beam of light hit Stevie's face, making her heart feel like she'd stepped off a ledge. The light swung past Stevie and she caught Miles' face in the shadowed place behind his phone's flashlight.

"The storm must have knocked out the power," he said.

Miles cast the light across the room, illuminating Bec as she crept out of the dark. She held her hand up in front of her face, blinking. Miles darted his phone to the ceiling, creating an eerie glow across the room.

"Are you okay?"

She didn't bother responding; instead she headed for the hallway.

"Where are you going?" Miles said, a touch of panic dripping from his voice.

Bec turned around slowly. Stevie could see the panic and shock had left her face. It was like she had expelled it all. A cold severity resided there now. Reality had hit Bec swiftly across the cheek. She was awake now. In a flash, her phone illuminated the room.

"I'm going to find a weapon."

A curious look washed over Miles' face. "Be safe and stay in the kitchen," he ordered. "I'll see you soon."

⁄ BEC ⁄

Bec set her phone face down on the counter, allowing the flashlight to shoot up onto the ceiling. The room came into focus dimly. She started searching the kitchen, opening cabinets and drawers with heavy tugs.

"Bec."

She ignored Stevie, continuing to rattle through drawers.

"Bec."

"What?" she snapped.

"Are you okay?"

A shrill laugh, cut off by her own words, slipped from Bec's mouth. "Of course I'm not fucking okay. Miles just told me that my boyfriend is—"

She stopped herself. She didn't have time for this. He'd be back to finish what he started soon enough. Whoever he was. Bec clenched her teeth together, staving off the wave of emotions threatening to leak out of her. Tyler? She thought back to all the times she'd tried to leave, all the times he'd somehow convinced her to stay. Had she really been that blind? She dismissed the thought by a shake of her head and walked across the room. *Focus.* They needed weapons, supplies, something. They had to be ready for him. She tugged at the closet that was tucked into the corner by the back door. It opened with a whine. Her eyes fought to see into the darkness of the closet. But it wasn't a closet. Bec's heart thumped in her chest as she stared down into a black stairwell.

"What is it?" Stevie said, moving towards her slowly.

"A basement," she stated.

"Oh fuck that," Stevie mumbled.

Clack clack.

A noise drifted up from the depths. Bec's stomach lurched. She wanted to slam the door, barricade them from whoever or whatever was down there. But another idea flickered to life inside of her. She knew it was stupid. She knew she shouldn't leave Stevie and Miles but there was only one thing that mattered now. She had started this. This was her fault. Now, she needed to end it before anyone else got hurt. Bec marched back over to the counter and grabbed her phone. The light splayed across the walls wildly before she aimed it in front of her. She hesitated, looking back into the kitchen. There were two knives left in the block. She stomped over and yanked one of them out before heading back towards the basement door.

"I'm gonna go check it out."

"Yeah-fucking-right," Stevie said. Her fingers gripped Bec's arm harshly, stopping her at the top of the stairs. "We have to stay together. You don't know what's down there."

"Exactly." She turned towards Stevie and let out a shaky breath. "If it's Tyler..." Her words caught in her throat. "Whoever is doing this—grab a knife and protect yourself. Okay? I'll be back in a few minutes."

"Wait. I'll come with you."

"No."

Concern rippled across Stevie's face.

"What do you mean n—"

"I need to do this alone, Stevs."

Stevie went to argue but before she could, Bec pulled her into a hug.

"I love you. Please don't follow me."

Stevie muttered objections as Bec pulled away and slipped down into the darkness. She took the stairs slowly, her sneakers pressing into the unfinished wood steps one at a time. They creaked with age and lack of use. There was a chill creeping up from the basement that seemed to permeate her skin. Bec shivered as she reached the bottom step and waved her phone out in front of her. Light painted the dank, darkened room in splotches. She couldn't see much, aside from a line of shelves on the wall immediately across from her.

Clack clack.

Bec nearly dropped the phone in panic. She froze in place as the sound came again.

Clack clack. Clack clack.

She took a sharp inhale as she held her phone out in front of her again. On the exhale, she took a step deeper into the room. The sound kept echoing through the darkness as Bec moved forward cautiously. Did the basement span the entire length of the house? After a minute she found herself in a hallway. There were no doors on either side of her, just thick concrete walls that seemed to close in the farther she ventured. She stopped and forced a deep breath from her lungs, trying to steady the quickening pace of her heart. She felt like she had entered a cave that wanted to choke her.

Her body lurched back as she heard the noise again. It was louder this time. This was stupid. She shouldn't be down here alone. The thought seemed to scream inside of her as she raised her phone higher, lighting up the hallway in a weak beam of light. Darkness edged in on both sides. She could only see a few feet in front of her. This was how people died in horror movies. She took a deep, shaky breath and continued on.

Bec stepped from the hallway and found herself in a larger room. The soft glow of the moon filtered in through a few broken shutters that covered small basement windows. The smell of wet, rotten wood crept into Bec's nose. She let out a quiet cough, trying to rid her lungs of the musty feeling.

Clack clack. Clack clack.

Bec's heart plunged into her stomach as the noise beat loudly through the room. She waved her phone around quickly, stopping the beam of light on the wall across from her. A soft, cynical laugh made its way from her throat into the air.

"Goddamnit," she muttered.

She stared at the source of the noise, feeling foolish. One of the wooden shutters outside had come free and was currently being slammed against the window by the storm.

Clack clack. Clack clack.

Bec pressed her hand into her forehead and took a few breaths. He wasn't down here. She'd come down here for nothing. She waved the light in front of her, searching for the exit. She paused. Maybe it wasn't for nothing. Across the room, her light lit up a workbench and some boxes. She hurried over, setting her knife and phone on the table quickly. She crouched down and began rummaging through everything. The first box was filled with dusty bedding. She ignored the dirty feeling on her fingertips as she pushed it aside and grabbed the next box. Nothing but cleaning supplies. She huffed as she pushed that one aside too. What was behind it made her heart soar. A toolbox. Her eyes lit up hopefully as she opened it, its old hinge whining with a stiff creak. Nails, wrenches, a rusted tape measure. She stuffed it all back inside before wrapping her hand around a screwdriver. She considered it for a minute, balancing the weight of it in her hand. It wouldn't do much to protect her, but it might come in handy. She tucked the screwdriver into the back of her shorts and continued milling around the junk in front of her. There were empty beer bottles covered in a thick coating of dust and cans of paint. She let out a sigh as she got up and brushed the dirt from her hands. Something on a shelf caught the light of her phone and raised a soft gasp from Bec. She grabbed the flashlight and pressed the button. Nothing. She slapped it against the palm of her hand roughly and tried again. Nothing.

"Shit."

She chucked the flashlight back on the shelf. Maybe there were more. She searched quickly. Just as she was about to give up, something else caught her eye. She snatched the small box up greedily. Taking a match in between her fingers, she struck it across the side of the box once, twice. Finally, the flame flickered brightly in the darkness.

"Yes," Bec whispered.

She pocketed the matchbox. If there weren't any flashlights, maybe they could find candles upstairs.

Clack clack.

She shot an irritated look towards the window, watching the wind slam the shutter back and forth violently until her annoyance morphed into something else. Could someone have gotten in the house through there? Her body tensed, suddenly becoming hyper-aware of her surroundings. Just because she hadn't heard him down here, didn't mean he wasn't here somewhere. The darkness seemed to creep closer, fading the edges of the room to black. She did nothing but listen for a solid minute.

Clack clack.

The shutter slapped against the house. The storm battered the roof and treetops above her. She tried to block it all out. If he was down here, he would have done something by now. Right? She slowly crept towards the broken window. She found her balance on a chipped cinder block as she stretched up on her tiptoes to see outside. There was nothing but darkness and the slashing pelt of rain. She reached her fingers around the window's latch, giving it a hard tug. It didn't budge. She tried to get a better grip, straining her body to grow taller but it was useless. She stepped off the cinderblock and released a tired puff of air from her lungs. She needed better leverage.

A thump pulled her attention towards the ceiling. What part of the house was she under right now? Dread crept over her. If he wasn't down here... She swore at herself for her stupidity and bolted across the room. She stumbled over something, sending both her and it crashing to the floor. Her hands met the ground harshly. Liquid sloshed next to her, like water gurgling out of a broken sprinkler. Bec pushed herself up and carefully walked the few feet to the workbench. She grabbed her phone but the smell hit her before the light had a chance to reveal it. Gasoline. Bec's phone illuminated two red plastic gas cans. One of the caps had shaken loose when she'd kicked it. Now the fumes rose into the air with a pungent toxicity. She held her breath as she grabbed her knife and painted the room in waves of light. Where was the exit? The tunneled glow of her phone's flashlight illuminated small sections of the room. Bouts of temporary light darted through the dark as Bec's movements grew more desperate. Where was the fucking hallway? Panic seeped into her chest as she staggered across the room, desperate for escape. The sight of the dark tunnel brought a strange sense of relief. She settled herself with a shaky breath and stepped into it.

⚔ STEVIE ⚔

Stevie wasn't just going to sit around and wait for something to happen.

She had taken the last knife from the kitchen after Bec had stupidly gone down to the basement alone. She shouldn't have let her go. Miles was going to kill her. Stevie had paced around the living room for a few solid minutes before she wondered what was taking him so long. Only bad thoughts had found her, so now, Stevie found herself fumbling her way through the dark, using the walls to guide her down the hallway.

Something was wrong. She rolled her eyes at the thought. Duh, everything was wrong. But aside from the obvious, something about what was happening now felt wrong. The house was too quiet. Miles should have been back by now. The fact that he wasn't meant something had happened. As she crept down the hall, trying not to bang into the walls, an unsettled feeling crept over Stevie. They were all doing exactly the opposite of what they should be doing right now. They shouldn't have split up. Stevie had taken some MMA classes a few years back to impress a girl she was dating, but she was crazy if she thought she could go one-on-one with some psycho killer. Especially if they were right about who it was. Tyler stood almost a foot taller than her and she'd seen him almost choke out Bec with barely any effort. Stevie gripped the knife tighter in her hand. She might not be able to take him out, but she'd do as much damage as she could. Her eyes darted through the darkness as she passed the other rooms. All of the doors were shut.

She found that more concerning than if there was a figure lurking in the doorway of each. She didn't know what or who waited behind the dark slabs of wood. Stevie stifled her fear as she reached Adrian's door. She held her breath and creaked it open an inch. Nothing stirred in the dark. She listened, hoping for answers. Rain. Wind. Silence.

"Miles?" she whispered. "Adrian?"

She cracked the door open further and slipped inside. Her eyes blinked, trying to adjust to the soft glow of moonlight that crept in through the window. There was a shape on the bed. Solid. Unmoving. She swallowed harshly as she stepped closer.

"Adrian?"

No response. She reached the bed. He was still lying on his back. It looked like he was asleep. Stevie's hand moved across the sheets carefully. When she touched his arm, she immediately recoiled. No—this wasn't right. He didn't feel right. She moved her hand over to his stomach. She didn't want to know, but she needed to know. As Stevie's touch met the sticky wetness of Adrian's shirt, she almost let out a yell. She pulled her hand away quickly. The raw, metallic smell drifted from her fingertips. She pressed her arm against her mouth as the rest of it wafted up from his body and the sheets. Her eyes adjusted to the dark slowly. Even in the dark, she saw more than she wanted to. Too much blood. How did a person have that much blood? She backed away slowly as a long smooth line under his Adam's apple dripped with thick, coagulated blood. The small nick they'd sewn up earlier had been sliced open—finished.

"Fuck," she muttered against her arm. "Oh fuck."

The slam of something down the hall made Stevie's skin jump. This was bad. This was so bad. She paused, listening for more.

Thump. Thump. Thump.

It was desperate. Forceful. Her breath grew more labored as she squeezed the hilt of the knife in her sweaty palm. She stepped out of the room cautiously. The hallway felt empty. But was it? She moved forward gingerly, the outstretched knife leading the way in the dark. Something thumped again but this time she heard the soft groaning that followed. It was coming from Tyler's room.

"Miles?" she whispered.

Tyler's door was open. Had it been a few minutes ago? A struggled murmur snaked its way up to Stevie's ears. Soft banging and muffled words. Stevie took a deep breath and stepped through the doorway. It was dark but she didn't need to see to know where the noise was coming from. Tyler's room had the same layout as hers. Stevie moved towards the closet, knife at the ready. One hand gripped the knife with protruding, white knuckles while the other reached out for the doorknob. She turned it, holding back a stream of profanities and prayers as she did. This was beyond stupid. She took a deep breath. A silent breath.

One. Two.

She counted in her head as she began to twist the brass knob.

Three.

She ripped the door open. Stevie took a step back, almost dropping the knife as she did.

"No way," Stevie whispered.

Her eyes went wide as she stared into the closet. Tyler was tied to a chair, blood dripping from his head with a t-shirt stuffed in his mouth. His eyes filled with panic and urgency but Stevie did nothing but stare for a few seconds. He rattled his bound hands against the chair angrily. The chair wobbled, scratching against the floor as he fought to get free. What the hell was happening? She stepped forward and yanked the shirt from his mouth. He coughed and sucked in a few deep breaths.

"How did you..." she stammered.

"A little help?" he grunted.

Stevie acted quickly, digging her fingers against the knots

of his bindings. She managed to get one hand free, despite the adrenaline that was making her hands shake.

"Where's Bec?"

Stevie's face grew pale as she looked up at him.

"Stevie, where's Bec?"

"In the basement."

"What?" he bellowed.

The screech of the sliding glass door made both of them stop. They watched the door for a few seconds, waiting for something to appear in the dark hallway. Tyler pushed her roughly with his free hand.

"Go," he whispered. "Get Bec. Get out of the house right now."

She looked at him like a deer caught in headlights, staring at his bound feet and then back to the blood on his face.

"Go, now," he urged her, already tugging at the tight restraints around his feet. "Get Bec. Head for the jungle. I'll slow him down and then come find you."

Uneasiness drifted over Stevie as she looked at Tyler—really looked at him. Aside from the slight cut on his forehead, he was untouched. Her eyes darted down his shirt, finding nothing out of place. Why wasn't he more hurt? As she started to back away slowly, another noise creaked from the living room.

"Go," Tyler ordered.

Stevie's blood seemed to rush through her ears as she raced out into the hall. Something in her gut was hounding her, scolding her for what she'd just done. She shouldn't have done that. Something wasn't right about Tyler. Something didn't make sense. Fuck. What was she thinking? She needed to find Bec and get as far away from here—and Tyler—as possible. As she stumbled into the kitchen, she saw that the patio door was open. Rain blew inside in wild torrents as the wind pushed it sideways. The door to the basement was shut. Stevie's heart leaped in her chest.

"Bec?" she whispered.

Silence filled the room. Stevie stepped into the kitchen, slowly and carefully. She made her way towards the door. Had Bec come upstairs? Or had someone gone down to find her? She felt a sickening panic slip down her throat. Stevie reached a shaky hand out towards the door. With one hand on the doorknob and the other on her knife, she heard the floor squeak behind her. Goosebumps prickled the back of her neck. She turned slowly, heart pounding so hard she thought she might have a heart attack.

"Bec? Miles?"

She held the knife out in front of her. All she could see was darkness and the faint glow of the moon outside. She swallowed harshly.

"Tyler?"

Her shoes sunk into the plush carpet. The rain pattered against the windows, every splat seeming to hit her ears with an unnerving sharpness. As she stepped back onto the kitchen tile, she felt a hot breath on her neck.

"Hiya, Stevie."

Dread washed over her. She tried to spin around to face him but it was too late. A growing warmth spilled down her chest. Stevie patted her shirt in confusion, feeling the warmth stick to her hands. Blood. Not Eleni's. Not the guard's. Not Benny's. Not Monique's. Not Adrian's. Hers. She staggered, the strength starting to leave her legs. As she finally faced him, she felt pressure. Pain radiated from her stomach. She looked down as he pulled the knife from her. Her breath was a jumbled gurgle in her throat. She stared into the darkness, her eyes finding the whites of his eyes and the evil that floated in them.

"Wh—why?"

Her words sloshed in her throat as blood drained from the line he'd slashed across her skin.

His faint smile glimmered in the shadows of the room. "Because I'm all she needs."

The knife struck her again and again and again and again.

She could barely feel it now as a cool numbness drifted over her limbs. Fear and regret gripped her. She should have seen this coming. She should have done a better job of looking out for Bec. She should have figured him out sooner. The creak of the stairs made Stevie's eyes bulge. He was done, slipping back into the shadows as quickly as he'd arrived. Like death, he was nowhere and everywhere. Stevie gripped her throat tightly, trying to ease the steady stream of blood. A bounce of light seeped out from the crack in the basement door. Bec. She needed to warn her. Stevie stepped forward but her body wouldn't take her there. She hit the floor with a heavy thud, her best friend's name choking in her throat.

✐ BEC ✐

Bec's light hit something solid.

She pressed her fingers against the door, the knife in her hands lightly scraping the wood. She hadn't closed it behind her. Had Stevie? Bec felt heat rise on the back of her neck. Stevie wouldn't have shut the door behind her, not unless something had happened. Bec took a breath, shallow and flighty in her lungs. She clicked her phone's light off and stuffed it in her pocket. Whatever was happening behind the inch of wood that separated her from the house, she wanted to see it before it saw her. She took another shaky breath before twisting the doorknob. It creaked, a gentle sound that felt like a shot in the dark. Bec stopped and listened for a few seconds. Silence. Rain pelting windows. The clack clack of the shutter back in the basement. She twisted the knob again, softer this time. The door opened soundlessly. As she stepped into the room, goosebumps sprouted up her arms. Rain blew in the house from the open patio door, tapping roughly on the tile floor. She didn't move an inch, waiting for something to happen.

"Stevie?" she whispered.

A wet gurgling sputtered from somewhere ahead of her, barely audible over the rattling storm. Fear stole Bec's breath. She looked across the room but only darkness stared back at her. Her body tensed. She listened. The noise rose and fell in volume, unplaceable in direction and origin. The only thing she could manage to hear over the storm was the unnerving, wet wheeze of it. It seemed to slide down to her eardrums and echo there. Bec's heart raced as she dug into her pocket.

Her hands were clumsy and nervous but finally, she clicked her phone's flashlight and shined it across the room.

"Hello?"

Every corner and shadow that the light illuminated was empty. Bec's stomach ached and swirled with a sickening fear. She began stepping forward slowly. Through the open patio door, lightning lit up the jungle in a blanket of white. Thunder rumbled overhead seconds later, causing her heart to pound harder than it already was. Bec clutched the knife in her hand. This was wrong. They should be here. As she stepped onto the tile floor, her sneaker slid a few inches out in front of her. She steadied herself, her arms flailing out against the empty air. Breath pumped from her lungs wildly. Bec tapped her foot around the floor, searching for what she'd slipped on. She felt the toe of her sneaker step into a slickness. She eyed the open patio door across the room. The rain? Her body grew still as a rattling rasp of a breath rose from the floor. Not the rain. Bec's fingers squeezed tightly around the phone's case as she aimed the flashlight down at the ground. Stevie's eyes shined back at her, pupils as big as saucers.

"No—" Bec choked.

The phone slipped from her grasp, clattering to the floor harshly and landing face down into the puddle of red. As Bec glared through the blare of light, her words spilled out of her in muffled cries.

"No-no-no-no-no," Bec pleaded, dropping to her knees.

Stevie looked up at her, gasping and choking. Blood spurted from the canyon-like gash in her neck, pulsing out with every labored breath. Tears swam in Bec's eyes and streamed down her face in vicious rivers.

"No, this can't—" Bec gasped. "You can't—"

Bec struggled to breathe, dragging each breath into her lungs with ragged force. Her hands reached out for Stevie unsteadily. She hovered them above the wound, unsure of how to subdue the flowing monsoon of red that rushed down onto the floor. The light from Bec's phone lit up the ceiling like a movie theater spotlight, casting long, eerie shadows across the room. Stevie's face was cloaked in darkness but Bec could see the glimmer of fear in her eyes.

"Please don't die," Bec sputtered as she pressed her hands against Stevie's neck desperately. "Fuck. God, please don't do this to me. Not again."

Salty tears dripped off Bec's face steadily, matching the way Stevie's blood flowed out of her body and onto Bec's fingers. Stevie lifted her hand weakly, dropping it against Bec's arm. Her eyes shot up at Bec urgently. Stevie's lips quivered against words that refused to come out. The only sound that came from her was the sickening sputtering of blood filling her throat.

"Hey, it's okay." Bec choked on her words as a ragged sob ripped from deep within her. "Everything is going to be okay. I promise."

She clutched Stevie's hand in hers while the other pressed harder against the wound. Her fingers slipped against Stevie's skin, slick with the blood that bubbled and oozed from her.

"You can't leave me," Bec yelled, her eyes cloudy with tears. "I won't let you." Her body convulsed as pain and panic ripped through her. "You promised me a drink after this. Don't you dare break that promise."

A tear dropped from Stevie's eye, falling down her cheek as the strength left her. Stevie's hand flopped against Bec's grasp.

"Stevie?"

Bec stared at her wide, unmoving eyes. The spasming in Stevie's neck stilled, her life slackening under Bec's fingers. In an instant, Bec's heart seemed to stop.

"Stevie?"

She stared down blankly as her brain fought to accept the truth. Bec shook her head, words spilling from her lips in a mumbled rush. "No-no-no-no..."

Bec pulled Stevie's face towards her gently. "Hey, hey, come on," she whispered, patting her friend on the cheek, trying to wake her up. "Stevie, please. Come on, wake up." Bec's voice grew louder until it resounded through the house with a feral panic.

"Stevie!" she demanded, shaking her friend's shoulders now. "Fuck, don't do this to me." She felt the dead weight of Stevie's body crumple against her chest as she tried to pry her up off the floor.

"Please, you can't leave me. I ca—" Bec's voice cracked. She stopped tugging at Stevie's limbs and let herself fall across her stomach. Vicious sobs tore through Bec as she pressed her forehead against the blood-soaked fabric of Stevie's shirt. "Come back!" she screamed, her voice a guttural wail fighting against the roar of the storm outside. "Stevie, I need you to come back. I can't do this without you."

"Bec?"

Her head snapped up, looking over Stevie's limp body at the figure in front of her.

"Holy shit," he uttered.

She watched Tyler carefully as he stepped closer. He looked down at Stevie's body and then to her. There was blood on his face. Bec could barely see in through the glow of her phone on the ceiling but it was there. It was unmistakable.

"We gotta get out of here, Bec. It's—"

"Get the fuck away from her."

Miles appeared behind Tyler, his dark silhouette stepping in from the patio. He clutched his side tightly as he fell against the kitchen counter. Bec stared in disbelief as the hazy glow of her phone's light slowly illuminated him. His eyes were wild—fearful. Bec's gaze drifted down to his body where fresh blood seeped from his side. It coated his hands like gloves. Bec felt chills ripple across her as she met his gaze.

"Run," Miles urged her through strained breaths. "It's

him."

"You son-of-a-bitch!" Tyler yelled, eyes blazing at Miles.

Bec snatched the knife off the ground, pulling Tyler's focus. His face filled with hollow shadows as the light beamed into his face.

"He's lying," he urged her. "He hit me and tied me up in the closet."

Tyler stepped towards her quickly. Bec jolted back and pulled herself up to her feet. He shot her an unbelieving look as he stepped over Stevie's body to get closer to her.

"You think I did this?"

She searched his face for the Tyler she knew but couldn't find him. With every step he took, Bec retreated further into the kitchen. "Stop." She pointed the knife out towards him, halting his advance. Anger filled Tyler's eyes as he hovered at the end of the kitchen's island.

"He wants this," Tyler growled, his voice flecked with frustration. "He wants you to think it's me!"

Bec shot her eyes across the kitchen towards Miles. He was still bent over the counter as shallow breaths heaved from his chest. His eyes pleaded with her.

"I was checking on Adrian. He's... he's dead. His window was open so I went to check outside and that's when he attacked me."

She was stuck in the middle of them, Tyler on her left and Miles on her right. In a cruel twist of fate, there was no more putting off her decision. She had to choose one. She wouldn't make it out of here otherwise.

"Bullshit," Tyler yelled. "He's lying!"

Tyler stepped forward, causing Bec to stagger back, bumping into the counter. She jutted the knife out in front of her, waving it towards him. "Stay the fuck away from me," she breathed.

Agitation pooled in Tyler's eyes. "You're being an idiot, Bec," he spat, gesturing towards Miles erratically. "It's him!"

"I said stay where you are!" she screamed, holding the

knife steadier now. She pointed it straight at his chest.

"Okay, okay," he offered, shooting a quick look over to where Miles rested against the counter. His eyes flickered back to Bec nervously. "Just calm down, okay?" he said, raising his arms up in front of him.

Bec wiped a rogue tear from her cheek and forced herself to look back at Miles. "Did you do that?" she rasped, nodding her head towards Stevie.

"No, of course not," he stated.

"He's lying," Tyler blared through gritted teeth. "How can you be so fucking stupid?"

"Leave her the fuck alone," Miles barked.

"Oh, you'd like that, wouldn't you?" Tyler snapped back. "Was that the plan? Go on a rampage to get me out of the picture?"

"How did you find me?"

Both men turned to Bec but it was Tyler who was on the receiving end of her stare. She held the knife in front of her with shaky hands.

Tyler stared back at her blankly. "What?"

"I changed my name when I left Reno. New name. New number. New life," she swallowed her fear. She was tired of being scared. Tired of falling for the wrong guy. Bec gripped the knife tighter and stepped towards Tyler. "How did you find me?"

"I have no idea what you—"

"Shut up," she yelled. "Shut up. Shut up!" Her voice wavered as emotion constricted her throat. Her eyes locked on him, searching for a clue, a flicker of guilt. She found nothing to quell the anger and pain surging through her. "Why are we here, Tyler?"

"I told you," he said, taking a step closer. "I was going to pro—"

"Stop," she hissed, halting the few steps he'd taken towards her. "I swear to God if you take another step." She took in a deep, shuddering breath to steady herself. "Why this island? Why here?"

His jaw clenched as he looked at her. He didn't say anything for a few beats of Bec's racing heart.

"My parents own it," Tyler sighed. "The island."

Silence crawled across the room like mist, only broken by the steady torrent of rain outside. Bec felt a knowing run through her, cold as ice, as her mind began to accept her reality. He planned this. He'd taken them all to the middle of nowhere. He'd made sure they couldn't get away and picked them off one by one. Had he known about her and Miles the entire time? Of course, he had. He was punishing her. It was him, after all. She felt her chest tightening, an expanding panic that seemed to push her insides tightly against her bones.

"Baby." Miles' voice pulled Bec back from her spiraling thoughts. "Run. Go. Head for the beach." His breath trembled as he palmed the bloody gash in his shirt. "Whatever happens. I love you."

"Shut the fuck up," Tyler spewed. He threw his hand out wildly, sideswiping a water glass that rested on the counter. It hit the floor with a sharp twang, shattering into a hundred pieces. The shards skirted at Bec's feet. "You did this. You ruined us."

Miles' focus stayed on Bec. "He's out of control. Baby, please. I need you to get out of here."

Tears flowed freely from Bec's eyes. She lowered the knife, her hand shaking. "No. I'm not leaving yo—"

"He's going to kill you," Miles pleaded, stepping closer to Bec.

"You're the one—"

"He planned this whole trip so he could make sure you'd end up with him," Miles yelled, cutting Tyler off. "He wants you to suffer like he suffered. He lied to you, tricked you."

"I can't let you d—" Bec started.

"I won't watch him kill you. Goddamnit, Amelia. Get out of here!"

Tyler was yelling now but Bec didn't hear him. Her vision tunneled, growing dark at the corners. She felt sick, the type of stomach ache you feel when your world comes crashing down. The sickness of realizing that you had been wrong—so very wrong.

"What did you just say?"

Miles tensed. His eyes locked on Bec but he stayed silent.

"You called me Amelia."

Tyler stopped yelling and stared at the two of them. Miles cocked his head to the side, his eyes full of dangerous curiosity. Fear tingled across Bec's skin. Her brow furrowed as she replayed memories, conversations, things he knew about her that she swore she'd never told him. It had been there all along—she just hadn't wanted to see it.

"Niko," she uttered softly.

He backed out of the kitchen slowly. He wiped his hands on the front of his shirt, straightening up from his pain easily—too easily. Finally, a smile flickered across his face.

"Hi, Amelia."

"Who the hell is Amel—"

Tyler doubled over as Miles thrust a knife into his side. Bec could almost feel the knife as Miles twisted it inside Tyler. She stifled a gasp as Miles yanked it out and wiped the blood off the blade.

"Did you miss me?"

Adrenaline coursed through her body. Tyler was clutching his side, grunting as blood ran over his fingers. Miles—not Miles. Niko. Niko was staring at her, a devilish grin spread across his face, lit up ghoulishly by the beam of light from Bec's phone.

"This is not how I wanted this to go," he laughed.

He took a breath before jabbing the knife in and out of Tyler once more. Tyler's hands slapped at Miles before desperately clutching the hole in his side. Bec's breath hitched in her throat as she watched. *Run.* She heard the command firmly in the back of her head. Her body tensed, from her taut grip on the knife to her toes that pressed the tips of her sneakers. Tyler groaned as Miles slid the knife inside of him once more. His arms flailed wildly, desperately trying to push Miles away from him. Bec's fear and guilt seemed to glue her to the floor. As Tyler's eyes met hers, she felt those feelings sink their teeth into her.

"I'm sorry," Bec breathed. "Tyler, I'm so s—"

His eyelids flickered heavily as he looked back at her. Short, sharp breaths ripped from his chest. "Run," he muttered.

Deja vu ripped through Bec as she shook her head firmly. His eyes burned into her. "Run."

A laugh rose up from Miles. He sounded different, like the role he had been playing for the past year had finally been dropped.

"Oh, come on Amelia," he smirked, twirling the knife in his hand. He raised his eyebrows at her as she inched closer to the patio door. He shoved Tyler away from him and stepped closer, blocking her exit. "You can't leave now," he smiled. "Not when we have so much to talk about."

Run. Her eyes flickered to her left. If she went now, she could make it. It wasn't a good option, but it was her only one. She had to be quick, but she was ready. Miles must have sensed something in her, like a wind-up toy ready to pop at any minute. His brow furrowed as the words began to leave his mouth.

"Don't—"

Run.

She took off into a sprint before he could finish the sentence, her sneakers slipping against the blood-soaked floor. She caught herself on the doorframe quickly, then threw herself down the stairs. The darkness swallowed her instantly. Without her phone's light, she was blind. Still, she raced downwards, missing the last two steps in a gut-wrenching fall. Her hands pawed at the dark, raking against the worn banister. Her back slapped against the bottom stair, ramming something into her spine. A sharp gasp left her throat as the pain radiated up her back. She fell to her side, reaching for the screwdriver she'd tucked into the waistband of her shorts. His footfalls pounded on the stairs above her. She didn't have time to waste. Bec ignored the pain in her back and scrambled to find the knife she'd dropped. Her heart pumped fiercely as she felt around the stairs. Finally, she clutched the handle and propelled herself forward without a second thought. As she raced through the black, only guided by vague memory and the touch of her outstretched hands against the walls, one thing gave her hope. Yes, she was blind down here but so was he. If she could get far enough ahead of him, maybe she could get out. Because she knew something he didn't—there was a window down here.

"Amelia!"

Bec's breath ripped from her lungs as she raced through the dark. She slammed into a sharp corner and felt pain radiate from her hip bone.

"Amelia, stop!"

She pushed around the corner and sprinted as silently and carefully as she could. He was trailing behind her, hunting her in the dark. Bec tried to still her breath but it came out in heavy, desperate heaves. She needed to keep going. She needed to get to the room, get outside, and get away from him. She didn't know what was going to happen after that but she didn't let her mind get that far. Her breath hitched as she ran into solid concrete. She slapped her palms against the walls—twice to confirm she was correct. She almost smiled. She was in the hallway. She picked up her pace, embracing the darkness that grew narrower and narrower. Where it had set her on edge before, it only motivated her now. She could hear the sound of heavy footsteps behind her. He was moving slower than her but still, he was getting closer.

A dim glow ahead shot every nerve in Bec awake. The room. She had made it. As her hands left the hallway's walls, she felt the room open up around her. The air was still as damp and dank as when she'd first plunged into the basement, but it felt better now. Spacious. Safe. She took a deep breath in, welcoming the dust and mustiness that slid down the back of her throat like an old acquaintance. She stifled a cough and flickered her eyes towards the windows. Three were closed, shutters sealed shut from the outside, not a lick of moonlight slipping through their crevices. Bec's eyes fixed on the other two. The one she'd tried to pry open earlier seemed like the best option, its broken shutters still banging against the storm above.

Clack clack. Clack clack.

Quickly, too quickly, Bec darted across the room. The toe of her shoe kicked something, sending a deafening rattle across the floor. An empty paint can. It clattered like an alarm in the dark. She froze, holding her breath as she strained to listen. If he hadn't known where she was, he did now. She shuffled her way toward the windows, her foot stepping into a puddle. A sharp smell crept up, burning her nostrils. The gas cans. She'd forgotten to pick them up earlier. She tried to stifle the smell with her arm but it was no use. She let the fumes burn into her throat as her foot tapped out the darkness. It hit something solid. She dropped her knife on the tool bench with a soft thud and hoisted herself up onto the cinderblock. Like before, her fingers brushed the window, fumbling around the little plastic piece that kept it from sliding open freely. She panted as she stretched higher, desperate for even an extra inch of leverage. She felt the window pane shudder against her efforts but nothing more.

"Come on, you son-of-a-bitch," she rasped, pressing her fingers against it harshly. Her fingers slipped, losing their progress. "Fuck," she hissed, straining every muscle in her body as she gripped the edges of the lock with white knuckles.

"Baby, I just want to talk."

The sound tore through the darkness. She stilled instantly. He was here. Bec's eyes darted out into the room, desperate to find salvation. There was no other way out. She was trapped. Fear pricked at her, pooling water at the outer corners of her eyes. Against the shadows of the room, her gaze found a pile of boxes. She took a step towards it before glancing back. The shadowed outline of her knife greeted her eagerly. She snatched it up before scurrying across the room. She had barely tucked herself behind the dust-coated stack of cardboard when a presence filled the air around her.

"Amelia?"

His voice was softer now but his breath came out in long, heavy puffs. It sounded like any predator recovering from the chase, gearing up for the kill. As Bec watched his shadowed figure step into the center of the room, she gripped the knife tighter in her hand.

"I know you're in here," he cooed.

He turned around in a circle, trying to sweep his eyes over every inch of the dark to find her. His attention whipped to the window as a clack clack screeched from the broken shutter. He stepped up to the window and gave it a solid tug. It budged enough for a lick of chilled air to drift into the room, but no more. Bec's heart sank at the realization. She was never getting out of that window. She'd led herself to a dead end. Her own basement-sized coffin. As he turned back around, she felt a stir of hatred rush through her. It had been him. All this time, there never was a Miles. He had played a role—played her. And he had done it well. Bec's throat grew achy and hollow. He had killed her friends. Just like he had done with Brennen, he had taken them from her. And Stevie. Bec barely stifled the sob that threatened to tear from her throat. Stevie was gone. He had gotten what he wanted. She was all alone now. She had no one left but him. Bec bit the inside of her cheek harshly. Silent tears warmed her cheeks as she glared at him through the dark. She had let him get away the first time out of guilt and fear. But now? Her breath drug slowly through her lungs and out her nose. She wouldn't make that mistake twice. Bec's eyes burned against salty tears and the bitter waft of gasoline as she watched him.

"Amelia, don't do this to me," Miles uttered. He was on the other side of the room now. He peered behind the shelves, searching for her. "I don't want to hurt you, baby. This is all just a big misunderstanding."

Liar.

Bec took a deep breath in, trying to steady her breathing, gasoline choking her. She bit back a dry cough as her eyes widened in understanding. She patted the front pocket of her shorts and took a steady breath into her lungs. She wasn't going to die down here. She wasn't going to let him win. Her fingers slipped into her pocket as she watched his shadowed form prowl through the dark. He'd taken everything from her. Not once, but twice. He was a monster. He belonged in Hell. If she had to help him get there—so be it. Bec stepped out from her hiding place. Miles turned around swiftly.

"There she is," he cooed. "Ready to talk?"

Light flickered through the room, then glowed brightly, dancing across the walls as the flame Bec held swayed. Bec watched the smirk slip from his face as he sniffed the air.

"What are you—"

Bec tossed the match. She felt his hand scrape her arm as he dove towards her. It didn't matter; she was already running. She heard the flame ignite the gasoline behind her. It whooshed violently, like it had the other night when Benny had lit the bonfire. Miles was yelling, screaming. The hallway filled with light. For a brief second, Bec thought the power had come back on. As she felt the heat growing against her back, her heart thundered in her ears and she sprinted through the basement. Already she could hear him on her heels, thrashing and yelling. The smoke burned into Bec's lungs as she panted and raced forward.

"You bitch!"

She slammed into the wall as she emerged from the hallway. Almost there. She pumped her legs harder. Something sliced through her arm as she bumped against a shelf, sending a cry from her lips. She felt the blood seep from her skin but kept going. Her body stumbled forward as her feet slammed against the base of the stairs. She scrambled against the old wood, pushing herself up on all fours. Her fingers curled around the banister, hoisting herself upright as she took the stairs two at a time. Her body screamed at her to stop, legs tired and lungs full of smoke. When she saw the soft glow of light shining into the air above her, Bec felt a shudder of relief. Her phone. She was almost there. Behind her, objects toppled and crashed. Was it him or the fire coming to take her? Bec reached the landing, hurling herself up into the house and slamming the door shut behind her.

Her eyes instantly flashed to the patio door. It was wide open—waiting for her. Smoke wafted from bedrooms. The fire was already burning up through the floor, desperate to reach the air above. Her lungs hacked against the smoke as she staggered forward, bumping into something. The sight almost dropped Bec to her knees. Stevie. A sick, cavernous ache filled her heart. She knew she would never forgive herself for what she was about to do. Her lips quivered as she mouthed a silent apology before stepping over Stevie and stumbling towards the patio. Bec couldn't take her body with her, not if she planned to outrun him. As Bec's hand gripped the doorway, a thought sent her reeling back. Where was Tyler? Her eyes darted around desperately. There was no sign of him. No body. Nothing other than a trail of blood, and she couldn't even tell which way it went. Her eyes searched the room wildly until the floor underneath her shifted with a heavy crack. The hallway was a wall of black now, smoke drifting from it like death's embrace. The house was surrendering. It was only a matter of time before it was swallowed. Bec ran towards the patio door and plunged herself into a new darkness.

If the storm had sounded bad from inside, the reality was even worse. Rain pelted Bec like needles, ice cold and piercing. She paused for only a second, taking in her new surroundings, before her heels kicked against the ground beneath her. Strands of hair slapped at her face, sticking in wet streaks as she sprinted across the lawn. She didn't know where she was going. *Run* was the only thought she had. Soggy grass shifted into pebbles underneath Bec's feet. She staggered, fighting the uneven surface for traction. Rain-beaten palm fronds smacked against her chilled skin as she entered the jungle.

Bec could barely hear anything above the wind but what she did hear drove her forward even faster. Miles' voice yelled out against the storm, angry and violent. He'd made it out of the basement—and he was coming for her.

⚔ MILES ⚔

The rain seemed to burn into his skin as he pursued her. Miles screamed against the wind, both in fury and pain. His left arm was seared, peppered with burns and dead flesh from the fire that had leapt at him like a hungry beast. But it wasn't the fire's fault. It was hers.

His sneakers sent a spray of pebbles and dirt in his wake as he barreled towards the jungle. He could barely see her, her pale silhouette peeking out occasionally through the dark fauna of the trail. She was faster than he expected. This would be fun. The pain etched across his face transformed into a sly grin. She couldn't outrun him, not forever. As he entered the jungle, the thick canopy shielded him from the brunt of the storm. Only a light drizzle of rain and fading wind followed him as he twisted and turned down the trail. His lungs burned from the fire. He forced in long, deep breaths, savoring the wet freshness in the air. His eyes squinted against the dark night and mist of rain. He felt alive. The feeling that coursed through his veins was even more delicious than it had been with the others. Eleni had been easy, too easy. The others had been more of a challenge, but not like this. He hadn't expected this. It wasn't part of the plan. But as pain rippled across his flesh with every branch and leaf that slapped at him, he realized he wouldn't have had it any other way.

Thunder rumbled overhead. The booms seemed to penetrate into Miles chest, energizing his heart and driving him further. He was going to catch her. With every glimpse he caught of her, he felt a ripple of pleasure run through his body. She had tried to kill him. She could argue otherwise—and he was sure she would, once he caught her—but the truth was obvious. Like a trapped animal, she had done the only thing she could think of to survive. She had been quick and resourceful. Brutal. He was proud. Miles grinned as he pressed his feet harder into the earth to propel himself forward. She was more like him than she even realized. The ghostly figure ahead of him disappeared as Bec rounded a corner.

"Am-e-lia," he yelled, the violent sing-song-y sway of his voice piercing through the dark jungle. "Getting tired yet, baby?"

He gritted his teeth and picked up his pace. He didn't want to lose sight of her, even for a second. A branch swatted across his face as he sprinted down the trail, drawing a thin line of blood. The wind whipped against his cheek, stinging the cut flesh, but he was too focused on what was ahead. Rage and pleasure drove him forward as he caught sight of her again. This was what he had been waiting for. For years, over a decade, he had wanted her. And now? Now he would finally get what he deserved. He would have preferred if Tyler had taken the fall for everything as planned, but this would do. He could talk his way out of this. He knew Amelia better than anyone. He knew how her parents died. Knew the reasons she hated her aunt. Knew where she used to cut herself in high school. He knew all of it—so he knew that she would forgive him. He was certain of it because one thing had gone according to plan. He had made sure that he was all she had left.

A wide smile crept across his face. He sprinted through the jungle effortlessly now, all pain and strain leaving his body. Every moment from now on was priceless. After all, he was about to get everything he wanted. He and Amelia would have a quiet life. No more killing. No secrets. No betrayals. No pain. Tomorrow, they would start fresh. But tonight? He ran down the trail, letting the thrill of the chase pump him full of adrenaline. Tonight she needed to be punished. He would make it quick. He still loved her, after all, despite the pain she had caused him all these years. But he would teach her a lesson so she knew how much he had suffered for her. And after that? After that, all would be forgiven. Their relationship would be a clean slate.

Miles lost traction for a split second, his sneakers slipping against the trail that had grown thick and wet with mud. The palms of his hands slammed against a tree trunk as he broke his fall. His breath tore through his chest in vicious, painful huffs. A flash of blonde hair disappeared behind the dark sway of vines and palm fronds. Miles stared down the empty trail, desperate to spot her again.

"Amelia!" he screamed into the wind, his voice swallowed by the storm.

He swore under his breath before sprinting after her again.

↗ BEC ↗

Nothing made sense to Bec—yet at the same time, everything did.

The world flew by in a blur as she hurled herself down the trail. The mud sucked and smacked at her shoes, seeming to reach out like hands, eager to hold her back. She was soaked down to her bra, the chill of the rain numbing her skin. But still, she urged her tired legs onward. She didn't know how deep she'd ventured into the jungle, if she'd suddenly find herself at the base of a cliff with nowhere left to run. All she knew was she had to keep moving. Away from the house. Away from him. The sight of Stevie's gaping mouth, like a fish out of water, haunted her as she ducked under a downed palm frond. She thought of Tyler and the desperate pleading in his eyes. Bec's heart ached. She had been so wrong. The muffled yell of Miles' voice tore through the jungle behind her. Not Miles—Niko. The constant correction in her mind made her sick. She forced herself to run faster despite the heavy ache in her legs. What would happen if he caught her? Or was it a *when*, not an *if*?

Grief and fear tugged her insides. She had been so drawn to Miles. She had thought it was lust or love or some irrational combination of the two but now she knew it hadn't been either of those things. It had been familiarity. She felt like she had known him all her life because she had. Like a wolf in sheep's clothing, he had pretended their connection was fate when really it had been by design. Niko had always been there, waiting for his moment to devour her.

Bec was getting so tired, but she couldn't stop. She had to

keep going. The trail veered to the left and a glimmer of hope came alive inside her. Something was familiar here. The trail widened slightly, the dense foliage flanking her on both sides growing more sparse with each new stride. Fear screamed at her to keep going while her body urged her to give up. The muscles in her legs felt like sandbags. She tried to suck in a full breath but her lungs were raw and strained. Her side cramped. *Rest. Take a break, just for a second.* Her mind seduced her as every step brought more pain. What did it matter? There was no way off the island. She was stuck here. He would leave no survivors. He would make her suffer. She was already suffering. It was time to join the rest of them. Just as Bec started to slow her pace, something up ahead pierced the dark thoughts that lulled her into submission. Even in the dark, the glimmer appeared like a lighthouse calling her to safety. Was she seeing things? Bec pushed soggy wet strands of hair out of her face as she drove forward with a burst of energy. She would survive. She had to.

The beach. She could see it now, glimmering under the moonlight like a patch of diamonds. She ran faster, desperate to leave the danger and darkness of the jungle.

She felt the tug first, then the unnerving feeling of her stomach dropping. Her hands sprawled out in front of her, her chest colliding with the earth in a brutal slap as she fell. She laid in the mud, elbow deep, and felt the rain beat down on her softly. It plopped against her skin with a terrifying cadence. Every drop was a second wasted. Every second wasted was a moment he had to catch up. She yanked her arms free from the mud with a heavy grunt and stumbled forward, only to slip back into the muck. Her breath tore through her lungs in a panic as her hands dug herself out until her feet found their way under her body again. A guttural yell left her throat as she propelled herself towards the end of the trail. Sand mixed with mud, clumping in a mess that pulled at Bec's ankles. She fought and struggled against it until all that was left was sand.

It was dense and compact from the weight of the rain and provided new stability. Bec wiped her face with the back of her hand as she stood up and took in the world around her. She had made it to the beach. In her panic, she had chosen the trail that she and Stevie had discovered the other day. The relief was short-lived as she realized she wasn't alone. Bec staggered forward a few steps, moving her hand to her mouth. Although the smell had been subdued by the downpour, bloating the stiffly pale body, the sight still rose a rush of bile to the back of Bec's throat. She turned away quickly, barely swallowing down the sting of vomit that curdled in her throat. She was sorry. So sorry. Eleni hadn't deserved this. None of them had.

A yell flitted through the rain, trailing out onto the beach like a ghostly threat. It took a minute for Bec to decipher it through the rumble of the storm around her.

"There's nowhere left to run, Amelia."

Her eyes widened in terror at the voice that bellowed from the jungle. The voice that had sent chills of pleasure down her spine now chilled her in a different way. His words hit her ears with a deadly clarity. He was close—too close. Bec's body exploded to life with an ugly jerk, ripping her muscles from the idleness they had briefly settled into. She pounded her feet against the sand. The wind fought her with every stride like it wished to deliver her into the arms of death itself. Bec urged her body forward with every breath. Now that the treetops had fallen into the background, the moon seemed to light up the beach like a stage. But it wasn't just the moon that showed her the way. Over the dune, red and orange flames danced wildly across the rooftop of the house. Black smoke wafted into the air, meeting the darkness of the night in a seamless embrace. The house was ablaze. There was nowhere left to hide. Bec swallowed the dread that ached deep in the back of her throat. She kept running. She didn't dare look back, already knowing that she'd see him closer than she hoped. The rain had slowed to a soft patter, plopping against her skin in steady drops as she sprinted through the sand.

Plop. Plop. Plop.

She blinked feverishly as the water slid into her eyes.

Plop. Plop. Plop.

Still, she moved forward, driving her legs harder and harder.

Everything stopped at once. The rain, the wind—even her breath. Her body slipped through the air, seeming to hang in the balance of life and death until everything came crashing down with an unholy ferocity. Miles rolled on top of her as he tackled her to the ground. The weight of his body pressed her firmly into the sand, seeming to hold her in place like a caved-in roof. His bright white smile beamed down at her with an eagerness that made her sick.

"Fuck," he grunted, breath heaving from his lungs in powerful bouts. "You're really making me work for this, huh?"

Her hand swung at him desperately, knife still gripped tightly in her fingers. Miles swatted it away, sending the knife flying across the sand. A small gash of red prickled on his forearm from where the blade had caught him. His eyes flashed back to her wickedly as he pinned her down.

"Really, Amelia?" he smiled. "If I didn't know any better I'd think you were trying to kill me."

Bec thrashed and screamed underneath him, kicking her legs against the sand. His weight held her in place, her efforts wasted.

"Easy," Miles cooed.

He withdrew his own knife, pressing it up against her cheek. The cool touch of metal made her flinch. She stopped squirming and watched breathlessly as he dragged the glint of silver slowly across her face.

"That's a good girl."

Bec gritted her teeth as frustrated tears slipped down her cheek. Had he used that same knife on Stevie? Monique?

Tyler?

"You wanna know something?" he laughed softly as he stared down at her. "I honestly thought you would have figured it out months ago."

Her heart hammered in her chest. She tried wiggling her legs an inch, careful not to alert him. They didn't budge. His weight had her pinned down, right where he wanted her.

"When you didn't, I thought it was for the best. I thought we could have a fresh start. Bec and Miles."

He smiled at that. Bec trailed her hand out to her side slowly, keeping her eyes on him. As she patted the sand, her gut twinged hopelessly. Her knife was nowhere to be found.

"But then you wouldn't break up with him."

Bec snapped her focus back to Miles as he pressed the blade harder against her cheek.

"And you made me do all this."

The knife slipped through her skin. Bec yelped as pain spread across her in a hot stream. Miles drew the blade in a curved line along her cheek, sending blood pooling down the side of her face and into the sand. She tried to shake him off as he finished the cut.

"Aht, aht, aht." Miles breathed, a soft smirk twitching at the corner of his mouth. "This will be a lot quicker if you behave."

Bec tried to block it all out but it overtook her senses. *Touch.* The feeling of metal against her chilled skin. *Hearing.* The storm that now rumbled in the distance. *Taste.* Soot and blood on her tongue—mixed with salt. *Smell.* Charred, dead skin. It reminded her of rotting meat. *Sight.* The way his eyes gleamed down at her like a hyena's over its latest kill.

She shot awake as he split the skin on her collarbone. Her teeth sunk into the flesh of her cheek, biting back a whimper of pain. She pulled her focus from his face for just a second—a moment's peace—and stared up at the sky, void of any light except for the glow of the moon and a soft speckling of stars. Bec pretended she was home. Not in LA, but Reno. She pretended that she was lying on the hood of that shitty old Jeep of Stevie's, staring up at the stars. Instead of the exhaustion that ached though her body, she pretended it was the buzz of alcohol—whiskey she'd stolen from her aunt. Bec took a deep breath and closed her eyes as Miles dragged the knife across her shoulder slowly. But Miles wasn't there, at least not in Bec's mind. It was just her and Stevie. Ever since meeting in middle school, they had been partners in crime. The Three Musketeers, if the third one had been bad decisions. A deep heave of emotion welled inside Bec. There was no more trouble to get into, no more adventures to be had. Stevie was gone. Grief ripped her from her daydream. It grew into a wild thing, a hateful thing. Heat spread across Bec's skin like spiders. It was subtle at first, almost like an itch. But soon it engulfed her, a fire burning inside her chest.

"You took her from me!" Bec yelled. She thrashed under him, not caring where the blade rested on her skin anymore. "I hate you!" She was frenzied, unable to contain the fury that pulsed through her veins as she spat her words through vicious sobs. "You psychotic motherfucker," Bec bellowed. "You killed Stevie!"

"And you abandoned me," he barked, pressing the tip of the blade into her flesh. "You chose that stupid mechanic over me. Then Tyler—Tyler? Are you fucking kidding me?" Miles slammed the knife into the sand, inches from Bec's ear. "I understood Brennen. He was convenient, a distraction. But that rich piece of shit?" Miles yanked the knife out of the sand and waved it in Bec's face. "You're lucky I didn't gut him the night you met him."

Bec stilled. Her eyes grew wide as she started to put it together. It had been Tyler who had introduced her to Miles. They had been friends. Not for long, but still. It had been thought out. Planned. Miles had known exactly how to slither his way into her life. Her throat grew dry and achy.

"How long?"

He smiled down at her. "How long what?"

"How long ago did you find me?"

Miles held her gaze, as if savoring every flicker of panic that blinked through Bec's eyes. "Two years."

Everything felt dizzy. She replayed his words over and over in her head until their meaning sunk in. Two years he had watched and waited. Two years he had planned how to cozy up to her, her friends, and then he'd pulled the strings like a puppet master. And the whole time, she had been oblivious.

"What do you want, Niko?"

He took a slow, steady breath. "God, I missed that." He twirled the knife in his hand, Bec's blood still dripping from it. "It's been too long since I heard my name on your lips." His eyes grew heavy with desire as he pointed the knife at her. "I want what I've always wanted. I want what you promised me so many times, yet always took away." He brushed a stray piece of hair out of her face with the tip of the blade. "I want you."

Bec was shaking, her anger and fear sloshing dangerously in her stomach with the sickly ache of guilt. She had tried to pretend before, to ignore the simple truth in front of her, but now there was no escaping it. He had killed them all because of her—*for* her. She reared up towards him, screaming and clawing her hands at any part of him she could find. She was feral in her grief, sick in her desperation. He wanted her to believe that this was her fault, and in a way, it was. But she wasn't the one who had slipped the knife into the skin of so many people she'd cared for—loved. That had been him and him alone. Her nails sliced into his cheek before he managed to pin her back against the sand. A single drop of blood spilled from his face onto her own as he gained control of her once more.

"You can be mad all you want now," he snarled down at her. "In time I know you'll forgive me."

"Fuck you," Bec spat, tears streaming down her face.

Tsk tsk. He clicked his tongue against his teeth as he gazed down at her with dark eyes. "Oh come on, Amelia. You don't really mea—"

"I wish you'd burned in that house."

"Shut the fuck up."

His body shifted, compressing her against the sand. Bec fought to pull a breath into her lungs. Fear prickled across her skin as he leaned in close and let out a throaty groan. He danced the tip of the knife across her face and down to her neck. "You're really testing my patience here," he breathed, his lips grazing her ear.

Bec took in a wavering breath as she fought through the pain that seared from every cut on her body. "If you're going to kill me," she uttered. "Just get it over with already. I'm tired of your fucking games."

"Kill you?" he said, pulling away so he was sitting on top of her hips. "Now why would I do that?"

Her brow furrowed.

"Like I said before," he stated, wiping the blade clean on his shirt. "This isn't how I wanted this to go, but the ending doesn't change."

"What—"

"After this, we're going to start fresh. Move to the East Coast. New York, maybe? I know you've always wanted to go there." He glided the tip of the knife down to her stomach. "We can still say Tyler killed everyone. His little college murder night was a fucking amazing coincidence. It makes it even more convincing." He lifted the hem of Bec's shirt and trailed the blade across her skin. "Billionaire brat with troubled past goes on massacre after finding out his girlfriend was cheating. Only two survivors—it's perfect." Miles smiled, pausing for a brief moment to look at her. "There's just one thing we need to really sell the story."

A shriek left Bec's throat as he plunged the knife deep inside of her. He dug it around the soft flesh of her stomach, seeming to relish the little screams that left her mouth. He pulled the knife from her as quickly as he had shoved it in. Bec heaved in a sharp breath. Tears welled in her eyes as she tried to process the pain that overloaded her nerves. Miles let his eyes grow wide and hungry as they drifted across her body. He was planning the next place the blade would puncture her skin, she could see it in the sick grin that contorted his face. Bec felt a violent sickness boil in her gut. He was going to enjoy every second of this and if she did survive, it would only be to live through the next phase of whatever horror he had planned. As Bec shifted her weight underneath him, desperate to get away, she felt a painful lump dig into her back. Her body stilled but her mind buzzed. Her eyes bore into Miles as he considered the tender flesh of her side, knife at the ready. No—this wasn't going to end like he wanted.

Bec took sharp, labored breaths as he sliced the knife across her waist, leaving a jagged cut that traced the shape of her ribs. Her eyes flickered to the right, where her hand laid flat against the sand. She had one shot at this. If she hesitated, she would die. Even if she did it perfectly, she still might die. She closed her eyes and let the faces of all the people he had taken away fill her heart with a jittery rush of adrenaline and hate. Only one person was making it off this island and it was going to be her. As Bec opened her eyes, she dug her fingers into the sand.

"Hey, Niko," she uttered, feeling the open wounds across her body seeping blood with every breath.

Miles looked down at her with a wide grin.

"This is for Stevie," she rasped.

Bec's hand rushed into the air, her fist unclenching as it released a blast of gritty sand straight into his face. He reeled backwards, startled by the biting flecks. As he sputtered and raked his fingers across his face to clear the grains of sand from his eyes, Bec rolled over onto her stomach and crawled through the sand. A heavy groan ripped from her lungs as her stomach pressed to the ground, alighting every cut and gash he had left with searing pain. Her hand flung to her back and under her shirt as she gripped the smooth plastic shaft. Miles was on her seconds later. His fingers dug into her hips as he flipped her over and climbed on top of her. He held her down, furry seeming to drip off his face.

"You had to make this hard, didn't you?" he seethed. His skin was coated in specks where the sand had stuck to the rain drops on his face. "This could have gone differently, but I can see you still don't understand." He pressed his knees into her stomach, sending a muffled cry from her lips. He fumbled for his knife. When he turned back around and held it up in front of her face, that jester's smile slid into place once again. "I'll spill as much blood as it takes for you to understand who you belong to." His eyes grew dark as he raised the knife in the air above her.

Bec took a wavering breath, trying to prepare herself.

"I'm going to enjoy this," he grinned.

"Me too."

Her hand collided with his neck and for a second, all was still. It wasn't until she yanked her hand away, pulling the screwdriver from his jugular, that his pupils widened and wavered. His mouth trembled as words formed at the tip of his tongue but failed to make it any further. He slapped at his neck wildly. A steady stream of blood poured from the hole like a spigot. His fingers squirmed around, trying to plunge their way into the opening and stop the flow. Bec watched as his eyes darted side to side before locking on her in a daze. There had been times when she was younger, maybe seventeen, when she'd dreamed of meeting Niko. What did he look like? Was he everything she'd hoped? Now, as she looked at that handsome face with its panicked eyes, she wished she had never found out.

He toppled in one swift, heavy sway like a chopped-down tree. The wind sucked from Bec's lungs as his body fell on top of her. Panic devoured her as his weight seemed to crush her bones. She flailed, digging herself out from under him until she was finally free. She scurried away from him as a final gurgle babbled from his mouth. As the rain came back, pattering against the sand in thick drops, she watched quietly and cautiously, searching for the telltale rise and fall of breathing. Minutes ticked by without so much as a shudder. In an instant, everything hit her. Sobs heaved from her chest. Bec tipped her head back to the sky. The rain slid down her face, mixing with blood and tears. Her fingers clutched her stomach as the sobs turned into wailing howls. She was covered in blood, his and her own, and the rain did little to rid her of the burden. She sniffled against a shuddering breath and steadied herself. Finally, she looked back at him. She'd watched enough horror movies to know they never really died.

With a painful groan, she heaved herself to standing. Her hand clutched her gaping side as she swayed on shaky legs, blood dripping off her hands into the sand. She jutted her foot out to kick his side, holding her breath as his body swayed and returned to its original position. There was no lurching moment where the monster returned. He was gone. Dead. Bec let a few more tears spill down her cheek before she began a slow shuffle across the sand, wincing with every step. Her head spun as she reached the top of the sand dune, her vision momentarily dizzy and black. Cracks and groans pierced the air as the fire raged in the distance. As Bec watched the hot flames spit through the roof, a cynical rattle left her throat.

"Happy birthday, Amelia," she muttered to herself. "Make a wish." She managed to smile before her body collapsed into the sand.

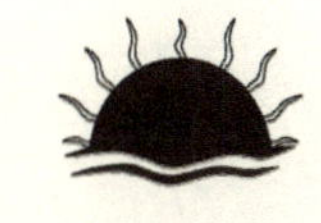

MONDAY

☀ MARTA ☀

She steadied herself at the bow of the boat, a fine mist grazing her face. Marta patted a few loose strands against her taunt bun, and tucked the hairs back into place.

She hated the ocean and the swell and sway it caused in her stomach, but she barely noticed the feeling now. There had been a darkness lingering on the horizon for the past thirty minutes. With every minute that passed, she grew more restless. The plume of billowing, black smoke that marred the blue sky was like a sign from God. The closer it got, the harder it was to ignore. She could see it clearly now, not that she needed to. The smell of smoke tainted the ocean air.

Marta shook her head softly. She had heard stories of the boy. It was hard to work for the family and not hear the gossip. The bad one, they called him. The troublemaker. She had told her staff to keep eyes on him and they had. They had noticed something amiss—something stirring in the group like a fever. Marta had been hesitant to grant Tyler the solitude he had requested. Now, she saw that her reluctance had been credible. Call it woman's intuition. Her knuckles turned ghost-white as she clutched the railing. She shouted at the captain to go faster. The boat bounced over waves as it accelerated. Marta didn't dare retreat from the bow; something had caught her eye like a mouse in a trap. Someone was on the dock, a shadowed blur against the morning sun.

Marta leaned forward, her crisp white pants pressed up against the railing and grew wet at the ankles. She blinked against the glare coming off the water. The dock was a hundred yards out now.

As the boat's motor slowed to a lull, guided closer by the current, the crews' panicked mutterings filled the air. Marta heard someone begin to recite a prayer in Spanish behind her. She didn't know if God could protect them from this. A girl sat on the dock, leaning against one of the wooden beams. Marta lurched away from the railing, quickly blessing herself with the sign of the cross. Fear crawled up her spine with a shiver. The girl's skin was red from head to toe. As the boat pulled up to the dock, the girl moved and one became two. Bodies untangled their blood-coated limbs. Marta's eyes grew wide as the boy hoisted himself up, seeming to struggle with the effort. She watched Tyler help the girl stand before the pair limped towards the edge of the dock. Just as Marta saw the whites of her eyes, Bec dropped a screwdriver from her hand.

A NOTE FROM THE AUTHOR

By purchasing this book, you have supported an indie author with big dreams. I am so grateful for everyone who has taken a chance on me by reading this story.

Thank you for diving into this birthday trip gone wrong and living through all of the drama one little friend group could possibly endure. I hope you enjoyed reading it as much as I enjoyed writing it.

From the bottom of my dark and twisty heart—thank you for supporting my work!

ABOUT THE AUTHOR

Angie Caedis is a lover of all things dark and twisty. She loves crafting stories that suck you into a world of thrills, chills, and a whole lot of drama.

When she's not writing until dawn, she enjoys watching horror movies, curling up with a good dark romance book, and counting down the days until Halloween.